Angela Thirkell

Angela Thirkell, granddaughter of Edward Burne-Jones, was born in London in 1890. At the age of twenty-eight she moved to Melbourne, Australia where she became involved in broadcasting and was a frequent contributor to the British periodicals. Mrs. Thirkell did not begin writing novels until her return to Britain in 1930; then, for the rest of her life, she produced a new book almost every year. Her stylish prose and deft portrayal of the human comedy in the imaginary county of Barsetshire have amused readers for decades. She died in 1961, just before her seventy-first birthday.

"[Thirkell's] satire is always just, apt, kindly, and pleasantly rambly. Blended in with the satire, too, are all the pleasures of an escapist romance."

—*New York Herald Tribune*

"The happy outcome of her tale is secondary to the crisp, often quaint amusement one derives from discovering how deftly Angela Thirkell makes the most unexciting incident appear important."

—*Saturday Review of Literature*

Table of Explanation

Roads..................
Railways.............
Rivers................
Towns............... HOGGLESTOCK
Parish Villages... Puddingdale
Small Villages.... Little Misfit
Mansions........... Pomfret Towers

0 1 2 3 4 5

Scale of Miles

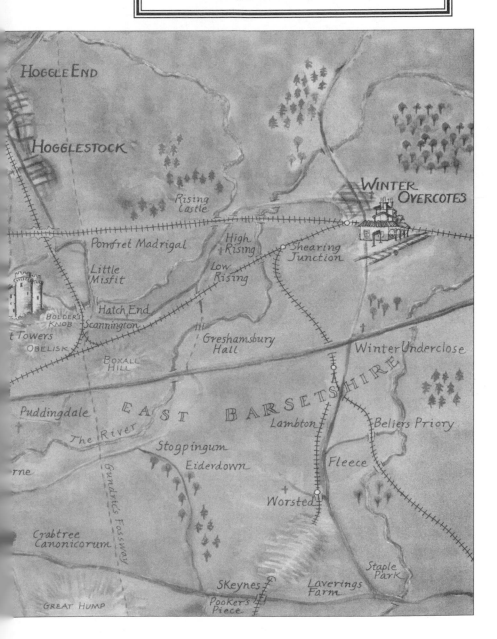

A Map of the County of

BARSETSHIRE

Showing the Situations of the various great Estates and Seats

Close Quarters

A Novel by

Angela Thirkell

MOYER BELL

Wickford, Rhode Island & London

Published by Moyer Bell
This Edition 2001

Copyright © 1958 by Angela Thirkell
Published by arrangement with Hamish Hamilton, Ltd.

**LIBRARY OF CONGRESS
CATALOGING-IN-PUBLICATION DATA**

Thirkell, Angela Mackail, 1890–1961.
    Close Quarters / by Angela Thirkell. — 1st ed.
       p.   cm.
    ISBN 1-55921-290-X
    I. Title.
    PR6039.H43 C55 2001
    823'.912—dc21   00-052547
                                      CIP

Printed in the United States of America
Distributed in North America by Publishers Group West, 1700 Fourth
Street, Berkeley, CA 94710, 800-788-3123 (in California 510-658-3453).

CLOSE QUARTERS

CHAPTER I

It is, or would be if one bothered to think about it, a well-known fact that there are far more surnames than Christian names. A cursory inspection of the four London Telephone Directories is sufficient proof of the variety of surnames from the *A.1. AAA Building Bracket* to the *Zzymbla* who closes those massive and useful volumes. And useful not only in life but in death. For if one can avoid the plea of the kind bringer of the new issue to have its predecessor returned to him (and what is done with the old telephone books we do not know, unless they join the Gargantuan cubic packages of waste paper which we see piled in steamers on the far side of the Thames from the Borough of Riverside), there are a thousand uses for it. As a kitchen adjunct it beats most other gadgets hollow. You can stand on it if that bit of lino in front of the cooker is all greasy where the fat splashed over just as I was dishing up. It is invaluable on the kitchen table because you can stand the big saucepan on it, so sparing that nice new red and white check oilcloth. You can test the iron—whether stove-heated or electric—on it before risking a burn on those cloths I washed out after breakfast and they're dry enough to iron now. Two of them are as good as a small step-ladder if you want to reach something you think you had put away at the back of that top shelf only I'm not sure if it was there I put it or on top of the spare-room cupboard. Whether the old volumes are sold to the new self-governing State of Borrioboola Gha as a token of civilization, or re-pulped and made into more telephone-directory fodder, we shall never know, nor do we care. But in the home they are deeply valued, in spite of the yearly argument, nay almost hand-to-hand struggle, with the P.M.G.'s representative whose wretched job it is to try to take them away from us.

This slight divagation was suggested to us by considering our many Barsetshire friends and how difficult it is to find enough Christian names of a normal kind which do not already belong to someone else; whereas surnames are ten a penny. The three sons of John and Mary Leslie, who have now for some years lived in the Old Rectory at Greshamsbury, are Henry (after his paternal grandfather), John (after his father) and Clive (after a maternal uncle who was killed in the 1914 war). Each of these is a good solid name, but for many years has been almost buried under Major, Minor and Minimus. How old they are now we can never remember and should probably get it wrong if we did, but we have a strong impression that the eldest, Henry, is now down from Oxford after a happy and hard-working three years, with a good first. The second, John (usually known as Johnny to distinguish him from his father), has been a passionate climber all his life of any church, monument, college, or other building to which he could cling with one hand, one foot and an eyelash. He was still at Oxford and had beaten the Oxford Alpine Club's record by walking round the quad of St. Jude on the outside of the second floor, frightening the eightieth son of the Head Chief of Mngangaland almost out of his wits and thus causing him, though a devout atheist and sceptic, to summon his father's Head Witch-Doctor from Mngangaland by aeroplane. Clive, or Minimus, now in his last term at South-bridge School, had decided on the Royal Air Force if it would pass him, because he had no head for heights at all and thought it might cure him. So far Cupid's darts had not affected the young men except in so far as one or more of them were always in and out of love with everyone unsuitable from the film star

Glamora Tudor (now starring with Pietro Nasone in a film about Cyrano de Bergerac who had to be an Italian condottiere because then Nasone's strong Italian accent, copied ad nauseam by all the older girls at the Barchester High School, seemed more in keeping, or so the producer Czemschk Kpozcz said, and he was getting such a huge salary that no one contradicted him), to the lovely Mrs. Fairweather formerly Rose Birkett. As for their cousin Edith Graham, she was now officially engaged to the Reverend Lord William Harcourt, younger brother of the Duke of Towers, so a possible marriage between first cousins did not come into the question.

Let it be granted (as Euclid used to say, before he regrettably turned into geometry) that there comes a time in the life of every parent when he has to approach his offspring on the subject of a profession. This approach is met in various ways. Happy is the father who has succeeded his own father in an honourable calling and finds a son who wishes to follow it. Quite happy also may the father be who was a West India Sugar Broker (though without suffering the dire misfortune that befell the poor wretch in the Bab Ballads) and finds that a son wishes to desert the parental business for the stage, or a scholastic career; provided the son is agreeable about it and really knows his own mind—as much as one ever knows that strange hinterland.

John Leslie had been in business; though what business we do not know, for we were only once in his London office, in 1933 to be exact, just before his second marriage. But whatever the business was, he had by now retired from it in comfort and taken up the life of a small county gentleman who can afford to give much of his time and his intelligence to public work. A great deal of England is still managed and controlled by unpaid labour, and long may it be so. All over Barsetshire, in both divisions of the county, the gentry and what one might still call the squirearchy were giving their time and their brains in service to others and still doing it remarkably well. In East Barsetshire young Mr. Crosse, son of Lord Crosse at Crosse Hall over

Boxall Hill way, had been gaining influence and had more than once been able to put down Lord Aberfordbury (formerly known and disliked as Sir Ogilvy Hibberd and equally disliked now) firmly and successfully. But at Greshamsbury there was a peaceful unanimity of purpose. No one was very much richer than anyone else and no one very much poorer. Things went quietly and smoothly along and even the peculiar inhabitants of the new part of the little town were gradually and peacefully conforming, even if their houses were a horrid art shape with small poky rooms and cubic or spiral furniture. There was a nice church in the new part for those who prefer a rather low service, while in the little church in the old town Canon Fewling kept to his rather high service, but always tempering his ritual to his flock. And as both high and low liked and admired him personally, he and the rather low-church vicar in the New Town got on very well.

It was now high summer, and those of our readers who have survived that summer will remember how bitterly cold it was; how one could never properly put one's winter clothes aside, had to go on wearing the near-camel-hair coat which one had hoped would see one through the next winter, saw one's coal and gas bill soaring to Arctic heights, and longed to become permanently bed-ridden with an eiderdown and a roaring fire. At least that was what the grown-ups felt, for most children and young people are mercifully immune to cold; though curiously enough they can feel heat. The Leslies had plenty of coal and coke laid in and so could look forward to the summer with equanimity, but there were others with less foresight or less space, who would probably feel like the foolish virgins as winter approached. This subject Mrs. Leslie and her husband were discussing on a chill August afternoon with their friends Captain Gresham, R.N., and Mrs. Gresham who lived in a wing of Greshamsbury House, now under the National Trust.

"Of course we are fairly all right, Jane," said Mrs. Leslie to

Mrs. Gresham, "because we filled the old pigsties with coal and coke and we are on the gas and electric mains."

"I wish we had a pigsty at the Big House," said Mrs. Gresham. "I mean there is one, only it's in the bit of the yard that belongs to the ground-floor tenants and as they keep their coal in it I don't quite like to ask them."

"I say, Mrs. Gresham," said Clive Leslie who, so his elder brothers considered, was never backward in putting himself forward, nor had they ever by force or persuasion cured him of it, "it's a shame. I could easily come up one night and move your coal for you. I'd bring a shovel and a broom and leave everything tidy. Where's your coal?"

Mrs. Gresham said in a bunker that her husband had made in the toolshed.

"You see," she went on, "we've got gas and electricity, but sometimes the electricity goes off and we have to wait till it goes on again."

"Still, there's one thing about electricity," said Mrs. Leslie. "If it goes off when it's on it's quite safe."

Her husband asked what on earth she meant.

"I think I understand," said Captain Gresham. "If the current is off and you haven't turned your electric fire off, it comes alive again when the electricians have got the thing going. But if the gas goes off and you don't turn the tap off as well there may be an explosion when it comes on again if there's a light in the room. Right?"

"Rather!" said Clive Leslie. "One of the fellows turned the gas on in the prep room in summer just for fun, to see if anyone would be gassed and the maths master came in and said What a stink and lit a match to see where it was and everything went off pop and Matron came in and there was a frightful row."

Mrs. Gresham kindly said How dreadful, but in a voice whose lack of interest was so plain that Minimus collapsed and pretended to have business elsewhere. Nor was his absence regretted by any of the grown-ups, including his elder brothers who felt that if ever a head needed punching it was young Clive's.

"What's the next trouble, Mary?" said Mr. Leslie.

"The Bring and Buy for the Mixo-Lydian miners' relief fund," said his wife. "In the New Town, thank goodness, but we'll have to send something."

"And buy something," said Captain Gresham. "That's the real trouble with bazaars. It's all right to send the things you don't want along, but there's nothing one could bear to buy, only one has to buy something, just for face. Last time someone had a bazaar—it was the Yates Umblebys I think—I got there a bit late and had to buy a basket of carrots and three penwipers that were hanging fire."

"And for why," said Mr. Leslie. "Because no one uses penwipers now with fountain-pens."

"Oh, but they *do*, John," said his wife, "because fountain-pens do spew so unaccountably and suddenly make blobs."

"Not only that," said Captain Gresham, "but sometimes you take the cap off and find the pen has been spewing all on its own and the cap is half full of ink."

"There was a boy at school when I was a kid," said John Leslie, "who had a pen with three different inks. His uncle in America sent it him and he did his Latin prep with it and old Squobs went right off the deep end."

Mrs. Gresham enquired who Squobs was.

"Oh, *him*," said John. "He took us for Latin. His real name was Mr. Stanhope and he told young Wilson to write his prep all over again in ordinary ink."

"And did he?" said Mrs. Gresham.

"No!" said John, in a voice of profound scorn. "He let Squobs look at his pen and write with it and Squobs said All right but don't do it again."

"So didn't he—or do I mean did he?" said Captain Gresham.

"Well sir, he *had* to, because we dared him to," said John. "But it was Geometry and Mr. Carter took us because the Maths master had flu and Mr. Carter said it was all right this time, but next time he'd confiscate it and so Wilson got off."

"Wilson being the boy in question?" said his father.

"Of *course*, father," said John. "He's not bad at Alpine work. He did that nasty bit by the Dean of Paul's study without a rope when he was staying in Oxford last hols."

His father, who knew and liked Mr. Fanshawe the Dean and also Mrs. Fanshawe, asked if the Dean knew.

"Of course he did, father," said John. "He knows everything somehow. He ticked Wilson off like anything and said when he was a young man they called that the Muffs' Walk and Wilson was awfully ashamed. When Mr. Fanshawe was an undergraduate he climbed round the whole of the outside of the college without coming down once."

His mother then made a rather motherly face at him and said if they were really going to oil the garden roller they might do it now. Pleased at the thought of a good deal of licensed dirt and oil, the young gentlemen jostled one another out of the room.

"Oh, Henry!" Mrs. Gresham called to him. "If Frank comes, do let him help you."

"Right-oh, Aunt Jane," said Henry, for a kind of reciprocal aunt-and-nephewship had grown up between the younger and older members of the two families. We always feel flattered if our friends' young adopt us as an aunt, though we score ourselves by having had once a beloved Scotch Grannie, who was no connection at all but always known to us by that name of affection.

"Oh, Aunt Jane," said John, suddenly reappearing. "It's all right. Frank's down by the garden roller and has got an oil-can."

"That," said Captain Gresham, "tears it. I will *not* have Frank taking my oil-can. I had it with me when I was torpedoed."

"Oh, it's all right, sir," said John. "It's one he bought with his own money, it's pink plastic," and shutting the door quickly and quietly he disappeared.

"*Plastic!*" said Captain Gresham with deep scorn. "And *Pink.*"

"You'll have to get used to it, darling," said his wife. "The kitchen garbage tin is plastic now and so is the big washing-up basin and that red broom with red bristles that you admired. And Lady Graham's housemaid's new teeth, because she told me so."

"You can't even get an anagram out of Plastic," said Captain Gresham, happy to discover a new grievance.

Everyone at once tried to get an anagram, the only one approximating to a possible hit being SCALP IT, which was ruled out by John Leslie as unfair because it ought to be one word.

"Here! Fair play for the Royal Navy!" said Captain Gresham. "What about the Horatio Nelson one—HONOR EST A NILO?" but John Leslie said that was different, as indeed it is, even if not a very good argument. Then the talk divagated to palindromes and other academic forms of amusement and Mrs. Leslie said it was time they had some sherry, which they accordingly did.

Mrs. Gresham said she must collect Frank and go home, picking up on the way her daughters who were having tea at the Umblebys, a pleasant family who had been lawyers in the town for several generations and had at the moment some very nice grandchildren on tap. Frank Gresham was called in from whatever he was doing, which included a good deal of dirt on his hands and a three-cornered tear in his shirt sleeve, and the Greshams took their leave.

There is something in common, physically, between the best sailors and the best lawyers. Both are apt to be clean-shaven (and with the greatest respect for the Law, a moustache does look rather out of place with a wig). Both are apt to approximate to a type which we can only describe as an intelligent and well-educated hawk. But this is only with barristers; solicitors are allowed to look as they please. Be that as it may, there was a

distinct physical resemblance between Captain Gresham R.N.
and Mr. Umbleby, though Mr. Umbleby was the older man and
also had the immense advantage of his very respectable safe
background, for the Umblebys had for over a century owned
their house with its pleasant garden and its brick-paved stable
yard whose coach-houses and stables were now let to a riding
school, whereas the Greshams during that time had gently
decayed and were only too glad to sell most of their land for
building and live in a wing of their own house.

The front door was in pleasant country fashion on the jar.
From the house came the noise—only to be compared with the
Zoological Gardens at feeding time—of some dozen nicely
brought-up children eating as one. And if it seems peculiar that
the tea-party was still going on, we must explain that there was
a tradition in the Umbleby family that after tea and games—
outdoor or indoor according to the season—the party should
return to the dining-room and polish off such of the cakes and
sandwiches as were left.

It is one of the fictions still kept up in well-behaved families
that if there is too much noise at a children's party each
mother—though convinced that her own children are guilt-
less—shall fall upon them with fire and sword and threats of
dire penalties such as going to bed early. So did Mrs. Gresham
at once fall upon her elder daughter Beatrice, named after a
long-defunct Gresham and better known to her young friends
by her brother's affectionate if unfeeling name of Batty. But the
difference in age between the two was so great as to prevent
much squabbling, for Frank was born before the war and Captain Gresham was missing in the Far East for a long time, so it
would have been highly unsuitable if he had returned to find his
wife with a second child.

Sherry was of course produced for the newcomers. Mrs.
Gresham took some for politeness. Her husband hesitated
between the lovely Rose Fairweather who had brought her
younger children and Mr. Umbleby, his host. But it is well

known that men on the whole prefer any man, however dull, to
the most delightful woman, so the lawyer and the sailor, glass in
hand—and in Mr. Umbleby's case firmly grasping the decanter
in the other hand—retired to the large bay window whence they
could observe the passers-by while they talked, which was
mostly about the Parish Council and how important it was to
keep the New Town off it; or at least to hold it at arm's length till
it had given proof of its worthiness.

"We do want one or two more solid people of our own sort,"
said Mr. Umbleby, "or we may be swamped. They've got a new
parson down there and I hear that he is rather up-and-coming.
It mightn't be a bad thing. Pity there aren't any Oriels left here.
Funny how those old families disappear. There's only the parson
over at Harefield now and he's not married. Now his great-uncle
who became a bishop married one of old Squire Gresham's
daughters and they had a large family but it tailed out as families
do."

"That was my great-aunt or great-great-aunt I always get
muddled about generations Beatrice," said Captain Gresham,
and the gentlemen plunged blissfully into county marriages and
would probably be there still if Captain Gresham hadn't asked
what the name of the incumbent of the New Town living was.

"Parker," said Mr. Umbleby. "No, it isn't, it's Parkinson. Same
thing. He was at Pomfret Madrigal. Married, nice little wife,
some children, not out of the top drawer—nor's she—but
making the grade. Her father was Welk, the Barchester undertaker, and she was an only child. I hear that he is very sound
about the Palace."

"Well, that's what really matters," said Captain Gresham who
had very proper ideas on what the incumbent of any Barsetshire
living should be. "I must tell Jane to call. Or would that upset
them?"

"A few years ago I think it would," said Mr. Umbleby, "but
they have made the grade now. At least I hope that's what I
mean—it's what the young people say and we must listen to

them. There was an old Lord Saltire who used to come to
Greshamsbury in my grandfather's time—a great gentleman by
all accounts—and he said to my grandfather 'I always take my
time from the young men.' And it's not a bad thing as one gets
older."

"Well Umbleby, if I had taken my time from all the young
lieutenants and midshipmen I've had under me," said Captain
Gresham, "I shouldn't have been very popular with their Lordships of Admiralty. Taking it by and large I daresay it's good
advice, but one has to go carefully. Sunt modus in rebus if that's
what I mean."

"I don't know what you think you mean, Gresham," said Mr.
Umbleby, "but you should verify your references. *Est* modus in
rebus, sunt certi denique fines—good old Horace. Old Walker
at St. Paul's would have given me a few of the best and a
whacking impot if I'd made such a howler. I can just remember
him," at which Captain Gresham said Kamerad and accepted
the topping-up of his sherry proffered by Mr. Umbleby, who
was certainly taking Lord Saltire's advice.

By now the young guests had eaten their tea and their rere-tea
to the last crumb and were getting a little above themselves, and
mothers began to say it was time they were getting home. So
with good-byes and thanks the party dispersed. The Greshams
with their son Frank and their daughter Beatrice took the short
cut by a wooden door in the park wall to which only residents at
Greshamsbury Park had the key. This was a grace and favour
gift and much prized, though if one came from the other end of
the road it was much quicker to go by the tradesmen's entrance.

"Can I go in over the wall?" said Frank Gresham.

"I shouldn't think so," said his father, treating his son's request
as a supposititious case. But Frank, who had been biding his
time, paused below a chestnut tree whose branches came well
over the wall, jumped, seized a branch and managed by its aid to
scrabble up the rough flint and mortar surface (much to the

detriment of his shoes), hoisted himself onto the wall and let the branch spring back.

"Do take care of glass, Frank," said his mother anxiously.

"Oh, Minimus and I knocked that all off and put some mortar along the top when the workmen were making the new garage," said Frank in an airy and insouciant way, and jumped down on the far side.

"That's what comes of having a sailor father," said Captain Gresham.

His wife asked what he meant exactly—she meant, she said, did he mean it was a good thing that came or a bad thing.

"Both," said her husband. "A good thing that he has the wits—or the cunning—to think of it; not so good if he goes on doing it and all the young ragamuffins of the neighbourhood follow suit. Then we'll have trouble with the Estate people," for Greshamsbury House and a certain amount of the grounds had been taken over by the National Trust some time ago. This had the advantage that the various tenants of the flats were hand-picked and the disadvantage that the Trust would suddenly send an official with instructions—more or less—to see what the tenants were doing and tell them not to. But the agent in this case was an ex-naval man and hand-in-glove with the Noel Mertons' agent Mr. Wickham, so all went very well.

"Then you'd better speak to him," said Jane and her husband said he would; and what was more, he added, he would forbid Frank to spoil his boots on a flint wall. If he wanted to climb he could tie his boots—or shoes—round his neck.

"Then he'll wear his socks out at *once*," said Jane Gresham.

"Well, you can't have it every way," said Captain Gresham peacefully, and the subject was dropped. Beatrice had not joined in the argument, for she was a quiet, though very happy and good child (except of course at parties, when a yell that rent the firmament was often heard from her) and found it far less trouble to do what she was told, unless it was something that she very particularly didn't want to do—but she usually did it.

*   *   *

Time passes, whatever we may do about it, and the day of the Bring and Buy for the Mixo-Lydian miners came round in its appointed course. As a rule local shows were held on a Saturday, but the promoters of the sale had decided to make it a Thursday because that was early closing day in Barchester. Between the Old and New Towns there was not a customs barrier, nor a red flag, nor police with truncheons, but—in the words (with music) of Couperin—a Barricade Mystérieuse. The Old Town had no objection to the New Town—oh, none at all. Some of its supporters had indeed done quite well by selling bits of land to the Cubist, or Hexagonal, or Functional entrepreneurs, known more simply in our young days as Speculative Builders. Very few of the old houses and cottages had been pulled down, for demolition is an expensive job unless you are certain of a quick return on the empty waste that is left. But various people interested in the building trade had raised money and done their utmost to modernize. In case the S.P.A.B. hears of this and is smitten by a pang that they might have saved Ancient Buildings but didn't, we should like to reassure them at once that there was nothing worth saving. In the few cases where there was a cottage that looked a little Morland-ish it was only because the lath and plaster Barsetshire walls were crumbling, the tiles were falling from the wooden pins of (possibly) Tudor days, the thatch was mostly green with moss and sprouting grasses and full of holes, and every fireplace (one to each cottage) had a large chimney down which soot fell all through the winter, and rain, hail, birds' nests and occasionally birds all through the year. So in spite of an anxious visit from the Barsetshire branch of the Society for the Preservation of Rural England, it was really cheaper and more sanitary to rebuild.

It is very difficult to judge fairly of a place where one's childhood has been spent and everything—however hideous or inconvenient—is nostalgic of the Golden Age, but wattle and daub cannot last for ever, nor can the carelessly built walls with cheap, bad bricks, no foundation, no damp course and seldom more than one brick thick. It is possible that the horrible pre-fabrications may outlast everything, though only below ground, we think. The rest will have its exists and its entrances. But the non-porous base of concrete, poured in like a giant's treacle from huge metal pots, will probably endure as long as Persia or Rome, though we shall not be there to see—or to feel.

In any case we think that the older part of Greshamsbury was and still remains a relic of older days. But the so-called working class were comfortably housed in the new building estate on the Barchester side, with their own Parish Hall and everything handsome about them and had become a horrible Palace of Art under the name of New Town. Art ramped in every direction and with every form of uninspired dullness—hardly even worthy of the name of hideousness. Small tumble-down cottages were shaved and manicured and concrete-emplacemented and centrally heated (with the very doubtful approval of the County Surveyor) and became perfect Naboth's vineyards to the house-agents who usually managed to buy them for double their value and sell them for tenfold and a hundredfold. Pastel colours ran riot on their pebble-dash walls; cosy corners and inglenooks were installed where a nice sensible kitchen range used to be; furniture was all built in, as in many cases were beds—at least their heads were part of the wall so that they could not be moved; the neon strip lighting reminded the older people of the horrid colour one's face used to look over a great flaming dish of snapdragon; chairs were triangular or hexagonal and very heavy; looking-glasses had motifs engraved on them, very thwarting to the human countenance; cupboard doors were flat and shut with a kind of ball-bearing which sometimes clicked with its socket and mostly didn't; the kitchenette, or dinette, or cook-and-eat alcove, like Cerberus three gentlemen in one, was too small even for a comfortably stout couple, let alone their friends; the built-in fridge (so-called because it stood firmly in a corner and was not built in) whined and roared according to its temperament; the electric washer had an unerring instinct for breaking down on washing day.

Such of the real cottage-women who came as morning helpers first refused to use the labour-saving implements and if they did use them later always managed to turn something the wrong way and fuse either the light or the power. And so the catalogue might go on to the length of Leporello's. In fact the only reliable thing was the water supply, but this was never recognized because so far we have lived in a civilization where water is cheap and accessible. Also the Greshamsbury water was of a hardness calculated to fur up the inside of any pipe and even choke the kettles. A great many people had an old belief that if you put a glass marble in the kettle, all the lime in the water which furs the inside would rush to the marble. But this had not so far been proved, largely we think because people used glass marbles instead of the common stone sort. As for the rim of dirt round the bath from the hard water, it took seven maids with seven mops to get it off unless they used one of the advertised water-softeners which took the skin not only off their hands but also off the bath itself. In fact everything was as up-to-date as it could possibly be.

Meanwhile the Old Town went on living in the perfect comfort of not-quite-up-to-dateness.

However there was a general feeling that the Bring and Buy should be supported and most households were able to do some Bringing, though they doubted whether there would be anything to Buy. Still, what you Buy at a bazaar can always go into a drawer in the spare room till you can Bring it, and most housewives had a Glory Hole where objects suitable for selling to other people were stored.

Mary Leslie found an art tea-cosy that she had been obliged to buy at the Little Misfit Sale of Work and several other depressed articles. The Greshams disinterred a bundle of old lace, of good and strong quality, but yellow with age, which Mrs.

Gresham boiled and then rinsed with the blue bag; but all she got for her trouble was having to iron it as the blue did not take. Everyone else was hunting madly for white elephants and finding little more than black beetles. Canon Fewling's housekeeper Mrs. Hicks sent some jellied brawn made by her own private recipe and instructions to send it back to her if it didn't fetch the price she put on it. She also sent a few useful objects on the side, feeling pretty confident that her employer would not notice and would be lenient if he did.

And so, with the generosity of giving something that you yourself like and the different generosity of giving what you have had put away for ages and never found a use for, the New Town was really very well provided with more or less saleable objects.

The Bring and Buy was to take place in the old Drill Hall, because the Old Town Hall was condemned. The New Town had a Communal Centre, so called, but as the funds had run out it only had tarpaulins over the roof, pending the collection of more donations, and they had rather shamefacedly had to seek shelter elsewhere.

The Drill Hall was a large wooden building with a small wash-house attached to it. Its well-wishers called it Functional though that was hardly the word for four wooden walls that let in draughts in spite of an asbestos lining about three feet high, a corrugated iron roof that became almost red-hot in warm weather, and one cold-water tap. It had been built outside the Old Town but was now comfortably englobed in the New Town where it found plenty of buildings like itself but smaller. To this horrid place well-wishers were bringing their gifts.

There had been a faint hope that Lord Pomfret might be induced to open the bazaar, but his wife had firmly taken him to Cap Ferrat where the family had a villa and didn't even let him see the invitation, which was acknowledged from the Agent's Office at Pomfret Towers and declined with suitable regret. This was rather a set-back, till the new Vicar, Mr. Parkinson, had suggested Sir Edmund Pridham, now very old and crippled but doyen of West Barsetshire and knowing more of that part and its people than anyone living. This Sir Edmund consented to do on the understanding that he would only do the opening and then go home; and of course would make a donation to the bazaar funds.

We have seen something of the new Vicar Mr. Parkinson in earlier days and have watched his struggle upwards, always helped by his very nice, capable, affectionate wife and—we are glad to say—by her father who was a Master Undertaker and knew more about wood than most people. When we first made Mr. Parkinson's acquaintance at a dinner party in the Deanery some ten years or so ago we were almost overwhelmed with shame and pity for him, especially when—in the Dean's hearing—he had made a quotation from the New Testament about one Oneasyforus and had then realized, from the Dean's eyebrows, that he had made some horrible blunder. But his real goodness and determination (backed by his wife who had managed three children and very little money with courage and good temper, though she had her father Mr. Welk and his funereal connection behind her if the worst came to the worst) had carried him on and up, and much as he regretted leaving his country cure of souls he was not sorry to go to a larger and more rising town and nearer to Barchester.

The chief difficulty when a cure of souls was established in the New Town was a house. No provision for a vicarage had been made by the first settlers and as the population increased some people went to the Old Town, some to a very small tin chapel belonging to a small sect called Cokelers whom no one had ever heard of. What their creed was nobody knew, but they sang a great many hymns to a harmonium and kept a very good General Store. Gradually, funds had been provided and the new church was already half built. The East End had been consecrated by the Bishop (which act made many right-thinking people feel that the church was doomed to fall down or be burnt) and funds for the work came slowly in. But no provision had been made for the priest as yet.

Canon Fewling—we call him Canon or Doctor indifferently though we think he likes his Doctorate of Divinity almost the better of the two—had of course done all he could to be kind to his young coadjutor and his wife, and before long they both trusted and loved him and were eating metaphorically out of his hand. It was he, through the medium of his housekeeper Mrs. Hicks, who had found for the Parkinsons a nice little new house in the New Town, quite solidly built, two storeys, a good kitchen and offices, a nice not too large dining-room and drawing-room, besides a small room with a window onto the garden, already fitted with bookshelves, for Mr. Parkinson's study. There was an easy-to-run small garden, a garage with a door into the house and a good dry basement with a new water heater which supplied really hot baths. Upstairs were three bedrooms, a very nice bathroom and a linen cupboard heated by the hot-water pipes. There was also a large dry attic where odds and ends could be kept and Harold and Connie Parkinson could play up there and fasten their toy railway to the floor, while their young brother, named Josiah after his godfather the Dean but known commonly as Joey, could rampage about as much as he liked without anyone having to bother about him.

As so often happens, it was Mrs. Parkinson who was the man of the family. For this there were two reasons. Firstly that her mother had always been master in the house (though a devoted wife to Mr. Welk) and Mrs. Parkinson took it for granted that wives—especially when also mothers—were always master. Secondly that what with the regular services and—as must happen in a growing community—the increase in marriages, christenings and burials, not to speak of the Boy Scouts' special service and the Mothers' Union service and other special services, and a good deal of parish work as well, Mr. Parkinson's time was very fully occupied. But we are glad to say that his health which, owing to poverty in his young days and never having quite enough food till he married, had not been of the best, was now almost indecently good and he thought nothing of bicycling over to help a brother priest when wanted, or taking the Greshamsbury Boy Scouts for a Nature Tramp. In earlier days he would have come back exhausted and his wife would have given him—as Mrs. Crawley the Dean's grandmother had done to the Reverend Josiah Crawley—a small modicum of spirits from a secret hoard. But now he appeared refreshed rather than exhausted by his pastoral cares and enjoyed a glass of beer with his supper like anything.

We need hardly say that his wife was on the Bring and Buy Committee. Not as Chairman, lest all should think that she was proud (as Mr. John Gilpin feared when he would not let the chaise drive up to his door), but as a very useful hard-working member, ready to make suggestions and equally ready to listen to and approve intelligent suggestions by other people. Her official title was Honorary Secretary, a title invented to describe some-one who is not paid for doing most of the work rather better than anyone else, and seldom had the New Town of Greshams-bury been so well served.

Luckily for the Old Town it was able to keep the noiseless tenor of its way undisturbed, except by sending such gifts to the Bring and Buy as it could spare which, owing to a murrain of sales earlier, was not very much, but the willingness was all. There appears to us to be a flaw here, for whatever Shakespeare may say, willingness however willing cannot always produce objects suitable for bazaars.

The New Town had united in what is known as a Drive, pestering all the inhabitants for contributions in money or kind and starting a kind horrible Snowball by which one person had to press two other people to come, and each of the two other people were to do likewise. By these means what is now called an astronomical number (whatever that slipshod phrase may think it means) of helpers would be produced. Mr. Umbleby, who was good at figures, had calculated that as a geometrical progression it should raise at least two hundred thousand helpers, almost at once; but no one else subscribed to this theory, which indeed every attempt at snowball-making disproves. For Mrs. A. will always fall out and Mrs. B. will say she's ever so sorry but she'll be at Brighton then and Mr. C. will say he will give them a quid to get rid of them and will be damned if he'll do any more. Still, even with these disadvantages enough money was collected to make the position fairly safe and the rest was in the hands of heaven, which would undoubtedly do its best to spoil the fun of the bazaar by pouring water on it out of the upper window.

Accordingly on the appointed day most of our friends in the Old Town crossed the barrier (invisible to mortal eye, but strongly defined) between Old and New and moved towards the Drill Hall. Luckily it was a normal summer day, that is to say not very warm, and rather cloudy with occasional showers, so the Drill Hall was—as yet anyway—not at asphyxiation point. Greshams, Leslies and Fairweathers arrived at about the same time and, as usual, coalesced. For if you go to a party or function it is much more restful to talk to Aunt Mary or the sexton's wife than to someone you don't know in tweed and raffia, or Victoria, Lady Norton, better known to West Barsetshire as the Dreadful Dowager. There was already a good sprinkling of buyers, many of whom had come provided with bags and baskets to hold their purchases, much to the annoyance of the Packing Stall, where your parcels could be done up for you in paper bags which had already seen a good deal of wear and tied with synthetic string at a gross overcharge of threepence.

"Do let's stick together if we can," said Rose Fairweather, who was looking as ravishing as ever, the Summer Girl of magazines. "I'll ask Mrs. Hicks to keep a tea-table for us," and she went to the stall where Canon Fewling's house-keeper was presiding. Mrs. Hicks was of course delighted by this tribute to her powers (as Rose had intended she should be) and said she would certainly keep a table for the party; the table with four good legs,

she added, because some of them were a bit rickety ever since the
Scouts had mended their legs in the carpentering class. Rose
than paid in advance for all the teas.

"That's all right," said Rose to Mrs. Gresham. "Now let's go
round and see what there is. I always buy things like cake and
home-made jam, but I'm afraid this is going to be raffia hats and
embroidered guest towels—dreadful expression," which made
Mrs. Gresham laugh and did her a great deal of good.

"Bless you, Rose," she said. "I was really annoyed at wasting
an afternoon here when the garden needs weeding so badly.
Anyway I've only brought a pound with me and ten shillings of
silver. And why we should give good English money to Mixo-
Lydian miners, I don't know."

"Perhaps it's to keep all the other miners out," said Mrs.
Gresham. "I mean whenever anything nasty happens in Europe
we are bound to get Mixo-Lydians and Slavo-Lydians by the
hundred. I wonder what the next lot of refugees will be. Most
of the ones that were in Barsetshire in the war didn't go
home. There's one of them," and she looked towards a stall
where a stout woman with black eyes and hair, accompanied by
a depressed-looking man in a sheepskin coat and a béret, was
selling fancy articles.

"Gosh! that's Madame Brownscu," said Rose. "She was a
refugee in Southbridge in the war when John and I were at Las
Palombas on an Admiralty job. She's perfectly ghastly and so's
the boy friend."

"If you mean the man in the béret he doesn't look like either,"
said Mrs. Gresham. "I mean he's certainly not a boy and I'd hate
to have him for a friend."

"Sorry," said Rose. "John always says I say the wrong things,
but no one else minds. Nobody really knows who he is because
she always calls him Gogo. The only Gogo I ever heard of was
Peter Ibbetson."

Mrs. Gresham could hardly believe her ears. Rose Fairweather, that combination of perfect wife and mother, famed for

her real kindness and her almost complete want of education in a book sense, apparently knew about George du Maurier, and she congratulated Rose on the same.

"Actually it's Daphne du Maurier that writes the books," said Rose. "*Real* books I mean—they've been filmed. That's why I saw Peter Ibbetson. Spike Flanagan was wonderful in it, or perhaps it was Trilby."

Mrs. Gresham gave it up. Rose went over to the Brownscu stall and Mrs. Gresham followed her, wondering What Next.

"Hullo, Madame Brownscu," said Rose. "Do you remember the time mother had the party at Southbridge School and you and Mr. Brownscu had a sale of Mixo-Lydian embroidery?"

"Ha! which joy of re-seeink you," said Madame Brownscu. "I am rememberink myself at Southbridge. Bog! which pleasure, which joy! I have here excessively fine articles of sale. We shall chaffer, yes?"

"She means bargain," said Rose to Mrs. Gresham, "but don't let her. Just say what you want to pay and put the money on the table."

Following her own excellent advice Rose, who had bargained in every port and country where her husband's ship was stationed, picked up a rather dirty strip of embroidery and said One shilling.

"Ha! hark me this one who says a schelling!" said Madame Brownscu, contemptuously.

"All right, sixpence," said Rose. "That's fifteen thousand lydions in their currency," she added to Mrs. Gresham. "Or I will buy three for a shilling."

This offer was considered by Madame Brownscu who then said "One and threepence. It is a bargain, yes? For so do you get one good one and two bad ones. Oll are bad except those weech are en évidence."

At this moment a very large well-dressed woman bore down on them accompanied, to Mrs. Gresham's horror, by Victoria,

Lady Norton. On seeing them Madame Brownscu wreathed her face in a very unbecoming smile.

"Ha! it is her Excellency the Mixo-Lydian Ambassadress," she said. "Now shall oll be joy and you will pay thirty thousand lydions for two embroideries, yes?"

But Rose Fairweather had turned to greet Her Excellency and was evidently telling her about the high price of Madame Brownscu's embroideries, for the Ambassadress spoke quite sharply in Mixo-Lydian to her compatriot. And as if things were not already bad enough, the majestic form of Victoria, Lady Norton, loomed over them.

"Well, I've come over to the Sale," she said, putting up her face-à-main.

"Then," said the Ambassadress, ready to champion a Mixo-Lydian, however disagreeable, against all comers, "you must buy these embroideries. One schelling only. It is a bargain. Oll made by hand. You see the workman's thumb which is an English idiotism," and she held up a piece of embroidered linen on which dirty finger-marks were far too visible.

At this point Rose and Mrs. Gresham felt a fit of the giggles coming and went on to the stall for toys and children's clothes. Here the Vicar's wife was industriously selling, with Harold and Connie doing up the parcels very neatly, while their young brother sat on the floor, building a house with wooden bricks.

"Hullo, Mrs. Parkinson," said Rose. "How are the children?"

"They're fine, thank you," said Mrs. Parkinson. "Harold and Connie are doing nicely at school and Joe is as good as gold. Of course he was christened Josiah after the Dean but it seemed a bit too familiar, so Joe he was and Joe he is."

"And *what* a darling," said Mrs. Leslie. "Will you come to tea with me some day? We live in the Old Rectory, down the lane past the church."

Mrs. Parkinson looked alarmed.

"Not a party," said Mrs. Leslie, guessing Mrs. Parkinson's thoughts. "Just ourselves and bring the children of course.

There's a swing and the see-saw and they can use them as much as they like. And there's a sandpit where they can dig."

While she was speaking she had observed Mrs. Parkinson's pretty, rather harassed face behaving like a kaleidoscope with hopes and fears, with pleasure at the invitation, gratitude to Mrs. Leslie and, at the back of her mind, a fear that neither her clothes nor the children's would be good enough.

"And please let them come in their oldest clothes," said Mrs. Leslie, "so that they can get as dirty as they like. I am always dirty in the garden when the wind comes from the Hogglestock side."

"Oh, isn't it *dreadful*," said Mrs. Parkinson, finding a subject fit to her hand, "and the laundry so expensive and all. We're going to get one of those electric washing-machines some day when our ship comes in. At least I want to, but Teddy says he doesn't want to buy anything on the Never-never because you never know."

Mrs. Leslie, taking this to be hire purchase, said everyone did it now, but Mrs. Parkinson said Mr. Parkinson didn't like the idea and her pretty, tired face became so sad that Mrs. Leslie wanted to buy the newest model and give it to her at once. But one can't always be a fairy godmother simply by wishing to be one, so she smothered her regrets and went on to visit the other stalls. Among other expenses were the raffle tickets that were pressed upon her from all sides. Like Gaul she was divided into three parts on the subject of raffles. The first said if one ever did win anything in a raffle it was something one loathed and all you could do was to offer it for re-raffling. The second said it was really gambling and as she was not a gambler it was useless for her to try backing her luck. The third said in a rather common way Why not have a shot—so she bought quite a number of tickets for the good of the cause. Therefore she was rather bored when one of the New Town ladies, unknown to her, approached her with the offer of more tickets for another raffle.

"It's quite a good raffle," said the New Town lady. "It's a surprise one and nobody knows what the prize is, but it's frightfully good. Only sixpence a ticket. I've sold them nearly all and what my feet are like now is just no one's business. Just look at them."

Mrs. Leslie did not at all want to look at anyone's feet, for grown-up feet are seldom a really pleasant sight. It is one of life's little tragedies that the divine feet of babies, so soft and exquis-itely rounded, "les pieds ronds" as our peculiar neighbours the Gauls say when they mean someone is tiddly or has had one over the eight, inevitably turn into the average human foot with all the knobs, corns, whelks and bubukles that civilization brings. Women have been blamed for deforming their feet by their folly in wearing pointed shoes or high-heeled shoes, or indeed any shoes, but it is in their nature. When M. Anatole France made the Devil introduce the female penguin who has turned into a woman to a pair of corsets and he begins to tighten the laces, what does the female penguin say? "'Vous pouvez serrer un peu plus fort,' dit la pingouine."

It is no use crying over spilt milk, so she looked down compassionately at the New Town lady's feet, shutting her eyes as she did so and then expressed a sympathy which, she hoped, would conceal her compassionate disgust.

"I've only five tickets left," said the New Town lady, and so moved by the sight of her feet was Mrs. Leslie that she bought them all and asked for them to be put in the name of Mrs. Parkinson.

"Well, thanks ever so," said the New Town lady, "and I hope they'll bring you luck. They'll say what the prize is when they draw," and away she went, having done her good deed for the day.

By this time Mrs. Leslie was bored with the whole affair, but duty must be done, so she bought some home-made jam and cakes and then had to buy a raffia bag to carry them in. And then by great good luck she re-met the Greshams and Fairweathers and Canon Fewling so they all had tea together.

"And what awful things did *you* get, Canon Fewling?" said Mrs. Gresham.

"Well, I couldn't see anything I could bear to have in the house," said Canon Fewling, "so I gave all my raffle tickets to my housekeeper Mrs. Hicks. I understand that she has hopes of a mauve silk nightgown case embroidered with pansies.

"I once met a nightgown case which was puce-coloured silk with a flat artificial poppy made of sequins sewn onto it," said Mrs. Leslie, "and Slumber Dear Maid was written on it in shells—I mean those little iridescent shells. But I gave it to the daily woman we had then."

Canon Fewling asked what the daily woman did with it.

"Well, her little boy pulled all the shells off and put them down the scullery sink," said Mrs. Leslie, "because she said Maid wasn't a nice word and everyone said Daily Help, or The Lady as Obliges. Though why whoever translated that song into English said Slumber Dear Maid I can't imagine."

Captain Gresham, who held as a rule to the tradition of the Silent Navy, said it was always awkward if a word had two meanings: like maid, he added.

Canon Fewling said maid appeared to be used now only for a domestic help, whether she were a maid or not.

"Well, Fewling, we all know what you mean," said Captain Gresham. "Goes a bit near the bone," to which his wife said not to be common.

"But ackcherly no one says maid like *that* now," said Mrs. Fairweather. "Besides there was a very nice hairdresser when John and I were at Malta and he sang it in Italian and the words were quite different. They were about There never was a nice shady vegetable that was so dear and amiable, which was awfully silly, but of course the words were in Italian so it didn't matter anyway."

"They aren't bad words," said Canon Fewling. "If you don't mind my attempt at a voice I'll sing it to you sometime. That's the best of Italian. However silly the words are they go nicely to music. Think of Funiculi, funicula."

It may be that this excellent song, so loved by us in our youth, is not sung now; not even under its English form of "The day we went to Brighton in the famous motor-car," but John Leslie remembered it because his mother's sister Lady Agnes Foster, she who had a passion for the celibate clergy and died unmarried, used to sing it for the nursery. It is true that there is an English version, beginning, "Puffing, snorting, most pe-cu-li-ar," but we have forgotten the rest of it.

By this time the original subject of discussion had been lost, while the party recalled the nostalgic songs of their childhood; songs discouraged by the grown-ups but immensely popular in the kitchen where the nursery was occasionally invited to tea and allowed to see the cook's comic papers. Mrs. Leslie said she would certainly hold Canon Fewling to his promise and it was his turn to dine with her and when would he come. An evening was fixed and the Greshams were begged to join the party.

"You know you do make an *enormous* difference here, Tubby," said Mrs. Leslie. "I can't think how we ever got on without you," which might have embarrassed Canon Fewling—in a quite pleasure way—but at that moment the tea-urn gave a loud shriek (by kind permission of the baker's wife who understood its ways and had undertaken to chaperone it) and all were silent and held their countenances intently.

The grocer's wife, who had been one of the most active members on the bazaar committee, got up and said the raffle results would now be given out. There was a kind of fluttering and scuffling and then everyone settled down to silence.

The grocer's wife then read the names of the prizewinners aloud. As usual the people who always do draw a lucky ticket again had the luck and smugly came up for their prizes. John Leslie said the maths master at school when he was a boy had calculated that the chances for anyone in any raffle were at least a hundred to one but some people just couldn't help getting the winning number; which is perfectly true and never in our long and fairly respectable life have we ever won anything anywhere when it was a matter of chance.

"And now we come to the last lot," said the grocer's wife. "The Mystery one. Prizewinner is Number Sixty-six."

There was a gentle rustling as people looked for their ticket stubs (which they had mostly lost, or crammed into that little extra pocket in one's bag, or put down just for a moment and when I looked they were *gone*, absolutely gone.)

"Didn't you have some tickets, Mary?" said John Leslie.

"Oh yes," said his wife and grabbed about in her bag. "I bought some for Mrs. Parkinson—I mean I had them put in her name. Here they are. Oh, Lord!" but these words she said under her breath, for among them was the winning number.

"I think this is the winning number," she said. "It's Mrs. Parkinson's. I was taking care of it for her while she gave the children their tea," and she passed the winning ticket up to the grocer's wife.

"Electric washing-machine, number sixty-six, please come forward," said the grocer's wife.

But who can fully describe the emotions in Mrs. Parkinson's kind bosom. First she hardly heard and didn't quite believe; then she knew she was dreaming. Then various friends shoved and pushed her up to the platform and the washing-machine was formally introduced to her and she began to cry.

We do not know whether the Parkinsons had as yet established themselves in the affections of the New Town, for, like most rather artificial settlements, it still tended to look with slight suspicion on any newcomers who were more newly come than the earlier newcomers—which we hope is clear. But within her modest sphere Mrs. Parkinson had gained the goodwill of a number of the New Townites, many of whom knew what it was to have three children or more and not much money to spend on them. After a moment's silence the loudest applause ever heard in the Drill Hall broke out and continued, and what with clapping and stamping speech was impossible. The New Town chemist, a Welshman with a large beard, was suddenly inspired after the manner of his race to burst into song, which was "Men of Harlech." He of course sang it in Welsh, and everyone else in English if they happened to know the words and the effect was extremely impressive, especially when the sexton who also played the harmonium in church sat down at the old upright piano and banged out an accompaniment, thus practically forcing everyone to sing in the same key.

At the same moment an elderly man unknown to anyone there, came into the hall and took the tearful Mrs. Parkinson into his arms, saying "What on earth's the matter, Mavis?"

"Oh, dad, I've won the electric washer in the raffle!" wailed Mrs. Parkinson.

"All right, girlie," said Mr. Welk. "You've won the electric washer. That's fine. I've come over in the big car because I was doing a job over Southbridge way, so I'll run you home and see it properly fixed. Ted's a good lad but he got a double number when thumbs were given out."

So happy was Mrs. Parkinson to see her father that she quite forgot to go on crying, overlooked the slight upon her husband, and rather shyly brought Mr. Welk to talk to the Leslies. Most luckily they had heard of him from Mrs. Morland and received him as a valued friend—which indeed a good undertaker can be—and when Canon Fewling joined them he and Mr. Welk plunged into a deeply technical talk about funerals and the preparations therefore; Mr. Welk from a true love of his art and Canon Fewling from kindness.

"Well, Canon Fewling," said Mr. Welk, "it's always a pleasure to meet a gentleman of your cloth. Teddy—that's my son-in-law—has a great respect for you. He's a bit Low and I dessay it's just as well for the New Town, but I'm all for a bit of High myself."

"And I have a great respect for your son-in-law and for your daughter," said Canon Fewling. "They will do more good in the New Town than all my sermons. And a nice family."

"Ah, that's where you've missed the boat," said Mr. Welk kindly. "Not a sebbylate are you?" he added suspiciously.

"Not a professional celibate," said Canon Fewling calmly. "But a wife hasn't come into my life," and whether he said this with a slight tinge of regret we cannot say. There *are* chords in the human breast—as Mr. Jobling alias Weevle so truly and far too often said to Mr. Guppy.

"Well, we can't all have everything," said Mr. Welk broadmindedly. "I lost Mrs. Welk when Mavis was a toddler, but we managed to rub along, Mavis and me. And when I look at the kids—Harold's after me, you know—I often think how pleased Mrs. Welk would be to see her grandchildren so nicely brought up. Well, I suppose we've all got to die some day. Funny idea though, to think the world'll go on just the same."

"Still, some people are missed and for longer than you would believe, Mr. Welk," said Canon Fewling. "I can think of some. Friends I had in the war—I was in the Royal Navy then."

"I know," said Mr. Welk sympathetically. "Makes you wonder, doesn't it? What Mother will say when she sees me coming in at the Golden Gates an old man and she's only twenty-seven. I really don't know, but there's a scar on my arm I got trying to kiss her before we were engaged, when she was ironing. She'll remember that. Well, pleased to have met you, sir," with which tribute—both to Canon Fewling's character and his cloth we think—he went away with his daughter and son-in-law. The electric washer was manhandled by the New Town Boy Scouts who got it onto the trek-cart and wheeled it to the vicarage, and we are glad to say that Mr. Welk, being a man of his hands which Mr. Parkinson with all his goodness was not, connected the electric washing-machine to the mains in a most skilful way and had the pleasure after tea (which was a kind of tea-supper with sausages and mashed potatoes) of seeing his daughter's happy face as the water swished and swirled on its trial trip and a pile of the children's underwear emerged shiningly clean.

"It's too good to be true, daddy," said Mrs. Parkinson when her father took his leave.

"Rubbish, Mavis," said Mr. Welk. "You deserve it all, girlie. But don't let those kids meddle with it or you'll be having a short."

"Of *course* not, dad," said Mrs. Parkinson indignantly. "And I'll be able to do Teddy's surplices and the tablecloths and all. I *am* lucky."

"Well, you're like your Mother, girlie," said her father. "If she wasn't washing she was baking and if she wasn't baking it was something else. I miss her. Every day."

Mrs. Parkinson, who had never before known her father speak of his own feelings, found nothing to say, so she hugged him tightly and then he went away, contented that his daughter was happy.

The party from the Old Town walked homewards, glad to be released from a long act of courtesy. At the Leslies' gate they parted company, the Greshams towards Greshamsbury House, and Canon Fewling to his Rectory, pausing for a moment, as he nearly always did, to visit his church and let its peace sink into him. Never had he come away uncomforted, not even on the day when, some half-dozen years ago, he had heard from Miss Phelps, daughter of old Admiral Phelps at Southbridge, of her happy engagement to Mr. Macfadyen the wealthy manager and part-owner of Amalgamated Vedge. Canon Fewling liked and respected Mr. Macfadyen and knew that with him Margot Phelps would be loved and cherished till death them did part, but his heart had been very heavy. As time passed his burden, like Christian's, had been loosed from off his shoulders, and he could truly give thanks that his lines had fallen unto him in pleasant places and no longer did his old wounds bleed anew; but he remembered.

Then he went down the path and through his wicket-gate to the Rectory where there would be peace and an excellent evening meal prepared by Mrs. Hicks and a glass of good port, for Canon Fewling although a moderate eater and drinker did not mortify his flesh. And we think he was right, for it would not have done the slightest good to anyone else and possibly made him cross — a thing unknown to any of his large circle of friends. After supper he sat down, as was mostly his custom, at his very good piano and sang "Ombra mai fu" softly aloud to himself, rejoicing in the miracle worked by one George Frederick Handel almost two hundred years ago.

CHAPTER 2

The more Canon Fewling saw of the new vicar in the New Town the better he thought of him (his wife being hors concours) as in a fair way of becoming a valuable coadjutor in the parish. Up till now the Old and New Towns had not mingled, the Old Town resenting the spread of building over what it remembered as pastoral and arable land, the New Town looking upon the Old Town as a lot of old stick-in-the-muds. Not that Canon Fewling wanted the two to mingle any more than the Greshams and Leslies did, but he thought Mr. Parkinson was going to be a valuable link. Nor was he the only person to feel this. The Leslies had also found Mrs. Parkinson's simplicity and her perpetual adoration for her husband and children rather touching, with never a thought for herself. As for the Greshams and Fairweathers they had yet to make her better acquaintance and Mrs. Leslie sounded her husband on the question of a dinner party to which the Parkinsons should be invited. This subject they were discussing one afternoon about six o'clock when Mr. Wickham, the Noel Mertons' agent, dropped in on one of his many county rounds, not without hopes of a modest quencher. He and Canon Fewling who had both been naval men in the 1914 war had much in common, including strong heads. Mr. Wickham's was well known to be the strongest in the county, but as Canon Fewling in his position only drank in moderation and with his meals—except for a pre-dinner glass or two of sherry—their backers had little or no hope of seeing the contest of Thor and the dweller in Jotunheim.

"Well, here's mud in his eye to old Nasser and pretty well everyone else down that way," said Mr. Wickham, drinking his first glass of sherry at one gulp as Brother Laurence did his watered orange-pulp in Mr. Browning's poem; but not with any intention of frustrating Arians, his only aim being to enjoy a quick one and then take the succeeding sherries more slowly. "I've been trying to make an anagram out of Nasser but you can't do it. Shows the sort of man *he* is," to which Mr. Leslie replied that no one could make an anagram out of Wickham either, so what. Nor out of Leslie said his wife sadly.

The word anagram naturally led to a discussion of *The Times*'s contributions and a decision that it had far the best crossword in the British Press, but the quality of its paper for wrapping one's boots when packing was not what it was.

"Well, most of one's pals die in *The Times*," said Mr. Wickham. "First thing I do every morning as soon as I've had a good stiff one and a shave is to read *The Times* front page. I'd have missed a lot of pals without it."

Mrs. Leslie said she mostly looked at the Forthcoming Marriages so that she could remember to give presents to children of her old friends. And then, she added, the births, for the same reason, as most of her contemporaries had had daughters, which put them well forward in the Granny Stakes, though she was very fond of her boys.

"But there is one thing that I *do* think the Editor of *The Times* ought to see to," she said earnestly. "You know the way *The Times* is always folded in four and then folded again when it's pushed through the letter-box."

Mr. Wickham said the newspaper roundsman in his part had strict orders to throw it into his, Mr. Wickham's bed-room window which was on the ground floor and always open day and night, and not to fold it more than once.

"How *clever* of you, Wicks," said Mrs. Leslie. "But ours comes through the letter-box and by the time it's pushed through, the people who have died just where the fold comes get rather scraped and sometimes one can't read them and then you can't write to them and say how sorry you are and they might think you just didn't care. And I don't see what the Editor could do about that, so I shan't bother him by writing about it," she added kindly.

"Anyone who didn't know you as well as I do, Mary, would think you were very silly," said her husband, with a kind of loving pride that took any sting from his words.

"So I am," said Mrs. Leslie, quite truthfully, for if we come to examine ourselves we are all pretty silly in one way and another. "I think it was the war that did it—two wars for the older ones like us. Oh dear! But now, you men, do pay attention for a moment. I've asked the Parkinsons to dinner next Wednesday as it seems to be the only day Mr. Parkinson isn't being a Youth Club or a Confirmation Class or something. Will you come, Wicks? Tubby's coming and I want you to come too. The only thing is," she added, frowning as she considered social difficulties, "that I did want to ask the Fairweathers and the Greshams, but now I've asked you and Tubby I can't fit four more in. What shall I do?"

This question was considered in the light of special politeness and several very useless suggestions made.

"Well, I'll be the mug," said Mr. Wickham cheerfully. "Count me out if you like. But bless my soul if I hadn't forgotten it's the annual dinner of the Barchester Navy League, men only. *What* a night! I'm not going this year though. Wine and song are all very well, but you need a woman or two. Last time I went the fellows on each side of me went to sleep and I had the devil of a time to keep them from falling under the table. But Fairweather and Gresham are going and their wives aren't. Thank God we keep that Navy League dinner clean," he added unchivalrously. "How do we stand now?"

By this time everyone felt rather addled, but Mrs. Leslie who had been putting names down on a bit of paper and frowning, suddenly saw light.

"It's all right now," she said. "There's John and I, and two Parkinsons, and Tubby and you and Rose and Jane. Four of each."

"What a mind, what a mind!" said Mr. Wickham admiringly. "A giddy Harumfrodite, guests and arithmetic too—that's what you are. Well, I must be off. Here's to more and better dinners," with which words he finished his sherry, gave himself another one and took his leave.

It does not perhaps really matter if one has not an equal number of men and women to dinner, but it becomes a matter of personal pride to oneself and Mrs. Leslie was much relieved. Also, much as she liked both Fairweathers and Greshams, it would have made things easier if she sometimes could have a spare husband or a spare wife. This she could quite well do if it was just herself and her husband and neither of them would have taken the faintest umbrage, but when it was a party—and for the new vicar in the New Town—it would seem a little discourteous. Also, the Parkinsons probably Knew Etiquette and might feel it awkward to come as a united couple and meet wives who had no visible husband. But there is no book of etiquette, so far as we know, that deals with the difficulties when different social circles meet.

Still, no one was an offence-taker and the invitations were accepted gratefully. Time passed. The Bring and Buy brought in so large a sum that the committee decided that when all expenses were paid they would give the Mixo-Lydian miners half and keep half for the needs of their own town. By great good luck the most prominent Mixo-Lydians, including Madame Brownscu and her husband (if husband he was, but no one will ever know) had all gone to a Mixo-Lydian-Get-Together meeting at Southend, so a cheque for half the amount was sent to them, received with ingratitude and not acknowledged except

by the bank to which the committee very wisely sent its contribution. The two towns then relapsed into their normal state of
peacefully ignoring each other.

Any of our readers who are kind-hearted may have been
wondering how Mr. and Mrs. Parkinson would cope with a
dinner party in the Old Town, but if so, they have not realized
Mrs. Parkinson's quietly masterful influence. We are sorry to say
that Mr. Parkinson, in a kind of lapse into a long-buried class
consciousness, began by saying that (*a*) he knew the Leslies
didn't really want them, (*b*) that he knew Canon Fewling
despised him and (*c*) that those posh people didn't really want
them. But he had a most salutary shock when his wife Mavis,
whose love and devotion he well knew and valued, turned upon
him like a tigress bereft of her young and said if he wanted
Harold and Connie and Joe to grow up all Communist, that was
the way to do it and if he wouldn't go *she* would, so *there*. She
then burst into tears, a thing which in her courageous, hard-
worked life she hardly ever let herself do, and all the children
began to cry too, so of course Mr. Parkinson had to say how sorry
he was and eat all his words.

"All right, Teddy," said his wife. "It's at half past seven and
Mrs. Leslie said not to dress. You just come as you are, she said,
and she's going to wear just an ordinary summer dress. I shall
wear that one I got at Luke and Huxley in Barchester and all you
have to do is to see your hair's nicely brushed," and she kissed
him.

"But what about the kids?" said Mr. Parkinson.

"Well, Teddy, you *are* a one to look for trouble," said his wife.
"Mrs. Smith at Green Close says she'll come and sit in the house
while we're out and bring her mending and I said you'd see her
home," to which Mr. Parkinson replied that she had managed
beautifully and of course he would see Mrs. Smith home,
though he didn't think anyone would look at her twice.

So on the appointed evening Mrs. Smith came with her
sewing and her Patience cards and said not to worry about being

late because before Mr. Smith passed over she was quite used to
sitting up till all hours and it was a blessing he passed out once
too often and she had to put a nice cross on his grave with
Underneath are the Everlasting Arms on it and all his pals said
that name for a pub was a new one on them. And then the
Parkinsons went off to the Old Town.

By this time their blood was up and they went in at the
Leslies' garden gate as bold as brass and were at once received
into an atmosphere of warmth (for summer was as usual pretending it was chill autumn) and friendliness, with a wood fire in
the open fireplace. Mrs. Parkinson took a quick look at the
ladies, saw that they were wearing light summer dresses just like
hers, and determined to enjoy herself. Canon Fewling she and
her husband knew as well as they would allow themselves to do;
Mr. Wickham was an unknown quantity, as were Rose Fairweather and Jane Gresham. Mrs. Leslie took care to do what
introducing was needed in a clear voice and not too fast. Mrs.
Parkinson's general feeling of being in a fog and under Niagara
in a bad dream gradually subsided and with a glass of sherry she
really began to enjoy herself. And so quickly were the newcomers absorbed and acclimatized that when Mr. Leslie went round
refilling the company's glasses, Mr. Parkinson, who had not
quite drained his, said "Top it up please," in a most dashing
way and then wondered if the Bishop would have objected. This
of course shows how ignorant he was, as yet, of the Palace's
ways, for at its dinner parties the sherry was Colonial and no
second helpings were offered. Not that we wish for a moment
to denigrate crypto-Spanish sherry, finding ourselves that a
Colonial brand (for there is no word for Dominionishness
unless we may borrow Dominical) keeps us quite happy, but we
do maintain that the Palace should at least have made a gesture
of topping up, even if the second helping was watered—of
which the Palace was, we believe, quite capable.

Mrs. Leslie, feeling that too much Old Town gossip might
bore or even intimidate Mrs. Parkinson, asked her about her

children and was glad to hear that Mrs. Smith from Green Close was to be with them while their parents were out and said what a good thing it was to have kind neighbours.

"Oh, it *is*," said Mrs. Parkinson. "I've been lucky here. At Pomfret Madrigal where Teddy, that is, where Mr. Parkinson was before we came here, I couldn't hardly ever get anyone to take the children so I had to stay at home."

Mrs. Leslie sympathized in a very kind way, though behind her words her lower mind was off on a track of its own, rather snobbishly (so her upper mind considered) wondering at what point of acquaintanceship, if ever, one could possibly explain delicately, yet understandably, the curious convention of not calling one's husband Mister. It was evident that Mrs. Parkinson was conscientiously putting herself to school in these matters and that to say "my husband" would be a little like trying to talk French in France. But she liked Mrs. Parkinson all the more for it and decided that the matter was better left alone. Then she took her guests into the dining-room where she put Mrs. Parkinson comfortably between her host and Canon Fewling.

The Bring and Buy was a very safe subject to start conversation and Mrs. Parkinson found Canon Fewling most sympathetic on the subject of bazaars. Not that he knew anything particular about them, but having accepted them as one of the necessary evils of a parochial life he had determined, as he mostly did, to make the best of things, and was considered by the best authorities to be a very present help in time of trouble. He had a good private income and could well afford alms, yet offered them in a quiet and almost humble way and if possible did good by stealth, though he certainly would not have blushed to find it fame. But this trial had not come upon him.

"You know, Canon Fewling," said Mrs. Parkinson, "we are so lucky to have such a nice house in the New Town. I don't mean our old vicarage was nasty but it was a bit old and the kitchen grate simply *ate* the coal and it needed such a lot of polishing, and the kitchen floor was all stone and it *did* get cold and we couldn't afford a new carpet then."

Canon Fewling said he fully sympathized with her as he had been in the Royal Navy before he took Holy Orders, and the brasswork alone was several men's work. Not that he had to do it himself, he said, but if you had to supervise other people's work it was as well to know all about it first and he had apprenticed himself as it were to a pretty severe course of brass-polishing before he began to chivvy those under him. But blackleading, he had to confess, was beyond him.

"Well, the kitchen range in the old vicarage was in a *dreadful* state when Teddy and I first went there," said Mrs. Parkinson. But I did a bit at a time and it came up really lovely. In our new house all the kitchen fixtures are white enamel. It's lovely and easy to wash but of course once it gets chipped, it's had it. That's the only thing about the fridge. Oh, did you know I got the electric washing-machine at the New Town Bazaar? I can't think how it got into a bazaar. There's hardly a mark on it."

"I can tell you how it got in," said Canon Fewling, a little bit bored, but with a feeling that this nice clergy-wife must be helped and protected. "My housekeeper, Mrs. Hicks, made me send it."

Mrs. Parkinson, unable to digest so extraordinary a statement, stared at him.

"You see, she is a very good housekeeper," said Canon Fewling, "and she said she really needed a bigger washing-machine now and I thought it was reasonable, so I bought a larger size and sent the old one to the bazaar. I am extremely glad that you got it. I hope it's working all right."

"Oh, it's *ever* so nice and useful," said Mrs. Parkinson. "It was reely Mrs. Leslie that got it, at least she bought the tickets and wrote my name on them only I didn't know she had till it was read out. I am *ever* so grateful to her—and I look after it very carefully and don't let the kids touch it," she added, lest Canon Fewling were anxious about the present state of his washing-machine. "But why didn't you trade it in, Canon Fewling? They'd have given you quite a lot off the new one."

It was quite impossible for Canon Fewling to explain to his new friend that he was very comfortably off and—partly through generosity and partly through laziness—preferred just to get rid of it and have done, so he evaded the question and asked about her children and then each had to turn to the other side. Canon Fewling, though he had liked Mrs. Parkinson, was a little exhausted by her conversation and grateful to relax with Rose Fairweather, while Mrs. Parkinson was left high and dry. But only for a moment, for Mr. Leslie was a thoughtful host and felt that Mrs. Parkinson might be a little out of her depth, so he turned from Jane Gresham and applied himself to Mrs. Parkinson very agreeably, and their conversation was so dull that we really cannot invent it.

Meanwhile Mr. Parkinson had been alternately terrified and attracted by Rose Fairweather who was being, as she always was, her own kind, slapdash very individual self, expressing the deepest interest in Mr. Parkinson's children; perhaps rather a mean way of finding common ground, but a safe one, as it gave Mr. Parkinson infinite pleasure to expatiate on the good looks, good behaviour and intelligence of his children, while Rose was able to think about the large spare bedroom and whether she ought to have it repaired and repapered.

"If it wasn't that they keep on growing," said Mr. Parkinson, "there couldn't be nicer children. Mavis got some nice things for them at the Bring and Buy Sale, but they'll be out of them by Christmas."

Rose asked how old they were. Mr. Parkinson gave their ages, adding that he never saw youngsters grow as fast as those kids of his and Mavis's. Eating their mum and dad out of house and home they were. And out of clothes too, he added.

"Oh, I *do* know the clothes, said Rose. "My sister Geraldine had to wear my old dresses when we were small and I don't think she ever got over it."

Mr. Parkinson said Was it a fixation, like?

Rose said she didn't know what a fixation was, but whatever it was Geraldine was bound to have it.

"And I know what happens," said Rose. "Your wife gets nice new things for the children and doesn't buy any for herself. These unselfish women!"

Mr. Parkinson was not sure if he quite liked the criticism of his wife implied in Rose's last remark, and remained silent.

"Look here," said Rose. "My sister Geraldine who married my brother-in-law—he's a Colonel now—sent me a couple of dresses for the Bring and Buy but they were much too good so I kept them. They aren't my size—Geraldine's shorter than I am. If your wife would care to try them on I would simply adore her to have them. Now let's talk about your plans for the New Town."

Rose had not been a senior naval officer's wife all about the world for nothing and knew—or perhaps sensed as a wild animal does—that if Mr. Parkinson could be encouraged to talk about himself, he would eat out of her hand, and that without this encouragement he would be quite capable of having Proper Pride and saying his wife had a hundred and eight new French gowns, thank you. Mr. Parkinson said, from a truly grateful heart, that he daresaid Mavis wouldn't mind if she did; but Rose knew what he meant.

"Well, we'll make a plan after dinner," she said, "and not a word to your wife."

Apart from that nice Mrs. Fairweather's use of the expression Your wife, she appeared to Mr. Parkinson a Heavenly Visitant and he went so far as to answer for his wife's willingness.

"But don't *you* say anything," said Rose. "You'd be bound to spoil it all. Leave it to me," and she gave him a conspiratorial look that almost made his heart flutter.

By this time a great deal of ice had been broken and Rose was able to turn to Canon Fewling with a clear conscience, leaving Mr. Parkinson to their hostess who asked him to tell her about his children and thought of other things while he did so, though always getting into the straight before the post was reached.

"Well, Teddy, how is everything?" said Rose.

Canon Fewling said everything was remarkably well as far as he knew and what had Rose been doing.

Rose said Nothing much, as the children would be back from their various schools and universities shortly and she would then have her hands full, but she had been over to Framley to lunch with the Luftons which was always fun. And old Lady Lufton was very well and her garden prettier than ever.

Canon Fewling asked if she had seen the Macfadyens, for Mr. Macfadyen the big master market gardener, if there is such an expression, lived in a wing of Framley Court and some four or five years earlier had married Margot Phelps the not very young daughter of old Admiral Phelps at Southbridge.

"Of course I did," said Rose. "If it wasn't for me she'd never have got married at all. I mean she didn't know a thing about clothes or a hairdo and cared less, so I took her in hand, and look at her now."

Canon Fewling said he hadn't seen her for some time.

"No, she hasn't been over this way much," said Rose, "because her husband isn't very well."

"I'm *sorry*," said Canon Fewling. "He is an extraordinarily good fellow. I always looked on him as a particularly healthy one."

"Of course he's a good bit older than Margot and she's no chicken now," said Rose. "She's much older than I am. I think she's rather worried. If only Dr. Ford were over that way. All these Health doctors are too busy."

"I quite agree," said Canon Fewling. "We badly need some more men like Ford. There's young Perry over at Harefield—all old Dr. Perry's sons are doctors or surgeons, but only one wanted to be a G.P., and God bless him for it," he added fervently.

"Well, he's certainly next best to Dr. Ford," said Rose, "and I told Margot she *must* have him even if the whole British

Medical Association say no. When you're ill you want a *doctor*. I mean someone who will give you enough *time*. You can't hurry illness. It's no good just rushing in and giving people a prescription and rushing out."

By this time nearly all those present had joined in the discussion, mostly with regrets for the older doctors who found time to be family friends as well, and so raised up for their own children an inheritance of friendship.

"You have only to go back to where we used to be," said Canon Fewling. "The doctor who is the Beloved Physician— Saint Luke. You can find a ruling for most things in the Bible— if you read it," he added, and most of his hearers felt rather guilty.

"Well, Mr. Macfadyen read some of it every day, so he would have known," said Rose. "Margot told me so. And we all *ought* to, even if we don't. It's such a *useful* book."

Her host asked what exactly she meant.

"Well, you can find something horrid you can say to pretty well everyone you don't like if you try hard enough," said Rose. "There's a very good bit about how awful the people are who get up early and make a cheerful noise. You ought to know, Tubby," for by this affectionate name, appropriate to his stout unbending form, Canon Fewling had long been known to his friends.

"I think—I say *think*—I know what you mean," said Canon Fewling. "'He that blesseth his friend with a loud voice, rising early in the morning, it shall be counted a curse to him.' It's somewhere in Proverbs."

The party were silent, partly digesting that very true pronouncement, partly in deep admiration of Canon Fewling's memory, though not one of them could vouch for its correctness from personal knowledge.

"Well *done*, Tubby!" said Rose.

"One had that well drummed into one at sea," said Canon Fewling. "When I was a midshipman I learnt not to make a noise at the wrong time, especially anywhere near the Old Man's cabin."

"But is Mr. Macfadyen *really* ill?" said Mrs. Leslie, speaking across Mr. Parkinson to Rose Fairweather.

"I don't know," said Rose, "but I'm afraid he is. I don't know who his doctor is. But they're having a specialist from London. Oh *dear!*"

And indeed that was the only possible comment. Most of those present had known Mr. Macfadyen and had come to respect and admire him, for his unrightness and his excellent good sense; and also for his remarkable aptitude for all business that he undertook.

"*Poor* Margot," said Mrs. Leslie in heartfelt tones.

"I don't really know Macfadyen well," said Mr. Wickham, "but we've knocked up against one another pretty often one way and another and I have a great respect for him as a man of business with a heart. All we can do now is not to bother Margot. I had a word with Lufton and he'll let me know what's happening," for it was on Lord Lufton's estate that Mr. Macfadyen had lived for some considerable time, on terms very advantageous to his Lordship.

There was a brief silence, broken by Mrs. Parkinson who with rather choked utterance said she wished she could do something for that poor Mrs. Macfadyen, adding that if one couldn't do anything one could always pray. There was a brief silence during which Mr. Wickham, with a kind of quiet reverence that very few expected in him, remarked "Out of the mouth of babes and sucklings," and though Mrs. Parkinson certainly was neither, everyone felt the remark was well placed. The point of emotion was passed. Mrs. Leslie took her ladies away to the drawing-room where there was a not-unwelcome fire on an English summer evening. The talk was, not unnaturally, a good deal about the Macfadyens, so Mrs. Parkinson would have felt rather out of it had not Rose Fairweather come and sat by her and asked who was looking after the children while she and her husband were out.

"A nice woman, Mrs. Smith who comes in for an hour in the mornings," said Mrs. Parkinson. "There's only the one thing, we haven't the telephone, and I don't really like leaving the children at night, even with Mrs. Smith. I mean if anything happened she couldn't let me know. We've applied for one, and filled in the form but they say there's a long waiting list and I *do* worry."

"So I should think," said Rose warmly. "Good gracious! Suppose the Dean wanted to ring your husband up and couldn't!"

"Oh, I don't think he'd ring *us* up," said Mrs. Parkinson.

"Well, I don't see why not," said Rose. "I'll get on to the Deanery tomorrow and I'll tell Palmyra Phipps."

Mrs. Parkinson asked who she was.

"Well, she was at one of the local exchanges—Worsted I think," said Rose, "and she was so good she got promoted and she's a kind of Queen Telephonist now, but she's awfully nice and will do anything for old friends. If you get another form and fill it in I'll send it to Palmyra. The Dean will be furious. Why, if he wanted to come and see the church in the New Town he wouldn't know how to get at you."

We must admit that Rose had rather overplayed her part, but it is perfectly true that she immediately pulled every wire she knew and our reader will be glad to hear that the Parkinsons had a telephone installed within the next few weeks with an extension to Mr. Parkinson's study. Also that Mrs. Parkinson insisted on having two telephone books, one for general use and one for her husband in the study and, what is more, got them.

The expressions of sympathy for Mrs. Macfadyen were very genuine but one can't go on being sympathetic all through a dinner party for someone about whose state of health one only knows by hearsay, so the talk veered to other subjects, including the complete horribleness of practically all African and Asia, most of Europe and large parts of the Americas; pride of place in horribleness being of course awarded to the Middle East. Mrs. Parkinson felt a little out of it, though quite happy, we think, to be a spectator. Mrs. Leslie, realizing with a good hostess's sixth sense that her guest was feeling rather lost without her husband's support, asked her if she would like to see the rest of the house, an invitation that every nice woman will gladly accept.

Accordingly they visited the bedrooms and the two bathrooms and the ironing-room (which Mrs. Parkinson particularly admired) and then the top floor where there were several more bedrooms, a bathroom and a very large kind of attic playroom.

"You know we have three boys," said Mrs. Leslie, "so when they have friends to stay we can pack them all in up here and they can make as much noise as they like. Mr. Carter at Southbridge School told us about a man who puts something under the floor that deadens the noise, so we had it done."

"I *do* like the attic," said Mrs. Parkinson. "Sometimes Harold and Connie do make *such* a noise and then Joe begins to yell too, and if my husband is writing a sermon he nearly gets cross. We've got an attic too only it's smaller. I wonder if it would cost an awful lot to make it nice."

Mrs. Leslie said it was rather expensive, but well worth it if one could manage it.

"Well, I'll ask Dad," said Mrs. Parkinson. "He's always got plenty of wood and Old Jasper's a good carpenter."

Mrs. Leslie asked who old Jasper was.

"He's nephew to Jasper, that's the keeper up at Sir Cecil Waring's place, Beliers Priory," said Mrs. Parkinson, "and Dad says he's the best hand with wood he's ever known. Of course it's mostly elm with Dad, but I daresay Jasper could manage something for us and there's always plenty of saw-dust."

Mrs. Leslie, much impressed by Mrs. Parkinson's practical outlook, said how nice it must be to have such a useful father and as there was nothing else to be seen they went downstairs again and found the men in the drawing-room. On seeing them Mrs.

Parkinson was again stricken with paralysis and dumbness, but when her husband looked at her, as a sailor clinging to a plank may look at a friendly light, her courage rose to help him. Her host put her into a comfortable chair and everything began to feel safe and ordinary again.

"I *do* like your house, Mr. Leslie," she said. "It's given me some lovely ideas. There's only the one thing—" and she paused.

Mr. Leslie asked what it was.

"Well, I was wondering where the girls slept," said Mrs. Parkinson.

As the Leslies had only boys, her host was at a loss and said he was sorry he hadn't any.

"Oh, but who was it waiting on us at dinner then?" said Mrs. Parkinson.

Light broke upon Mr. Leslie.

"Oh, the staff, the maids that is, have their own bedrooms in the kitchen wing," said Mr. Leslie. "We built on a bit so that they could have it all to themselves."

"That *is* a good idea," said Mrs. Parkinson, "because then they can have their friends in without disturbing you and Mrs. Leslie."

"They not only can, but do," said Mr. Leslie, and as these words seemed to alarm Mrs. Parkinson he turned the talk to more peaceful subjects, such as the nice little pub, The Greshamsbury Arms, which straddled over the border line between Old and New Town and had red curtains in the Snug.

Mrs. Parkinson said what a pity it was that each parish didn't have its own licensing laws, because then if the Old Town closed earlier on one day and the New Town on another one could have a glass of beer in the Tap, or what was untruthfully called the Coffee Room, according to the day and hour. Mr. Leslie thought this an excellent idea and complimented Mrs. Parkinson on her knowledge.

"Oh, it isn't me, it's Dad," said Mrs. Parkinson. "He says a good undertaker ought to know everything, because you never know in the profession," which rather addled remark seemed to Mr. Leslie to have something in it. And with what he afterwards attributed to Direct Inspiration, he said he was sure Mr. Welk had an excellent all-round knowledge of affairs and evidently his daughter had inherited it.

He then rather wished he hadn't spoken, for Mrs. Parkinson, who under the influence of a good dinner and pleasant company had begun to feel most comfortably at home, was overtaken by a fit of self-consciousness which again caused her to twist her hands and go rather pink in the face. But with great presence of mind he said what a good thing it was that Her Majesty was going to Canada and the United States. This at once started a conversation about the Royal Family which, he felt, might go on for ever.

Luckily Mrs. Leslie, who had the good hostess's gift of seeing and hearing what her guests were up to and—if necessary—telling them not to, said, "Tubby! You did say you would sing us that song in Italian. My piano's nearly as good as yours. Would you? John could go over and get your music," but Canon Fewling said, with modest assurance, that he thought he had it all in his head and his fingers and would be delighted.

The Leslies' piano, though not quite so perfect as Canon Fewling's (perhaps because the boys played it so often and so loudly when they were at home), was a very good one. So he sat down and felt the keys, which were obviously pleased to meet him and the more horsy of them said to the others that this new bloke had damned good hands and they must give him a good run for his money. But these remarks were drowned by the Canon's preluding.

"Slumber Dear Maid," or "Ombra mai fu," whichever you prefer, for both sets of words are extremely silly (though we think the Italian are rather less shame-making, even if ours are even more vapid) is undoubtedly one of the World's Great Songs. There are a few airs which seem to have no real home and can be found almost from Asia to Peru, or at any rate from Russia to the Hebrides, the Calling Song from the Immortal Hour being one. Handel's aria is apt to be oversung or overlooked, but nothing can touch its immortality. We ourselves prefer it in Italian, probably because we first heard it sung in that language, but what matters is the singer, even if four different languages are sung in one opera.

Canon Fewling chose to sing it in Italian and very well he did it, without any fuss or pretension, almost as if he were singing aloud to himself, as we think he probably was. Several of his audience felt they would like to sniff, or even blow their nose, so much were they affected, but like Aeneas's audience in Carthage they were silent and held their countenance intently. And when he had brought the song to its lovely close they remained silent for a few seconds.

Mrs. Parkinson, all her fears and inhibitions temporarily swept away by the music, left her seat and went over to the piano to thank the singer, with tears in her eyes.

"Oh! I *did* like it," she said. "It's like being in church only almost better," which remark Canon Fewling took in very good part and thanked her.

"Well, it's Handel we ought to thank," said Mrs. Parkinson. "And he really ought to thank you, Canon Fewling, for singing it. I used to sing in the church choir at home and I loved it, but I hadn't much time when we were at Pomfret Madrigal and now I've really no time at all. The New Town hasn't got a choir yet, but Teddy thinks we could get one together, and then perhaps I could sing in it. And perhaps we could put on an oratorio. It would be wonderful, if I could sing in the Messiah!"

"I wish you would," said Canon Fewling. "If I played one of the arias quite softly, would you sing? No one will want to listen," he added with great cunning, certain that she would take this double-edged remark as kindly as it was meant and he began—as if improvising for his own pleasure—to play the air of "He shall feed his flock," humming it a little to himself in his

pleasant baritone. What he had hoped then happened. As the
fly that tastes sugar is lost in the sweets, so did Mrs. Parkinson as
the lovely harmonies made passionate her sense of hearing,
begin to sing almost unconsciously in a small voice, true and
clear. The talkers paid little attention to what was going on at
the far end of the room and even Mr. Parkinson, well away by
now with Mr. Wickham on the fascinating question of the
drains in the New Town and the way the kitchen sink had a
horrid habit of regurgitating till he thought of unscrewing the
bottom of the U-joint, clearing out the muck, screwing it up
again and putting boiling water well laced with soda down it,
paid little or no attention to what his wife was doing. But Mr.
Wickham had been listening with one ear and when the aria had
come to an end hardly knew what to say. So far as an ex-naval
man, now for many years agent of the Noel Mertons at Northbridge, could judge, that little Mrs. Parkinson was a Winner.

"You didn't tell me your wife sang, Parkinson," he said
accusingly.

Mr. Parkinson, who had always liked to hear Mavis singing
about the house and in church, didn't see why he should have to
discuss the subject with Mr. Wickham and nearly said so.

"But mind, Parkinson. She must *not* have lessons from anyone if it's Melba herself come back from the grave. They'd only
spoil a lovely little natural voice," said Mr. Wickham.

As Mr. Parkinson had no thoughts of having his wife's voice
trained seeing that (*a*) it was a nice voice anyway, (*b*) he couldn't
afford it and (*c*) Mavis wouldn't have time with the kids and all,
it was all the easier for him to say Certainly not, in a very manly
way and try to hide from himself the fact that it was a thing that
had never crossed his mind. But in his mind there began to come
to life a thought—no bigger than a man's hand—of more and
better singing in his church and perhaps raising enough money
to put the little organ into order so that they could use it instead
of the harmonium. Mrs. Leslie was now dispensing drinks and
the question of music was allowed to lapse, rather to Mrs.

Parkinson's relief. Mr. Leslie had gone out of the room. When he came back his wife looked at him enquiringly.

"Did you get on to Framley Court?" she said.

"I did," said her husband. "Lufton says Macfadyen is much the same. Young Perry had been today and will come again early tomorrow unless they have to ring him up earlier. He isn't in pain—drugs and things."

"That's what doctors say," said Mr. Wickham darkly. "I know when I had something-or-other-itis in the war and our gunboat going up and down and sideways and practically standing on her head, our medical bloke said I was doing nicely. I'd have done *him* nicely if I could have got at him, with a scalpel and a pair of surgical scissors, and throttled him with a bandage and put a mustard plaster in his mouth."

Mr. Leslie said Mr. Macfadyen was having sedatives and dozing comfortably.

"*I* know their tricks and their manners," said Mr. Wickham. "They stuff you with things till you're stupid and then say you had a quiet night. I'd give them quiet nights. I'll go over myself tomorrow. I've known Macfadyen ever since he came to these parts and what he didn't know about market-gardening wouldn't fill a wren's egg. How was Margot?"

Mr. Leslie said, rather unconvincingly, that he hadn't had time to ask.

Mr. Wickham's lips could have been seen to form and indeed heard to utter in a very low voice the words "You had all the time there is," but luckily no one saw or heard. The party was over and the guests dispersed with many thanks. Canon Fewling said he would run the Parkinsons down to the New Town, which he did, and then asked if he could look at the children in bed. All three were buried past the depth of plummet in that dreamless sleep that most of us will never know again till a longer sleep comes upon us. He looked at them, with affection and without sentiment, said good night and drove home thinking of a great many things and of the past. When he had put his car away he went, as he often did, into his dark silent church and earnestly prayed for comfort. Not for himself but for a friend who might very soon be a widow. Then resolutely turning his mind from the past and the future he walked back to his house, went to bed and presently slept.

Over at Framley there was much sorrow and anxiety. Mrs. Macfadyen, she who had been Margot Phelps, had not married the wealthy market-gardening expert till she was a young middle-age. The marriage had been a very happy and peaceful one. Her husband could give her everything she wanted as far as money was concerned, but having known comparative poverty nearly all her life she had continued to live simply, which suited her husband very well. And having kept open house during many years for all her parents' naval friends, it was quite easy for her to switch over to her husband's gardening and agricultural friends; it was little more than exchanging the talk of one trade for the talk of another. Instead of halyards and bowlines and high seas it was green vegetables and root vegetables and agricultural improvements. Instead of Captains and Lieutenants it was big growers from Holland and Denmark and elsewhere. Men are much the same all the world over, and where she used to feed and entertain her parents' naval friends, so had she entertained and fed the growers—unknown to the ordinary world—who altered or improved the growth and pretty well controlled the price of green things from mustard and cress to the outsize pumpkin which is of little use except as a Jack o' Lantern, if there is anyone left who has the skill to scoop it out when at the proper ripeness and carve its horrid eyes and mouth through which the candle will terrifyingly shine.

Accordingly on the following day Mr. Wickham drove himself in his disgraceful little car to Framley and so to Mr. Macfadyen's half of the Court. As he neared it he looked up at the windows. Most of them were open, and there were not any blinds down, so he drove on and ran his car into the kitchen yard, where the cook was washing the worst of the dirt off some vegetables under the tap.

"Well, cook, here you are as large as life and twice as natural," said Mr. Wickham as he got out of the car and shut its rickety door with repeated bangs till it finally came to rest. "Anything to eat here? I've hardly had any breakfast."

Cook, who was a local woman and old acquaintance of Mr. Wickham, said there was plenty of eggs and bacon if he liked to come to the kitchen. So in he came and seated himself at the kitchen table while cook began to fry the breakfast for him.

"I s'pose you heard about poor Mr. Macfadyen," said cook. "Gave me quite a turn it did and I let the potatoes boil dry. Look at the saucepan," and she showed him a large saucepan with a horrid mass of black sticky cinders in it.

"It'll take me half the morning to get that clean," said cook, "and then I expect there'll be some of the bottom chipped and that's the way you get the stomach ulcers. Dreadful they are. My auntie had them and sometimes she couldn't hardly eat her dinner and she'd always been a hearty feeder."

Mr. Wickham, after a little more of the badinage which is better than a tip to the servants that know you well, asked how was Mr. Macfadyen. Cook said she couldn't rightly say because Dr. Perry hadn't been yet and yesterday she had missed him because she was having her afternoon off in Barchester. But when she did see Mr. Macfadyen last—yesterday it was—cook said, it give her quite a turn. He'd all fallen in, gone thin-like, and his face, well you could nearly see his teeth through his cheeks so fallen in he was, and his nose you could have sharpened a pencil with it. He said he felt cold and she'd put a fresh hot bottle in his bed and his poor feet were like ice, but she didn't like to trouble Mrs. Macfadyen because she'd been up for two nights and was having a nice lay-down.

"Well, well, Shakespeare isn't dead," said Mr. Wickham aloud to himself. Cook said rather tartly there was lots of people not dead like old Nasser and old Cruskoff—whom Mr. Wickham privately identified as one of the nastier Russians—and all them Syprots said cook and if she didn't get on with her work there wouldn't be any dinner and a nice bit of lamb it was, and she bustled about so violently that Mr. Wickham thought retreat was indicated and went through the passage to the other side. In the hall he found Mrs. Macfadyen sorting the post which had just come and putting a large pile of business letters aside.

"Hullo, Wicks," she said. "You're early."

"That's as maybe," said Mr. Wickham. "I came over to see if I could do anything. If I can't I'll go away," but this he said very kindly.

"Oh no *don't*," said Mrs. Macfadyen. "Come into the sitting-room," and she took him into a large comfortable room, half office, half sitting-room with rather large manly chairs, very fat and comfortable.

"Donald isn't any better," she said and for a moment Mr. Wickham could not think what she meant, for very few people used Mr. Macfadyen's Christian name and he signed letters and cheques with his initials. "Dr. Perry has been as kind as he could be, but there we are. I don't know, Wicks; I *don't* know," and she looked out of the window.

"Cheer up, Margot," said Mr. Wickham. "You're a *Good* girl. Always have been. Chin up and all that. What does young Perry say?" for though Gus Perry was now in his forties his father was still fairly active and all his older patients, though wishing good fortune to the young doctor, naturally preferred the older man who had seen them through childbirth and then seen the results of that interesting phenomenon through all their childish ailments.

"I don't think there is anything he *can* say," said Mrs. Macfadyen. "I mean Donald is dying. Of course Dr. Perry says he isn't, but I know. You see he has really stopped wanting to live."

"You're a plucky girl, Margot," said Mr. Wickham. "Most people can't face that. But when people don't want to live that's that. We used to see it in the war—I mean the old war when I was with the navy. If a fellow had stopped one, sometimes he was so angry that he swore he'd get well and sock some bloody Germans. Some of them just said Thy will be done."

"But that was all right, Wicks, wasn't it?" said Mrs. Macfadyen, for the moment almost forgetting her own unhappiness in a philosophical discussion.

"Not on your life it wasn't, Margot," said Mr. Wickham. "How the dickens did they know whose will it was? It was certainly the Hun's will, but what God was thinking about nobody knows—nor never won't," he added, his double negative— though perplexing—ramming his point home. "You've got to leave that to Him. No arguing, no pack-drill."

Though not entirely convinced by Mr. Wickham's arguments, Mrs. Macfadyen couldn't help laughing which of course did her a great deal of good, and she asked Mr. Wickham if he would like to go up and see Mr. Macfadyen, which invitation he at once accepted, with the rider that if Mr. Macfadyen was too tired she mustn't press it.

"You can trust me, Wicks," said Mrs. Macfadyen. "I'll go and tell him," and she went away.

Mr. Wickham looked at the cattle sales in the *Barchester Chronicle* and a very similar account of the same sales in the *Barchester News*; glanced with a great lack of interest at the leaders and—as he knew he would be mysteriously forced to do—settled down to the *Chronicle*'s Crossword Puzzle. Not without some annoyance though, for ever since that form of puzzle, or quiz, or rebus first crossed the Atlantic, nearly forty years ago now, only the *Thunderer* has kept up its remarkably high standard. No longer though, alas, do we have EME and ORLOP, those favourites of the early 20's. While he was still struggling with 26 across, "How to break up that infernal shadow (8)", Mrs. Macfadyen came back and said her husband sent his thanks to Mr. Wickham and didn't feel up to visitors yet.

"Don't think it's unfriendliness, Wicks," said Mrs. Macfadyen. "It isn't. It's just—" and she paused.

"Yes, I know. Turning one's face to the wall," said Mr. Wickham sympathetically. "I turn mine like billy-o if anyone tries to visit me when I've a hangover."

"But Donald doesn't have hangovers," said his wife indignantly. "He's practically teetotal except for wine at dinner. He knows all about wine," she added proudly. "Especially claret."

"Why the dickens claret of all drinks?" said Mr. Wickham.

Mrs. Macfadyen said because he was Scotch.

"All right, I'll be the mug," said Mr. Wickham. "Why because he's Scotch?"

"Because the Scotch always drank good French wines," said Mrs. Macfadyen proudly. "The old friendship between France and Scotland."

"Oh, well, good luck to them," said Mr. Wickham, whose notions of the Old Alliance were sketchy if even that. "But look here, Margot, is there *anything* I can do? Because if there is I'll do it, even if it means stealing the Bishop's apron."

"Good old Wicks," said Mrs. Macfadyen, half laughing, almost half crying. "Look here. If you want to come upstairs, come. He won't really mind when he sees you."

Much as Mr. Wickham would have liked to see an old friend, he felt that if not really minding were Mr. Macfadyen's condition, it would be as depressing for him to see his old friend as it would be tiring for the old friend to see him, and told Mrs. Macfadyen so.

"Good old Wicks," she said gratefully, to which Mr. Wickham replied that a wink was as good as a nod to him and he would go over to the Luftons and see what was cooking. With which elegant words of farewell he gave Mrs. Macfadyen a brotherly hug with one arm and went away. Mrs. Macfadyen looked after him regretfully. Not that she had any tender feelings for him, but he was an old friend and one could talk freely with him, which would lighten her burden of loving anxiety.

Faithful to his rule of always killing two birds with one stone if they were both there at the same time, Mr. Wickham walked back to the Old Parsonage where the Dowager Lady Lufton lived in quiet comfort, being pretty sure that he would find one or other of the Luftons there. Nor was he wrong. Old Lady Lufton (a title which she much preferred to Dowager, insisting also that her friends should address letters to her as Mary, Lady Lufton) was as usual in her garden which, as always happens in late summer, was far too full of reds and yellows but this cannot apparently be helped.

"Good morning, Lady Lufton," said Mr. Wickham to the Dowager. "May I pay a call on you? I've just been up to see Mrs. Macfadyen."

Lady Lufton asked, most earnestly, whether the news was better.

"We don't like to bother Mrs. Macfadyen too much," she said. "When my husband was very ill the end of his life, *so* many kind friends wrote or called or telephoned and it was most difficult to answer them all. I did of course, but I had the girls to help me and dear Ludo. Poor Mrs. Macfadyen has no one. Not that one would have expected it of course at her age, and her parents are too old and rather ailing I am sorry to say—though I have never met them," her ladyship added.

Disentangling her ladyship's obiter dicta as best he could, Mr. Wickham said Margot was a fine girl even if a bit long in the tooth and he felt quite sure she would rather be alone with her husband and there was an excellent nurse and young Dr. Perry came every day. And when he said "young," he added, none of us were as young as we were, adding chivalrously, "Except you, Lady Lufton."

"That is most kind of you, Mr. Wickham," said Lady Lufton quite unmoved, "but I am getting on for seventy."

"Comes to that, we all are," said Mr. Wickham. "What's happened to the years between *I* don't know. Can't say that the locusts have eaten them — we don't get locusts over here luckily, nasty plaguy things. I saw too much of them in North Africa."

Lady Lufton who like most people thought of Mr. Wickham as adscriptus glebae, part and parcel of Barsetshire, asked when that was.

"Oh, a spot of trouble in old World War One," said Mr. Wickham. "Can't remember why I was out there, but I was. Everyone with leprosy or flies in their eyes. Give me Barsetshire for peace and comfort," which made the Dowager laugh and she asked him what he had been doing lately.

"Oh, going to and fro in the earth and walking up and down in it," said Mr. Wickham. "Just the usual."

"But you are *not* the devil, Mr. Wickham," said Lady Lufton.

"Kamerad!" said Mr. Wickham. "It isn't many people that know their Bible now. We had a good talk about it at the Leslies the other evening. Rose Fairweather began it. That girl's a fair startler. Looks like an ingénue and she's the mother of a good family and reads the Bible."

"I have noticed," said Lady Lufton, "that when people quote the Bible it is nearly always against someone or something. I suppose we all feel like that."

"Rum thing," said Mr. Wickham. "Lots of things there's no accounting for. Well, I must be getting away myself. Give my love to Lufton and Grace. If there's any change in Mr. Macfadyen, or Margot needs any help, will you be so very kind as to let me know, because I know *she* won't. Her parents are a bit failing, too. Hard lines."

Lady Lufton said, quite truly, that they had all come to like Mrs. Macfadyen very much and would certainly keep an eye on her and Mr. Wickham got into his disgraceful rackety car and went away on his own concerns.

There was not enough cheerful news that summer for older people to want to travel very much. As usual the United States and Canada were out of bounds for the simple reason that the

pound was only worth a little over two dollars unless you were
Big Business and travelled on expenses, or had relations in
Hickville or Saskatoon. The young, we are glad to say, got
themselves abroad in what to us would seem horrible discom-
fort, going all over Europe in small rackety cars with sleeping-
bags and all came back full of good food and their noses peeling.
The Bishop and his wife went on a Hellenic cruise on the cheap,
as his Lordship gave talks on "The Mediterranean Culture."
Unfortunately for him Miss Hampton and Miss Bent from
Southbridge were among the passengers and when they passed
the island of Lesbos, off the coast of Mysia, and the Bishop
mentioned it by its present name of Mitylene, those redoubtable
ladies had an impromptu lecture of their own in the nasty little
room called Ladies' Lounge and told their tightly packed audience all about it. And not only that, but a very pleasant undergraduate, one of the Dean's many grandchildren, offered to sing
at the ship's concert in the large saloon and chose a charming
Victorian song called "My Lesbia hath a beaming eye," which
was subsequently sung all over the ship by the young tourists of
both sexes with several quite original versions of the words, and
nearly all the passengers said it was *such* a charming song and *so*
English.

But we divagate—and we may say that without divagations
our immortal works would be uncommonly short.

Mr. Wickham who in his capacity as agent to Sir Noel
Merton, Q.C., over at Northbridge, got about the county far
more than was really necessary—though we have to admit that
he did make many useful friends in every class—now rather
neglected his employer and was over at Framley a good deal. A
few years earlier when Mrs. Macfadyen was still Miss Phelps
and weighed down (though she never thought of herself in that
light) by elderly parents poor in health and in pocket, Mr.
Wickham had kindly offered to marry her—more from strong
benevolence of soul than from deep affection—and to his

sincere relief she had told him that she had just promised to marry Mr. Macfadyen. Mr. Wickham had been vastly relieved by the good news which not only let him safely out but also meant a comfortable future for Miss Phelps. We cannot say that it broke his heart, nor his rest, and he went on having a very comfortable friendship with both Mr. and Mrs. Macfadyen. Someone who has once cared for you a good deal can be a great comfort when you are in sorrow—a kind of souffre-douleur to whom you can say anything. But though all West Barsetshire began to arrange that the wealthy market-gardener's widow should marry again, we may say that no such idea was in her head—nor in Mr. Wickham's. Still it was very comforting to her to know that she could talk freely to her old friend and it did her a great deal of good.

When we say widow, Mr. Macfadyen was not dead, but Dr. Perry and two specialists knew they could do no more. There was talk of calling in Sir Omicron Pie, but Mrs. Macfadyen said very firmly that her husband was to be left in peace, encouraged thereto by all her most trusted friends. For though Sir Omicron Pie's position in the medical world and his beautiful hands and his admirably tailored clothes and his air of sympathy are all excellent in their way, there is a tide in the life of man when no doctor or surgeon can do more and it is kinder to let the little wandering pleasant soul, no longer guest and companion of the body, go alone on its own way, as a Roman Emperor's did more than eighteen hundred years ago. He was not in pain and was often back in his own country and in his youth and almost his last words were regarding the growth of ingans and syboes and neeps, and the policies of the big house where he had worked as a boy in the Kingdom of Fife.

The funeral was in the church at Framley. His body was laid in the little churchyard and life went on. The Luftons begged Mrs. Macfadyen to stay in the house as long as suited her and she was not unwilling to do so, for there were many friends and acquaintances in the world of big commercial growers who wrote to her with sympathy and sometimes to ask a question or two, most of which she could answer, as she had learnt a good deal from her husband and had a very clear practical mind. There would be a good deal to clear up and she would be able to help the lawyers considerably. The Luftons were very glad to have her there and for the moment the question of her moving did not arise. But she realized that the Luftons would not want their tenant's widow as a fixture and that therefore she must make some kind of decision about a home for herself. Her husband had made ample provision for her financially and as the Luftons had not any new tenant in view, it was for her to decide how soon she could give up the house and where she would settle. So it was with satisfaction to both sides that things remained as they were for the time being and she was able to deal with her husband's affairs.

If Mrs. Macfadyen had told anyone the real truth, she did not at all want to leave the house where she and her husband had so happily lived. And even less did she wish to stay with her parents at Southbridge, for though she was truly attached to them and a dutiful daughter, they were getting old and she was determined to do everything in her power to help them but not to live in the same house. Mr. Macfadyen when making a new will after his marriage had discussed everything with her and she knew exactly where she stood. And though no money can make up for the touch of a vanished hand there is no doubt that sorrow is easier to bear if one has an assured background. And with money one can do many things that the departed owner would have wished.

West Barsetshire, at any rate that part of it, had wondered whether Mrs. Macfadyen would wear mourning. Not that anyone expected black crape and a heavy black veil and note-paper with a black edge half an inch wide (though gradually tapering to a fine Italian edge as the time passed), nor would they have liked it if she had flaunted in orange and scarlet. And we think she did quite rightly and as the county expected. To wear black in daily life and about the garden and the policies (as her husband had continued to call them) would be affected and silly. Also, though she was not vain, black was to her not a becoming colour. So she went about her daily work in her ordinary clothes and did get herself one good black coat and skirt and one good black dress which would do for evenings or afternoons, only she mostly forgot to wear them.

And had she known it, Admiral and Mrs. Phelps at Jutland Cottage were feeling much the same. They truly loved their only child, were glad that she was happily married and grieved with her for her loss, but to have her home again would never do. They had got used to being alone together. Both were always busy, there was a coming and going of Southbridge friends, and even now naval men would turn up who had served under the Admiral when he was first a Captain, and Mrs. Phelps enjoyed fussing and giving them a bed, or even two beds, in what had been their daughter's bedroom. And we may say that her daughter's marriage had been a good thing for Mrs. Phelps, who had rather got into a habit of depending on her stalwart Margot and yet wanted to run her own house. For many of us, as we get older, become in a way more fiercely independent, just to show that we are not incapable drivelling idiots. Our young have a fairly low opinion of our capacity to look after ourselves and sometimes quite unnecessarily put a kind hand—we speak figuratively—under our elbow to help us walk; but in moments of crisis they will still mostly look to us—which is our reward. But Mrs. Macfadyen was no chicken and had now considerable wealth and nothing particular to spend it on and did not in the least wish to live at home again.

Nor did the Luftons wish to lose her. Mr. Macfadyen had been of real help to them as a tenant, his wife had become a pleasant friend and his widow would always be welcome at Framley Court. The dowager Lady Lufton knew what it was to lose a beloved husband who was also a pillar of strength and though neither lady spoke of it this was a bond between them.

Still one's parents are one's parents, however trying, and even Mrs. Wilfer, however irritating to her daughters Bella and Lavinia, was a good mother, and so were Admiral and Mrs. Phelps good parents to their daughter Margot and never gave Mr. Macfadyen any cause to say, as Mr. George Sampson said to Mrs. Wilfer, "Demon, with the greatest respect to you, behold your work."

And as Mrs. Macfadyen was a good woman, in the very nicest and least priggish sense of that word, she thought a good deal about her parents. One plan would be to ask them to come on a visit to Framley, but she knew that her father, now of a considerable age, hated leaving his own home, and her mother certainly would not leave her husband with only a village woman to come in for a couple of hours and do for him—a sinister expression but also used for the rough and ready and quite kind service that untrained help can be. The only alternative she could see was to go and stay with them which she didn't in the least want.

However Providence, casting about to see what meddling it could do, was inspired to make a suggestion to Mrs. Everard Carter, wife of the headmaster of Southbridge School, that she should invite Mrs. Macfadyen to come on a visit. This invitation Mrs. Macfadyen accepted with great pleasure. The Carters were old friends, they had all worked together in various ways during the war, and Mrs. Macfadyen, an only child, accustomed all her life to the society of boys and men in the Royal Navy and elsewhere, found the school much to her taste. Accordingly she told the Luftons of her plans—who wholeheartedly approved them—and drove herself over to Southbridge, passing through Greshamsbury on the way but not stopping there. Canon Fewling, walking up the village street, recognized her car, raised his hat and smiled. Mrs. Macfadyen smiled back and with a wave of her hand sped on her way.

"Ships that pass in the night," said Canon Fewling aloud to himself. "Now, where does that come from? It's Longfellow; but which poem?" and when he got home he looked it up in the *Oxford Book of Quotations* and it came not from "Evangeline" as he had thought, but from a very dull poem in English hexameters called "Elizabeth." And then, for we all have some superstitions in us, however unsuperstitious, he shut the book, opened it again and put his finger down at random, a kind of Sortes Oxfordianae, and lit on Fluellen's excellent aperçu on the wars of Pompey the Great where there was no tiddle-taddle or pibble-pabble in Pompey's camp. He then gave it up and set his mind to his sermon for next Sunday.

It was with a rather pleasant feeling of nostalgia that Mrs. Macfadyen drove down to the river valley and saw the hideous mid-Victorian Neo-Gothic chapel of Southbridge School (built by the same architect who had designed Pomfret Towers) rising among the School buildings with the playing-fields beyond it and the river in its winding course marking their limits. Old familiar places, and still there. And several familiar faces too, both old and young, as she drove up to the School, one being the Carters' butler Edward, who had been odd-job man with their predecessors the Birketts and had every intention of seeing them into their graves or their retirement, being himself of course immortal. Edward graciously took charge of her. Kate Carter came out to welcome her and said Everard would be back for lunch and there were already several invitations for her from friends in the village. So Mrs. Macfadyen went with Mrs. Carter into the house and felt that this was—for a time at any rate— the Land of Lost Content.

CHAPTER 3

Southbridge School has not changed much since we last saw it. Most of Everard Carter's staff were interested in their work and happy in their surroundings. Year after year the stream of boys poured in at one end round-faced, apt to be unwashed about the neck and behind the ears, given to frightful boasting about what they had done in the holidays, a prey to whatever collecting was in vogue at the moment, whether stamps, autographs, insects or cigarette cards. Year after year they had their physical, moral and mental mumps and measles. There were—as far as we know—no Young Woodleys, no bullies, hardly any prigs, and the very few who tried to show off by secret smoking were made to smoke one very strong cigar which discouraged them for a considerable time. In fact a nice average set of nice average boys. Rather to Mr. Carter's disappointment there were very few originals and eccentrics, but we fear that this breed is becoming rarer. No one kept a chameleon in his desk, nor did the Upper Fifth tie wet towels round their heads during the prep. period in emulation of Sydney Carton.

These grievances he let loose on Mrs. Macfadyen and as they did not in any way affect her, she took them very calmly.

"Now, about plans," said Kate Carter. "I expect you want to go and see your people tomorrow. I met your father yesterday and he said he was looking forward to hearing all your news. He is getting rather deaf."

"I thought so last time I was over," said Mrs. Macfadyen, "but we didn't talk about it. If I get deaf I'll have one of those little things you stick in your ear and there's a cord that goes into a little box."

Mrs. Carter said she had an aunt with a thing like that, but it used to buzz and click so much that she gave it to the Barsetshire Red Cross. Her aunt said it was much easier to hear people without it if only they would speak clearly and slowly and above all, Not Shout.

Everard Carter capped this with a great-aunt who had an ear-trumpet, relic of an older civilization, slightly curved, with a kind of decoration of thick black silk cord, rather like a military bugle. They all agreed that being deaf was a Bad Thing, chiefly because people got bored with you, and then the talk shifted to more local matters such as how the nice vicar Colonel the Reverend Edward Crofts and his wife were, and whether Eileen (formerly barmaid at the Red Lion who had married Colonel Crofts's batman and had now for some years been cook to Colonel Crofts and his wife) still dyed her hair gold: which she did, only now it was red-gold.

Kate, who felt that her husband would probably want to take his guest round the school, said firmly that Mrs. Macfadyen would want of course to see her parents before embarking on further gaieties. Her guest said Oh *please* say Margot as she always had been Margot in Southbridge. Kate as in courtesy bound said then she must call her Kate and the consequences were—as they always are—that for at least twenty-four hours each lady felt both self-conscious and rather rude, after which they settled down pretty much as they were before, and got on very well. Although it was not a Sunday, on which day the Carters always had a couple of masters to supper, Mrs. Carter had invited two of the junior masters and had asked Matron to join them.

"You won't mind, will you?" she said to Mrs. Macfadyen. "I mean having people to supper," to which Mrs. Macfadyen said she was rather tired of living alone and the more the merrier and might she ring up her parents, which she accordingly did and arranged to go over and see them next day.

The dinner party was quiet and pleasant. The two new masters were nice young men with good manners. One of them had a sailor uncle who thought his father had known Admiral Phipps, but when Mrs. Carter said she was sorry but it was Phelps, he said he was always making an ass of himself one way or another and the chap he was thinking of wasn't Phipps but Stephens. Everyone agreed that the mistake was quite understandable. The other master, who had been thinking of some remote claim to naval colour because his great-aunt married a paymaster who died before the year was out, took warning by his colleague's fall and kept his own counsel. But what Mrs. Macfadyen really wanted to know was all about the School and the Old Boys that she had known as knickerbockered little boys, so the young masters were rather left out of it and argued about forthcoming cricket matches.

But the outstanding success was Matron, in a semi-evening dress of beige lace, dispensing graciousness in an almost overpowering way. Luckily Mrs. Macfadyen had a very good memory and though it was several years since she left Southbridge she could put some kind of memory to most of the old boys that Matron mentioned. She also asked after Matron's eldest nephew, the one that was radio operator in the largest Atlantic liner and was always known as Sparks (his name being Empson) and was delighted to hear that he was doing extremely well. Then everyone went to bed; Mrs. Macfadyen rather relieved, though we do not think she realized it, by being in a house where everyone was very much alive, read some of Mrs. Morland's last Madame Koska book which Kate had thoughtfully put by her bed and only just managed to turn off the light before she slid into a deep dreamless sleep.

Next morning her breakfast was firmly brought to her in bed. When she had dressed she went downstairs and found Kate

Carter in the back drawing-room which was also in a way her sitting-room and her seat of judgment for all domestic squabbles.

"You are out to tea, I remember," said Kate, "with your people. Oh, and Mr. Feeder and Mr. Traill are having a party after tea. Will you come? Miss Hampton and Miss Bent will be there."

Mrs. Macfadyen said she would love to, for though those strong-minded and hard-drinking ladies were not exactly her style, they were old Southbridgians and as such she accepted them in a friendly spirit.

The morning passed very pleasantly in talking with Kate Carter and making with Everard a brief tour of the school, which had changed very little. The boys in the lowest forms still had round faces and their hair starting from a little whorl at the backs of their heads and mostly in need of brushing, except with those dashing chaps who used hair fixative, which was sternly forbidden by Matron because it messed up the pillow-slips and even the laundry couldn't get it out.

"Dreadful it is, Mrs. Macfadyen," said Matron, who had added herself to the tour as a V.I.P. (which indeed she was.) "Of course when it's the lower school, I've told Matron there just to confiscate all the bottles and see that none of them have any vaseline, but the pillow-slips were just as bad as ever because those two Dean boys—grandsons of Mr. Dean over at Worsted you know—got the groundsman to let them have some of that oil he uses for the big mower. I can't tell you what the pillow-slips were like. Matron was terribly upset."

Mrs. Macfadyen, who having been brought up among the Royal Navy found all males an open book, said she had read in a newspaper that Hicky Heinz, the very popular new American boy-film-star, slabbed his hair down with a wet brush with just a few drops of Smartikreem which was guaranteed not to stain. Matron said, quite kindly, that there was *nothing* that didn't stain as The Laundry would tell anyone.

"But my father," said Mrs. Macfadyen who had been ransacking her brain for some way to help Matron, "always uses just a little water mixed with fixative on his brush. I mean he puts his head in the basin in the morning and then gives it a rub and then brushes it with some fixative while it's damp. But of course he hasn't got much hair now," she added, feeling that her contribution had not helped in the least. Matron said it was funny the way everyone had different ways.

"Have you tried nylon pillow-slips, Matron?" asked Mrs. Macfadyen.

"Well, that's an idea," said Matron cautiously. "I was going through the linen room the other day, though linen is quite a faux pas if you see what I mean being all cotton or some kind of mixture now, and really we do need some new pillow-slips. I'll speak to Mrs. Carter about it. There's all sorts of nylon now, at least the names are different though I daresay it's all the same really. Now I come to think of it I did see some in Bostock and Plummer's window last time I was in Barchester. The only thing is," said Matron, who took her duties seriously, "there's not much warmth in it and it doesn't absorb."

Mrs. Macfadyen asked if that was important. After all, she said, one didn't really want the pillow-slips to absorb *all* the hair fixatives because that would mean more trouble with the laundry. Matron said her eldest nephew, the one who was chief wireless operator in the biggest trans-Atlantic liner, had told her the trouble they had with the pillow-slips on every voyage you wouldn't believe. It wasn't only the laundry but the way they disappeared.

"Do you mean the passengers *steal* them?" said Mrs. Macfadyen.

"Well, that's what it comes to," said Matron. "At least they have a fancy dress dance and what they do with the pillow-slips is absolutely *beyond*. There was one passenger used his to wipe his razor on, one every day. And there was a lady passenger taking her pet hedgehog with her and some of its quills got in a pillow-slip and the ship's laundry swore quite dreadfully. Still, it's all in the day's work as they say. You remember Jessie, Mrs. Macfadyen?"

Mrs. Macfadyen did indeed remember the valued but hideous spectacled housemaid and shook hands with her. Jessie, who being of the old school, didn't hold with ladies making themselves cheap, said she had her brights to do and bolted through a green baize door. Mrs. Macfadyen asked Matron if she still had trouble with Jessie about wearing her spectacles and was rewarded by a long excursion into what was known among the Carters and their friends as Jessie-land. Mrs. Macfadyen thanked Matron warmly for the treat and so parted from her at the green baize door. She found Mrs. Carter in her sitting-room and they were able to have a really good talk about the School and the way it was changing.

"We are so lucky in our Governors," said Mrs. Carter. "People like the Dean and Sir Robert Fielding who really know their job and have good business heads. Just think if it were the Bishop!" but this was unthinkable.

"You know I'm going to spend the afternoon with the parents," said Mrs. Macfadyen. "I expect I'll have to stay to tea because I haven't seen Mother and Father lately, but I'll be back by half past five or six. Will that do?"

Mrs. Carter said it would do perfectly, as the party was nominally for six o'clock, but everyone knew that when Adelina Cottage threw a party it always went on till the last bottle of gin had been drained. Mrs. Macfadyen laughed and said she didn't believe there had ever been such a thing as a last bottle, because the hosts always had at least a dozen of everything in reserve.

So then they had lunch, alone, as Everard Carter was lunching in Barchester with his solicitor brother-in-law Robert Keith, now head of the firm of Keith and Keith, who handled all the legal business of the Cathedral and hence (with considerable profit to himself and his firm) a good deal of the private affairs of the Close. We must of course except the Palace who used a rather second-rate firm of the name of Stringer, one of whose predecessors had been mixed up in a shady affair about a cheque in old Bishop Proudie's later days. During lunch the two ladies relived a great deal of the war, finding, as all those of us do who were not in perpetual danger and saw their sons and brothers and husbands come back in safety, that they looked back upon it (in the light of a post-war world) as a kind of oasis of safety where none were for a party (as the parties had made a Politicians' Agreement to be a Coalition) and all were for the State— very broadly speaking. Mrs. Macfadyen enquired after a number of old Southbridgians, for having been brought up with the Royal Navy she had a great liking for boys who mostly accepted her as a good sort of chap; which indeed she was.

So then Mrs. Macfadyen drove down to the village, where she went very slowly, the better to see any old friends who were about, and so to the right up the hill to Jutland Cottage. It seemed to her a little smaller than usual, but this shrinking of a once familiar house is a quite common occurrence. As the road was rather narrow she ran her car into a little lane that skirted her parents' garden and field, and walked up to the house from the back. The kitchen was empty, so she pursued her way to the sitting-room where her father was asleep in his big chair, as he often was after lunch, but not looking in any way an object for ridicule for he had, unconsciously, the gift of going to sleep almost upright with his face composed and had never been known to snore; nor even to wake up with the short but severe struggle that so many people unconsciously make before they surface, as it were.

So Mrs. Macfadyen took up the newspaper which had fallen from the Admiral's hands when he slept and tried to finish a crossword puzzle that he had begun. Presently she heard sounds from above and knew that her mother had woken from her after-lunch nap, or lay-down in Modern English Usage, so she went upstairs and was received with joy. We think that both mother and daughter felt a kind of change in their relationship. When Miss Phelps had been at home she had been not only a daughter but pretty well everything else as well while her mother, quite unconsciously we think, rather took the role of mild invalid. But when she went away to Framley her mother had reverted to the earlier days when she was a poor naval lieutenant's wife and had found herself cooking again and enjoying it. She also had a quite good morning woman who could do the heavier work and most of the laundry, and as her husband liked gardening and carpentering, things went very well. But neither of them was young.

Mrs. Macfadyen had expected that her mother would want to hear what was happening at Framley and what her widowed daughter's plans were but, as we all do, she wanted to speak of herself and what she had been doing. So her daughter sat quietly and thought of other things and of the day when Mr. Macfadyen had found Miss Phelps crying among the hen-coops because her mother was ill and her father had a heart and oughtn't to go upstairs except to bed, and had taken her in his arms and comforted her and she had found that she was engaged. And then she thought of her happy, busy married life, now at an end; but she was an unselfish woman and took a great interest, or made an excellent pretence of doing so, in her mother's talk of Southbridge affairs and how kind Sir Cecil Waring (himself an ex-naval man) and his wife Lady Cora had been, dropping in to see them and letting the Admiral fight the Battle of Jutland as often as he liked.

Mrs. Macfadyen felt curiously removed from it all and blamed herself for not being more interested, but we think she was (as most of us are) too ready to feel guilty. For curiously enough we do, in many matters, judge ourselves more severely than we would judge others. Whether this is inverted pride or what it is, we cannot say, but most people have experienced it. Then they went downstairs and Mrs. Macfadyen helped her mother to get the tea and the Admiral woke up. But he did this neatly and precisely, as he did everything he turned his hand to, without yawning, or stretching, or looking madly about to see where and who he was.

When Margot Phelps, penniless daughter of a retired naval officer, married a wealthy man, he had settled money upon her, and from her money she had done a great deal for her father and mother. And we must say that never for a moment had either of them taken it for granted and what is more they had openly expressed their gratitude to their wealthy son-in-law and to their filially-minded daughter. This grant-in-aid Mrs. Macfadyen had now privately decided to increase, but not until her husband's estate was finally settled which, as always with wealth, was an unconscionable time a-doing. But this was not the moment to begin discussing ways and means and she settled herself to listen to the Annals of the Parish; whose hens were laying, how the new bit of field the Admiral had taken into cultivation was doing, whether Sans Souci a little farther up the hill was going to be taken by the new games and swimming instructor at the School who had a wife and two children, and several other faits divers. All fascinating to the locals; and to a certain extent to Mrs. Macfadyen as she picked up the threads.

Owing to her insistence one of the village women, who found her cottage dull with all her family out at work, now came every morning to Jutland Cottage, washed up the breakfast things, made the beds, washed what is known as "the smalls" and, what was more, insisted on bringing the wash-house with its copper into use and on Mondays there was—weather permitting—a fine sight of sheets, pillow-cases, underwear, the Admiral's soft shirts and practically anything else that Mrs. Brown, wife of Police Constable Haig Brown, could lay hands on. If they weren't dry enough to iron she would roll them up and do them another time and when there was a breakdown in the electricity she had brought her own irons with her, one to wash the other so to speak, made up the kitchen range nice and hot, set the irons on it and enjoyed herself vastly, while the Admiral, who but seldom interfered in the kitchen, came in to see what was smelling so pleasantly and it was the iron being pushed over the linen by a practised hand. And when the iron got too cool and Mrs. Brown put it back on the stove and picked the other one off and spat on it to test the heat, the Admiral almost cheered.

In honour of Mrs. Macfadyen's visit Mrs. Brown had stayed on to oblige, so they all had to go into the kitchen where Mrs. Brown gave a virtuoso display with a goffering iron, which implement is now to most of us only a name, largely because we haven't got anything to goffer now like the white drawers, petticoats and frilled frocks of our extreme youth.

Mrs. Macfadyen had felt a little nervous about her visit, for though she was a dutiful daughter and had always come over to Southbridge when she could, her own life and the market-gardening jaunts to Holland and other places that she took with her husband occupied much of her time and so often she had found one or both parents asleep or drowsing and felt that she was almost an intruder. But her parents seemed quite pleased to see her though she had a secret feeling that even as she left the house her image would fade from them. Not from their hearts, but the heart has a will of its own and sometimes keeps things to itself. So she enquired after various old friends in the neighbour-hood and of course the Vicar, Colonel the Reverend Edward Crofts. He appeared to give great satisfaction to her father, who was vicar's churchwarden, and to her mother who had known and liked Mrs. Crofts as Miss Arbuthnot before she was mar-ried.

The time passed pleasantly and Mrs. Macfadyen was begin-ning to wonder if she could escape without giving offence, when to her great relief her mother looked meaningly at Admiral Phelps who was gently dozing. His daughter gratefully took the hint, hugged her mother, pushed into her hand a parcel contain-ing a very large book on Admiral Benbow which the Admiral could not get from the Branch library and several most enchant-ing kitchen objects in plastic of various colours.

"Oh darling, they *are* lovely," said Mrs. Phelps, stroking a pale blue plastic plate rack and a pale pink refuse container (for no less genteel name could be applied to it) made of something called (we think) polythene.

"And these ties are for father," said Mrs. Macfadyen. "They're orlon, I think, whatever it is. They're like Richard Hannay's wife—they can't scare and they can't soil. Only NEVER iron them or they'll all fall to bits. Just drip-dry them. I'll come again soon," and away she went. She had given real pleasure to her father and mother by her presence and by the gifts. And now she had gone they could be as sleepy as they liked. How much Mrs. Macfadyen realized this, we do not know; but we think she understood and sympathized.

When she got back to the School House, she found the Carters in Kate's sitting-room. At least that was what the Carters called it, though Matron always said boudoir. Everard Carter had more than once expressed a wish that a meeting between Matron and the late and lamented H. W. Fowler could take place at the school on the subject so well illuminated by him of genteelisms. Matron, he said, could run rings round Mr. Fowler in that line, her latest contribution being "on the verge" for any article of food that had gone, or was obviously going, bad. Not, Matron said, that there was any need for things to go off when they had those two nice big fridges, but if cook wouldn't put the milk in the fridge as soon as it was delivered in the hot weather, well if the milk was a bit on the verge it was really not to be surprised at. But as Matron had been in a state of guerrilla warfare with cook—and cook with Matron—for at least ten years, no one paid much attention and the milk, which cook stood on the slate shelf in the old-fashioned larder, popularly supposed to be built over a disused well and always nice and chilly, remained fresh all through the hottest weather, if any.

"I can't help feeling rather a beast sometimes," said Mrs. Macfadyen, "when I see father and mother in Jutland Cottage and I'm rattling about like a pea in a pod in our big house. At least I suppose I ought to say the Luftons' house. They have been extremely nice about it and said I could stay on as long as I like while I am looking for somewhere to live."

Now the subject of where Mrs. Macfadyen would take up her widowed life was one of deep interest to many people. Not so much at Framley where, apart from the Court and the Parsonage, she had several pleasant acquaintances but no intimate friends, but very much at Southbridge where she had been well known for many years and where her devotion to her parents and her cheerful readiness to help anyone in any way within her power had won the admiration of all her friends, high and low.

"Do tell us a little about your plans, Margot," said Mrs. Carter. "Where do you *want* to live? We all hope you may come over this way."

"I really don't know yet," said Mrs. Macfadyen. "It will take some time to clear up Donald's papers, and lawyers are always slow about wills. I mean I shall be quite well off as far as money goes. Donald had no near relations and he did always think about me. You don't know how kind he was," and the Carters began to realize that the middle-aged widow, well-dressed, travelled (for her late husband took her on all his professional trips abroad and across the Atlantic), competent and very pleasant to look at and talk with, was still Margot Phelps, the Admiral's fat good-natured daughter, willing slave of her parents.

"I have been thinking about it," Mrs. Macfadyen went on, speaking aloud in an effort to clarify her thoughts—a thing many of us do and though we usually emerge even woollier in the intellect than when we began to try to think, we may have made some slight progress. Westward, the land may be bright, as an incredibly tedious Victorian poet with flashes of poetry in him so truly wrote. But Mrs. Macfadyen was not at the moment looking east or west; only inwards, a strange land though we live in it, unknown to us when we enter it, still unexplored when we leave it for yet further wanderings.

Then Mrs. Carter said they had better be starting, as whenever Wiple Terrace gave a party there were so many guests that those who came late were almost squeezed out of the windows like lanoline and she would like to take up a safe position.

"By the way, Margot," she said, "have you heard about the new discovery in the Terrace?"

Mrs. Macfadyen said she hadn't, but she could not think of anything so peculiar that it couldn't happen there and it must be one of the rummest places in England.

Mr. Carter said, rather violently, Thank God, NO. He then explained his interjection, saying that England was still simply bursting with rum places and rum people and he wouldn't be in the least surprised if a Druid turned up in the School Grounds.

His wife asked what he would do if one did turn up.

"Tell Matron," said Mr. Carter without a moment's hesitation. "She would have all his robes off and tell Jessie to wash them at once and borrow my dressing-gown for him and take him to the bathroom to clean himself and if he wasn't careful she would personally inspect his finger-nails and toe-nails. And then the Chaplain would take over."

His wife wondered what language they would talk. Mrs. Macfadyen said she expected a Druid, if he was a modern Druid, she meant one of the ones that were there when the Romans came, would know some Latin.

"Well, God help them in that case," said Everard. "Holy Joe," for by this affectionate name the Chaplain was mostly called, "still speaks proper Latin. Seezer; none of your Kysers. Goodness knows how the Romans talked—I wish we *did* know."

Mrs. Carter said it was wonderful to think that Romans talked Latin so naturally with the words in that extraordinary order always, and even Mrs. Macfadyen, whose acquaintance with the classics was extremely limited, had to laugh, at moment which the Chaplain came in and wanted to know what it was all about and he had to laugh too, and Kate felt rather flattered.

The Chaplain, encouraged by the laughter, said it didn't matter two hoots how you pronounced Latin so long as you got the quantities right. He had, he said, lately heard a golden-voiced announcer on the local Regional Programme say fons et orrigo. Mr. Carter shuddered.

"What *ought* he to say?" said Mrs. Macfadyen.

"Fons et orīgo," said Mr. Carter, adding rather crossly, "any schoolboy would know that."

Mrs. Carter said perhaps the announcer wasn't at a good school.

"If I had made a howler like that when *I* was at school," said Mr. Carter, "I'd have been beaten for it. At least I'd have deserved beating," and then the company had a competition in mispronunciations in high wireless quarters, the palm being awarded of course to contròversy with despìckable as a good runner-up. Then Mrs. Carter said they really must be going or they would never get into the party at all.

"But what *is* the new discovery in Wiple Terrace?" said Mrs. Macfadyen.

"Oh, Maria and Louisa apparently were made into one house a good many years ago," said Mrs. Carter, "and then they were unmade, and a bookcase was put up on each side of the communicating doors and everyone forgot about them. That's why Mr. Feeder and Mr. Traill heard each other's wireless and gramophone so clearly and made such a fuss. So they had the bookcases moved and the doors made so that they opened again, so that when they gave a party they would have more room. Only of course there isn't really *very* much more room, because you have to leave room to open and shut the doors or people couldn't go through from one room to the other. I'm afraid I'm not very clear. I had to say 'room' so often that I got muddled," but her audience appeared to have grasped her meaning. So they all walked down to the river and over the bridge to Wiple Terrace.

On the face of it, having communicating doors between the two houses sounded all right, but as our reader has already thought and has been longing to point it out to us, the mere fact of each of the rooms having an extra door in it made much more crowding because people were always squashing themselves through in one direction while other people were doing the same in the opposite direction, and those behind cried Forward and those in front cried Back, as they did in Rome, teste Lord Macaulay. But the Carters were used to squashes in Wiple Terrace, and so had Margot Phelps been used to them before she went away to foreign parts at Framley, so they had no fears.

Luckily they were among the first-comers and found Mr. Feeder and Mr. Traill each at his own front door. Both gentlemen greeted the party warmly, especially Mrs. Macfadyen whom they appeared to look upon as the lost sheep providentially returned to the fold and hence more valuable than any other possible visitor. But within the next quarter of an hour there was such a rush of visitors that the Carters and their guest were almost submerged and went up to the top rooms where they could stake a claim to the window seats and watch the crowd below as it surged in.

"Are you all right?" said Mr. Traill, who had forced his way upstairs with a relay of bottles and glasses.

Mrs. Carter said Quite all right and it was fun to look out of the window and see the guests arriving.

"Well, you're all right in the window seat," said Mr. Traill. "I got Snow to look at it—you remember the school carpenter, Margot?—Oh, I say, I'm sorry, Mrs. Macfadyen I mean."

"I like Margot," said Mrs. Macfadyen. "It's like old times."

"Good girl!" said Mr. Traill. "Well, I got Snow to look at the floor and he says the joists aren't in bad condition but the floorboards are simply *rotten* and one might go right through them in any old place or any old time, so I thought I'd tell you. If the floor does go you'll be quite all right in the window seat and we'll borrow a ladder to get you down."

Whether he wanted to make their flesh creep we do not know, but the ladies only laughed at him.

"I say," said Mr. Feeder, who had come upstairs while they

were talking, "would you mind just shoving people along a bit, Mrs. Carter, when they come upstairs? Spreading the load, you know."

"*I'll* do that," said Mrs. Macfadyen firmly. "Now, you men go downstairs and leave it to me." The two masters said "Kamerad," saluted and went downstairs. But almost before Mrs. Carter and Mrs. Macfadyen had settled themselves, Mr. Traill appeared again.

"I say, Mrs. Carter," he said. "Could you and Margot—oh dash it, Mrs. Macfadyen—"

"You always used to say Margot," said Mrs. Macfadyen. "What's come over you?"

Mr. Traill went bright red in the face, feeling quite unable to explain that Miss Phelps the Admiral's hard-working daughter was different from Mrs. Macfadyen a widow and well off.

"Oh, all right, Margot," he said. "I mean I always think of you as Margot, but—oh well, you know what I mean."

"No I don't," said Mrs. Macfadyen firmly. "Margot it is. We always called you Traill without a Mr. when I was living at home—behind your back I mean."

"I wish you would now," said Mr. Traill. "I'm Donald, if you like that better."

"I think not," said Mrs. Macfadyen, "but it's nice of you to think of it."

"Oh LORD! I am a beast!" said Mr. Traill. "I'd forgotten about Mr. Macfadyen—I mean I suppose I oughtn't to mention him—but I *am* a fool. I'm most frightfully sorry, Margot, oh GOSH! I mean Mrs. Macfadyen."

"Look here, Mr. Traill," said Mrs. Macfadyen with something of her father's quarter-deck voice, so that Mr. Traill almost jumped to attention.

"Need you really say Mister?" said he.

"All right, we'll make it Traill," said Mrs. Macfadyen calmly. "I'd like to come downstairs now—that is if there's room."

Mr. Traill, delighted by this friendly advance, said there jolly well *should* be room and what about the back verandah as it was a nice evening. Mrs. Macfadyen said she didn't know he had one.

"No more I didn't," said Mr. Traill, "but I thought I'd like one and Snow the carpenter had some of the wood from the old cricket pavilion in his workshop. He hadn't any business to have it there, but that's no one else's business neither. Anyway he made a good job of it. Come down and I'll show you," and he escorted her and the Carters down the stairs and made way for them to the kitchen and so into a charming little verandah along the blank wall of the scullery, sheltered from the wind and gathering the late afternoon sun.

A hammock was slung from the verandah roof and there were some garden chairs and a table with bottles and glasses on it.

"Look here, Margot, if you like to sit here I'll bring some of your old friends to call on you. It won't be so tiring for you that way," said Mr. Traill.

Mrs. Macfadyen, touched by his thought for her, said that would be delightful. So she sat down, thankful that the chairs were not deck-chairs in which it is difficult to sit with grace and from which it is almost impossible to rise with grace or with ease. It was all rather a dream to be back in Wiple Terrace and for the moment her life at Framley became a dream and she was Margot Phelps again. But not for long. Mr. Traill had skilfully cut out Colonel Crofts the vicar, with his wife, both delighted to see her again, and they were able to have a peaceful gossip while the cocktail guests bellowed and roared and got in each other's way inside.

Colonel Crofts, partly in his clerical capacity, said a few extremely kind and understanding words to Mrs. Macfadyen about her late husband. Then in her turn she asked him about his own affairs.

"Extremely satisfactory, thank you," said the Vicar. "I can't say that the church is full, but it isn't as empty as it was. You remember Bateman, my ex-batman, who married that nice

Eileen that used to be barmaid at the Red Lion. He is the sexton now, since that dreadful drunken old Propett died, and he rounds people up for Sundays as if he were a recruiting sergeant with a cockade in his cap. Hullo, Wicks!" for Mr. Wickham who had an unerring sense of where the best part of any social gathering would be, had ignored the party—now a howling mob where no one could hear himself or anyone else speak— and come straight through to the verandah, the large pockets of his old shooting-jacket bulging suspiciously.

"Sorry I'm late," said Mr. Wickham, laying a couple of flattish bottles on the table. "Gin from Holland. A hundred degrees overproof if that means what I think it means—and how it got into my pocket don't ask *me*. Fellow called Pancart—funny name but there's no accounting for names. There's an old farm-labourer over Chaldicotes way called Wamber. Ivanhoe and all that of course. Makes you think," he went on, opening a bottle as he spoke.

Mrs. Macfadyen, who was genuinely fond of Mr. Wickham as well as being grateful for the attention he paid to her parents, asked if Wamber had a brother called Gurth.

"Might have," said Mr. Wickham. "Oh, you mean Gurth. I thought you meant Girth."

"But I do," said Mrs. Macfadyen. "I mean I didn't mean a horse's girth, I mean *Gurth*. Ivanhoe, you know."

Mrs. Carter said she had seen a film of Ivanhoe when she was quite small. A silent film, and about three thousand supers pretending to be Normans had to pretend to storm a Saxon castle. Mr. Carter suddenly said "Tring, Wing and Ivanhoe," and on being pressed said it was some kind of old rhyme his nurse used to say to him.

"Tring and Wing rhyme all right, Carter," said Mr. Wickham, "but where does Ivanhoe come in? You can't find a rhyme to that."

Mrs. Macfadyen said Piddinghoe, which led to an ill-informed discussion as to where Piddinghoe was and a general feeling that it was in Sussex and probably on the Ouse. Then Mr. Wickham, who was very fond of Mrs. Macfadyen as a good fellow with no demned nonesense about her, put a few searching questions to her about her plans. So she told him how considerate Lord Lufton had been in offering to renew the lease of the house if she wanted it, although she knew that he really needed it himself, and said she was going to begin house-hunting soon, but there was no hurry. Mr. Wickham said the Luftons had always been good landlords and young Lady Lufton had a head on her shoulders.

"Get her onto it, Margot," he said. "The Grantlys know as much about property as anyone in the county and if there is a good house going, her father will know. You know him, the Rector over at Edgewood."

Mrs. Macfadyen asked where Edgewood was.

"Good God, my girl!" said Mr. Wickham. "Over Chaldicotes way of course, my side of the county. I'll have a look-see for you. They can't do *me* down on the price of a house."

"It's awfully kind of you, Wicks," said Mrs. Macfadyen, "but I don't want to live out there. It's too far," and then she wondered if these words sounded hard.

"Far is as far does," said Mr. Wickham sententiously. "We'll think up another one. But look here, Margot, you must *not* be too near Southbridge."

Mrs. Carter who had been listening with interest, for every woman likes to hear about houses, and to go over them even if she has not the faintest idea of buying or leasing it, asked why.

"Well, they say a nod's as good as a wink to a blind man," said Mr. Wickham sententiously. "I mean if you come and lie over here, Margot, you know what will happen."

There was a second's silence. Mrs. Carter looked anxious.

"Yes," said Mrs. Macfadyen. "Mother and father will want me. At least I don't mean that, Wicks. I mean—"

"No need to invent any lies, my girl," said the ungallant Mr. Wickham. "They'll swallow you whole. And you jolly well know

Macfadyen wouldn't like it. When he married you he had his eyes open and he took you away to Framley. And your parents got on perfectly well without you. They're very fond of you, and so am I, Margot, and you're a damned fine girl—well anyway a good sensible woman—but if you come and live here you'll be eaten alive. Spurlos versenkt as Jerry said in the war."

Luckily the others had got off onto the subject of the possible death-watch bettle in a part of the Red Lion, which respectable inn was known to be seventeenth century behind its more modern façade, so no one noticed Mr. Wickham, nor did they see Mrs. Macfadyen go rather red in the face and then quickly bang her eyes with handkerchief.

"It's all right, Wicks," she said, in her normal voice. "I was only being silly. You win, Wicks, but I *am* fond of them."

"Of course you are," said Mr. Wickham, "and they are fond of you, and so am I, and we're all fond of each other. But live together—NO!"

"If you mean me living with you, Wicks, you're perfectly right," said Mrs. Macfadyen, "and it's not the first time I've told you."

"You're telling *me*," said Mr. Wickham. "It was five years ago, at the back door of Jutland Cottage and you were sitting on an old box in the backyard with a pail of that stinking chicken food, crying. And listen, Margot. The whole of Southbridge is keeping an eye on Jutland Cottage. Your people are in pretty good form and all their old friends are round the place. You've got to live your own life, my girl. Like me."

"No. *Not* like you, Wicks," said Mrs. Macfadyen.

"No? Well, perhaps better not," said Mr. Wickham generously. "You haven't got the head I have. But there's one thing, I'm not a secret drinker. Never have been. I always get a pal in when I feel like a quick one. Well, Gob-bless, my girl. Mind you ask me to the wedding. It's bound to come," and sketching a kind of salute he went away, leaving Mrs. Macfadyen slightly

outraged but—as her sense of humour came to her rescue—
quite amused.

Pleasant as it was to be safely on the back verandah, and out of
the crowd, it could not last. Mr. Feeder appeared.

"Oh, you're there, are you," said Mr. Feeder. "It makes a nice
place to sit in, doesn't it? I say, Mrs. Carter, will you all come
inside? Mother's here and she would love to see you. She's in the
front room and she's bagged four chairs. She's sitting on one and
she's frightening everyone else off the others, but she can't go on
for ever. Do come in."

So the party from the School followed Mr. Feeder. Mr.
Wickham, who was very neat-handed in household matters, put
the glasses on a window-sill, got a cloth out of the scullery,
wiped the table, put the cloth back and holding eight glasses
upside down between his fingers carried them into the kitchen
where Eileen, the ex-barmaid from the Red Lion, was washing
glasses and drying them with lightning speed.

"Hullo, Eileen," said Mr. Wickham. "Younger and lovelier
every time I see you. Here, take these glasses like a good girl or
I'll drop them all."

Eileen disentangled the glasses from his fingers with practised skill.

"You did ought to have a tray, Mr. Wickham," she said
reproachfully. "I'll wash them and bring them in with the next
lot. Isn't it nice to see Miss Phelps again? I thought she'd be in
mourning, por thing. I'm sure I would be if Bateman was to die.
Not creep. Just a nice black suit and a nice black dress. Bateman
says when Colonel Crofts's first wife died, por thing, he had a
creep band round his arm. Bateman says if I was to die he'd have
a nice creep band and wear a black tie for the funeral."

Mr. Wickham, always more than ready to discuss any subject
of human interest, said he didn't go much to funerals himself
unless it was an old pal and then he wore a black tie and his best
suit and didn't go to bed till he'd put down one or two neat
whiskies to his old pal's memory.

Eileen said she was sure she didn't know what the Government would do if Mr. Wickham stopped drinking whiskey and they couldn't get the taxes, and so with coquettish giggles put her glasses—now clean and polished—on a tray and carried them to the front of the house, followed by Mr. Wickham.

Rather to Mr. Feeder's relief none of the ceilings had yet fallen in. The noise was deafening. In the front room Mr. Feeder's mother, a very active elderly woman in black who looked rather like a witch, was holding court with a number of old Southbridge friends round her, Mr. Traill was penned into a corner of the room by Miss Hampton and Miss Bent who had come in from Adelina Cottage, bringing several bottles with them, so Mr. Wickham wormed his way towards the party, who greeted him warmly.

"Put it down," said Miss Hampton, who was as usual in an impeccable black suit of a rather military cut and smoking a thin cheroot in a long amber holder, and she pushed a glass towards Mr. Wickham.

"Not on your life, my girl," said Mr. Wickham, "till I know what it is. If it's Greek wine, no. Resin and methylated spirits, better known in the Royal Navy as rotgut."

Miss Bent, always ready to defend her Friend, said it was true Samian wine.

"Come off it, my girl," said the unchivalrous Mr. Wickham. "You ought to read Byron. He had a go at it and said what he thought of it."

This conversation, which had been carried on in rather a loud and argumentative way as it was extremely difficult to make oneself heard without shouting, now began to attract general attention, which in no way embarrassed the speakers.

Miss Hampton, also wishing to defend her Friend, said rather truculently, "What did Lord Byron say? 'Fill high the cup with Samian wine,'" at which there was a kind of murmur of applause from those standing near whether they knew what it was about or not.

"Always verify your references, my girl," said Mr. Wickham, this time apostrophizing Miss Hampton. "He did say. Fill it high, but when he'd had a taste of it, what did he say? 'Dash down yon cup of Samian wine!' and he didn't mean dash it down inside you either. He meant chuck it down the drain because it's pure rotgut—like this," and suiting the action to the word, Mr. Wickham put his now empty glass down on the window ledge. It swayed, toppled and fell into the garden.

"It's all right," he said to his audience who had gradually gathered round the disputants, eager to hear these great minds striking sparks from one another. "It's a flower-bed outside. Well, I must be going, Feeder."

"You can't, Wicks," said Mr. Feeder. "Mother wants to talk to you. She hasn't had a chance yet. Come over here."

A gentleman could do no less. Mr. Wickham, who feared no man and had but a faint interest in women except as good pals if you took them the right way, followed his host, collecting another drink as he went. As no one who has met Mrs. Feeder is likely to forget her, we will merely remind our reader that she was of an unknown age that might be anything between seventy and ninety, always dressed in black, thin (not to say bony), devoted to her son whom she bullied unmercifully, and though by no means unkind could have a scarifying tongue. Partly owing to her son's attention, partly through her own determination, she was one of the few people who were seated and, what was more, had several chairs beside her to which favoured guests were summoned.

"Well, Mrs. F., here's to your bright eyes," said Mr. Wickham as he sat down, raised his glass and ceremonially drank to her.

"And here's mud in yours," said Mrs. Feeder, raising, emptying and putting down her glass all in one movement. "Is that Margot Phelps that I see?"

"She was, but she's a widow now, poor girl," said Mr. Wickham.

"And *that*," said Mrs. Feeder, "is *not* the way to talk. What's wrong with widows? Too many of us, I admit, but whose fault is that?"

"All right," said Mr. Wickham. "I'll be the mug. Whose?"

"Yours," said Mrs. Feeder, fixing him with an Ancient Mariner's eye. "Men's. No stamina. My dear husband, *his* father," she added waving her glass towards her son, "would be alive today if he hadn't let himself die."

"Suicide?" said Mr. Wickham, with friendly interest.

"They didn't bury him at four cross-roads with a stake through his inside," said Mrs. Feeder severely, "if that's what you mean. But if he'd downed his drink like a man he'd be alive today. Look at *me*."

"I do," said Mr. Wickham. "I can't take my eyes off you. Nothing wrong there."

"Because I know how to live," said Mrs. Feeder. "You've got to know how to live if you don't mean to die. When my dear husband was dying he said, 'Mind *you* don't die, Little One.' He always called me that."

Mr. Wickham, for all his worldy experience feeling slightly confused, said it was the last thing he would dream of calling her and then wondered—as we all so often do—if he had said what he meant, and even if he had meant what he said. But most luckily the co-host Mr. Traill, who had been absent in the kitchen, came in with a tray of fresh drinks and while Mrs. Feeder was changing old glasses for new, he was able to join in the general conversation.

As nearly always happened with the parties in Wiple Terrace, no one showed any disposition to leave. Some because they were truly enjoying the friendly atmosphere of people they met every day (which perhaps really makes the best kind of party), some because drinks flowed, some because it would have felt horrid not to be there. Mrs. Macfadyen was much in demand, for all the older guests remembered her valiant work during the war when she had run Jutland Cottage with her parents as a kind of Miss Weston's Home for Seamen, and those who knew most about Admiral Phelps and his wife, living on his pension, not always in good health, and relying more and more on their unselfish capable daughter (selfishly relying many people felt, but as Margot Phelps had never thought of her parents' attitude in that light we can leave that question alone), were sincerely pleased that she had married the wealthy market gardener. They had been sorry too for her when her short years of happy peaceful married life had been brought to an end and everyone said she was sure to marry again. We think that no such idea had ever come into her head. She had found calm happiness rather later than most of her contemporaries and with the unclouded memory of those years always present to her, she had taken up again the burden of living and was making a good job of it. Sometimes she wondered if she was doing enough for other people; if it were not rather selfish just to go on being alive when one ought to be on committees and being a Mrs. Pardiggle to the poor. But charity—in Lady Bountiful deeds as apart from any affection for those that need it—is not always easy. Anyone can sign cheques if they wish to and have the necessary funds, but the giving of time, and of time on settled days and at definite hours, is not always easy and Mrs. Macfadyen sometimes felt that she needed a friend who could give her real work to do and set definite bounds to it so that she would use time and money to the best advantage.

Victoria, Lady Norton had once, at a Victoria League Meeting, got Mrs. Macfadyen into a corner and practically ordered her to join several societies for Doing Good to people who didn't want to be done good to. Those who were present were annoyed by her Ladyship's rather arrogant way of treating their fellow-member and there were a good many murmurs of "Meddling old woman" and "A lot of good she does." But the British Navy in Mrs. Macfadyen's blood enabled her to stand up to her ladyship and make it quite clear that she had already as much voluntary work as she could undertake over at Framley, even with the able assistance of young Lady Lufton, and clapping her glass to her sightless eye (tropically speaking), said her naval charities and the charity that begins at home were all she could undertake, especially since her husband's death and Lady Norton must know what *that* meant.

The few who overheard this were delighted, as Lady Norton had worn the trousers ever since she married the late and down-trodden Lord Norton (a Lloyd George peer we think) and would have worn the trousers of the whole county if given her head, and if her husband had lived longer; his death being attributed to a nasty chill contracted while waiting for his wife to come out of a Young Liberals' meeting in Barchester Public Baths. The happy few who knew all about it then enjoyed themselves immensely in an informal discussion group. Lady Norton said her time was not her own, alas, and she must go. As no one attempted to stop her, she went, and the meeting raged on as if she had never existed.

In their joy at re-finding an old friend, Miss Hampton and Miss Bent tried to persuade Mrs. Macfadyen to come back with them to Adelina Cottage for an impromptu extension of Mr. Feeder and Mr. Traill's party. Luckily she could say with perfect truth that she was staying with the Carters and must go back with them to the School. The party was thinning now and only the stalwarts, headed by Mrs. Feeder, were left. The Carters and their guest said their good-byes, thanked their hosts and walked home in the cold summer evening.

So immersed had Mrs. Macfadyen become in Southbridge life during the last few days that she had almost forgotten that Framley was there and that she must presently go back to her task of sorting and arranging. Not only her husband's papers, but the furniture, the curtains, the bolsters, all the comfortable impedimenta of life. The Carters, who would in due time be retiring, were also concerned with the question of what to get rid of when you go from a house, with large rooms and all repairs done by the School Governors, to your own house where it is just as well to know how to put a washer on a tap. Mrs. Carter's sister Lydia Merton, whose husband was the eminent Q.C., Sir Noel Merton, had very much wanted them to be near her, but houses were not easy to come by.

When Mrs. Macfadyen came down to breakfast next morning her host and hostess were talking so hard that they almost jumped when they realized her presence. She asked what the matter was.

"Probably a mare's nest, or Carter's Folly," said Mr. Carter. "The Rector of Northbridge, that Mr. Villars with the very nice wife, is resigning. He wants an easier job. We're all getting on."

Mrs. Macfadyen said she wasn't getting on, she had *got* on, and that was why she would have to look for a house too.

"I expect it will be rather fun when I've made up my mind," she said. "I'd really like to live in one of the small towns, like Greshamsbury. There are some nice retired naval people there; some of them war-time sailors and some real ones. It's not a long drive to Southbridge and I could get over at once if the parents needed me. You don't think I'm selfish, do you, Mrs. Carter?" she added.

"I shan't ask you to call us Kate and Everard again," said Kate Carter. "I've asked you twenty times and you always shy away from it. How would you like it if we began calling you Mrs. Macfadyen when we've known you for—how long is it?"

A great deal of arithmetic with permutations and combinations then took place and it seemed that algebra and geometry might have to come in too, not to speak of the very reasonable solution: counting on one's fingers. The only drawback to this, said Everard in his pleasant, slightly donnish voice, was that after you had used both hands, you could never remember how often you had used them and anyway hands were on the decimal system.

"I *hate* decimals," said Mrs. Macfadyen violently. "It was the one thing I didn't like when Donald and I used to go abroad."

Everard enquired what her special grudge was.

"Well, there's nothing to hang on to," said Mrs. Macfadyen.

"It's all in tens and you can't divide anything into three. And if you once put the dot wrong you lose hundreds of pounds—or else the other people do. Donald was very good at it. But he was good at everything," which she said very simply.

"You know, Margot, you are a remarkable woman," said Everard. "You have never lost the childlike in the larger mind."

"Haven't I?" said Mrs. Macfadyen. "Who said that?"

Mr. Carter said Tennyson.

"Oh, a quotation," said Mrs. Macfadyen. "Donald was always saying bits of poetry and bits of prose too. His people were very poor and he taught himself to read and saved up his pennies, when he got any, to buy books off the second-hand stalls on market day. But I don't think Tennyson was one of his poets. It was mostly Scott and Burns and the metrical psalms. He would have liked that line you quoted just now—*he* never lost the child's mind."

"I think the biggest people don't," said Mr. Carter. "That's why one can meet them so easily."

"And he knew all the children's rhymes too," said Mrs. Macfadyen. "If we had had any children he would have taught them everything."

There was a silence. In common with her many other friends the Carters had sometimes wondered, idly, if Margot Phelps would take kindly to babies and small children, though with the older ones, especially boys, she was perfect.

"I don't know why we didn't," said Mrs. Macfadyen thoughtfully, yet in a detached kind of way. "One doesn't know. Donald would have loved them and so would I. But we didn't have any and we were very happy together in the short time we had— very happy. I want to find something to do now. Some kind of work that helps people. You see I don't need to earn. Donald saw to it that if he died I would be safe—or as safe as anyone can be now. If I had died first I couldn't have left him anything—I never had anything of my own."

All this she said, more as if talking alone, to herself, and neither of the Carters wished to break her self-communing, when luckily the bell of the big clock over the School Hall sounded. Mrs. Carter said they might drive over to Northbridge after lunch as she wanted to see her sister Lydia Merton, and then they could go on to the Vicarage and see those very nice Villarses. Mrs. Macfadyen asked if they were high or low.

"I never thought about it," said Mrs. Carter. "I think they're just ordinary. I mean they have the proper prayer-book and don't mess up the service."

"What on earth do you mean, Kate?" said her husband.

"What I said. Mr. Villars just has the proper service, and doesn't alter things or leave out great chunks. Not like St. Horrificus in Barchester where they have a prayer-book quite of their own. I went there once by mistake and nearly threw the sops all in the sexton's face."

"Oh, that's Shakespeare," said Mrs. Macfadyen. "Donald loved him and we used to read him aloud together just for fun. We were going to Stratford this year. I'll go and see the parents this morning, Kate, unless I can do anything to help you," but Kate said no thank you and Mrs. Macfadyen went away.

"She *is* a nice woman," said Mr. Carter. "I'd say a nice girl if it weren't rather ridiculous at her age."

"Well, darling," said his loving wife, "you *have* said it once— about the childlike and the larger mind. You'd better go and see Snow about that sash cord. I want it mended before the children get their fingers squashed."

As arranged, the Carters and Mrs. Macfadyen went over after lunch to Northbridge. It is a pleasant drive, partly by the river and partly by the lower slopes of the downs, over the beautiful old stone bridge that spans the river, up the steepish hill of Northbridge High Street and so round to the left between the water-meadows and the downs to Northbridge Manor.

Here they were received enthusiastically by Sir Noel and Lady Merton. There had been a time when Noel had been rather silly about a charming woman who liked him but no more, being—as are most nice women however attractive—entirely on his wife's side if he did a little mild straying. Jessica Dean, the well-known young actress, had then spoken to him for his good, telling him exactly what a fool he was making of himself, and though he had the good sense not to smite his breast or go about in sackcloth, he had shown his Lydia, without words, that he had been a fool and knew it and wouldn't do it again. They had never spoken again of the subject and had continued in a busy life, with deep affection each for the other.

Everard Carter and Noel Merton, who were old friends besides having married sisters, at once coalesced as men always do, leaving the women to talk with one another, which gave satisfaction all round.

"If the weather weren't so foul," said Lydia, "we could sit outside on the terrace."

Mrs. Carter said it would be much nicer inside, so they all sat in the drawing-room whose long windows looked over the garden down to the river, and Mrs. Carter and Mrs. Macfadyen, in strophe and antistrophe, gave the Mertons a brief account of the party in Wiple Terrace, and the Mertons were mildly amused. But only mildly, for the really amusing things are what happen among one's close friends and are best told to an audience who is of the same circle. To outsiders it all sounds like any other account of any other party. We think Mrs. Macfadyen might have gone on talking for longer but Mrs. Carter wisely started another subject and Mr. Carter asked Noel Merton about his dairy herd and Noel had to admit that he really knew nothing about cows and left it all to his bailiff—which sounded very well. A very good man, he said, had been found for him by Wickham.

"Do you know Mr. Wickham?" said Lydia to Mrs. Macfadyen, who said she did, quite well, and then stopped; but as if she might have gone on if she felt like it.

"He's a rum bird," said Noel, "and a first-class manager. A

born bachelor too. Give him his pipe and his glass and he will be happy anywhere. I don't think he's got a heart, but what he doesn't know about West Barsetshire isn't worth knowing."

"But he *has* got a heart," said Mrs. Macfadyen, almost violently.

The other ladies were consumed with curiosity, but hardly liked to ask questions.

"He asked me to marry him when father was so ill and I was feeding the hens and everything was *dreadful*," said Mrs. Macfadyen rather defiantly.

There was complete silence for a few seconds. Mr. Wickham was well known to them all, much liked by them all and in the case of the Mertons also deeply valued as agent and friend, but never had it occurred to any of them to look upon him as anything but a confirmed bachelor.

"It's quite true," said Mrs. Macfadyen stoutly. "I was feeding the hens and I was crying all the time because of father being so ill and mother being so tired and the hens being so horrible and Donald—my husband you know—asked me to marry him and I said yes and then he had to go on somewhere else so I went on feeding the hens and crying and then Mr. Wickham came— he'd been letting father talk to him about the Battle of Jutland— and he was so kind and said would I marry him."

Never before, we think, had Mrs. Macfadyen spoken of this idyll to anyone. Her hearers were completely flabbergasted, for it was well known that Mr. Wickham, though no misogynist, had firm views about the nuisance women were if you had them about the house and only allowed the woman from the village who "did" for him to come at stated hours and for stated periods.

"So what happened?" said Lydia, feeling that someone must carry on.

"Well, I said I was engaged to Donald," said Mrs. Macfadyen, "and Wicks said 'Great holy cripes,'" which heart-felt exclamation released the tension and everyone began to laugh.

"And then," Mrs. Macfadyen continued, rather enjoying this

emotion recollected in tranquillity, "Mr. Wickham said That was that and even if I didn't marry him I could let him have what I'd been trying to write about how to keep goats—horrible things—and so I gave him the typescript of a book about looking after goats that I'd done and he sent it to his uncle Mr. Johns the publisher—Johns and Fairfield, you know—and it got published. Of course it wasn't a Best Seller like Mrs. Rivers's books, but all the Goat Clubs bought it and it goes on selling. I think it was *very* nice of Wicks."

There was a buzz or murmur of applause as Mrs. Macfadyen, rather flushed, finished speaking. Everyone felt that the whole affair reflected great credit on everyone concerned, though if pressed no one could have explained why. Noel Merton voiced the opinion of the party when he said that though he knew nothing about goats, he felt certain that their lives were more interesting than those of Mrs. Rivers's heroines.

"But she has been a Book of the Month twice," said Mrs. Macfadyen.

Everard Carter, an omnivorous reader of fiction, said hers were exactly the books that one would expect to become Books of the Month.

"Donald didn't like them either," said Mrs. Macfadyen. "He said that the subject of a middle-aged woman who has a comeback with a young man was all right for once and there was no need to make a habit of it."

This of course led to some more talk about recent books and how good Lisa Bedale's latest thriller, *Rattle His Bones*, was and how extraordinary it was that a marchioness should write thrillers; for it was now pretty generally known that Lisa Bedale was an anagram of Isabel Dale, the heiress who had married Lord Silverbridge, the Duke of Omnium's heir. But she had then been, if not exactly poor, kept on a very mean allowance from her rich invalid mother and had begun writing thrillers as a kind of escapism after a beloved friend had been killed—all now a good while ago.

"But you won't tell Wicks I told you, will you?" said Mrs. Macfadyen. "I think he must have proposed to lots of people, just out of kindness, but he wouldn't like people to know it."

Noel said Mr. Wickham did good by stealth and would blush like anything to find it shame, but as Mrs. Macfadyen looked rather puzzled he said it was just a bad habit he had of misquoting.

"Donald wasn't like that," said Mrs. Macfadyen. "He said he had never thought of marrying till he met me," and though countless millions of men must have said that since the Fall, it is true of some. Love can come early or late or whenever he feels like it he will find out the way.

"Margot is looking for a small house," said Mrs. Carter. "If you hear of anything, do let us know."

Lydia asked where she wanted to be.

"I don't really mind much," said Mrs. Macfadyen, "except that I don't want to be in Southbridge. I mean—" and she paused.

"What Margot means," said Kate, "is that—very sensibly— she doesn't want to be too close to her parents."

The Mertons, who knew a little of Mrs. Macfadyen's life before her marriage, thought she was wise in her decision, but naturally did not say so. Lydia said she would certainly enquire and keep her ears open.

"And we shall be moving too," said Kate. "Not just yet, but Everard will be thinking of retiring some day and we rather want before he retires to find a house where we can have the children, and in the holidays they can have their own friends, which seems to be really why parents have houses at all."

As Noel had not been at Southbridge School he was not deeply interested, but Lydia had always had a feeling for the school since her beloved brother Colin had spent a term teaching there and her elder sister Kate had married Everard Carter, then an assistant master. She asked them where they thought of settling.

"We haven't really thought at all," said Everard. "I have a vague hope that if I don't worry the gods they may look favourably on me. We are going on to the Villarses and I'll ask them. There are some good houses going in Northbridge sometimes—and we'd be near you."

"That *would* be fun," said Lydia. "I did hear that Mrs. Dunsford was going to sell Hovis House. She and her daughter think of settling on the Riviera. There's a good garden."

Kate said that she didn't really want to live *in* Northbridge. Somewhere up the river she would like, so that she could see more of Lydia and all the young cousins could make friends.

"You have heard I suppose that the Villarses are leaving here," said Lydia. "Not just yet, but he wants to have the sort of clergyman's job that would give him more time for writing. Something in the Close would suit him," and the Carters felt sure that if that was what he wanted, he and his wife would get it, because they were so nice.

"As a matter of fact we are going on to them," said Mr. Carter. "If the subject of their moving crops up, well and good. If it doesn't, there is no hurry. But I'm glad you mentioned it. If I see any hope I'll get Robert onto it," for Kate and Lydia had an elder brother who was now head of the family firm of solicitors in Barchester and generally considered to be the best lawyer the town had known for some time. Their younger brother Colin was also a lawyer, but he was a barrister in London, which is quite different.

So the Carters with their guest went on to visit the Villarses. Though the Rectory was only half a mile or so by the river it was almost two miles by road and they had to go back to Northbridge, cross the river and drive back along its farther bank. As they drove up to the Rectory they saw Mrs. Villars in the garden, where indeed she was mostly to be found, wearing gardening gloves and a hessian apron with large pockets.

There is no accounting for tastes—nor indeed for colours if we are to believe a Latin tag, though whose we regretfully cannot say as neither the *Oxford Dictionary of Quotations* nor the excellent Dr. Brewer have given us any help. But soft! M. Larousse in his "Locutions Latines et Estrangères," a thirty-page supplement of a vivid pink separating Zythum (*bière que les Egyptiens fabriquaient avec de l'orge fermentée*) from the second section "Histoire—Géographie" which begins bravely with Aa (*fleuve côtier de France, qui baigne Saint-Omer et se jette dans la mer du Nord*), labels it as *Proverbe des scholastiques du moyen âge, qui est devenu français*. All which could lead to a consideration of why the French are on the whole better at dictionaries and Grammars than we are. But of this also *non est disputandum*.

We must now return after this pedantic digression to where we left off, namely Mrs. Villars's gardening gloves. All we can say is that some can garden in gloves and some can't. We, being town born and bred, have but small knowledge of gardening but are willing to weed for days on end, a job in which one cannot do much harm beyond pulling up the green sprouts of spring onions as noxious weeds. And we have come to the conclusion that the ungloved human hand is the best implement. If you have a little fork you at once come to a weed that needs a kind of long lobster-pick to deal with it, and it is almost inevitable that if your attention is distracted by a colony of small snails, you may lose the lobster-pick among the irises; and as by that time you remember that you stuck the trowel in the ground so that you would know where it was but cannot remember where you stuck it, there is nothing to do but to lose your temper.

Mrs. Villars looked up when the car stopped, saw friends and went towards the gate to meet them, stripping off her right-hand glove in greeting, as they came up the path.

"May we come and call on you?" said Kate. "We've got Mrs. Macfadyen with us. You remember her—Margot Phelps she was. The Admiral's daughter."

"Yes indeed," said Mrs. Villars. "You did hens and goats, didn't you? I remember getting a clutch or a setting or something from you in the war, because Hibberd said I must. He's our sexton and does the hens and the vegetables, but I don't let him do the flowers."

"Your border *is* lovely," said Mrs. Macfadyen. "I always meant to have a really good herbaceous border at Framley when my husband was alive, and I did begin one, but we had to go abroad so much that it rather went to pieces. And Donald—my husband—did so truly love flowers," she added rather wistfully, and Mrs. Villars felt a small pang of compassion for this pleasant woman, so obviously a flower gardener and not a market gardener. While Mrs. Macfadyen had been speaking Mrs. Villars had taken off her other glove and put it to join its fellow in her apron pocket. She then took off her apron and laid it and her trowel in her trug—a local name for a kind of basket (only it isn't a basket) of thin strips of wood, familiar to our youth in Sussex and still, we hope, being made today.

The Rectory, as visitors to Northbridge may remember, was originally a biggish house with ten bedrooms and old-fashioned rambling kitchen quarters. When families were large and money was cheap (and all that money buys) it had served its purpose. During the war it had been chosen as a headquarters for part of the office staff of the Barsetshire Regiment. The big laundry and servants' hall were converted into offices, central heating and fixed basins had been installed. Mr. and Mrs. Villars had found themselves the heads of a large and quite pleasant family and except for the undercurrent of anxiety about their sons (who we are glad to say both came through the war unscathed) passed a not unpleasant war-time. And when we look back upon those years it is extraordinary how little (except in cases of personal bereavement) they seem to have altered the lives of many of us.

"Come into the study," said Mrs. Villars. "It is so good for Gregory to be interrupted—it stops him working," words which both Kate and Lydia understood from their own experience of husbands who unless watched would always drive themselves far more fiercely than they would drive others.

So into the study they went and there was Mr. Villars sitting at his large writing-table, getting on with his sermon for the following Sunday, but whether lest all should think that he was proud, or for other reasons, *The Times* was lying on the top of his sermon with its back page uppermost. He rose as the visitors came in and greeted them warmly. Mrs. Macfadyen he hardly knew, but had heard of her via Colonel the Reverend F. E. Crofts at Southbridge and entirely to her advantage.

His wife asked if he was busy and he replied that if it had been the Income Tax or Lord Aberfordbury he would have been very busy indeed, but for friends from Southbridge his door was wide open. Mr. Carter, who had felt a distinct draught between door and window, quietly shut the door and everyone sat down comfortably.

As was only natural Mrs. Carter wanted to hear all about the Villars's plans.

"You are leaving Northbridge, aren't you?" said Mrs. Macfadyen.

Mrs. Villars said indeed they were and she was rather dreading the break after so many years there. Kate asked how many.

"I haven't the faintest idea," said Mrs. Villars. "I mean if I began to think very hard I might remember, but just now I don't. It was when Gregory stopped being a school-master. When was it, Gregory?"

Her husband said, rather unclerically, that he was blessed if he could say off-hand but before the war began. Say nineteen thirty-seven he added after a brief interval during which, so Kate afterwards said to her husband, she had distinctly seen him counting on his fingers under his desk.

"That's right, Gregory," said his wife. "Because John was twenty-one in 'thirty-nine. I remember because his birthday was just before the war began."

Her husband said that didn't prove anything but he was pretty sure it was 'thirty-seven, because it was engraved on the clock that the Governors of Coppin's School gave him when he left, with the welcome addition of a cheque.

"Twenty years in one place," he said, "and sometimes it feels like a hundred and sometimes like a week. Time's a queer thing. Are we going to have tea, Verena?"

At almost the same moment tea announced itself by the voice of Edie, formerly rather half-witted slave to Mrs. Chapman the cook, now for many years the rather half-witted but affectionate wife of Corporal Jackson of the Barsetshires. Many slightly mentally defective people have gifts of their own and Edie's was cleaning. She had learnt in a hard school under the Villars's old cook Mrs. Chapman (now honourably retired on her Old Age Pension) and was very willing. Her husband who had been an electrician before the war absorbed him had taken up his trade again and was doing very well in Northbridge and was much in demand by the gentry. To no one's surprise they had no children, which everyone said was just as well seeing what Edie was like, and were a very happy couple.

So the party went into the dining-room which was large and full of sun, and had a comfortable gossip about things in general over their tea. But presently Mrs. Carter could contain herself no longer and asked Mrs. Villars what her plans were.

"Well," said Mrs. Villars, "I really oughtn't to talk about them, because nothing is signed yet, but we are leaving Northbridge. Not just yet but it is more or less settled and I might as well tell you. There will be a Canonry vacant in the Close and Gregory has been chosen. It is still unofficial but as everyone knows it one might as well mention it. But don't tell anyone," which contradictory remarks made everyone laugh.

Her audience almost cheered, so good was the news. But kind Kate Carter at once thought of the shepherdless flock and asked what would Northbridge do without them. Mr. Villars said it would do much as it had done with them; i.e., it would go to church when it felt like it and not when it didn't and would be generous with subscriptions and gifts for the Harvest Festival and there were still several very devout elderly ladies who would make the new incumbent's life hell by showing their devotion with woollen comforters and slippers. His wife said he had been reading too many Victorian novels and was quite out of date and they were far more likely to want to do a play by Sartre in the church.

"But, seriously," said Mr. Villars, "although it is settled and we shall be moving, I haven't told anyone here yet except my churchwardens."

"Who undoubtedly haven't told a soul except their wives," said Mrs. Villars in a resigned voice.

"Well, the great thing is that you are going to Barchester," said Everard. "We shall miss you here, but it is a far far better place that you are going to," which echo of Sydney Carton made everyone laugh and yet feel a little sad. "And who is succeeding you?"

"I don't think anyone knows yet," said Mr. Villars. "But whoever they are, they won't be here. The Rectory is too big and expensive and it is going to be secularized so to speak and my successor will have a modern house, easy to run and not so expensive to keep up, at the Plashington Road end of the town. That is where Northbridge is developing and one has to look ahead."

"Yes, I suppose one does," said Everard, "but often one would rather not. Have you any idea who is likely to want to live in the Rectory? Kate and I shan't be at the School for ever and we are beginning to look for a house and we'd like to be near Lydia and Noel. And I shan't go near the School for a year after I retire. That's what Birkett did when he retired and I think he was right. I would very much like to get into trouble with the right people."

"But, my dear fellow," said Mr. Villars, "Keith and Keith are handling it. They do most of the Cathedral business. Hasn't your brother-in-law told you about it?"

"Not a word," said Everard. "He's quite right not to. But if I see him, may I tell him what you have told me?"

"Certainly," said Mr. Villars. "It would be very nice to think of you and your wife here, and so near the Mertons. But I must warn you about the cellars. If the river is very high they do sometimes have water in them. I think the river wall at the end of the garden needs repairing, or a better drain put in the cellar. My predecessor kept a lot of wine there, so it must have been dry then."

"By the way," said Everard, "will your gardener want to stay on? That is, if we do take the house."

"So long as you don't interfere with the kitchen garden—he always speaks of it as *his* kitchen garden—you can have a pretty free hand," said Mrs. Villars.

"I suppose you don't happen to know what kind of lease we'd be likely to get," said Everard. "I mean how long a lease."

"Not the faintest idea," said Mr. Villars. "But," he went on, rather reminding Everard of the delightful game of Happy Families (now so debased in the drawing and colour of its cards that we can only hope it may die), "can you give me any idea of how soon you would want it? I might be able to put in a word."

"Well, I can't say exactly, because my retiring date isn't definitely fixed," said Everard. "Kate and I would like the house if we can get it at a reasonable price and will keep it in good repair. And it will be so nice for the children to be near their Merton cousins. All mine can swim quite well. But I want to get hold of it well before I retire. We should use it for the holidays and I could make any alterations we need a bit at a time. We would meet the ground landlords at any reasonable price."

"You must remember," said Mrs. Villars, "that the river can be tricky. You get some nasty eddies, like small whirlpools, here and there and whenever you find thick rushes along the bank you'll find nasty, oozy mud. Gregory had posts planted in the worst places and keeps them painted white, just to guide people. And you must lock the boathouse always. Quite a lot of hooligans from Barchester come this way in the summer and they'll pinch everything out of a boat if it isn't in a locked shed and the magistrates won't convict. They say the boys need psychic treatment. And if you wallop them yourself their parents tell the police. We shan't ever have peace till there is juvenile conscription."

Everyone laughed and the Rector laughed too, but it was uneasy laughter, for anarchy was in the air and so many of the young were inveigled by it; brutalized themselves and deliberately brutal to anyone weaker than themselves, while cringing and sucking-up (horrible expression—but justifiable) to the stronger.

"If only all these Billy Grahams and people would really get at them," said Everard, "they might do some good."

"If *we* could get at them—the church I mean," said the Rector, rather crossly, "*we* might do a great deal of good. Well, once in the Close all this will be as the fierce vexation of a dream. I look forward to vegetating like anything. I shall probably write a dull and very inaccurate book about St. Ewold. No one knows much about him; nor indeed if he ever existed."

"My nurse used to tell me," said Everard, "that he lived in a hut in the forest—it was all marsh and forest where St. Ewold's is now—and used to play cards with the devil on Sunday nights."

Kate said that didn't sound very saintly.

"But, you see, he had made a little cross on some of the cards and when the devil touched them they burnt his fingers," said Everard.

Mr. Villars said people had been asked to resign from their clubs for less than that, quite apart from the religious aspect, and then the talk wandered to the Palace and then Kate said they really must be getting home. Partly because she meant it, but also because she had a guilty feeling that Mrs. Macfadyen must have had a very dull time and she blamed herself for not having pushed or pulled her guest forward and tried to make her talk.

They drove back to Southbridge by another road, but all the roads in Barsetshire are lovely. When they were back in the Carters' house Everard went to his study to get some letters written that he ought to have written that morning, so the ladies went to Mrs. Carter's sitting-room.

Mrs. Carter asked her guest what she thought of the Rectory.

"It is a lovely garden and I did like the Villarses," said Mrs. Macfadyen. "But I wouldn't like to live there."

Mrs. Carter asked her why.

"Partly the river," she said. "Mrs. Villars said something about damp in the cellars. It's very lovely, but I wouldn't like to live there, I would rather be higher up. That was one nice thing about Jutland Cottage—it did stand higher than most of Southbridge, but even so the mists used to creep up the hill and I'm sure they aren't good for the parents. Still, there it is. I would like somewhere like Greshamsbury where there isn't a river and you are fairly high up. Framley was well away from the damp too."

Kate, interested by her guest's words, asked more about Framley and was touched by Mrs. Macfadyen's real affection for the Lufton family.

"I hardly know the people there," Kate said. "It's curious how one can live in a county and have so many friends and then find there are a lot of other ones. But young Lady Lufton is very lovely. I *do* like good looks. I always enjoy watching Lydia."

"So do I," said Mrs. Macfadyen. "I think being pretty plain oneself makes one like people who aren't plain even better. I mean it *is* so nice to look at someone beautiful. I always want to give Grace Lufton sixpence, just to express the pleasure she gives me."

Kate said that was a very good idea and they chose some other Barsetshire acquaintances who would qualify for the sixpenny dole, Lady Cora Waring coming first (partly because she was a Duke's daughter) and young Lady Lufton second, followed by several names of people known or unknown to us.

"You know, it is rather nice to be ordinary," said Mrs. Macfadyen. "It's like a disguise and you can go about looking at people and they don't look at you."

"And the older I get," said Kate, "the more I find I admire the older faces where the bones mean so much. Old Lady Emily Leslie—I only saw her once—had the most beautiful bones I have ever seen. I wished I could draw, just to remember them," and then they had a delightful talk about the Dreadful Dowager and how you couldn't call her ugly, because it was too good a word for her, but no one in their senses could call her good-looking, or even passable.

"You know," said Mrs. Macfadyen, "if it hadn't been for Rose Fairweather I would always have been awful," which roused Kate's curiosity and she begged to hear more.

"Well, I never bothered about myself," said Mrs. Macfadyen, "because I was always pretty busy at home and then there was the war and I was nearly always in trousers—you remember. I must have looked *awful*," at which Kate, in whom the words evoked memories of Margot Phelps, her bounding bosom but imperfectly confined and her even more bounding behind even less under control, so valiantly looking after her parents and the hens and doing A.R.P. and Civil Defence and anything else that came her way, not to speak of keeping goats and taking their horrible milk on her bicycle to the parents who thought cows' milk was poison for their children, felt a kind of shame for not having taken the trouble to realize what was behind it all.

It had been left to Rose Fairweather, the lovely incredibly silly daughter of the late headmaster Mr. Birkett, to take real trouble to help the fat, overworked, unselfish Margot Phelps and make her conscious of her own good points. Since then Margot had never looked back and when she married the wealthy Mr. Macfadyen she had made it her duty and her pleasure to keep herself groomed and dressed as became the wife of a wealthy man of business who liked his wife to accompany him wherever his business led him, and to shine quietly among other wives.

"You know, Margot, sometimes I almost envy you," said Kate.

"You needn't," said Mrs. Macfadyen with a sadness that made

Kate feel she had been a beast. "You see, I was nobody. Then Donald gave me everything. Now I am back in my mud hovel, like the fisherman's wife. Donald gave me courage but when he died my courage mostly went with him."

"It *didn't*," said Kate indignantly. "Anyway you had the courage to start life again. Let Everard and me know if you want any help or good advice. Everard is frightfully good at advice and it's quite often right."

"I do want help," said Mrs. Macfadyen. "But I do want to be what Donald let me be. I mean the person that asks and it is given to them. Sometimes I think it is more blessed to receive than to give."

Kate did not feel equal to arguing on what seemed to her almost a doctrinal point, but with great presense of mind she pointed out that if everyone gave there would be no one to receive, so it was really rather blessed to receive because then you are helping the people who gave to be blessed, which original piece of casuistry seemed to comfort Mrs. Macfadyen a good deal.

"I'm sorry your visit is so nearly over," said Kate. "We'll keep an eye on your people and ring you up if there is any real need. If you are in Greshamsbury give Rose and all the Fairweathers my love, and that nice Canon Fewling. And someone told me—oh yes, it was Mrs. Francis Brandon—that the Vicar who used to be at Pomfret Madrigal had gone to Greshamsbury New Town. He's got a wife and family and she thought they might be a bit out of it. Do ask Rose Fairweather, and if you are over there you might visit them and say a few kind words. Parkinson is their name."

CHAPTER 4

So Mrs. Macfadyen, much refreshed by her holiday and seeing so many old friends, went back to Framley. She had been afraid that the break in her work of sorting and tidying might have spoilt her hand, as it were. But the "nice change" which everyone had recommended seemed to have done its work, and though she still missed the smell of her husband's tweeds and his tobacco and the row of boots and shoes most shiningly kept by his own hands and every day's most quiet needs by sun and candlelight, she found that she was gradually remaking a life of her own, and the Luftons, especially the elder Lady Lufton in the Dower House, made much of her. Perhaps her most poignant regret, apart from the mere sense of irreparable loss, was for music. Mr. Macfadyen, the son of poor parents, working his own way up in the world, had the true Scotch passion for education and in no narrow sense. Though the terms trivium and quadrivium were probably unknown to him, he had pursued several of their studies as far as he could, music being not least among them. A year spent in Holland near the German border to learn more about bulbs had been well employed in other ways as well and the Dowager Lady Lufton, for one, would always remember the evening some six years ago when Mr. Macfadyen had sung Schubert songs to her accompaniment, for it was on that same evening that her son had clearly shown his love for Grace Grantly. Now Grace was Lady

Lufton and her mother-in-law the dowager; and Mr. Macfadyen was dead.

"I remember when I was a little girl," said the elder Lady
Lufton to Mrs. Macfadyen who had come over for tea and to
report on her travels, "my father was talking to my mother about
the death of a friend and she told me that I said 'What is death?
I shall never die,'" at which Mrs. Macfadyen had to laugh. But
most of us in youth have felt the same, for it is impossible to
imagine a world existing except in so far as we ourselves exist.
Who was it who said "Je pense, donc je suis?" We might equally
say "Je suis, donc le monde existe."

When a young peer, with a widowed mother who is not so
very old, is getting married, there is always the question of the
change of title for the widow. The name Dowager, a title not
unpleasant, is not now in favour and after some family consul-
tations it was agreed that it should not be used and when, after
the wedding, the guests attended the reception, the bride-
groom's mother had been announced publicly (by Mr. Tozer of
the Barchester caterers Scatcherd and Tozer who were responsible for the excellent arrangements) as Mary, Lady Lufton. Her
new daughter-in-law had wondered if the dowager would
mind losing her status, as it were, but it was made abundantly
clear to her that her mother-in-law only wanted to love and to
give. As usually happens, her old friends and most of the county
went on speaking of her as Lady Lufton or Old Lady Lufton and
of her daughter-in-law as Young Lady Lufton and as neither of
them was likely to take umbrage, however addressed, everyone
was satisfied.

Perhaps the only lapse from perfection that Lady Lufton
could see in her daughter-in-law was that so far she had not
produced an heir though she had two delightful small daughters. But when she considered that she herself had started with
Maria, now the Honourable Mrs. Oliver Marling with a young
family, she felt she was not in a position to throw stones. Not
that she would have thrown them in any case. But when you

have a barony of quite respectable age in the family you do want it to go on in the male line. The Granny-sense is very strong in some women and Lady Lufton had already begun to accumulate Granny-fodder from her two daughters, but their children (though far more beautiful, clever and intelligent than any other children) were not, she considered, suitable heirs to the barony. Darling Grace had certainly done well, but it was, in her mother-in-law's opinion, necessary that she should do better. Of this interesting and vital subject she did not speak as a rule, but she somehow felt that Mrs. Macfadyen, who had never had children nor even been suspected of any tendency in that direction, was a very suitable person with whom to discuss it. And we think she was right in this, for Mrs. Macfadyen had the rational and unsqueamish attitude towards the producing of young that is not infrequently met in people whose lives have been largely dealing with farm and domestic animals. Some, it is true, are quite nauseatingly forward with the accouchements and/or miscarriages of their domestic animals, but Mrs. Macfadyen, even when she was Margot Phelps, rendered unto the goat-pen and the chicken-run the things that were theirs and rarely troubled to speak of them unless with professionals.

Not many people knew that the Dowager (as it will be really more simple to call the elder Lady Lufton) had not only a very friendly feeling for Mr. Macfadyen's widow, but admired her greatly for her practical sense. A few years earlier, Margot Phelps, as she was then, had met one of the widowed Lady Lufton's daughters who had asked her to come over to lunch at Framley, where her mother had moved from the Court to the Old Parsonage. This was a pleasant house which had been brought up to date with plumbing and bathrooms so that there might be a Dower House for whoever needed it, while the clergyman had been moved into a smaller and more modern house in the village. During Miss Phelps's visit Lady Lufton had offered to take her over the house, a treat which no nice woman can refuse, and as they went over the house Miss Phelps had made several such sensible suggestions for improvements as had greatly impressed Lady Lufton. The most outstanding of these was that there simply must be a gate at the top of the stairs so that when Lady Lufton's grandchildren came to stay with her they could be kept on their own landing, and that a second gate was also indicated at the top of the other staircase that led down to the kitchen quarters.Both these gates had been put in by the estate carpenter and ever since then Lady Lufton had felt the greatest admiration for Miss Phelps. So when Mr. Macfadyen brought his bride to Framley there was always a warm welcome for her at the Old Parsonage and since his death she had been there a good deal.

Now that she was home again, without her husband, it did not feel much like home to her. She had made up her mind to finish the clearing of the house and then to begin to look for a small home for herself, all of which agreed very well with Lord Lufton's plans. We think that earlier in his life he might have been rather weak—or it would not be unreasonable to say silly—and have suggested that the widow should remain in what had been her home. But as he went about his county affairs and talked with various people he began to realize that any agent—and an agent he really needed now and could well afford, for his wife had come to him not undowered from the Grantly money—must have somewhere to live and the obvious place was the house Mr. Macfadyen had rented from him. When he had made this decision he felt rather like the judge in the Gospel according to St. Luke who feared not God, neither regarded man. But even as the unjust judge did eventually listen to the widow, Lord Lufton (who was eminently just) spoke to her very kindly about it, saying that he did not wish in any way to press her. For this she was grateful, but did not wish to prolong her stay, and began to look about for a new home.

Soon after his marriage Mr. Macfadyen had decided that for his wife it would be better to have a lawyer of her own and thought of Mr. Updike at Harefield, lawyer to the Beltons and other families of high county standing, with the additional advantage of a son who would succeed him, for a family business is very useful in the county where the lawyer is more often a friend than he is in London. To this his wife was perfectly agreeable and never having been used to dealing with business and money she was glad that a competent friend would look after her interests and Mr. Updike, who had known and liked Mr. Macfadyen at the County Club, was glad to do so.

So Mrs. Macfadyen packed all her husband's papers neatly in a large suitcase, rang Mr. Updike up, asked for an appointment, and drove herself and the suitcase over to Harefield. The little town, as we still think of it, though it has spread up and down the valley and up the northern slopes much more than we like, still kept its air of self-sufficiency. Harefield House up on the slopes still looked like a Gentleman's Mansion though now as we know a flourishing preparatory school for boys. The melodious jangling bells of the church still sounded up and down the river valley; the High Street was very little changed. Even Messrs. Sheepskin and Messrs. Gaiters had obligingly toned down—or arted up—what we believe are called the Fascias (only we have never dared to pronounce the word) of their shops. On what was still called market-day some of the county still turned up in a pony cart with their children; still were there some real slums (and a county slum can be just as slummy as a town slum) where children played happily with dirt and went to bed as late as they saw fit, if not previously slapped into bed by their mother. Still, we are glad to say, are most of the lovely red brick houses lived in by gentry—among whom we of course include the Beltons, Dr. Perry and also Mr. Updike the lawyer whom Mrs. Macfadyen was visiting by appointment.

The lawyer's house was Clives Corner—most of the better houses, as we know, being named after Clive of India and his victories. Mr. Updike's family had been for several generations in Harefield, lawyers from father to son. More than once a young Updike had been tempted to move to Barchester, but in every case the older generation had won. And we think they were right, for a country town lawyer has in many ways a better time than his perhaps richer colleagues in town, and also, which is really important, lays up an inheritance of friends for his children. So Mr. Updike with his elder son continued the family firm and widened the circle of their business and of their friends.

Mrs. Macfadyen had corresponded with Mr. Updike, but this was her first professional visit to him and she felt certain she would say something foolish, or forget all the things of importance that she had to say. Like all the older houses in Harefield Clive's Corner was of fine mellow red brick with some good stonework on its front. She rang the bell and waited. Nothing happened, so she rang the bell again. A face appeared at a window and disappeared. In a very short time a door in the large stable-gate was opened and a tall fair woman looked out.

"Oh, do come in this way," said the woman. "The front door has stuck again. I *am* so sorry."

"I am Mrs. Macfadyen," said that lady. "I have an appointment with Mr. Updike. Is that right?"

"Oh, *Phil*," said the woman. "He did say he was expecting you—I mean if it is you. Do come in."

So Mrs. Macfadyen followed her through the door and across a cobbled yard into the house. Like all the older houses in Harefield, each of which was quite different from the others, Clive's Corner had its own peculiar beauties. Nothing to astonish, but the composed symmetry that is so difficult to copy and an air of saying "Here I am. Take me or leave me. I am perfect and do not care."

"Don't fall up this step, it's rather dark," said Mrs. Updike, stumbling as she spoke. "Oh dear! it's that place where the carpet got burnt when I dropped the iron on it and I meant to mend it, but it's nailed down to the steps and I couldn't get the nails out and broke the kitchen scissors because I couldn't find Phil's tools. He *will* lock them up. It's this way."

Much to Mrs. Macfadyen's relief they came out into a hall of pleasing proportions from which a staircase spiralled upwards to the floor above.

"Oh *what* a lovely staircase," she said, looking up to the elegant lantern above it which lighted the hall. And when we say lantern we hope that our reader knows what we mean, a kind of elegant, glazed cupola.

"Oh, *isn't* it," said Mrs. Updike, pleased that the house should be admired. "I can't tell you how many times I've fallen up it."

"And down?" said Mrs. Macfadyen.

"No, I don't think so," said Mrs. Updike, "though why not I really don't know. Phil! are you there?" and she opened a door.

"He is," she said proudly, holding it for the guest to enter, so Mrs. Macfadyen said thank you and went in.

Mr. Updike, who must now be described as an elderly man, we suppose, though he didn't look it and was a very hard worker, got up and shook hands.

"You, I hope, are Mrs. Macfadyen," he said. "I don't suppose Betty asked you. Do sit down."

"Well, no, she didn't," said Mrs. Macfadyen. "But I didn't ask her either. I was thinking how very pretty she is."

Such a remark from a new and unknown client gave Mr. Updike considerable pleasure and he said he had always thought so himself.

"And I brought a large case of papers and things," Mrs. Macfadyen said, "but I left it in the car in case you didn't want it."

Mr. Updike said he would get it and went away while Mrs. Macfadyen admired the curve of the large bay window and the elegance of the mouldings on the plaster cornice, till Mr. Updike came back with the case or trunk, and put it on a table. Mrs. Macfadyen handed him the key which he took with a smile of thanks and put on this desk.

"Oh, aren't you going to open it?" said Mrs. Macfadyen, rather disappointed.

"'I don't think that is necessary now," said Mr. Updike. "I

should like to look at the contents thoroughly and then I shall be able to tell you more about them."

"I have docketed them all as neatly as I could," said his client.

"I am sure you have," said Mr. Updike. "But there is no need to trouble you with business at present. Will you come and have some tea? I know my wife will be disappointed if you don't," and he opened the door for her to go out.

"It *is* a lovely door," said Mrs. Macfadyen, as indeed it was, being gently curved to the curve of the room which at that end was a kind of apse, though from the hall this was not visible.

"Some of the houses in the High Street are more handsome, or more magnificent than ours, but I think ours is the loveliest," said Mr. Updike.

"And I suppose everyone thinks theirs is the loveliest," said Mrs. Macfadyen, at which her lawyer laughed and stood aside for her to go out.

"Just across the hall," he said, and opened a door. Mrs. Updike was discovered sitting on a sofa with a tea-table in front of her and seemed pleased to see them.

"Broken anything, Betty?" said her husband, but very affectionately.

"Not yet," said his wife. "Did you do all your business?"

Mr. Updike said they hadn't even begun and he was sure Mrs. Macfadyen wanted some tea and apart from Mrs. Updike emptying into the sugar basin the hot water from a cup which she was warming, everything went well. Mrs. Macfadyen enjoyed herself very much. It was the kind of pleasant, homely feeling which she had missed so much since her husband's death. Just so, only on other subjects, had he and she talked together alone and to her horror she felt the pricking behind the eyes that heralds tears. She put her cup down rather abruptly.

"Oh, Phil!" said Mrs. Updike. "*Poor* Mrs. Macfadyen! I can't find my handkerchief anywhere unless I left it in my other pocket. Oh, here it is," but Mrs. Macfadyen had mastered the crisis.

"I'm sorry," she said. "It was only that I was tired. And Donald did like that suitcase so much. You must think me very silly."

"But my dear Mrs. Macfadyen," said Mr. Updike, "I don't want to keep the case. I shall put all those papers in my safe."

"It isn't that," said Mrs. Macfadyen. "I suddenly couldn't help remembering how we came back from Holland with it and there was a scene with the customs when we got back and how well Donald handled it. I'm sorry."

And so were the Updikes, or rather they were very sorry for her and most kindly and tactfully talked of dull things like the weather and how horrid it was to have such a cold summer.

There was the sound of a door being shut. Then the drawing-room door was opened and in came Mrs. and Mr. Belton from Arcot House, for Harefield came in and out of each other's houses very freely, though woe betide any new-comer who did so till he or more often she had been made free of the liberties of the little town. They and Mrs. Macfadyen had met several times, so there was nothing to explain. There was some more general talk and then Mrs. Macfadyen thanked Mr. Updike and said good-bye to everyone. The Beltons pressed her to come over again soon and see Arcot House, which she promised to do. Then she drove herself home. Luckily she was dining at Framley Court with the Luftons and by the time she got to bed she was able to go to sleep quickly, and slept through the night.

Rose Fairweather, driven by strong benevolence of soul, now rang Mrs. Macfadyen up and asked if she would come to Greshamsbury for a week or so, an invitation that Mrs. Macfadyen, secretly glad to have a respite from her sorting and tidying, gladly accepted and drove herself over. It was a nice English summer day with an occasional gleam of sun, spatters of rain, and bitterly cold. As few hardy, insensitive people said one couldn't call it cold when the thermometer was nearly sixty, but that—as Mr. Wickham who had dropped in to greet Mrs.

Macfadyen said—was where their toes turned in: a locution enthusiastically adopted by the young Fairweathers who were home for the holidays. We are not quite sure how many of them there were, but there were several. All we can definitely say is that Rose's first baby was born in 1940 in South America where her husband was stationed at the time and she certainly had two more children if not three, the youngest having been born in 1946. We think that the two elder were boys and are certain that the two younger were girls.

"It's a rum thing," said Mr. Wickham, "but you can't go by the thermometer nowadays."

Rose asked what he meant.

"Well, when I was a kid we had a thermometer in the nursery," said Mr. Wickham. "Our nurse used to look at it every day, though what good that did I don't know. When it went up to sixty nurse said it was a very hot day. Well, when it's sixty now I don't feel any warmer. And there was something marked Sick Room Temperature. But something's happened to the weather. I haven't felt really warm for years."

Rose, who was wearing a thin sleeveless frock and looking as charming as ever, said she felt quite warm enough.

"Well, I don't," said Mrs. Macfadyen stoutly. "All my tweed suits wear out twice as fast as they did because I can hardly ever give them a holiday."

"Trouble with you, Margot," said Mr. Wickham unchivalrously, "is that you're too sensitive."

"I'm *not*," said Mrs. Macfadyen emphatically. "And never was."

"Now, come off it, my girl," said Mr. Wickham.

"Look here, Wicks, I'm *not* a girl now," said Mrs. Macfadyen, who was very fond of Mr. Wickham.

"Well, you weren't as young as all that either when I proposed to you down by the hen-run," said Mr. Wickham with sad want of chivalry.

"Did you really?" said Rose Fairweather, much intrigued by this sudden outburst of romance.

"Yes, he did," said Mrs. Macfadyen. "It was *most* kind of him. Father was rather ill then and mother was so tired and I was feeding the hens and Donald came into the field and saw me crying and said would I marry him. So I said yes and then he had to go."

"And then I turned up," said Mr. Wickham, "and she was looking like the morning after the night before, so what could a kind-hearted old codger do? Ask the girl to marry me of course. And when she said she'd just got engaged to Macfadyen I could have spliced the mainbrace."

"But didn't you *want* to marry her, Wicks?" said Rose, much interested in the story which she was hearing for the first time.

"God bless my soul, my girl, of course not," said the unchivalrous Mr. Wickham. "But I was in the Navy for a bit of the '14 war and there was she, an Admiral's daughter, with a pail of that stinking hen food, crying like a good 'un, and I said to myself, 'Wicks! what would Nelson have done? His duty.' So there and then I asked the girl to marry me—all honourably you know, separate bedrooms and all that if she wanted it—and Lord bless me if she didn't say she was engaged to Macfadyen."

"Poor old Wicks," said Rose, who thought this a most peculiar courtship.

"Not on your life, my girl," said Mr. Wickham. "Who was the fellow that said he never saw a chap give a penny to a blind beggar but he was bound to be run over by a bus next minute? Well I was the mug that tried to give the penny and I may say I've never been more relieved in my life than when Margot told me what she'd done."

At this Mrs. Macfadyen began to laugh in a most undignified way, as did Mr. Wickham. Rose, who with all her charm and her real kindness was not very quick at understanding hunour, looked at them with interest and said it was a good thing Margot hadn't married Mr. Wickham because it would have been so awful if they hadn't got on together.

"I say, Wicks, do stop to tea," said Rose. "The new clergyman and his wife are coming."

Mr. Wickham asked what new clergyman. He hadn't heard that Tubby had gone away.

"Oh don't be so silly, Wicks," said Rose. "Of course he hasn't. It's the Vicar from the New Town. He's called Hopkinson—no he isn't—it's Parkinson. I can't think why I get so muddled."

"Well, it might be Atkinson, or Tomlinson; you never know," said Mr. Wickham liberally. "Oh Lord! though—isn't she a daughter of old Welk the undertaker? *He* knows a bit of good wood when he sees it. I've run across him once or twice up in the woods above Gundric's Fossway. He's hand in glove with the bodgers."

Neither of the ladies had the faintest idea what he meant and showed it.

"Lord! where were you brought up?" said Mr. Wickham. "Woodsmen they are. A rough lot but they've been handling the woodman's axe ever since axes were invented. Like Sherwood forest and all that. They'll bring a tree down within an inch of where they want it to lie and they know how long it ought to lie and season and when to begin cutting it up and how to stack it. Of course they've got a circular saw and so on now, but every one of them knows how to use an axe. There's an old man there who used to work in a sawpit when he was a boy and rose to top sawyer."

"Well, you've only got to stay to tea, Wicks," said Rose, "and I'll tell them to bring your brown teapot," for those who knew Mr. Wickham best also knew his addiction to spirituous liquors and liked to pander to his taste. It had often been a subject of discussion among his many friends as to when he knew when he had had enough, but as no one had ever seen him even mildly under the influence of drink, no one could give a ruling or even an opinion on this fascinating theme. "I think that bell's them."

"They, my girl; do mind your P's and Q's," said Mr. Wickham. "And why are they a bell and who are they?"

"The Parkinsons of course," said Rose. "Mr. and Mrs. and
three children. I know I shan't remember their names. Harold
and Connie and Joe. *Do* help me to remember."

"There's someone else with them," said Mr. Wickham who
had been looking discreetly out of the window. "By Nelson and
Bronte it's old Welk. I'll let them in, then they won't mind so
much," and he went out of the room.

"But why *should* they mind?" said Mrs. Macfadyen. "I mean,
there isn't anything to mind about, is there?"

"Good old Wicks," said Rose. "I think he thinks the Parkinsons might be frightened if Edie opened the door. That's my
parlourmaid and ever since she had her new false teeth she
thinks everyone will want to look at her and mumbles. Still, I've
got her to wear them and that's something. At first she wouldn't
because she said it didn't seem natural-like. Now she does wear
them, but she usually takes them out for her meals. She says her
gums are quite hard. Cook doesn't like it because she says it
turns her stomach to see teeth in a glass of water," but any
further information on this fascinating subject was cut short
by Mr. Wickham, personally conducting the party from the
Vicarage.

It would be difficult to say which of the Parkinsons looked the
more alarmed. Mrs. Parkinson, with the courage of the wild
animal defending her young (which appeared to include her
husband), said How do you do to Rose and told the children to
shake hands nicely, which they did. She did not exactly tell her
husband in so many words to shake hands nicely, but Mr.
Wickham said afterwards that she had pinched or shoved him in
a very expressive way. Mr. Welk, whose profession demands far
better manners than most, shook hands warmly with Rose.

"You won't remember me, Mr. Welk," said Mrs. Macfadyen.
"I used to be Margot Phelps—the Admiral's daughter at Southbridge."

The Royal Navy is a passport almost everywhere. Mr. Welk shook hands warmly with Mrs. Macfadyen and said Sir Edmund Pridham had brought the Admiral over once during the last war to give his opinion about some wood that was needed for something in the naval line.

"A find old gentleman he was and I hope he is still," said Mr. Welk. "In our profession we have to be careful the way we speak about old people, because some people are always out to take offence, but I'm sure no offence meant in this case," to which Mrs. Macfadyen replied that her parents were neither of them as young as they were and on this theme they talked very restfully for several minutes, agreeing that one wasn't what one was, nor ever likely to be and he, Mr. Welk, rather liked being older himself. One was able to look back and be thankful.

"And I have something to *be* thankful for," said Mr. Welk emphatically. "My Mavis never gave me a day's trouble. Teddy's a good husband and I hear in the Close that he is well thought of, but it's Mavis that made him. He *was* a poor weedy thing when first he came in these parts. But he's been a good lad and worked hard. I help them a bit. Mavis is all I've got now and I'm not badly off and I'm going to see that those children get on. I have to keep an eye on them all because my Mavis she's like all these young mothers and if things are sometimes a bit tight it's Mother that doesn't have the extra bit of meat or the glass of port. I'm not a teetotaller myself, and I'm not a drinker neither, but you can't live on water. So I give them a proper lot of stout and some port and when Teddy next gets a holiday we're all going to France."

Much interested by these details, Mrs. Macfadyen asked which part of France.

"Well, I'm making enquiries," said Mr. Welk cautiously. "I'm not going to do this on the cheap. We're going to some place where there'll be sun and a nice sandy beach and Mavis won't have a thing to worry about. I've an old army friend at Mentone and he's a pal of the English chaplain there and will find a nice hotel along the coast where the kids can be in the sea all day. And if they've got any good undertakers there," said Mr. Welk, warming to his subject, "'Funeral Pumps' they call them, but there's no accounting for foreigners, I might pick up a hint or two."

Mrs. Macfadyen praised his plan and said she was sure that it would work both ways and they would pick up a hint or two from him. Like Maud, he took the hint sedately, for he had a very good idea of his own value.

Mrs. Macfadyen, who had been an elder sister or aunt to so many midshipmen, took the children into the garden where there was a swing and a seesaw. Of course the children all wanted to go on both, but Mrs. Macfadyen very firmly said that Harold and Connie could go on the seesaw and she would give Joe a very gentle swing.

One never knows what effect anything will have on children. They may find that swinging very high (which would make us sick at once) is pure bliss and on the other hand may be terrified of the seesaw whenever their end is high in the air. They may be openly bored by a little artificial rivulet bordered with flowers and diversified with a waterfall at least nine inches high, or they may ask nothing better than to dabble in an old trough half-full of green slimy water behind the potting shed. Luckily the young of the human race were an open book to Mrs. Macfadyen who from her earliest years had helped to run children's parties wherever the Flag of England flew; the highlights in her memory being the Christmas when the Phelps family were all at Trincomalee and the Khansamah had draped the box the tree was in with yards of coloured muslin, and the year her father was stationed at Flinders with H.M.S. *Gridiron* and H.M.S. *Andiron* and they celebrated the scorching Australian Christmas with a young gum-tree in a huge block of ice which stood in a shallow tank from the Navel Barracks with plenty of freezing salt.

We regret to say that Joe, unworthy namesake of his god-

father, began to yell as soon as Mrs. Macfadyen began to push
the swing. Had they been alone she would probably have spoken
sharply to him, but a yelling child is heard at a great distance, so
she stopped the swing and firmly took Joe to a very small shallow
concrete pool with a green slimy bottom and some little clumps
of iris. Here Joe was at once perfectly happy. Mrs. Macfadyen
turned up the legs of his very short knickerbockers, rolled up his
sleeves, took off his shoes and socks and told him he could do
what he liked but if he sat down in the water he would go
straight home. He was a good child, so he paddled quietly in the
pool, picked up various pebbles that took his fancy, washed
them in the rather muddy water and laid them out on the iris
island. It was quite obvious that he was doing something very
important and did not wish to be interfered with, so Mrs.
Macfadyen sat herself on a stone by the pond and thought her
thoughts. What they were we do not know, but we think it was
mostly a remembering of her own childhood, without regrets,
without nostalgia, thankful for parents who had loved and
sheltered her. The horrid imp who likes to spoil our moments
of peace did put his head up and say What about her Parents
and oughtn't she to Do More For Them; but she very sensibly packed him off to where he came from and thought of
Harefield and the kind lawyer Mr. Updike and his charming,
rather touching wife, and how nice it would be to get over to
Harefield from time to time and become better acquainted with
some of the people. And also perhaps to make some friends at
the Hosiers' Girls' Foundation School which had been housed
at Harefield during the war and for some time afterwards and
was now in its brand-new home over near the Southbridge
Road. Also the Priory School owned and run by Philip Winter
and now settled in Harefield House whose owner, Mr. Belton,
was glad to get a good rent for it. And so far had those thoughts
taken her that only the tca-bell, energetically rung outside the
house, called her back to her lost self.

With a firm hand she led Connie and Joe into the house,

followed by Harold. All three children washed their hands well and also rinsed them well before drying them, which Mrs. Macfadyen noted with approval, as most children if left alone will damp their hands in the basin, smear some soap on them, dabble them perfunctorily in the water and smear the soapy dirt all over the towel. They ate their tea most correctly and said Please and Thank You.

"They *are* beautifully brought up," said Mrs. Macfadyen to Mr. Parkinson who, we are glad to say, appeared to have got over his shyness and was making a very good tea.

"It's all Mavis," he said. "I'm pretty busy now. I'm giving Harold some Latin lessons. I never knew very much myself but I know enough to start him. He's going to have a good education whatever else he can't have. Mr. Welk," and he lowered his voice, "is insuring Harold for his education when he gets to the expensive age, but he'll have to work hard and try for scholarships too."

Mrs. Macfadyen said an educational endowment was the best thing you could give a boy, or a girl either.

"Well, me and Mavis have been thinking," said Mr. Parkinson, "and we can start Connie with an educational insurance, but it's a bit worrying when we don't know if we can keep it up. But it's the last thing we'll give up. And Dr. Crawley is doing an insurance for his godson. It's more than I deserve, but the kids do deserve it and I hope they'll do their godparents credit."

Mrs. Macfadyen said she was sure they would and then led Mr. Parkinson—by no means loath—to talk of himself and the New Town and the work he was doing there. She gathered that he was finding it interesting work but rather uphill because nearly everyone got into the car on Sundays and went out for the day and the ones that didn't had a nice long lay-in and then had to get the family dinner cooked.

"I must say I'd like a Sunday lay-in myself sometimes," said Mr. Parkinson, "and if I ever have a curate I will," which he said with a frankness that made Mrs. Macfadyen laugh.

"And I'll tell you another thing," he went on. "I can't be grateful enough to Canon Fewling. He has given me some very good tips and he said if ever I was in difficulties to let him know and by—I mean I certainly will," at which Mrs. Macfadyen found it difficult not to laugh.

After tea Mrs. Parkinson made as if to go, but Rose got her into a corner, enquired when the children went to bed and how long she needed to get the supper ready and said they must stay a little longer and she would run them all back in the car.

"Oh, it *is* kind of you, Mrs. Fairweather," said Mrs. Parkinson, "but really we can't bother you. Father left his car at the garage to be cleaned, that's why we walked, but it's not far."

Rose was sorely tempted to say Don't be so silly, but felt that Mrs. Parkinson might take it hardly. Luckily at that moment a roar was heard outside and as suddenly stopped and in came Canon Fewling, delighted to find Mrs. Macfadyen with Rose and pleased to see the Parkinsons.

"Oh, *be* an angel, Tubby," said Rose, "and run Mrs. Parkinson and the family home," to which Canon Fewling of course replied, and quite truly, that he would be delighted. And we are glad to say that Mrs. Parkinson, who had a quick mind, realized that she must take the good the gods provided and be thankful, and before Mr. Parkinson had time to arrange scruples or professions of unworthiness, Rose had kissed the children, given them each a box of chocolates to take home, kissed Mrs. Parkinson (which surprised that lady very much), shaken hands warmly with Mr. Parkinson, asked them all to come again soon and waved to them as they drove away.

"Ouf!" she said as she stretched her elegant legs out on the sofa.

"Yes, indeed," said Mrs. Macfadyen who had been plumping up the cushions and generally tidying the room. "I never had any children, so I don't know if I'd have liked them or not, but the Parkinson children though most exhausting are *beautifully* brought up."

"Give yourself some sherry, Margot," said Rose. "I don't want any just yet, John ought to be back any time now."

Mrs. Macfadyen asked what Captain Fairweather was doing now. Rose said it was all office work and she didn't ask and he didn't tell her, but if she waited till John came back he would tell her or else he wouldn't. After which both ladies were rather silent in a friendly way till Canon Fewling's car roared up again and he came in.

"Well, Tubby," said Rose. "Give yourself some sherry till John comes."

"He's practically here," said Canon Fewling. "I saw him coming up the hill as I left the New Town and I very meanly went all out, just to annoy him," and even as he spoke in came Captain Fairweather, to be greeted with a hug and a kiss from his wife and a rather terrifying handshake from Mrs. Macfadyen.

"Lord! Margot," he said, massaging the injured hand, "you're like Tartarin when he said he had *doubles muscles*. You've torn my tendon Achilles or something. Help!"

"Oh, John, I *am* sorry," said Mrs. Macfadyen. "I suppose it was dealing with those awful goats for so long. You've got to have muscle for that."

"Now sit down, Tubby, and re-lax," said Rose, slightly affecting an American accent as heard on the movies. "And tell me all about Château Parkinson because I want to know."

Her husband asked what on earth she was talking about.

"Only the new Vicar in the New Town, darling," said Rose. "He is as good as gold and nearly as dull, and his wife is gooder than gold and will push him along I think and they've three children and her father is Welk the undertaker and knows everyone and the Dean is the elder boy's godfather. Fill my glass again, there's an angel."

"Your wife is one of the most delightful women I know," said Canon Fewling. "Her account of the Parkinsons—whom I *know* I shall call Hopkinson by mistake one day—is a fine bit of reportage, but not altogether accurate. It is the younger boy who is Crawley's godson. They have had a hard time, but I hope and think the worst is over. My housekeeper Mrs. Hicks, who is hand in glove with the churchgoing people in the New Town, says everyone likes her and they are getting to respect him."

"I never knew Mrs. Hicks went to church in the New Town," said Rose, "and I do know most things here," she added with a simple assurance that made her hearers laugh. "Why doesn't she go to our church here?"

"As far as I can make out, she feels that it is the abode— broadly speaking—of the Scarlet Woman," said Canon Fewling mildly. "And while she cooks for me so well and looks after me so kindly I see no reason to quarrel with her belief. Her religious activities never interfere with her admirable cooking and her pleasure in the dinner parties I occasionally give. I think I must have one for the Parkinsons. Will you come, Margot, if you are still here as I hope you will be?"

"She will have to be," said Rose. "I want her here as long as she will stay. But, Tubby, do you think a dinner party would frighten Mrs. Parkinson?"

This was an interesting social problem. Canon Fewling very meanly said he hardly knew them well enough to judge.

Mrs. Macfadyen, who perhaps had seen more of life on a small income than anyone else present, said she felt pretty sure that the Parkinsons would enjoy a real dinner party very much, adding with a slight touch of malice that if they were asked they would say they had thoroughly enjoyed it, which led to one of those endlessly interesting discussions as to why some words were all right and some weren't. On being pressed for examples of what she meant, she said serviette and lounge were among the more obviously wrong ones. On the other hand if someone said they would give you a tinkle it was unreasonable to object to it, as one said ring up oneself, which was obviously rubbish, and the only correct word would be telephone. And after this there was such a noise and discussion of words that no one could hear anything anyone else said—nor did they wish to. Canon Fewling, feeling rather like a schoolmaster whose senior boys are being a bore, removed himself to the piano and began to play for his own amusement.

As was always happening in Greshamsbury, an unusually friendly community, one or two other friends dropped in for sherry and gossip. We were going to say small-town gossip, for the Old and the New Towns constituted a whole, but the older part round the church still kept itself to itself, which was remarked on by Canon Fewling.

"It is curious," he said to Mrs. Macfadyen, talking while he played, "how we go on up here with our heads buried in the sand. I don't think its snobbery."

"Nor do I," said Mrs. Macfadyen. "And I don't think it's snobbery in the New Town either. I think you pretty well don't exist for them except as a place one has to drive through to get to Southbridge."

Canon Fewling said, rather unkindly, that as far as the Old Town was concerned the New Town wasn't even a place to drive through to Northbridge as it was just as quick to by-pass it by the new road if one was going in that direction. He then felt he had perhaps been unjust and said he was sure there were a lot of very nice people there.

"Well, of course there are," said Mrs. Macfadyen, "only they don't happen to be our sort of nice people any more than we are theirs. But isn't it lucky that you've got a link now?"

Canon Fewling asked What link in a voice that showed him to be sceptical of any such thing.

"The Parkinsons, of course," said Mrs. Macfadyen.

Canon Fewling said he didn't know them much.

"Then you ought to, Tubby," said Mrs. Macfadyen severely. "After all he *is* a clergyman."

"I know he is," said Canon Fewling, "and that's what makes it more difficult. But he seems to me to be the right man in the right place," to which Mrs. Macfadyen replied that he might seem to be but his wife certainly was.

"I'm a snob," said Canon Fewling sadly. "Mrs. parkinson seems to me to be just the kind of wife a young vicar needs. Mrs. Hicks tells me that everyone down there likes her."

"Well then, that's all right," said Mrs. Macfadyen. "If the women like her then they'll take on her husband. Give him time. And her father will be a help. Undertakers *have* to get on with people. It's part of the job. When Donald died I can't tell you how considerate the men from Tozers' were. I'd seen some of them being waiters at parties in the Close and they have such kind manners and I think Donald would have liked them. He got on with everyone."

"Except with Lord Aberfordbury," said Canon Fewling and Mrs. Macfadyen had to laugh, for her late husband had signally worsted that very unpopular peer over a bit of land.

"Listen, Tubby," said Mrs. Macfadyen. "We've got to keep an eye on the Parkinsons. After all the younger boy *is* the Dean's godson. Look here, Tubby, I'll bet you five shillings that the Dean will help Mr. Parkinson with the service one Sunday," which prediction rather shocked Canon Fewling. Not that he saw anything wrong in a godfather being kind to the father of his godson, but—and there were several buts and though they seemed valid enough to him he also realized that other people might think differently. And in any case if Margot Macfadyen thought a thing was so, it probably was so. Margot Phelps had changed very little and if there were any change it was for the better—if anything could be better than what she was.

"A penny for your thoughts," said Mrs. Macfadyen.

"Certainly not," said Canon Fewling. "They are quite good thoughts, but you are completely out of date. A penny doesn't buy anything now."

I *know*," said Mrs. Macfadyen with a heartfelt sigh. For the rapid debasing in the value of money was irritating even more people than it really hurt. "There's not a thing that hasn't gone up in price this year. And I can't see that anyone is doing any better for it."

"If I hear the word vicious spiral once more I shall bark like a dog," said Canon Fewling violently, which made Mrs. Macfadyen laugh.

"I do like to hear you laugh, Margot," said Canon Fewling.

"So did Donald," said Mrs. Macfadyen. "And he had a pretty good laugh himself. I wish you had known him better. But living over at Framley and then having to go abroad so much we did rather lose touch with Greshamsbury. Anyway it's fun to see you again, Tubby. Look here, I'm staying on with Rose for a bit. Could you ask the Parkinsons to dinner and get Dr. and Mrs. Crawley? You could ask me too if you like. You need a spare woman. And I'm *very* spare," she said with sudden melancholy. "It comes of always having had Donald to go about with, I suppose. Oh, well."

Canon Fewling did not quite know what to say. So he said, "He was a good man and a good citizen and what matters more to me, he was a good husband to you. I'll certainly ask the Parkinsons. I know Mrs. Hicks will be pleased because then she can boast in the village that she knows them. With the Dean and Mrs. Crawley we shall be six. Whom else shall I ask? Six is an awkward number if two of them are unknown quantities. Greshams? Fairweathers?" but Mrs. Macfadyen said she didn't know why exactly, but she thought not.

"Well, I don't know why either, but I'm sure you are right," said Canon Fewling. "What about the Umblebys? It isn't a bad thing for newcomers to know the local lawyer and if I judge the Parkinsons correctly they won't have a lawyer and probably think it's rather out of their line."

That, Mrs. Macfadyen thought, was quite a good suggestion. Then they chose two dates so that the Parkinsons could have a choice and Canon Fewling said he would write to them.

"By the way, which had I better write to?" he said. "I feel that I ought to get my etiquette right with them. It is all rather an affair of protocol till we know each other better and I want them to feel quite at home and comfortable."

"Well, you're an angel, Tubby," said Mrs. Macfadyen. "Let me think. I believe—mind I can't swear to it—that if you write to him as a brother priest he'll be frightfully pleased. And anything that pleases him will please her. But all the same, she's the man of that couple," and Canon Fewling laughed and said the same idea had occurred to him.

Accordingly Canon Fewling wrote to Mr. Parkinson to the effect that he would very much like to make his nearer acquaintance and would he and Mrs. Parkinson (which he felt would be correct) come to dinner on the following Thursday at about half-past seven. Only a few old friends, he said, including the Dean and Mrs. Crawley, and the ladies would not be dressing. He then thought this might be considered bad taste, tore up his letter and began again, saying that the Dean and Mrs. Crawley were having supper with him on the following Thursday and Mrs. Macfadyen whom he thought they already knew was also coming and what a pleasure it would be if Mr. and Mrs. Parkinson would come too and everyone would be wearing ordinary afternoon clothes as it was quite informal. This letter he had composed, written and rewritten at least three times before it was shaped to his mind. He licked it up, addressed it and stamped it and then remembered, to his annoyance, that he had not mentioned the Umblebys. We regret to have to record that Canon Fewling then said Damn aloud to himself. But he did penance by opening the letter (by good luck just before the gum had hardened) and adding a postscript to the effect that Mr. Umbleby the solicitor and his wife would be of the party. He then relicked the letter and wished that life were simpler.

When Mrs. Hicks paid her usual morning visit to Canon Fewling to get any special orders for the day he informed her that they would probably be eight on Thursday and named the guests.

"So you're asking Mr. and Mrs. Parkinson, sir," said Mrs. Hicks.

Canon Fewling, though he had the courage of a sailor and of a beneficed canon with private means, said Yes with a firm voice but a rather shaky feeling.

"My niece in the New Town that's obliging at the Daffodil Cafe—and why some people call it Caffy is beyond me—says Mr. Parkinson is an ever so nice gentleman," said Mrs. Hicks.

Canon Fewling said he was very glad to hear it and what did Mrs. Hicks think they had better have for dinner. Mrs. Hicks said The Fish would be round any time now and she'd give him the order and what about some nice lemon sole first, because she'd got some lovely fat and it would be a sin to waste it and then what about a nice joint. She knew the butcher had some real South Down mutton though it wasn't everyone he'd allow to have it and what about a nice saddle of lamb. Ate beautiful it did, said Mrs. Hicks, almost with tears in her eyes, because she'd had some at Mr. Umbleby's with the cook and the staff the evening Captain and Mrs. Gresham were having their dinner at the Umblebys. And plenty of those young potatoes, just boiled and then done in the fat so as they'd be nice and crisp outside and nice and soft inside. And there were some nice lettuces now, and no thanks to The Boys, said Mrs. Hicks darkly, but she'd spoken to their mothers and those Young Turks wouldn't do it again. And, said Mrs. Hicks, fixing her employer with an Ancient Mariner's eye, a nice Summer Pudding because the black-currants were ripe and a good help of ice cream to go with it and what about a savoury?

Canon Fewling basely said he would leave it to her.

"Well, just as you like, sir," said Mrs. Hicks with the air of a peculiarly virtuous martyr. "I'd say mushrooms on fried croutons, but it's for you to say, sir."

Canon Fewling, wishing devoutly that he could take the whole party to the White Hart in Barchester where he could leave everything to the old waiter Burden and the chef, or even to the Country Club though the wine there was not quite so good, said mushrooms would be very nice and that was all.

"I'll see to the wine as usual, Mrs. Hicks," he said and went back to his study to consider, for he had found when he was given the living at Greshamsbury that, owing to the laziness or the incompetence of previous incumbents, the cellar was very badly ventilated and sprouting mushrooms (or more probably poisonous fungi). He had therefore, at some expense, got experts to install good drains and good ventilation and replace the rotting wooden stands by shelves of slate and had installed wine racks which made the inside of the cellar look rather like a giant honeycomb. He had a sound knowledge of wine though without any pretence to being an expert and always had on tap a large cask of beer. There were also compartments for liqueurs and for spirits, for it was one of the Canon's greatest pleasures to entertain old fellow seamen as well as his civilian friends.

When he had carefully considered the relation of food and drink he made a list in his careful writing, for the guidance of Mrs. Hicks, and a copy for his own use. The next question was the seating of his guests, a rock on which many a party has foundered. Mrs. Parkinson, who on her first visit must have place of honour, would of course be next to her host and he put Mr. Umbleby on her other side as he had an easy if slightly professional way with people. Then Mrs. Crawley who would have Mr. Parkinson on her right and beyond him Mrs. Macfadyen. This was a particularly kind and thoughtful move on Canon Fewling's part, as both ladies were used to dealing with parties, while Mrs. Crawley could easily have been Mr. Parkinson's mother or even at a pinch his grandmother. Beyond Mrs. Macfadyen would be Dr. Crawley, and Mrs. Umbleby would fill the gap between him and the host.

What wines Canon Fewling had chosen we will not attempt to describe, for we are very illiterate on that subject, but we know that they were good and suitable to the dishes that were served.

As it was summer Mrs. Hicks had seen that the fires in Canon

Fewling's study and in the drawing-room were lit and the
dining-room fire laid; but not lit because there is nearly always
someone at a dinner party who complains if the room is even
nicely warm, while the people who genuinely feel and hate the
old have to be cross for the rest of the evening.

The person most celebrated for the coldness of her entertain-
ments was Victoria, Lady Norton, who strong in her own virtue,
corseted almost from head to heel and incapable of feeling any
differences in temperature whether at the North Pole or in
Borrioboola Gha, gave her guests nasty food in an icy room. But
as none of our Barsetshire friends dine with her, it does not
matter.

The chief difficulty about fires is of course the dining-room
where each guest is adscriptus glebae—tied to his or her chair.
One can hardly ask to have the fire extinguished for oneself
alone, nor can one ask to have it lighted for oneself. But Canon
Fewling had lately installed a new heating system for the living-
rooms and the bedrooms, known as the Thermocontactic Bra-
sierette (which led Mr. Wickham and kindred spirits to make
lewd witticisms on the same), which really did all its illustrated
brochure said it would do. After sulking for several days because
she wasn't used to them things, Mrs. Hicks had discovered that
having warmth in her bedroom and her little sitting-room off
the kitchen was very soothing to her rheumatism and turned it
on with enthusiasm even in the dog days, so that Canon Fewling
had to choose between offending her and dying like Mr. Krook
of spontaneous combustion. At the end of an English summer
heating was of course essential and when the Crawleys, who
were the first arrivals, came into the house they were loud in
their praise of its mild climate.

"It is so good of you both to come, Mrs. Crawley," said Canon
Fewling. "Mrs. Macfadyen, whom you may remember as
Margot Phelps—her father is Admiral Phelps over at Southbridge—is spending two or three weeks over here and is looking
forward so much to seeing you."

"I hardly know the Phelpses, I am sorry to say," said Mrs. Crawley. "But their daughter—that is Mrs. Macfadyen I gather—did excellent war-work."

"You are an authority on the subject of good daughters, Mrs. Crawley," said her host and courteously enquired after them. As Mrs. Crawley had eight sons and daughters, she gave what we can only call a quick précis of their condition, and as they had all made successful and happy marriages it was all nice and dull.

"Happy the family that has no history," said Canon Fewling, slightly paraphrasing a better-known phrase, but as Mrs. Crawley did not quite grasp his allusion it was just as well that the Umblebys came in. The connection between Mr. Umbleby's firm of lawyers and the Close was of old standing and they saw eye to eye with the Crawleys about the Palace, but before they could get down to it Mrs. Macfadyen arrived, to be joyfully received by her host and the rest of the company who were mostly old friends.

We will not disguise from our reader the fact that Canon Fewling was slightly nervous about the last guests. He had thought of sending a car to fetch them, but feared they might think it presuming. The evening was fine, the walk was not long, he had particularly said that no one would be wearing evening dress. The Umblebys had walked as had Mrs. Macfadyen—a very short walk in both cases he must admit. But before he could do any more hostly worrying in came Mr. and Mrs. Parkinson.

"I do hope we're not late," said Mrs. Parkinson. "Joe was a bit off colour but Father was having tea with us so he said he'd stay with the children till we came back and he sent us up in his car. Not his professional car of course. He's got a lovely new one and Mr. Samson that has the garage up the road said he'd drive us, because he'd never driven a Crotona yet and he'll come and fetch us."

Canon Fewling said he was very sorry about the little boy.

"So am I, Mrs. Parkinson," said Dr. Crawley. "I feel rather

responsible for my godson." Mrs. Crawley also offered her sympathy and everyone said a few kind words.

"I think you know all my guests," said Canon Fewling, "except Mr. and Mrs. Umbleby. They live near me and have some children too."

Mrs. Parkinson said wasn't that nice. Canon Fewling offered sherry from an elegant glass decanter on a handsome salver of silver gilt, picked up abroad by him at some period of his naval career.

"Do tell me about your children, Mrs. Parkinson," said Mrs. Umbleby. "We've got three, but a bit older than yours, I expect," and the two ladies plunged into ages and sexes, which is quite a good way of making friends, and they might have been talking about them still, had not Mrs. Hicks come in and said dinner was ready. So the party, some taking their unfinished sherry with them, straggled into the dining-room and when they had circled the table often enough they each found their name card. Canon Fewling managed to go in beside Mrs. Parkinson and showed her where she was placed.

"Next to me," he said, "and Mr. Umbleby on your other side."

"Oh, I'm ever so glad," said Mrs. Parkinson, "because I've talked to Mrs. Umbleby. It's so awful to be next to someone you don't know," and when her host had sat down, she felt almost safe. "And it was ever so kind of you to ask us. Teddy was ever so pleased when he got the invite. He works so hard and it's lovely for him to get an evening out, like this."

Canon Fewling was more touched than he would have liked to admit by this artless confession and enquired after the washing-machine.

"Oh, it's *super*," said Mrs. Parkinson. "You can't think what a difference it makes. It's only half the time and half the work and if the children get very dirty playing in the garden or the school playground, I can just pop everything in and no trouble at all. But do tell me how your new one is working."

"Well, I'm afraid I don't really know," said Canon Fewling. "You see I'm an old bachelor and I leave all that to Mrs. Hicks."

"Oh, that's Mrs. Hicks that did one of the stalls at the bazaar," said Mrs. Parkinson. "She was splendid. She sold everything off her stall and she won the darts prize. Daddy said she was a fine woman and a fine business head and he *does* know."

Canon Fewling said he was sure he did, with a mental reservation that he did not really want to know exactly what Mr. Welk, though a highly respectable and worthy man whom he had often met professionally, did know.

"I wish you'd known Mother," said Mrs. Parkinson. "She died when I was a little girl and Daddy's never forgotten her. He puts a wreath on her grave every year. It must be *dreadful* to die when you've got children. I don't know *what* I'd do if I was to die with Harold and Connie and Joe so small."

"Dear Mrs. Parkinson," said Canon Fewling, touched by her artless talk, "pray don't think about it. You are as bad as the girl in one of Grimm's Household Tales," and then he wondered if he had said something silly which would need explanation and how to explain he did not know, so he did not try.

"Oh, I *know* the one you mean," said Mrs. Parkinson. "It's The Tree Sillies. Father taught me to read out of Grimm. It's a *lovely* book. I've read it to the kids again and again. Joe doesn't really read yet, but he's got a wonderful memory and once I start one of those stories he'll go on with it, right through."

"I have always liked and respected your Father, Mrs. Parkinson," said Canon Fewling, "and what you tell me makes me respect him even more. He must be very proud of his grandchildren and I know Dr. Crawley will be pleased to hear how well his godchild is getting on."

Mrs. Parkinson looked round, rather nervously her host thought. Then her face cleared.

"Oh, the *Dean*," she said. "I *am* a silly. I thought at first you meant we must tell a reel doctor—I mean like Dr. Ford. Doctors are very mixing."

Canon Fewling quite agreed. And in his calling it was, he said, more than usually trying, as the Archbishop could confer a Lambeth doctorate on any person in Holy Orders whom he saw fit to honour. And then, said Mrs. Parkinson, one might think it was a *real* doctor and ask him to come if anyone was ill. And then, she added, with growing concern, if the person who was ill thought he was going to have a doctor and it turned out to be a clergyman he might think he was going to die.

Even Canon Fewling, strong as his head was, was beginning to feel rather as if he were in Looking-Glass Land, when luckily Mrs. Crawley, who in the absence of a hostess felt rather responsible for the party, turned from Mr. Umbleby to Mr. Parkinson. The whole table followed her example and Mrs. Macfadyen who had been finding Mr. Parkinson distinctly heavy going was relieved to be able to talk to the Dean, or rather to let him talk to her, largely on Cathedral matters.

In common with much of West Barsetshire Mrs. Macfadyen had taken some interest in the engagement, formally announced early in that year, between Edith Graham, youngest daughter of General Sir Robert and Lady Graham, and Lord William Harcourt, younger brother of the Duke of Towers, at present a curate in Barchester.

"Would it be tactful to ask you about those young people?" she said to Dr. Crawley. "I know the Grahams a little, but Lord William I've not met."

The Dean said that Lord William was a gentleman and more than that one could hardly say and then he stopped, giving Mrs. Macfadyen an impression that something was wrong, but she did not like to ask in case it was something about Lord William that one oughtn't to know, like secret drinking or bigamy.

"Not," the Dean went on again, "that one can insist too much now. The doors of the Church are open wide to all who come if they can prove their worth," the last dozen words or so of which speech sounded to Mrs. Macfadyen like a line from a very bad hymn, one of those which have been unnecessarily tacked onto the English Hymnal (which we ourselves shall always consider an unnecessarily large and unwieldy upstart when we think of our Hymns Ancient and Modern); but each generation has its own views and if we cannot accept them it is better not to criticize them. "For instance," the Dean went on and then shot a very expressive look towards the quarter where Mr. Parkinson and Mrs. Crawley were talking.

"Yes," said Mrs. Macfadyen, who had quite taken in the implications of what was almost the equivalent of Lord Burleigh's nod. "I have met your godson. An extremely nice little boy. Joey, after you, I gather. Has anyone ever called you Joey, Dr. Crawley?"

The Dean laughed and said he would like to catch them at it. Josiah was not perhaps, he said, the name he would have chosen for himself, but after using it for the last seventy years or so he had got quite used to it. And if one had a name handed down in the family it was a link with one's forebears. Mrs. Macfadyen asked what he would have liked to be called. If, said the Dean, he had been given a chance, there were several names which, at various ages, he had coveted, among them being Percy and Nebuchadnezzar. Mrs. Macfadyen said she could understand Percy, but Nebuchadnezzar would have been difficult to live up to.

"Well," said the Dean, "there was a poem, much quoted by my contemporaries when I was at my preparatory school, beginning 'Nebuchadnezzar the King of the Jews, Sold his wife for a pair of shoes'," which made Mrs. Macfadyen laugh so much that she choked and had to drink some water.

"Quite unhistorical so far as I know," said the Dean, pleased with the effect of his quotation.

Mrs. Macfadyen said what extraordinary names people in the Bible did have, mentioning Ish-basheth who was very meanly killed by a friend at a place called Helkath-hazzurim; but the Dean said no funnier than Mephibosheth whose regrettable habit of staying in bed till after lunch enabled his ill-wishers to

kill him without much bother, and we must confess that both
Dr. Crawley and Mrs. Macfadyen laughed so much that the
other guests began to wonder what the joke was. But, which was
just as well, someone mentioned the iniquitous proposal lately
brought forward by Them to widen Barley Street, a crooked and
narrow road of considerable antiquity which was blocked by
traffic and a street market for six days out of every seven. And as
no one knew the real facts, or to whom the land belonged, or
what powers would be needed, the argument was free to all. We
may say that here Mr. Parkinson gained favour in the Dean's
eyes by his views on the monstrousness of the proposal, and had
the dinner party taken place some hundred or more years earlier,
the Dean would certainly have asked Mr. Parkinson to take wine
with him.

Then Mrs. Crawley, again as acting hostess, ushered the
ladies to the drawing-room where there was a nice wood fire,
suitable to any English summer evening, blazing on the large
open hearth. Here, for the first time, it was Mrs. Macfadyen
who felt herself a little outside the talk, for as a kind of compliment to Mrs. Parkinson on this formal introduction to Old
Greshamsbury, Mrs. Crawley and Mrs. Umbleby plied her with
questions about her young family, all of which she answered very
prettily, till the conversation turned to the question of how
much if at all one's children were improved by smacking, as and
when necessary. We are glad to say that all three ladies, from
their very different points of view, were at one on the subject
and agreed that a good smack in time saved nine, besides—
possibly—acting as a deterrent to other forms of disobedience
and evil-doing. Mrs. Crawley asked Mrs. Macfadyen's opinion.

"I don't think I've got one," said Mrs. Macfadyen, "because
Donald and I hadn't any children. But Donald said his mother
would skelp him as a boy if he was disobedient. And I think if I
had children I'd have smacked them if they were naughty.
Father did smack me once for telling a lie, so I went and hid in
the wood-shed."

Mrs. Crawley, hopeful of further light on the subject, asked what happened next.

"Nothing," said Mrs. Macfadyen. "It got rather dull, so I came out and went back to the house and it was tea-time and no one talked about it so I didn't either," at which anti-climax everyone laughed and Mrs. Crawley noted with pleasure that Mrs. Parkinson laughed too.

"That was very sensible," said Mrs. Umbleby approvingly. "I've hardly ever smacked mine. But then I was lucky and had a Nannie."

"But you wouldn't let a *nurse* smack your children, Mrs. Umbleby?" said Mrs. Parkinson, apparently with visions of whipping female 'prentices to death and hiding them in the coal-hole.

Mrs. Umbleby looked at her with a kind of affectionate pity.

"Nannies never needed to smack anyone," she said. "They just told the children not to and the children didn't. And if they told them to, they did."

Mrs. Parkinson, who didn't quite understand, looked slightly alarmed. Mrs. Crawley asked her to come and tell her all about the Dean's godchild, and Mrs. Parkinson's tongue was loosened and she told Mrs. Crawley—as all Mrs. Crawley's daughters and daughters-in-law in turn had told her—how marvellous the youngest was and unlike, and also superior to, any other children of anywhere near his age in intelligence and charm, and goodness only knew what he would say next, and could clean his own shoes and tie up his shoe laces.

"I mustn't forget the older ones though," said Mrs. Crawley. "How is my friend Harold, Mrs. Parkinson? I remember so well when you were in hospital with him in Barchester. And now you have three children," which words she said with so kindly and laudatory a manner that Mrs. Parkinson quite forgot that Mrs. Crawley had had eight.

"Oh, Harold's a good boy," said Mrs. Parkinson. "He's called after Father, you know. And Father's going to help pay for his education so it's wonderful. He wants Harold to come into his business when he's grown up, but he says if Harold really has a turn for anything else he'll pay for it just the same. Me and Teddy *are* lucky. Everyone's so kind."

And then Mrs. Crawley asked about the Vicarage and what the New Town people were like and if the attendance at church was good, to all of which questions Mrs. Parkinson gave most satisfactory answers.

"Teddy's wonderful," she continued. "He has a Children's Service on Sunday afternoons, it's lovely. And at Christmas we're going to have a crib in the church."

Mrs. Crawley, to whom the first associations of the word were a bed with bars round it for a small child and the second the rack from which stabled horses tear and munch their hay, pulled herself together and said How lovely, and how were they going to arrange it.

"Well, it's a most wonderful piece of luck," said Mrs. Parkinson, looking younger at every moment as she spoke. "You know Mr. and Mrs. Villars, he's the rector at Northbridge, well Mrs. Villars has a friend at Northbridge called Mrs. Paxon and she's wonderful at getting things up—she did their pageant for the Coronation and she used to be in the South Wembley Amateur Dramatic Society and she's going to help me stage it. Just some straw on the floor and a few branches up above. Of course it was really in a stable but we can't manage that but the branches will look nice with a lot of holly among them and Mr. Brown at Southbridge, he's the Red Lion you know, says he can get us some nice straw to put on the floor and he's got a bit of some old banisters that we could pretend were the animals' stall. And Teddy told his Children's Bible Class that the three that have had the best attendance and learned their texts can be angels. The blacksmith's going to be the black King and we'll easily get the other Kings. We can't do the ox and the ass, but I don't suppose anyone will mind. And Father's going to stand a big supper for all the actors in the Drill Hall. It's going to be *wonderful.*"

Mrs. Crawley said, quite truly, that she was sure it would be a great success and if the Dean was free she was sure he would like to come and so would she. And, she added, she had in her big box-room upstairs two large papier mâché heads for the ox and ass that her children used to wear when they had a Christmas pageant. If, she said, the heads were put on a bolster or something of that sort and just showed over the banister-stall, it would look very seasonable. And what about the star?

Mrs. Parkinson said she hadn't thought of that yet, but she was sure they could find one.

"Wait a minute," said Mrs. Crawley. "Mrs. Macfadyen."

Mrs. Macfadyen, who was talking to Mrs. Umbleby, looked up.

"Didn't you have a star on the Christmas-tree when you had the party for the evacuated London schoolchildren in the war?" Mrs. Crawley asked.

"It was a doll with a yellow wig," said Mrs. Macfadyen, "and a silver wand and a lovely silver star on her head. Matron at Southbridge School dressed her."

"You haven't still got it, have you?" said Mrs. Crawley. "Mrs. Parkinson needs one for her Christmas crèche," at which outlandish word Mrs. Parkinson looked slightly alarmed.

"It was given to the youngest child at the party," said Mrs. Macfadyen, "but when the schools went back to London they gave it back to us and I think it's at my father's house. I'm sure I could get it for you, Mrs. Parkinson."

"Oh, thanks *ever* so," said Mrs. Parkinson. "And there's just the one other thing I wanted to ask. I don't know many people here—I mean not like at Pomfret Madrigal where I knew everyone—and everybody says Mrs. Parkinson and I'd be so glad if you'd call me Mavis."

The moment of Christian-naming after a long period of Mrs.-ing is always a little awkward. Mrs. Macfadyen, feeling for the stranger among them, said she would love to say Mavis and her name was Margot if Mrs. Parkinson felt like using it. Mrs. Parkinson went a very pretty pink, choked a little and then said she was very sorry, but she reelly couldn't because it would seem so rude.

"Very well, Mavis. I shall love to call you that," said Mrs. Macfadyen, exaggerating her feelings in the cause of humanity, "and you can say Mrs. Macfadyen. But if you want to say Margot, I'll be just as pleased."

"It's most awfully kind of you, but I simply couldn't," said Mrs. Parkinson. "Besides you're much older than I am. At least I don't mean that," and she went bright red from her brow to as much of her bosom as was exposed by her pretty summer frock.

"I know what you mean," said Mrs. Macfadyen sympathetically, which meant nothing but soothed Mrs. Parkinson. "I'm looking for a house for myself and when I've found one you must bring the children to tea. They are such nice, well-behaved people."

At these kind words Mrs. Parkinson at once cheered up and talked away about the New Town and its life and activities, while Mrs. Macfadyen thought a perfect kaleidoscope of things and chiefly how nice Mrs. Parkinson was and how awful it would be to have to live at her conversational level for the rest of one's life.

Then Mrs. Umbleby took over and asked Mrs. Parkinson about her children and said she must bring them over to tea with her children.

Mrs. Parkinson looked round for help. None was forthcoming. In desperation she said it would be very nice and twisted her fingers like barley-sugar.

"I've got to go down to the New Town on Thursday," said Mrs. Umbleby, "and I can pick your young people up. And I hope you will come too."

"Oh, I *would* like to," said Mrs. Parkinson. "You see the

children haven't been to tea much with strangers and I don't know how they might behave."

"Like nice, well-brought up people, I am sure," said Mrs. Umbleby, which was a noble lie, for she wasn't in the least sure. But this pretty, shy clergy-wife must be befriended. "What on earth are those men doing?"

And certainly the men were tarrying unconscionably, as they were having a delightful talk about the things they talked about every day. The Dean and Mr. Umbleby had got well away on the approaching retirement of the Chancellor, Sir Robert Fielding, and Mr. Parkinson was listening with much interest and threw in one or two very sensible remarks, while Canon Fewling watched his guests, refilling their glasses (an action which, curiously enough, they never noticed till it was too late for the deprecating hand or shake of the head) and hearing what they said, but making no comment. Then he shook himself out of his remoteness and took them all into the drawing-room.

Very often when he had guests he would amuse himself at his piano, softly, while they talked, or play to them if asked. This evening he did not know which would be the better part for a host, so he amused himself by short improvisations and rememberings of old airs, wandering from one to the other. The talk went on and he played on, sometimes singing quietly to himself.

"You are like Frank Churchill," said a voice behind him.

"Hullo, Margot," he said. "May I ask what you mean? Sit down."

Nothing loath, Mrs. Macfadyen sat down near him.

"Don't you remember," she said, "in *Emma*, when Jane Fairfax is playing and singing and that conceited Frank Churchill takes a second, slightly but correctly."

"Of course," said Canon Fewling. "Bless that woman's heart. Do you know Kipling's poem about her? You know I am a Kipling fan—dreadful expression but come to stay. I know so much of him by heart."

Mrs. Macfadyen said she didn't think she did. Canon

Fewling, one of whose virtues was an almost complete un-self-consciousness, repeated it. The rest of the party, now all well away on the ever-fruitful subject of the Palace, paid no attention. Mrs. Macfadyen listened, not moving. When he came to the end there was silence, but the roar of six friendly people conversing in a drawing-room entirely drowned it. And if our reader thinks silence cannot be drowned it is because she is lacking in apprehension.

"It might always happen to one—we don't know," said Canon Fewling getting up.

"What might happen?" said Mrs. Macfadyen.

"Something one thought could not happen," said Canon Fewling almost to himself and they joined the gossiping circle. Presently Mrs. Hicks brought in word that Mrs. Parkinson's car was there and Mr. Samson said no need to hurry.

"I'm sure we don't *want* to hurry," said Mrs. Parkinson, "but Mr. Samson has been so kind I think we ought to go. It's been a lovely evening, Canon Fewling, and thank you *ever* so. Would you like to look at the car?"

Canon Fewling was, as we know, an extremely good if rather alarming motorist, only equalled—possibly surpassed—by Lady Cora Waring, so his acceptance of Mrs. Parkinson's offer was immediate and sincere. His other guests preferred to remain by the fire. The car was all and more than its makers said and it was only with difficulty that Canon Fewling could be prevented from getting under it to have a look at the auto-interrogation frisk lock—or if not that something very like it.

"By Jove! it *is* a piece of work," he said, taking his head out of the bonnet.

"You'd say so again if you could get underneath, sir," said Mr. Samson. "She's that easy to handle you wouldn't hardly credit it. A bit too easy to my mind. I was taking her up Fish Hill and when I put her into top, blessed if she didn't give a hop, skip and jump before she settled down into the collar," which was Greek to the Parkinsons, but we imagine that Canon Fewling understood it. Something passed from hand to hand, the Parkinsons embarked and the convoy speeded away. Canon Fewling went back to the drawing-room.

Here the Crawleys and Umblebys with Mrs. Macfadyen were peacefully discussing the exhibition of the Ultra-Phallic Group (an offshoot of the Neo-Phallic Group) which was being held (subsequent to the exhibition at the Set of Five Gallery off Tottenham Court Road) at Barchester Town Hall, and as none of them held advanced views about art and liked a picture to look like something that they could recognize, they were in friendly agreement about its merits, or rather its complete want of any merit at all.

"Well, what do you think of my fellow-priest?" said Canon Fewling.

Dr. Crawley, who did not like the word Priest—especially when applied to Mr. Parkinson—bent his shaggy eyebrows in disapproval and said "H'm." His wife said that wasn't an answer one way or the other.

"I think they'll do very well, Dean," said Canon Fewling. "She is the right stuff for a clergyman's wife—twice the man he is."

"Well! if *that* is your idea of a clergyman's wife!" said Mrs. Crawley, and everyone laughed. Then the Crawleys and Umblebys went away. Mrs. Hicks asked if she should lock up and Canon Fewling said he would do it himself. Mrs. Macfadyen said she must really go and Tubby mustn't dream of seeing her back to the Fairweathers' as it was only a step. She thought he was going to say something in answer, but he didn't, so they went down the garden path, Canon Fewling opened the gate for her, closed it behind her, waited politely till she had crossed the road and then went back to his Rectory. Mrs. Hicks had already tidied the room, shaken up the cushions and gone to bed. There was some fire left in the grate and Canon Fewling sat looking at it for some time. But there was nothing that he could see in it, so he hooked the fireguard onto the front of the grate and also went to bed.

CHAPTER 5

Life simmered on. The summer—if one could call it that—was short, brutish and nasty; also very cold and damp, merging into what was a blustery, cold autumn. People were cold on the moors, by the sea, in the Lake District, on the Norfolk Broads, and in the mountainous district of Mewlinwill-inwodd, where tourists with no qualifications for rock-climbing fell off or over precipices every summer and had to be rescued at considerable personal inconvenience by bored and angry natives. A good many people were away for the holidays and a good many other people stayed at home because in one's own house one knows the worst and can start the central heating again or, if the worst comes to the even worse, sham sickness and go to bed.

So far Mrs. Macfadyen had not found a house to her liking, but there was no very great hurry and her various friends were glad to have her to stay. She would have liked to go abroad and visit some of her husband's old friends in Holland and elsewhere, and see the new tulip, named Macfadyenensis by its growers, but when she thought of travelling, even her stout heart failed her. For four happy years she had gone everywhere with her husband and made friends with his friends and never had to think of passports, or tickets, or the rate of exchange as that was all done for her. Now she had to think for herself, as well as the responsibility for her parents which her husband had shared.

Now that was all at an end. Her visits to Mr. Updike had brought her into a new circle and when Mrs. Belton asked her to spend a week in Harefield she gladly accepted.

It was a nice chilly day when Mrs. Macfadyen drove herself over to Harefield again. There had not been much rain, everything looked pinched and cross and miserable. As the wind rushed down Harefield High Street, depressed leaves fell from the trees—remains of the avenue that used to lead up to the church—and the gardens had little to show except straggling Michaelmas Daisies and a few late roses which would have done better not to bloom at all.

Arcot House at least had central heating. It was already turned full on and even as Mrs. Macfadyen went in, her spirits rose. If we must stay with friends in the country it is safer to go in the winter because then the heating—if any—will be on. But during most of the spring, all the summer, and far too much of the autumn, one's tweed-clad country friends will live in what might just as well be an igloo—except that igloos, so we understand, are small, overcrowded and overwarmed by a paraffin lamp. Such is the custom of the country. But Mrs. Belton who hated the cold refused to stand any nonsense about economy in warmth and as soon as the first cold day made its appearance—usually about the beginning of July—the heating was turned on.

The houses in the High Street, some beautiful, some handsome, some plain but with character, all had gardens and most of them had some stabling, now of course used for cars. To this there was in most cases no access except by the lane that ran along the end of the gardens. Some of the houses—Mr. Updike's as we know being one—had a stable gate onto the street, but this was only on the North Side. The South Side where the Beltons lived had its garages at the far end of the garden most inconveniently opening onto the lane so that the car had to be fetched in whatever weather and brought round to the front.

Mrs. Macfadyen got out of her car and rang the bell. The

door was opened by an elderly woman who looked like a cross between an elderly nanny and a housekeeper—as indeed she was.

"Mrs. Macfadyen, isn't it, madam?" she said. "Mrs. Belton's expecting you. I'll get your luggage in and I'll tell someone to take your car round to the garage. You can't leave cars in the streets these days. Those boys up at Madras Cottages they'll be up to mischief. Stole the horn off Admiral Hornby's car—that's Miss Elsa's husband—they did."

Mrs. Macfadyen asked what happened to them.

"Admiral Hornby, he went up to the cottages and told their mothers if the horn wasn't back in five minutes he'd lather the lot of them. So their mothers lathered them instead and Admiral Hornby took the horn back."

Mrs. Macfadyen said she didn't know that mothers lathered the boys—she thought it was the father's job.

"Fathers!" said the woman in a voice of deep scorn.

"You must be Wheeler, aren't you?" said Mrs. Macfadyen. "You've got a cousin over at Southbridge. He does odd jobs for my father—that's Admiral Phelps."

"*Well*, you were Miss Margot Phelps, madam, weren't you?" said Wheeler. "Haig Brown, that's the policeman at Southbridge, his mother's a cousin of mine, he's often told us what a fine old gentleman the Admiral is, and he said Miss Phelps she had a rare hand with goats—mucky things I call them—and hens. If you don't mind driving your car round yourself, madam, I'll go and open the garridge door. Up the lane to the right and then to the right again and there's Arcot House painted on the garridge door, if it's shut."

So Mrs. Macfadyen got back into her car, drove up the lane, round to the right, found the garage open, drove in and ranged her car neatly beside a battered-looking old Ford.

"That'll do nicely, madam," said Wheeler who had come up the garden and so into the garage by its back door. She then pressed a button in the wall and a door came rolling forward from the ceiling at the far end and slipped down into place.

"Self-locking, madam," said Wheeler, with what was almost a simper of pride. "It was Admiral Hornby's idea, Miss Elsa's husband that is. Will you come this way?" and Mrs. Macfadyen followed her down the long garden with its herbaceous border and so by the back door into the hall. Wheeler opened a door on the right, said "It's Mrs. Macfadyen," and went away. Mrs. Belton welcomed Mrs. Macfadyen and they sat by the fire very comfortably till Wheeler brought in the tea.

"It *is* a lovely house," said Mrs. Macfadyen, who had been admiring the room, its unpretentious, well-proportioned deal panelling painted white, its good furniture obviously used by several generations, and on the walls the Scotch ancestors and ancestresses of old Mrs. Ellangowan-Hornby, daughter of a Scotch peer, aunt of Admiral Hornby, R.N., the present owner of the house, who had married the Beltons' only daughter. "But Harefield is full of lovely houses. I'd like to see them all."

"Well, we certainly will see some of them while you are here," said Mrs. Belton. "Harefield is rather like Cranford. None of us are particularly well off and we give a lot of tea-parties. The Updikes I think you know. Mrs. Updike said you had been there and she wanted to see you again," so Mrs. Macfadyen explained, very simply, that Mr. Updike was handling her interest in her late husband's will for her.

"Late is a funny word to use," she said meditatively. "I don't think Donald would like to be late. He never was. No more than I'm really a widow."

Mrs. Belton, slightly taken aback by this statement, could not think of the right thing to say, so sooner than have a silence which might be embarrassing she said the first thing that came into her head which was to ask why her guest wasn't a widow. Having said which words, she wished she hadn't. But Mrs. Macfadyen took it all as a matter of course.

"Donald didn't want me to miss him," she said, looking at the fire as if talking with it. "If I'd died it would have been much worse for him than it is for me now *he* is dead. He wouldn't have known how to get on. He got so used to me in the years—so few but so happy—that we were married, and he needed me. I daresay anyone else nice would have done, but I happened to be his wife. And I go on being his wife in a way. I just don't feel like a widow."

"But what *do* widows feel like?" said Mrs. Belton, who felt that if this kind of conversation pleased her guest it would be interesting to pursue it; though of course she would never have dreamed of discussing such a subject unmasked.

"The funny thing is," said Mrs. Macfadyen, "that they feel much the same as they did before. At least I do. I miss Donald nearly all the time inside myself, but sometimes I don't remember that I am forgetting him. It's like being two people."

Mrs. Belton did not answer. In her life there had been no one great loss. If there had been she would certainly have faced it with courage and dignity. All her three children had come unscathed through the war. Her husband, though not able to fell trees and help her with the tractor as he used to do and loved to do, was in good health and good spirits. Beltons were long-lived; so were her people, the Thornes. They were poorer than they used to be, but no need for unpleasant economies. And she had her children and her grandchildren. Having a practical mind, she spoke it.

"But it's quite right not always to remember," she said. "One can't remember everything. And surely your husband would rather you forgot than that you were unhappy in remembering."

She then felt that she had been talking priggish, unhelpful nonsense.

"That's exactly what Donald *would* feel," said Mrs. Macfadyen. "Thank you very much, Mrs. Belton," and before there was time for either lady to feel embarrassed by this conversation Mr. Belton came in, demanding tea. Wheeler brought some in freshly made, so of course the ladies had to have a rere-tea. Then

as often happened in the friendly and rather close society of
Harefield, a few friends dropped in for sherry. Mr. Carton,
whose editing of the fourth-century scholar Fluvius Minucius
had given him a place among scholars, with his agreeable wife
who had been Miss Sparling, Dr. and Mrs. Perry and then the
Vicar, Mr. Oriel.

On hearing that Mrs. Macfadyen had been staying at Greshamsbury, Mr. Oriel attached himself to her so that he might
tell her about his great-great-uncle Oriel who married one of old
Squire Gresham's daughters some hundred years or so ago,
which was much more interesting to him than it was to his
hearer. She expressed her sympathy and said she thought the
lawyer Mr. Umbleby's family also belonged to that period and
Mr. Oriel enjoyed himself immensely in relationship and pedi-
grees (as we all do) without much regard for the interest (or lack
of interest) of his hearer.

But Mrs. Macfadyen, who had been brought up in a stern
school to listen to her father's reminiscences of his naval experiences over most of the Seven Seas, bore up very well. And
though listeners may not always hear good of themselves, they
will undoubtedly be considered very pleasant and intelligent
by the talker. The donneurs de serénades will think well of the
belles écouteuses; what the charming listeners think of the concert offered to them we do not know—probably they are thinking of their dress for the next ball. So did Mrs. Macfadyen think
of the agreeable evening at Canon Fewling's house, while saying
the right things to Mr. Oriel.

"By the way, Mr. Oriel," said Mrs. Belton, "how is that nice
maid of yours that was mentally defective? The one that married
the brother of the Jorams' butler—Simnet wasn't it?"

Mr. Oriel said as far as he knew she was happily settled in
Barchester and got on very well with her mother-in-law. Mrs.
Belton, preening herself a little, said she got on extraordinarily
well with both her daughters-in-law—and with her son-in-law,
she added.

"I can't say I've much difficulty with mine," said Dr. Perry.

"I almost wish we *had* some difficulty sometimes," said his wife. "Mrs. Bob is so much better-born than we are that it's like trying to pick up a jelly-fish and Bob does whatever she tells him to do."

Everyone present who had met Mrs. Bob, more correctly the Honourable Mrs. Robert Perry, daughter of a well-known and very wealthy consultant with a title, agreed cordially with Mrs. Perry, but did not like to say so.

"And she is always so *very* kind to us," Mrs. Perry added with almost a sigh, and those who had been at the dance at the Nabob some years ago and seen Mrs. Bob inwardly despising her in-laws and her surroundings in the most gracious way, knew exactly what Mrs. Perry meant.

"Never mind, Dr. Perry," said Mrs. Macfadyen. "If I had a stroke, or leprosy, or the glanders, whatever they are, I'd rather have you than all Harley Street. You were so kind to Donald. Kindness is much more important than being a good doctor. At least I don't mean that—" and her voice trailed off into confusion. But Dr. Perry, not a whit taken aback, laughed loudly and said it was the best compliment he had ever had.

"Now, do listen everyone," said Mrs. Belton. "Mrs. Macfadyen is looking for a house for herself. She wants to be fairly near Southbridge because of her father and mother, but it needn't be too near. I mean I don't mean she doesn't *want* to be near"—and her voice trailed away as everyone began to laugh, though in a very kind way.

"But it's quite true," said Mrs. Macfadyen. "If I hadn't got married I'd have stayed at Jutland Cottage always. I'm *very* fond of mother and father. But when you get married it isn't the same thing."

Mr. Carton, in his precise, donnish voice, said that undoubtedly the celibate state and the honourable state of matrimony were different.

"I was a celibate once myself," he added.

"Well, *really*, Mr. Carton, considering how long you have lived in Harefield, we all know *that*," said Mrs. Perry. "But not professionally," which made everyone laugh, and a discussion arose as to which, if any, among their common celibate friends were professionals, and which amateurs.

"Oriel, for one, is a professional," said Mrs. Carton, who enjoyed mildly baiting the Vicar. "But of course he was born an uncle."

There was a brief silence. Being on the whole a country community, not too far from the farmyard, it occurred to at least three of the party that in their youth when kindly farmer friends had taken them round the fields or the sties and shown them the various animals, they had described them as the mum and the dad and the uncle; a description which had the great advantage of telling their young friends all about the facts of life in a way which conveyed to the young friends absolutely nothing at all.

Mr. Oriel asked Mrs. Macfadyen how her father and mother were.

She said they were well, but she wished they were better.

"Mother has always worried about father," she said, "but I'm more worried about mother. One doesn't want to talk about it much, but Dr. Ford, who has known her for a long time, told me her heart isn't very strong either. I sometimes wonder if I ought to have married," a remark which her hearers found it difficult to deal with as they had all felt, and continued to feel, that the best day's work the wealthy market gardener had ever done was to marry the Phelps's admirable and devoted daughter before they had—in all innocence—sucked her life juice away and ground her bones to make their bread. No one found it easy to make a comment till Dr. Perry, with his usual good sense, said it was the most reasonable thing she had ever done and Mrs. Belton asked how that nice Canon Fewling was.

Mrs. Macfadyen said he was very well and as kind as ever and she had dined there a few days ago with the Dean and Mrs.

Crawley and the new Vicar from the New Town with his wife—the Parkinsons.

"That's not a name," said Mr. Belton. "Feller with a name like that might be anyone," which made Mrs. Macfadyen feel rather uncomfortable, though she knew Mr. Belton did not intend any slight.

"His father-in-law is a Mr. Welk," said Mrs. Macfadyen. "He's an undertaker and he knows all those gypsy poachers and bodgers up in the woods above Grumper's End."

"Oh, *that* Welk," said Mr. Belton, though what other Welk he had suspected it to be we do not think he knew. "He's all right. He knows something about wood. I've had some dealings with the bodgers up there myself—so did my old father and *his* father—and they say he's forgotten more about wood than they ever knew, and *they've* been at it father and son since the Druids. Oldest blood in West Barsetshire probably. They leave the old families like the Thornes nowhere. Yes, Welk's all right."

"I don't really know him," said Mrs. Macfadyen, "but his daughter is very pretty and has three nice children and the Dean is godfather to the youngest. I think he's going to help with his schooling. He can present a boy to the Cathedral School he told me."

Although in the country interest in people and things tends to be local rather than general, this information interested everybody. Largely, we think, because of the introduction of the bodgers.

"A queer lot," said Mr. Belton. "I wouldn't trust them within ten miles of a rabbit or a hare—or a hedgehog for that matter. They still bake them in clay. But if they are working for you, you can be sure of good work. When my old father was alive and we had a lot of timber in the park, my governor used to have a dozen of them down sometimes and they'd bring their gypsy caravans and live in them like wild animals."

Mr. Carton was heard to register a mild protest. Wild animals, he said, were more apt to live in herds than in caravans.

"All right, all right, I daresay they do," said Mr. Belton. "But the bodgers lived in caravans. No one lives in caravans now."

At this point a number of voices were raised, all much to the same effect, that half the young people seemed to like living in caravans now, but as there were no young people present the point was not argued. Mr. Oriel said that his great-great-uncle the vicar at Greshamsbury had a brood of young turkeys stolen by a passing gypsy caravan. Mr. Carton, with his most tight-lipped smile, said aloud to himself, " 'When we lived at Hendon Barnes's gander was stole by tinkers.' "

"Tinkers?" said Mr. Belton. "No, no, Oriel said Gypsies."

"But Mr. F's aunt said tinkers," said Mr. Carton and a kind of hum of applause and sympathy rose from the party, most of whom were educated.

"Effsarnt? Never heard such a name," said Mr. Belton, thus causing his wife to feel mingled affection and irritation, while the rest of the party pretended they hadn't heard him and tried not to smile at one another.

Then as mostly happens the men, with their curious herd instinct that numbers give safety, managed to get closer together, which gave the ladies freedom to talk as they wished among themselves. The front-door bell was heard resounding through the hall and Wheeler announced Mr. Updike.

"*Don't* say my wife isn't here," was Mr. Updike's peculiar greeting. "I suppose she has tripped up on something. I never knew such a woman. If she were in the middle of a desert she'd find something to fall over. Oh, here you are, Betty," and Mrs. Updike came in, apparently limping.

"Oh, how do you do, Mrs. Belton?" said Mrs. Updike. "I *am* silly. I meant to put on my new shoes just to break them in and when I'd got one on I found a hole in my other stocking so I took it off and mended it because it wasn't really a hole but only where the seam had gone a bit and then I put it on again and I thought I had put the other shoe on again, but it was another one with a higher heel and I've only just noticed it. I *am* silly."

Harefield was of course used to Mrs. Updike's divagations. Mrs. Macfadyen who had only met her once was fascinated to find her again in trouble.

"May I talk to you?" said Mrs. Updike sitting down by Mrs. Macfadyen. "I *did* like it when you came to see Phil. I do wish you would come and live here, only there's such a lot going on that one hardly ever has time to see anyone. Have you found a house?"

Mrs. Macfadyen said not yet, and there was no hurry, but she would like to be settled before the winter, and have her own furniture out of store.

"Not that I've very much," she said, "because the house on Lord Lufton's estate where we lived was partly furnished. But I've a good many books in store and I *do* want to have them on shelves again."

The word books to many people is like jam to the wasp and several of the party stopped talking about whatever they had been talking about and began to relate their own experiences with those elusive objects, especially Mr. Oriel who had borrowed a book on Fluvius Minucius from Miss Sparling's grandfather the learned and deceased Canon Horbury in nineteen hundred and two; which book Miss Sparling had found by pure chance among an untidy heap of books in Mr. Oriel's study some forty years later. Mr. Carton said he wished he had had the strength of mind to copy an old Oxford friend of his who had a bookplate bearing the simple words "Stolen from S. W. Watkins" which he pasted into all his books.

"'Songs Without Words,' we used to call him at Paul's," he added.

Mrs. Updike asked if it was because he couldn't remember them.

Mr. Belton said Couldn't remember *what?*

"The words," said Mrs. Updike. "Like the 'Lost Chord' only that man forgot the music, not the words."

Mr. Belton, rather at sea but willing to pull a conversational oar, said Mrs. Updike was quite right and it was the Music the feller lost, not the Words, adding that his old aunt used to sing it only she couldn't do the high notes, which he appeared to find rather creditable to her.

Mrs. Macfadyen asked what she did then.

"Sometimes she just left them out and sometimes she transposed them," said Mr. Belton, and as Mrs. Macfadyen still looked a little at a loss he added, "Put some of them down."

"Oh, put them down an octave," said Mrs. Perry. "Now we *all* understand," and as nearly everyone present had understood for some time and everyone had lost the thread of the discussion, it was much easier to talk about a house for Mrs. Macfadyen.

All she wanted, she said, was a house within easy reach of Southbridge so that she could keep an eye on her parents. Everyone was most kind to them, she said, and the neighbours were in and out all the time. And people who had been sailors, like Mr. Wickham and Canon Fewling and Sir Cecil Waring, came and talked with her father about the Navy. But she did feel a responsibility for them.

Dr. Perry, who had attended the Admiral professionally when Dr. Ford was away, said he always enjoyed his visits because the Admiral didn't mind if one talked or not, so long as he did all the talking himself, which made the company laugh and Mrs. Macfadyen couldn't help laughing too, because it was kindly said and all too true. Owing to Admiral and Mrs. Phelps's active interest in various committees, and to speak of the war years when they had worked for every good or charitable cause and kept open house for naval men of all ages who needed a night's or a week's lodging, Jutland Cottage had remained a rallying-point for the Senior Service.

"But it's not easy now," said Mrs. Macfadyen. "Mother isn't very strong and father has a bit of a heart. Donald was so good to them. I feel I ought to settle near them—in case—" and she left the sentence unfinished.

Every person in the room, while admiring and sympathizing

with her filial piety, felt that—quite apart from any other consideration—it was a very good thing that Mrs. Macfadyen had escaped from the Daughter Who Is So Devoted To Her Parents position. But in a small town local interests will always win and the fact that Mr. Oriel had put his foot through a rotten plank in the vestry and the workmen who were mending it had found nothing of any interest at all except an early penny of Queen Victoria's reign when Her Majesty still wore her hair gathered into drooping ringlets at the back, looking—so irreverent Young People said—exactly like an elephant with its trunk, was far more important and interesting than any domestic or foreign news.

"We have had a little trouble over the penny," said Mr. Oriel, "because no one knows whose property it ought to be."

"Not that it really matters, Oriel," said Mr. Carton. "It's not rare enough to be Treasure Trove and one penny is neither here nor there now. None of the workmen would thank you for it. Even the smallest child despises a penny now."

Mr. Oriel said he was sorry to hear it. When he was a child, he said, a penny would buy four farthing buns, or take you in a horse omnibus from Hammersmith Broadway to Kensington Church. He used to spend part of his Christmas holidays regularly with an aunt in Hammersmith down on the river but thought it was all sadly changed now. When last he had been down there he hardly knew where he was. Those delightful little stone-paved streets too narrow for wheeled traffic and the romantic humpbacked wooden bridge over a little stream, tributary to the Thames; all were gone, alas.

"Like Barchester when I was a small boy," said Mr. Belton, yielding as we all do when we are old to the nostalgia of the past. "There were no drains to speak of in the Close and my old father used to say there was typhoid every few years if the river was low and The Poor never came into the Close. Well, we shan't see those days again, more's the pity."

We are glad to say that these highly undemocratic and antisocial remarks went down very well. Nearly everyone present could contribute something of the past from what their parents or grandparents had told them, the Vicar scoring highest marks as it was well known that during the incumbency of old Canon Umbleby the town had been left to the care of a curate for seven years.

Mrs. Macfadyen said she would certainly ask Mr. Umbleby about it when she was next over at Greshamsbury.

Mr. Oriel said the Church then was very different from what it was now.

"It's a pity Wickham isn't here," said Mr. Carton. "He says he likes the clergy because you never know what they'll say next," and he might have expatiated on this fascinating subject had not his wife looked at him. He was not the man to quail before any look, even from a woman who had kept some dozen mistresses and some hundred girls or so in subjection simply by existing, but his chief happiness was to please his wife in everything— except of course the doctrine of the enclitic *de* and the proper basing of *oun*—so he smiling put the question by.

"There was some talk a few years ago," said Mr. Oriel, "of converting the Vicarage into flats and putting me—or my successor—into one of those new houses along the Barchester Road."

Mr. Belton said that was something he didn't know, conveying by his manner that it was therefore probably something rather hole-and-corner that he ought to have investigated.

"It was the West Barsetshire County Council of course," said Mr. Oriel. "Luckily Adams is on it and he wouldn't stand any nonsense," for the wealthy ironmaster was a power in the county. "Do you remember his daughter, Mrs. Carton? She was at the Park," by which Mr. Oriel meant Harefield Park, tenanted during the war by the Hosiers' Girls' Foundation School of which Mrs. Carton had been Headmistress.

"Indeed I do," said Mrs. Carton. "I don't think I have ever had a girl who worried me so much as Heather Adams. I don't mean that she *worried* me, but she was so ill-trained and it was very difficult to help her to fit in. In fact if it hadn't been for Mrs. Belton, I don't think I could ever have done it."

Several people asked Mrs. Belton what her methods were. "But I hadn't any," said Mrs. Belton. "It was Freddy."

As her elder son, now Rear-Admiral Frederick Belton with several letters after his name, had been for some ten years happily married to Susan Dean, daughter of the wealthy business man Mr. Dean at Worsted, he was not often seen in Harefield and Mrs. Macfadyen only knew him by name. Several guests begged Mrs. Belton to tell them All.

"Well, there isn't much to tell," said Mrs. Belton. "Heather fell into the lake when she was skating with the school because she wouldn't pay attention to the DANGER board. Mrs. Carton will remember," and she looked at the ex-Headmistress of the Hosiers' Girls' Foundation School.

"Indeed I do," said Mrs. Carton. "But why Heather improved so much afterwards I have never known."

"It is all old history now," said Mrs. Belton. "The silly girl wouldn't pay attention to the danger sign and fell in and Freddy pulled her out. She *was* a silly girl and thought she was in love with him and Freddy, really very bravely I think, told her that the girl he was engaged to—a Wren—was killed in an air raid. Which was quite true," said Mrs. Belton, looking round for unbelievers, "and his heart was nearly broken. So Heather enjoyed the romance tremendously and concentrated on mathematics."

"The most brilliant and reliable pupil in that branch that we have ever had," said Mrs. Carton. "The present Headmistress, Miss Holly, could answer for that. What makes people be mathematical I don't know."

"No more than they know what makes you a classical scholar, Mrs. Carton," said Mr. Belton. "The brain's a very rum thing. I was at Rugby and King's, but when I'd taken my degree—I just managed to pull off a second—I had to think of the place. And here I've been ever since. I'm an old feller now and Freddy is carrying on while I'm alive and he'll have to carry on when I'm dead," which last words he said with a fine boastfulness, as of one who would back himself against any of his coevals to keep death at bay as long as it was necessary, and would then make a good exit.

"You are like Donald," said Mrs. Macfadyen, thinking of her good, utterly reliable husband. "He used to quote a saying he had heard in his childhood but couldn't say where, that there was always something to saw that he wanted to see sawn, or something to maw that he wanted to see mawn. But he died between the sowing and the mowing," and her hearers suddenly felt that there was here something beyond reach of their sympathy.

"That's Andrew Fairservice," said Mr. Belton, who was very well read in his Scott—far better than the next generation though he never rubbed it in and they were not conscious of a loss—for how can you regret something you have never had, nor perhaps known that you wanted? "Rob Roy," he added, the better to impress on his hearers his very poor opinion of their general culture.

Mr. Carton said, in his scholarly, rather didactic voice, that as no one read Scott now it was useless to quote him.

"Not only do they not read him," said Mrs. Macfadyen, "but they only know him from strip-tease—or whatever you call those stories all told in pictures with labels coming out of people's mouths saying 'Says,' or 'Thinks.' If Donald and I had had any children we would have taught them to read as soon as they could talk."

"And given them the run of the library," said Mr. Belton.

"There was only one book that my grandfather—who brought me up—said I mustn't read," said Mrs. Carton.

Naturally everyone asked what it was.

"The Picture of Dorian Gray," said Mrs. Carton. "I was only nine or ten then and of course I had read it and thought it a very

interesting story—as indeed it is. And as my grandfather had
given me the freedom of his library he couldn't very well protest."

Mr. Carton said it might be quite a good thing to let very
young people loose on a great many books now frowned upon,
because if you are young enough it all runs off you like water off
a duck's back. Encouraged by this, Mrs. Belton said that her
father had found her at a tender age reading Hardy's *Group of
Noble Dames* and told her not to, to which she had replied that
she liked reading about those Good Women: an equivalent title
which made everyone laugh. Everyone then spoke at once and as
far as the noise would allow the consensus of opinion seemed to
be that children should be free to read any books and all books
on their parents' shelves because the parents wouldn't be likely
to have disgusting or pornographic books.

"Speaking as a doctor," said Dr. Perry, "I have found that the
nastier a book is, the duller it is."

"But then you couldn't read any of your own books, Dr.
Perry," said Mrs. Updike. "I mean about leprosy and broken legs
and things. They would be too dull."

Dr. Perry gave it up.

"Do tell me, Mrs. Macfadyen," said Mr. Oriel, "how is my old
friend, and I may say pupil, Dr. Fewling at Greshamsbury? I
know he has the pleasure of your father's acquaintance. We meet
from time to time at a duty dinner at the Palace and compare
notes."

Mrs. Macfadyen said she didn't know Canon Fewling had
been a pupil of Mr. Oriel, but she would love to hear what they
compared notes about.

When, Mr. Oriel said, he had spoken of Dr. Fewling as his
pupil, he was exaggerating. Mrs. Macfadyen of course knew that
Canon Fewling had been a naval man during the first war.

"Yes," said Mrs. Macfadyen. "He likes talking about it and I
think he misses the navy sometimes. Does he ever talk to you
about his war service?"

Mr. Oriel said he had never heard anything about it except that he wasn't killed—not even wounded, which, to judge by his voice, he thought a poor war effort. "He is, I believe, an excellent parish priest. He was a Commander when he left the Navy," he added. "I remember during the war we did roof-spotting everywhere and Fewling was on the tower at Northbridge. He know how to look through a telescope which was a great help. Most people can only do it by screwing up one side of their face. Pray remember me to him when you are next there," which Mrs. Macfadyen was very willing to do, and hoped it would be soon, for then she would the sooner be able to give Mr. Oriel's message.

Gradually the guests went away, for even if one had a cook, or at any rate a someone, it was all the more necessary to be punctual lest one should give offence. And offence taken at close quarters can be most depressing, for the offendee will never explain anything, merely saying in the voice of a tired saint that it doesn't matter and we just won't speak of it again.

The departing guests asked Mrs. Belton to bring Mrs. Macfadyen to tea which she promised to do. Then the front door was shut for the last time—or rather slammed because it had taken to not shutting very well. Mr. Updike had lingered in the dressing-room where they found him when the door had at last consented to be shut.

"Only one more moment, if I may," he said to Mrs. Macfadyen. "I have some papers for you to sign and they might as well be done while you are here. I can easily bring them over tomorrow," but Mrs. Macfadyen said it was no trouble at all to go to Mr. Updike's office and seemed more business-like.

"Will that be all right for you?" she asked her hostess. "I mean you haven't any particular plans?"

Mrs. Belton said not in the least, unless Mr. Updike needed a witness or anything, though in what other capacity she thought he could need her we cannot imagine. Mr. Updike said he would not trouble her as it was simply a matter of Mrs. Macfadyen's signatures and so took his leave.

Supper—for most people still kept that war-time name for it unless having a real dinner party—was peaceful. Everyone was a little tired by the excitement of the party. Mr. Belton went to the estate room, and Mrs. Belton with her guest to the drawing-room. Here Wheeler had obligingly put more logs on the fire which was burning very handsomely with flames leaping upwards in endless chase, dying even as they reached their peak and as quickly replaced by fresh-comers. A large log, almost burnt through, suddenly broke and sent out a shower of sparks like golden rain.

"Wheeler will *not* remember the guard," said Mrs. Belton.

Mrs. Macfadyen looked round, could not see it and asked where it was.

"Oh, we don't use it now," said Mrs. Belton. "Christopher and Elsa were in America and came back full of new ideas and look what they brought me."

She touched a brass knob at the side of the fireplace and a shining gold mesh screen came rolling down from above till it touched the hearth. Like Man Friday Mrs. Macfadyen could only say OH.

"I thought you would like it," said Mrs. Belton, much gratified. "It makes all the difference. So safe and no live coals can jump out and the ashes stay where they ought to be. I believe there is another contraption that whisks the ashes away, but my husband thought it mightn't be safe in this old house. Most of the floors and panelling would burn at once. Lady Pomfret liked the screen so much that she is going to have some at the Towers. We might go and see her tomorrow."

Miss Margot Phelps might have said "Oh do you think she would really want to see me?" but Mrs. Donald Macfadyen had learnt to have—in the Doric of her husband's boyhood—a good conceit of herself and accepted with composure any honours or treats that came to her; though always wishing that

Donald were there to share them. Or perhaps not wishing it quite so often now, for grief must run its course and though its streams may still flow they run through caverns measureless to man towards the waters of Lethe. At the last hour they may rise again and gently overwhelm us and take us down again, painlessly, to a final oblivion—or to a renewed memory. We do not know.

But when tomorrow came it was even colder than the day before and the wind blew and the rain spattered against the windows and the place where there had been that damp patch at the top of the stairs just where the chimney-stack is began to look damp again. Or so Mr. Belton said when he came down a little late for breakfast, annoyed with himself for being late, though no one would have thought for a moment of blaming him in his own house, or anywhere else.

"I'll have to get Bill Wheeler over to see to it," he said.

Mrs. Macfadyen asked who he was.

"He's a remarkable man," said Mr. Belton. "A real trades-man."

Mrs. Macfadyen said she never knew tradesmen repaired chimneys.

This was a splendid opening for Mr. Belton to come the old English Squire; just as Mr. Marling would have done over at Marling Hall.

"I don't know how that word went down in the world," said Mr. Belton. "We used to talk of a good tradesman when we meant a man of his hands. The older people here still do. Wheelers have always been chimney-sweeps ever since the chimney tax and probably before that. They're all cousins of our cook. They keep themselves to themselves. When Wheeler first came to us she said she was S. Wheeler. Lucy did ask her what her Christian name was, didn't you, Lucy?"

Mrs. Belton said it was Sarah, but she would never have known it except for the census and identity cards and ration books, and believed that the older generation still felt that by giving away one's baptismal name power went out of one.

"They're all Wheelers over here," said Mr. Belton, getting away on one of his favourite topics. "Sid Wheeler is the landlord of the Nabob—he's our Wheeler's uncle. We must show you the Nabob, Mrs. Macfadyen. It's one of the prettiest houses in West Barsetshire. And Wheeler's cousin Bill Wheeler is a chimney-sweep. He's the only man who really knows the chimneys at Pomfret Towers. *They're* a rum lot. Pomfret told me—I mean old Lord Pomfret, this man's uncle—"

"Not *uncle*, Fred," said Mrs. Belton. "Old Lord Pomfret's only son," she went on, for Mrs. Macfadyen's benefit, "was killed in one of those Indian frontier affairs and the next heir was a *cousin*, a Major Foster, and they didn't get on. So then," she went on, seeing that all this was new and interesting to Mrs. Macfadyen, "he ordered Gillie—he's really Giles like old Lord Pomfret—who was Major Foster's son and the next heir, to come and stay at the Towers on approval and Gillie married Sally Wicklow, the agent's sister. Old Lady Pomfret died fairly soon after that and the young people came and lived there. Old Lord Pomfret used to ride about with Sally when he got older and the doctor said he mustn't ride alone. She had the best hands in West Barsetshire, but she doesn't ride now. They can't afford it. Old Lord Pomfret died just when the war began."

"He always knew what he wanted and got it," said Mr. Belton, rather unfairly we think, for though old Lord Pomfret was in a way The Last of the Barons (in spite of being an earl) he had made himself keep up-to-date in many ways and had left the estate in excellent condition and his death was natural and peaceful.

"But it isn't easy for Sally," said Mrs. Belton. "They've had to let nearly the whole of the Towers to those business people. Very satisfactorily, but it can't be pleasant to live in a corner of your own house. I'd hate it."

"We should have been living on a crust in a corner of Harefield House ourselves, if it hadn't been for that Girls' School that took it during the war," said Mr. Belton. "You know it's a boys' prep. school now and doing very well, Mrs. Macfadyen. We might go and see it."

After some rather inconclusive talk it was decided that the weather being what it was, and that was pretty nasty, they should put off a visit to Pomfret Towers and visit Harefield House School instead. And this was rather a relief to Mrs. Macfadyen who knew several of the masters and their wives and had felt rather depressed by the picture of Pomfret Towers with its owners cowering in a corner while Big Business rolled on. But she was quite able to laugh at herself inside for her own silliness, which is a saving grace.

So after lunch, mackintoshed and in good country shoes, they walked up to Harefield House, across the park. This walk, almost a regular weekly institution now, gave Mr. Belton a good deal of pleasure. Not only was he walking across his own land, but as a fair amount of it was now being cultivated by his tenants and very well too, he was able to condemn loudly all these newfangled ways, including every kind of mechanized agricultural implement that sped the plough and helped the agricultural labourer in general.

"I did see Harefield House once before," said Mrs. Macfadyen. "It was before I was married. Donald was going over on business and he took me and Justinia Lufton with him. I loved it all. I *do* like little boys. Then Justinia married that nice Eric Swan that's a master here."

"You know our younger son, Charles, is a master here too," said Mrs. Belton. "He married Clarissa Graham."

Mr. Belton said in *his* young days assistant masters *were* assistant masters and headmasters were mostly in Holy Orders. *They* had families, he said, but the assistant masters didn't. Headmasters *were* headmasters then, he said. Though Mrs. Belton was quite used to these fine atavistic outbursts and paid no attention to them, Mrs. Macfadyen felt that she ought to say something. But she could not think of anything particular to say so she wisely kept silence while Mr. Belton rapidly disposed of practically everyone in authority and said it was all very well, but farming was going to the dogs.

"I wish you could have a talk with my father," said Mrs. Macfadyen. "He feels *exactly* like that."

"I should like it too," said Mr. Belton, who had taken a liking to his wife's new acquaintance and might easily have described her in Mr. Edmund Sparkler's great words as a fine woman with no bigod nonsense about her.

"He is always saying that the British Navy isn't what it was," said Mrs. Macfadyen.

"Well, he's right enough there," said Mr. Belton. "All aircraft carriers and submarines now. In *my* young days you could still see proper ships with luck. Sails and all that. *My* old grandfather remembered hearing about the loss of the *Birkenhead*—all ranks standing to attention and getting drowned," and Mrs. Macfadyen almost felt that she ought to stand to attention and salute.

"It's rather like, 'What would your great-grandfather do, Who lost a leg at Waterloo, And Quatre Bras and Ligny too, And died at Trafalgar,'" she said aloud to herself. Mrs. Belton laughed.

"That's nonsense," said Mr. Belton, not rudely, but as one who states an incontrovertible point. "Feller couldn't have done it."

Mrs. Belton gave her guest a look as expressive as Lord Burleigh's nod; a look which managed to convey exactly what she felt for her husband's peculiar Olde Englishe manner of speech.

"But I *like* it," said Mrs. Macfadyen quietly to her hostess. "It's exactly the way Father thinks about things. I do wish Father could meet Mr. Belton."

Mrs. Belton said she hoped she would bring her parents to lunch at Harefield one day and though Mrs. Macfadyen was pleased and touched by the suggestion she had to tell Mrs. Belton that neither of her parents was in very good health and they found getting about too much for them. But if Mrs. Belton—and of course Mr. Belton if he felt like it—were ever near Southbridge she hoped they would let her know and she would love to take them to Jutland Cottage.

By now they were on the gravel sweep in front of the house.

"There you are. Not a weed to be seen," said Mr. Belton proudly, apparently under the impression that as the house belonged to him, so did the credit for all that its present occupiers were doing for it.

"It's that weed-killer, Fred," said his wife. "The best we ever had. What is its name?"

"Chokeweed," said Mr. Belton.

"Oh, that's one of Donald's things," said Mrs. Macfadyen. "It took him years to get it right, but it's wonderful."

"Donald? Never heard of the feller," said Mr. Belton.

"Of course it was only his *Christian* name," said Mrs. Macfadyen, thus adding to Mr. Belton's confusion. But his wife, with a conspirator's look at her guest, explained to him that it was Mrs. Macfadyen's late husband who had produced and patented this excellent preparation.

"I must apologize for my ignorance," said Mr. Belton, almost removing his plumed hat with a sweeping bow. "I should have remembered your husband's remarkable and most useful contribution. Of course I know his real interest was in market gardening, but the weed-killer does for *everything*. My fool of a man put some on the spring onions because he thought they were weeds."

Mrs. Macfadyen asked what happened.

"No spring onions," said Mr. Belton. "I had to buy some. My old father would have blown the roof off if such a thing had happened."

"Well, you did your best, Fred," said his wife kindly. "Old

Lord Pomfret was the best curser I ever heard, but you could be nearly as good when you tried."

"When I *tried*? When I *was* tried you mean, Lucy," said Mr. Belton. "Come on," and he went up the steps, under the pillared portico to what used to be his own front door.

As we have never been forced to let our ancestral home first to a girls' school during the war and then to a very flourishing boys' prep. school after the war, both institutions paying an extremely good rent besides repairing and keeping up both house and garden, we do not know how bitter Mr. Belton's bread was, but we are strongly under the impression that it was good and well-buttered, not to speak of marmaladed or jammed. The Headmaster Philip Winter and his wife Leslie, sister of Sir Cecil Waring at Beliers Priory, were excellent tenants and as both had money of their own they took true pleasure in keeping the house in good repair, even to the extremely expensive business of having the whole outside repainted, a thing which had not been done for far too long simply because its owners could not afford it. But now it stood out, so dazzlingly white and handsome, with its fine centre block and the two curved arcades that led to the small houses, or lodges, at each end, that artists of all kinds begged permission to take its portrait.

Mr. Belton was not at all averse to having the house immortalized, but it had to be his idea of immortality, not the artist's. And though he may have unnecessarily blighted one or two serious young men and several serious young women, he it was who—to the admiration of all who knew the facts—had taken the measure of that conceited and now not so young man Julian Rivers (a member of the Set of Five which had exhibitions in an out-of-the-way gallery off the Tottenham Court Road) and warned him off the Turf. Or, in other words, had found him planted in the middle of the drive with an easel, laying the house onto his canvas with a palette knife in Indian red, ochre and some highlights squeezed out of a tube of Chinese white, and had spoken his mind. The one or two gardeners—for he still had gardeners then—had looked and listened with heartfelt appreciation and it was with the greatest regret that he felt obliged to refuse their offer to chuck the gentleman into the lake. Since then Julian Rivers had not visited Harefield and if he ever mentioned it described it as that stinking hole; which was hardly fair comment.

We are glad to say that another artist, though in a very modest way, Mrs. Roddy Wicklow, wife of Lord Pomfret's agent, had asked permission to draw the house, using the word draw in the old sense of a water-colour drawing, and had produced a charming fantasy on a theme. When we remember that her father, Mr. Barton, was a distinguished architect it is easier to understand why Mrs. Roddy, as she was usually called, had the sense of form that marks the true landscapist—or housescapist if we may coin the word—and her delicate works were admired all through the county and beyond. And what is more they were bought by more than one collector who liked the true English school of cool, flat washes of colour, with no hesitation about a blob of Chinese whites where it seemed desirable, or even a small blob of brilliant scarlet.

We think that the house, after the long, lean years, had enjoyed having its portrait taken, and we know that it was pleased to shelter the chattering, cheerful little boys who would go on being young as long as the school existed and the flow of little boys continued. The school, on a smaller scale, had been in existence for several years previously and the only fear that Philip Winter had was that the increasing number of boys would burst the banks and bound—like the Tiber in "Horatius"—and force him to move again. But owing to a stiffish entrance exam and a quiet personal enquiry into parents and background, we do not think there is any danger of this. Nor will the perpetual depreciation of money seriously affect matters, for the Good English Parents will make every sacrifice and submit to any sort of privation sooner than lose the privilege of getting their beloved offspring off their hands for some three-quarters of the year—though even that is being pared down.

The front door was always open during the summer. The Beltons and Mrs. Macfadyen went through the vestibule (for we cannot think of any other word to describe the panelled room with its floor of black and white squares of marble) and so into the handsome hall from which doors led to the various large living-rooms, now all converted to class-rooms. From the hall a staircase with wide shallow steps and at the half-way landing a large window, led to the upper floors, the whole being lighted from above by a domed sky-light. This, during the war, had to be blacked out and as no one could devise any method of drawing black curtains over the inside of a dome to which there was naturally no inside access, it was regretfully decided that the whole skylight must be painted black outside; which was accordingly done. So good was the paint that the Winters had almost given up in despair all hope of removing it, when Mr. Adams, the wealthy ironmaster who had married Mr. Marling's daughter Lucy and had already put down his second child, a boy, for Harefield House, had offered to have the work done properly. To this end he sent his foreman who looked about and above and below, and put down a great many unintelligible notes with a very short pencil (which he licked for each fresh item) in an illegible (except to himself) handwriting in a small pocket-book secured by an elastic band which, having lost all its elasticity, was little or no good. These notes he handed to the right quarter and men with mysterious bundles and tools got out onto the roof and removed all the paint and polished the glass till it shone. Flown with the pleasure of work well done and, we may say, long-drawn-out, with frequent visits to the kitchen for strong tea and sausage rolls or bread and cheese, they had made an excellent job of it and also made an arrangement by which some of the panes could be made to open and shut on the louver system by cords to the balcony which circled the well below. As the opening of the panes almost always coincided with rain or a thunderstorm on Saturday night when on one could be got to clean up the mess till Monday, the dome was rarely if ever ventilated, but very pretty it looked when seen from higher up on the downs, and when Wheeler the sweep came he would always get outside and clean the glass.

Mrs. Belton took Mrs. Macfadyen straight to the Headmaster's private wing where Philip Winter was writing in his study, with his wife Leslie doing the family mending.

"Well, well, under your vine and fig tree, Winter," said Mr. Belton, adding with a deliberately old-fashioned courtesy which nearly gave Mrs. Macfadyen the giggles, "and Mrs. Winter with her embroidery."

"Not really," said Mrs. Winter, getting up and shaking hands warmly with the Beltons. "Only socks. Philip has claws on his toes and his heels. And how nice to see you, Mrs. Macfadyen. I heard you were going to be over here. How are your people?"

Mrs. Macfadyen said not too bad, and not too good, and though she spoke cheerfully Mrs. Winter felt that it was rather a mask. There was a good deal of pleasant talk, chiefly local, to which Mrs. Macfadyen listened with vague interest and thought of a day, some five years ago now, when her husband had proposed to her down among the hens in her parents' field— and of her first congratulations, which had come from that nice Canon Fewling. Oh well, all that was in the past. So she quickly brought herself back to the present.

The Winters had been abroad for part of the summer holiday and Mrs. Macfadyen had visited with her husband most of the places where they had stayed. This always makes a good basis for conversation, only if the other person gets in first you will have no chance at all, for to them the day they had to change at Basle and hadn't even time to get a cup of coffee bulks as far more important, looms much more imposingly, than the day you were in the Rome Express and thought you had lost your passport and made a frightful fuss and then found it was in the pocket or bag you had put it in.

The Beltons and the Winters of course fell into local talk. That is, Mrs. Belton asked about the School and what the prospects for next term were and Mrs. Winter asked Mr. Belton how his central heating was and if he had turned it off as yet, so that Mrs. Macfadyen was rather left out of their talk, but she was used to that when her husband had business people to entertain and was quite happy to listen.

"*I* didn't," said Mr. Belton. "My old mother always said 'Don't cast a clout Till May is out.' I leave all that to Lucy. Much the best way."

"Quite right too," said Mrs. Winter. "And as for clouts, I haven't cast mine all this summer. All my woollen things are wearing out and I shall have to buy new ones instead of waiting for the Christmas sales. And stockings too. Such a trouble!"

Mr. Belton, something of a ladies' man or so he always felt, said in his experience it wasn't the stockings that were the trouble but the legs inside them.

"*You* don't remember when the Hosiers' Girls' School was in this house in the war," he went on, addressing the company in general. "A nice lot of girls but half of them were beef to the ankle. That girl of Adams's—legs like pillars in a church," which unusual comparison made Mrs. Winter laugh.

"Not those twisted pillars like barley sugar," said Mr. Belton suspiciously. "Ordinary pillars. Can't think why one can't get proper barley sugar now. When I was a boy we bought a pennyworth at a time at the village shop—old Mrs. Hubback kept it then, she had hardly any hair and only one tooth and was a witch—none of this fuss about wrapping it up in shiny paper. That's what makes everything in such a mess. The children have too much money for sweets and no one tells them to put the paper in the dust-bin."

Mrs. Belton said they wouldn't do it if they were told and as they saw their parents and their school teachers throwing paper on the ground one couldn't expect them not to do it themselves. The pavement and the road outside the Barchester Odeon, she said, were quite revolting on Saturday mornings when hordes of yelling children were let in for practically nothing and ate sweets all the time and dropped the sticky wrappings on the floor and then came out and threw their tickets on the pavement and stormed the buses while housewives, laden with the weekend shopping, had to walk.

"Donald couldn't *bear* that," said Mrs. Macfadyen. "He said it was Ane Monstrous Regiment of Children and if he were Minister of Education he would get Herod to rise from the grave and do the Good Work."

The Winters agreed cordially to this suggestion and said the only difficulty was Where to draw the line.

Mr. Belton, who abhorred academic discussions (though not including arguments about the Government, the Russians, Central Europe, the Near East, the Far East and practically everything else), said it was all the parents' fault. He had a penny a week when he was a boy, he said, and made it go a long way and then it was raised to twopence.

"Ah, money bought things in those days, sir," said Philip Winter, which was extremely wrong of him and the ladies found it difficult not to laugh. But a just judgment fell upon him, for Mr. Belton fixed him with an Ancient Mariner's eye and gave him a very full and accurate account of his expenses when he went abroad as a young man and a franc *was* a franc, and money was money, not these bits of paper. Golden sovereigns, he said, would take you all over the world.

"And my mother," he added, "always took twenty five-pound notes in a linen bag pinned inside her stays. Stays she called them, not corsets."

"But no one calls them corsets now," said Mrs. Winter. "They say belts."

"Not in *my* old mother's time," said Mr. Belton firmly. "Not the ladies. There were some fellers had to wear a belt. You know, Winter. Shockin' cases of rup—"

But at this point the Headmaster, choking back his laughter

with a firm hand (or whatever one chokes laughter back with), said Would Mrs. Macfadyen like to see the dormitories and the kitchen quarters. She said not the dormitories, because they would look empty with the boys away, and this was so reasonable that no one questioned it. So Mrs. Winter took her ladies down to the kitchen quarters, leaving her husband to deal with Mr. Belton—or shall we say to allow himself to be dealt with by that gentleman, for once Mr. Belton was away on any subject that appealed to him it was like the water coming down at Lodore.

The kitchen quarters in Harefield School were of course in the basement, but as the front door with the hall and the surrounding rooms were approached by a flight of steps and practically a first floor, and the ground had been dug away at the back, most of the rooms were pleasantly light. Here ex-Sergeant Hopkins with his wife Selina reigned, Mrs. Hopkins as cook and her husband as general utility. But there was a power greater than both of them, namely Mrs. Hopkins's widowed mother Mrs. Allen. This remarkable character had been Nannie to Sir Harry and Lady Waring at Beliers Priory for their only child little George Waring who was killed in the First World War just before the Armistice. Later she had been Nannie to their nephew and heir, little Cecil Waring, and his sister Leslie, now happily Mrs. Philip Winter. As for the late Mr. Allen, a rather dashing commercial traveller, he had drunk himself and his business into the grave within a year or so of his marriage, leaving Mrs. Allen with one daughter Selina, who had married first a middle-aged grocer and some years after his death had been wooed and won by Sergeant Hopkins, then billeted at Beliers Priory. Nannie Allen, who like many resolute, self-supporting English matriarchs stood no nonsense from any of her family, had commanded Sergeant Hopkins to come and live with his wife and mother-in-law at the preparatory school which was the Winters' first venture and had then brought them both to Harefield. It all worked extremely well, for while Sergeant Hopkins had a passion for vegetables and was allowed a free hand to put as much ground under cultivation as he could manage, Mrs. Hopkins reigned in the kitchen, and had also constituted herself as a kind of unofficial Nannie to the newest and youngest boys and was adored by every one of them, while her mother sat all day in the kitchen and—as Mrs. Samuel Adams was still very apt to say—told everybody what.

"I've brought some friends to see you, Nannie," said Mrs. Winter. "Mr. and Mrs. Belton and Mrs. Macfadyen."

Nannie Allen, who was sitting in a comfortable chair darning socks, sketched a motion of rising (which she obviously did not intend to do in the least), and graciously acknowledged the Beltons.

"And if I'm not mistaken, madam," she said to Mrs. Macfadyen, "you came over here four or five years ago with Mr. Macfadyen. You weren't married then."

"No. I got engaged to him quite soon afterwards," said Mrs. Macfadyen. "You know he died not long ago. But we were very happy."

"Now, Mr. Macfadyen, he was a gentleman as *did* understand vegetables," said Sergeant Hopkins who had come in with a trugful of potatoes and greens from the kitchen garden. "When he was over here with you, miss, I mean mum, we had a good talk, him and me, and I told him a thing or two and he told me a thing or two. It's surprising how time passes. That was all of five years ago. Well, we've all got our number up. I hope you are keeping well, mum."

Mrs. Macfadyen thanked him and said she was doing pretty well and looking for a house.

Other people's houses are always a fascinating subject and Sergeant Hopkins described in some detail several highly unsuitable properties which were (or were about to be) in the market, and had very good kitchen gardens. She thanked him and said, very untruthfully, that she would certainly think of them. Mrs. Allen then said she daresaid they would all want to be going now, which was so clearly in the nature of a royal congé that the visitors and the owners of the house retreated, in good order but all conscious that they had been carefully weighed and kindly found a little wanting, and so by the scullery door into the grounds.

Mr. Belton, whose family had been landowners for several generations, always took a deep and real interest wherever cultivation of any sort was in progress. As he seldom left Harefield now except to visit his son-in-law Admiral Christopher Hornby, R.N., and his family at Aberdeathly (a large hideous family mansion built from local granite with pepper-pot turrets all over it on the southern slopes of Ben Gaunt, just above Loch Gloom, train will stop at Inverdreary twice a week, but if you know the guard he will stop it on any other day) he had not had much opportunity of seeing other people's properties and made up for it by coming over to Harefield House at least twice a week with a shooting-stick, so that he could rest himself while he told Sergeant Hopkins exactly how turnips—or asparagus or whatever green vegetable or tuber was in season—should be treated. Luckily Sergeant Hopkins, with the fine tolerance of the old soldier, told the outdoor staff that there was nothing wrong with the old gentleman and to give him his head, which order was carried out the more willingly as (a) it meant that one could stop work and lean on one's spade or one's hoe for an indefinite period and (b) that largesse at Christmas was on a munificent scale.

It is very doubtful whether one saves any money now by living on (or trying to live off) owe's own ground, but it gave Mr. Belton immense pleasure to believe that this was still possible and to boast to his friends about it, so no one discouraged him. The only person to whom he would listen was his elder son's wife, once Susan Dean.

We do not think that she was an authority on market gardening, but she knew everyone who was and picked their brains and served them up in a form easily assimilated by her father-in-law who, luckily for himself, had complete faith in her. He was also willing to listen to Mrs. Samuel Adams, once Lucy Marling, who could talk or bargain with any farmer or agriculturalist in Barsetshire and, though mellowed by time, was still ready to tell anyone what, whether they wished to be told or not.

Mrs. Belton, who did not enjoy standing about on a cold summer day, or indeed much at any time, having (as we all have as we get older) a growing conviction that legs were made to be walked with if necessary and not to be stood upon, looked at Mrs. Winter and Mrs. Macfadyen with a questioning eye and a tilt of her head towards the house. A wink is often as good as a nod. Both ladies at once grasped the situation and thankfully went back to the house with Mrs. Belton, glad to escape, leaving the men to follow when they wished, or when Sergeant Hopkins felt like saying Dismiss.

As they walked towards the house, the sun behind them, the back view was as handsome as the front and the wings curving away towards each side were a lovely line. On the parapet of the centre block were plaster urns of no particular period or style, but eminently suited to the building. The sash windows with their elegantly proportioned panes and the original glass, most of which was still there, glittered with the inequalities and slight flaws which at a distance give life and movement, though often annoying when one looks through them from inside.

"It's Perfect," said Mrs. Macfadyen with a deep sigh of content.

"There's only one thing wanting," said Mrs. Belton.

Mrs. Winters prettily said If anything was missing it was the family to whom it belonged; and we think she meant it.

"I didn't mean *that*, my dear," said Mrs. Belton, shocked lest any word she had let slip had ever put such a thought into her tenant's head. "I mean the statues."

Mrs. Winter said What statues?

"I think they were the Roman Emperors," said Mrs. Belton. "They were all along the parapet at the back but Fred's father had them taken down. We meant to put them back and then there was the war. They are in the original plans in the Muniment Room."

Mrs. Winter, overcome by the majesty of these words, asked where the Muniment Room was.

"Well, we always called it that, but it was really the second wine cellar," said Mrs. Belton. "When we had to give up the Park we arranged to keep our family papers there for safety, so that Fred could consult them. He has been going to write a history of the house ever since we were married," she added proudly, as a hen may cluck who had laid an addled egg. "Mr. Updike wanted us to let him keep them, because he has a very good safe, but Fred was suddenly obstinate."

"*Suddenly?*" said Mrs. Winter, and then she and Mrs. Belton had to laugh, for Mr. Belton had always been famed for obstinacy—nay, pigheadedness, his loving friends would say— and it had not left much room for sudden outbursts.

"Could one say characteristically?" said Mrs. Macfadyen, and this was so exactly the mot juste that all three ladies had the giggles.

So then they went to Mrs. Winter's sitting-room where there was a good fire and waited for the men and if Mrs. Macfadyen felt a little out of it as her companions talked of matters connected with the house as a school, she took it in quite good part. After all, if she had Mrs. Belton and Mrs. Winter to tea and her father and Canon Fewling got off into the Battle of Jutland, it would be very much the same position. So, after the fashion of a great historical character (not sufficiently known to our grandchildren, we fear) she laid low and said nothing.

As soon as the men came in Mrs. Belton asked her husband if he had the key of the Muniment Room and would he—with Mr. Winter's permission—open it and get out the original plans of the house, as the Winters had never seen them.

This was of course a splendid opening for Mr. Belton, who at once became the King Lear of Harefield, uncrowned, disowned, his few white locks disordered by the blast; home, name, fame all swallowed up by Chaos and Eternal Night. His performance was masterly—and indeed should be as it never varied. Everyone was much impressed and entirely unmoved, Philip Winter even going so far as to say to his wife, sotto voce, that Mr. Belton ought to be at Hollywood where his value would be recognized.

From his trouser pocket Mr. Belton extracted one of those long snake-like silver chains, fastened by a leather loop to one of his trouser buttons, with a bunch of keys dangling from it.

"I can't tell you," said Mrs. Belton aside to Mrs. Winter, "*how* often I have to get Wheeler to patch Fred's trouser pockets. The keys wear them out in a few weeks."

Leslie said she had much the same trouble with Philip and had tried putting the keys in a wash-leather bag, but Philip had said it was a nuisance and she had let the matter drop. The ladies looked at each other with a look of heavenly resignation mixed with some good wifely irritation and said nothing.

"Donald had only one key for everything," said Mrs. Macfadyen.

Mr. Belton glared at her and said One couldn't do that.

"But Donald *did*," said Mrs. Macfadyen calmly. "He had all the locks of important things the same and one key opened them all. He always had his key on a chain and I had one of my own and the bank had a couple of duplicates in case of need. It took a little time because we had to get the Lufton Estate Office's permission, but luckily Lord Lufton was very keen. This is it," and she opened her handbag. Moored to the handbag was a snake chain and on the snake chain one large ordinary key and one small key with a kind of little spiky coronet on the end of it.

"The big key was the lock of the front door of our house at Framley," said Mrs. Macfadyen. "I *must* remember to send it back to Lord Lufton's agent. And everything else—all the drawers and all his boxes of papers and my jewel box and the safe and the wine cellar and I forget what else, all had the little key."

There was a moment's respectful silence.

"To think that one never thought of that," said Philip Winter. "I wonder what it would cost to have it done here. Which reminds me, Leslie, where the dickens *is* the key of the Muniment Room? I borrowed it from Mr. Belton last week for something."

"Only for putting that awful silver challenge cup away, darling," said his wife calmly. "I expect you gave it back to Mr. Belton."

If temporary hate could have killed, Mrs. Winter would have been as dead as Browning's Soliloquizing Monk in a Spanish Cloister wished Brother Laurence to be. But her husband was very fond of her and willing to overlook what was entirely his fault.

"Well, that's all right now," said Mr. Belton. "And what the dickens *was* it we wanted this key for?" and while his wife was kindly repeating to him everything that had just been said, he took the key off his own bunch and handed it to Philip Winter.

"Thank you, sir," said Philip and went away, to return in a very short time with a large long book (if our reader sees what we mean).

"And here is your key, sir," he said.

"No, you keep it, Winter. I'm only an old fool," said Mr. Belton.

Used as she was to her husband's Protean performance as King Lear, the Vicar of Wakefield unjustly in gaol, Marius among the Ruins of Carthage, the New Zealander sitting among the ruins of St. Paul's and various other Historical Impostors, Mrs. Belton felt that he had surpassed himself.

Philip laid the book on a table. It was bound in red morocco, now in a rather crumbly condition, the family crest (or arms, we are very ignorant on these points) tooled on it in gold. He turned over the four or five blank pages that in those free days were at the beginning of any book suitable for a Gentleman's Library, till he reached a page where the printer's art was fully displayed by the blackest of inks—here and there a little sered by time—in a flowery Introduction to the *Views of the Perspective and other Aspects of Harefield House, Seat of Frederick Belton, Esq., Armiger, in the County of Barsetshire*, with such curves and curlicues of the penman's art as made one wonder what hand was sure enough to draw them.

For a moment no one spoke. There was a kind of sigh of mingled admiration and of regret that such things no longer were.

"Funny thing," said Mr. Belton when the audience began to breathe again. "The man who did the writing was a Goble."

"*What* was he, sir?" said Philip Winter.

"He wasn't anything as far as I know," said Mr. Belton rather peevishly. "His father must have bound him apprentice to someone who knew how to write though. Gobles are a very old family—Ancient British probably. You'll find his name somewhere in the tailpiece," and he turned over the pages with an apparent carelessness that impressed his audience very much (though we believe he knew very well what he was doing and would never have made a slip, or torn or dog's-eared a page) to where one of those beautiful, graceful whirls and inter-loopings of a line that has neither beginning nor end surrounded a tiny engraving of the front of the house, the fine flight of steps and the colonnades curving round to the two flanking buildings. And below the house the curves and whorls gradually formed themselves into a running script of the word Goble, with such lovely flourishes and convolutions as we have almost lost now.

No one had a word to say. When you meet perfection on any scale your tribute can be silence. Mr. Belton carefully turned the first two pages which showed the house from the front and the back, by an artist who knew his work. On the north façade above the front door and the fine flight of steps were six stone urns. On the south façade, facing into the sun, were six statues of exactly the right proportion for the house, some in that peculiar form of armour known to us in Roman and Italian sculpture where every muscle of the stomach, diaphragm and chest stands out as it would when a naked athlete was showing off, the better to intimidate his opponent we suppose.

"But who on earth taught whoever it was to do that lovely 'GOBLE?'" said Mrs. Macfadyen.

Mr. Belton said no one knew. One authority had said he thought it was German influence, and it was not unlike the signature of Johann Maria Farina which used to be so familiar to us on our Mother's and Grandmother's eau-de-Cologne bottles.

"Well, there you are. That's that," said Mr. Belton. "The Barsetshire Archaeological are after it, but here it stays as long as I'm alive. If Freddy wants to sell it—or more likely *has* to sell it," he added grimly, "well, I shall be dead then. Best thing to be now. Will you put it away for me, Winter?"

Philip thanked his landlord most wholeheartedly for having allowed them to see it and took it away.

"There's nothing like this house in the county," said Mr. Belton. "Omnium is a shocking architectural monstrosity, so is Pomfret Towers—all the big houses. There are plenty of good small ones—you've only got to look here, at Harefield. Barsetshire did best in the good red-brick period, with houses for the smaller landed gentry. When my hour comes and I have to go through the ropes"—by which his hearers were some amused, some irritated, and all entirely unimpressed—"there's only one thing I'll regret."

Mrs. Macfadyen, feeling that as an outsider she had the least to lose, said what was it?

"The glass in the Saloon windows," said Mr. Belton. "When I was a youngster those great sash windows had proper panes. Good carpentering, and the glass was the kind that goes a bit purplish in places. My old father wanted to be up-to-date and he had them taken out and replaced with plate glass. The house has never looked the same since," which indeed seemed extremely probable.

"Is there any of the old glass left, sir?" said Philip. "If there is, we might be able to use it when the boys break a pane, which they do now and then. They have to pay of course. I made out a price list of breakages for them."

Mr. Belton looked rather uncomfortable.

"It was one Guy Fawkes Day," he said, "between the wars. I was younger then."

This appeared so extremely probable that no one showed any surprise. Mrs. Macfadyen, who had nothing to lose, advanced to the breach and asked how Guy Fawkes came in.

"It was a fine Guy Fawkes," said Mr. Belton, "and the best show of fireworks since Queen Victoria's Jubilee when I was a lad."

As Mr. Belton was getting older every time he spoke, Philip, almost expecting to hear him remember the Battle of Waterloo, or at least Sebastopol, said wasn't Mr. Belton going to tell them what happened to the old glass.

"Happened? Nothing *happened*," said Mr. Belton. "It was all heaped up on the stone terrace and my father let the village boys throw stones at it. No use to us and no one would buy it and most of it was broken already. The boys got rid of a lot of high spirits that way. Boys will be boys. One myself once."

Philip said he was sure Mr. Belton was a boy once and he knew that the boys at the school would like nothing better than to throw stones at a lot of old window panes. And what, he asked, was done with the broken bits.

"My father sold the lot," said Mr. Belton. "Old Lord Norton had just built a six-mile wall round Norton Park and wanted broken glass to keep boys from climbing over. It's there till this day. And my old father got what he asked for it," he added. "He said to Norton, 'You can have the lot for two pounds if you cart it away.' Norton sent his carter and one of the men over with the biggest farm wagon and they took everything. My old father gave Norton's carter a good tip and the man said they would all drink his health."

"Did they?" said Mrs. Belton.

"They did," said Mr. Belton. "They stopped at the *Red Lion* and then at the *Cow and Calf* and then at the *Duke of Omnium* at the top of the hill above Norton Park. That was why they forgot to put the skid on the wheel and the whole thing went into the ditch. The road was in a shocking state, all covered with broken glass. Norton never heard the last of it."

This fascinating story, which everyone hoped would go on for ever, then came to an end. Mrs. Macfadyen asked what had happened to the statues on the south front.

"My father's architect—Barton his name was, over at Nutfield," said Mr. Belton, "arranged all that. His son does any work I need here. A good-looking wife he has, she writes books about Popes and Cardinals and things. Can't say I've much use for Italians but she's a handsome woman still. Their son married the Archdeacon's daughter over at Plumstead and their girl married Lady Pomfret's brother—Pickles or some such name. He's the Pomfrets' agent over at the Towers."

Mrs. Belton did not often interfere with her husband's meanderings but this was too much: facts are facts.

"Not Pickles, Fred," she said. "Wicklow."

"Oh, all right, Wicklow—that's in Ireland," he added. "I had some of the best hunting I've ever known in County Wicklow. They understand horses *there*."

"But Roddy Wicklow isn't Irish—nor his sister," said Philip.

Mr. Belton, the old lion at bay, set upon by jackals, said of *course* Wicklow wasn't Irish. Any schoolboy would know that the Wicklows were a good Barsetshire family. No land, but good family.

Mrs. Macfadyen, who was not an Admiral's daughter for nothing, then returned to the attack and asked where the statues were.

"In the Long Attic," said Mr. Belton. "*You* wouldn't know about it, Winter," which indeed was the case, for Mr. Belton when he let his house to Philip had reserved for himself the extremely inconvenient top floor with various rooms so low that dwarfs must have lived in them and windows wider than they were high that stuck if one tried to open them and could not be shut again when they were at last opened. "I asked Barton about the statues and he said if there was a bomb within a mile of Harefield they would probably be blasted. So I got him to have them moved and there they are. At least I suppose they are," he added, glaring round him for statue-thieves. "Like to look?"

There breathes not the man, no nor woman neither, even if by your smiling you seem to say so, who can resist an invitation to visit the attics. The thought of seeing the piano nobile, the best bedrooms, the conservatory, can be lightly dismissed; but in attics there is some kind of romance. And even though the romance is partially hidden by dust, windows not cleaned for many years, spiders, mice, birds and even a few bats, there is always the chance of some kind of treasure trove, even if it is only a brush and comb, the one almost bald, the other almost toothless, in a drawer that won't come out till one final pull brings it out with a jerk to hit you painfully in the stomach.

So the party went up to the second floor and then, led by Mr. Belton, up a steep unlighted flight at the top of which was a door with which Mr. Belton wrestled in vain.

"Let me, sir," said Philip who had been watching with much interest. "I think if we could pull that bolt back—it's probably rather rusty—" and after a good deal of pulling and banging the whole thing, the bolt, the thing it slides in and the thing you push it into, all came out of the rotting wood and fell on the floor with a loud noise, scattering rusty screws and worm-eaten wood.

Led by Mr. Belton, the party picked their way over the débris into a long attic, its windows almost obscured by the balustrade outside. All along one wall there was a dirty curtain. Mr. Belton pulled it back. Being now quite rotten it disintegrated and fell on the floor.

"Just look!" said Mr. Belton, and there were the six statues standing against the wall, their helmets, noses and even their stomach muscles in almost perfect condition.

"Good Lord!" said Philip.

"I'm not sure who they are," said Mr. Belton, "but you'll find a list of them in the book downstairs. I rather think they are Alexander the Great and Julius Caesar and Leonidas—who the deuce was Leonidas?—and Pericles—no, that's a play by Shakespeare—Scipio Africanus he is. Oh, and there's Pompey, you know, the one Caesar was killed at the foot of the statue of. I can't remember the sixth. They've each got the names of the battles they won."

Philip Winter, who had been examining the statues from head to foot closely and with much interest, straightened himself and said the sixth was George the Second. All were silent, for a respectful moment.

"But it *can't* be," said Mrs. Belton. "He wasn't born then. I mean he wasn't born till hundreds of years after the other ones."

"Well, it's got Dettingen on the pedestal, sir," said Philip. "and I think Leonidas is Scipio Africanus, at least that's the name on the base. And not a nose broken or chipped among them."

Having discovered his statues Mr. Belton did not know what to do next.

"I can get Sergeant Hopkins and one of the outdoor men to bring them down, sir, if you like," said Philip.

"That's very good of you, Winter," said Mr. Belton. "And I daresay the old fellows would like to see a bit of life. Damned dull up here and you can't see much out of the windows with that balustrade in front. Might put them round the hall."

"You can't just stand them on the floor," said his wife. "Think of the boys."

There was a short silence while Mr. Belton digested this true and unwelcome criticism.

"Oh! very well, very well," he said and walked away to the end of the attic humming a tune crossly to himself, which was recognized by his family and now also by the Winters as being his form of "Lilliburlero" and having apparently the same soothing effect on him as it had on Mr. Shandy senior's brother Toby.

"Mr. Belton," said Leslie Winter, who had followed him. "May I suggest something?"

It was obvious from his expression that nothing was further from his wishes, but she was a lady and—being his tenant—in a sense his guest, so he stopped humming and turned to her.

"I wondered," said Leslie, "about the wings. I mean the arcades that lead to the two pavilions. Of course you remember there are niches on the inside walls. Do you think the statues could go there? Some of the masters dressed up and stood in them for fun when we had a party and there would be quite enough headroom for the statues. Nobody would touch them there and it's out of bounds for the boys."

Mr. Belton did not answer, but it was obvious that he was bringing his mind to bear upon the matter. He looked out of one of the rather cobwebby windows and thought of past glories and the statues keeping guard from the high roof, as they had done for so many years, and now living in an attic, unseen.

"I think you are right, Mrs. Winter," he said. "I'm sometimes a bit quick in the temper. I'm sorry. If you and your husband agree I'll tell the men—no, I will ask your husband to deal with it. Hopkins is *his* man, not *mine*."

Leslie Winter had hardly dared to hope for so swift a surrender and thanked him, almost with a choke in her voice and a muddled feeling that he and King Lear had something in common, which was of course quite irrational, for Mr. Belton would never have been so misguided as that unamiable old egoist.

"Thank you, my dear," said Mr. Belton and they walked back to the rest of the party. Here Mr. Belton gave a rough outline of the plan, which of course was already becoming his, and they all went downstairs where, now full of zeal, Mr. Belton suggested that they should look at the two curved wings and the niches in them and decide how best the statues should be placed. Luckily there were three niches in each curved wing, so the statues could be well placed. There was a not very serious discussion as to which statues should be in which wing and it was finally decided that they should roughly be Greeks and Romans, in case they quarrelled. Though, as Philip Winter said, It was more probable that Alexander the Great and Leonidas would get on well with Julius Caesar as Moderator between them than with Scipio; while it would be just as well to put Pompey away from Caesar, with Scipio Africanus and George the Second. Mrs. Winter had quietly taken the height of the statues with some string and the niches would give plenty of headroom. Everyone felt that something had been accomplished, except Mr. Belton who was now concerned as to the removal of the statues and their careful replacement in the arcade.

"I think you'll find that will be all right, sir," said Sergeant Hopkins who had added himself to the party. "If agreeable, I will ask Dr. Perry if his young gentlemen would like to help. Being as they are doctors, sir, they did ought to be able to handle a statue, and there's always one of them about."

This plan Mr. Belton of course at once disapproved, on principle we think. But his wife knew him and Sergeant Hopkins had seized him up and after a certain amount of carping and questioning he gave it as his entirely original opinion that Hopkins, with some of the men on the place to help him, would be the right person and some of the young Perrys might be asked to help.

By this time Mrs. Belton was really tired. Mrs. Macfadyen saw this and said a word to Mrs. Winter who at once understood, and they all said good-bye outside the house.

"You must come again after term has begun," said Mrs. Winter to Mrs. Macfadyen. "It feels *horrid* here without the boys."

Mrs. Macfadyen said she quite agreed, though she would

never have said so if Mrs. Winter hadn't said it first and then all
the good-byes were said and Mrs. Belton and her guest walked
back to the quiet comfort of Arcot House while Mr. Belton went
into the park to see how the men were getting on and to reflect,
not altogether sadly, on the past glories of Harefield and how
good it was for the house to have young creatures in it. Term
would begin again soon and the pleasing anxious beings would
be spending a good deal of their spare time in the park. Mr.
Belton had given instructions to any men working there that the
boys were coming by his permission, but if any of them were
found doing anything mischievous they'd better have one or two
of the best on the spot. Word of this got round somehow,
probably via Sergeant Hopkins and his wife Selina, and we can
say confidently that there were hardly any complaints of tres-
passing or damage of any sort. Partly that Philip Winter and his
staff were excellent disciplinarians and partly that so much
licensed rough and tumble could go on in the grounds and the
park, not to speak of the organized games, as left little scope for
the fiends angelical to get out of hand.

CHAPTER 6

Ever since her husband's death, time had passed slowly for Mrs. Macfadyen. Not that she was bored, for that we think she would never be, such kindly interest did she find in her fellow creatures. But there was still with her the touch of a vanished hand and the sound of a lost voice speaking to her with the touch of the Doric that would move her heart for evermore, wherever she heard it. Her visit to Mrs. Belton was extended which was, we think, the best thing that could have happened to her, for in the small town there is a maximum of meeting and party-giving. Never anything very exciting, but an almost communal life with friends coming on their way to or from the shops, or catching the Barchester bus, all helped by the few servants that still existed and the old nurses, and by the occasional glimpses of an outer world when Lady Graham and some grandchildren came over in the pony cart, or the children—very much grown-up people themselves now—of Dr. Perry, or the Updikes, dropped in, and other friends turned up for a weekend, full of strange words and interests, but mostly very kind to what they considered the aged.

We need hardly say that the whole town was taking a deep interest in the rediscovered statues up at the park and on a fine Saturday the move was to take place, before the little boys came back to school, but not before the assistant masters had returned. Partly because their arms were needed, partly because the staff under Philip Winter was on the whole a very united band of brothers. The Beltons' younger son Charles with his wife who was Clarissa Graham and a very good fat little boy and an excellent small girl were in the house at one end of the colonnade. Eric Swan, with Southbridge School and an excellent war record behind him, had married Lord Lufton's younger sister Justinia and lived in the house at the other end of the colonnade. They were rapidly catching up with the Beltons and both families agreed that there could not be a nicer or happier place to live if only the children wouldn't grow up so quickly. This sad and ineluctable doom they had so far prevented (in the Prayer Book sense) by having more babies, but this could not go on for ever and both couples had decided on four. Whether they will keep to this we do not know, but think they will, for they are of their generation which is the best thing to be and all we ask is to be allowed to remain in ours and never be mutton dressed as lamb.

Mrs. Macfadyen's visit to Harefield had dawdled on into September and now the assistant masters were back at the School and the little boys' luggage sent in advance was already in the School. Her parents were rather on her mind, so on a day when the Beltons were going to Barchester she drove herself to Southbridge to see her parents and in spite of misgivings found them much the same. Her father on the whole not quite so well perhaps—but Dr. Ford said nothing to worry about. Her mother she thought looked better and Mrs. Phelps told her daughter that Canon Fewling was most kind about coming over to see them and letting the Admiral tell him about the battle of Jutland, because so few people remember it now. Except, she said, Mr. Wickham, who often looked in with some small present such as a bird, or a hare in season, which he had himself killed and most thoughtfully prepared for cooking.

"He always asks after you, Margot," said Mrs. Phelps. "He says you're a great girl. You certainly were pretty big, but of course he didn't mean that. And he has quite a joke about thinking he ought to have married you, only Donald was there first."

Mrs. Macfadyen laughed, but behind her laughter she had always liked Mr. Wickham and had truly valued him as a friend. When, some years ago, he had asked her to marry him, she had felt a pang for a moment, but she had only a few minutes previously plighted her faith to Mr. Macfadyen, and never had she regretted saying No to Mr. Wickham. We must say that Mr. Wickham had taken her refusal with great kindness and good-humour and though when he got home that night he had given himself several extra nightcaps to heal his broken heart, he had woken next morning in excellent spirits (of the mind, not liquor) and warmly congratulated himself on being a bachelor still. It had never occurred to him when Mrs. Macfadyen was a widow to renew his suit and she would have been distinctly annoyed, we think, if he had, though as a friend she continued to value him. All this her mother did not know, for Mrs. Macfadyen kept her own counsel.

Then the two ladies talked abut other things and Mrs. Phelps said she did hope Margot would soon find a house and settle down, not too far from Southbridge, to which her daughter gave kind answers but did not commit herself, for she was quite determined never to live in her old home. If her father died—when her father died—she would do all she could for her mother, even to coming to live in Southbridge, but never to share a house. And we think she was right. Then it was time for Mrs. Phelps's rest and she went upstairs. Mrs. Macfadyen went softly into her father's small sitting-room or den where he read his naval books and did a little writing of his own about his experiences when he first went to sea. Mr. Wickham, who had been at sea himself in his early life, said he would recommend it to his publisher uncle if it looked any good. Even his unskilled eye could see after a few pages that it wasn't good, but the Admiral got such tremendous pleasure from the writing that he was quite willing, nay eager, to go on; so Mr. Wickham cleverly suggested that he should add a lot of his other experiences, and it was hoped that this would occupy him for some time to come. Mrs. Macfadyen found him at work, but fast asleep, a state which we have all experienced, and she thought he looked very fine in his quiet repose. Presently a noisy car drove up to the front gate recognized at once by Mrs. Macfadyen as Dr. Ford, who drove abominably (which he attributed to having made so many urgent journeys at the behest of the goddess Lucina, though he had now told that deity that she must find a few of the younger fellows to help her, as he wasn't doing any more night calls at his age) and had never been known to have an accident.

"Not a professional call," he said as he came in. "I was going this way and someone told me Margot was here. Well, my girl, you look as fit as sixpenn'orth of ha'pence. What have you been up to?"

Mrs. Macfadyen said staying with the Beltons and asked Dr. Ford to come into the kitchen till the Admiral woke up.

"Nice old family," said Dr. Ford. "Landed gentry living in a house they can't afford to keep up," at which sweeping statement Mrs. Macfadyen flew to the defence of her friends.

"But they *can*," she said. "Not Harefield House of course because it's a school. But they can *quite* well afford to live in Arcot House."

"Kamerad!" said Dr. Ford, with a gesture of putting up his hands and Mrs. Macfadyen laughed and said he was a bit out-of-date and no one would know what he meant now.

"Oh! they wouldn't, wouldn't they?" said Dr. Ford. "There are quite enough of us at our annual Not Forgotten dinner."

"I am sure there are," said Mrs. Macfadyen, "but you are all old soldiers, aren't you? I don't think the young people now pay much attention. You and I are grandparents, Dr. Ford, and back numbers."

"Well, I like that, Margot!" said Dr. Ford. "Considering I never got married and you married pretty late, I don't see where the grandparents come in."

Mrs. Macfadyen said, with a dignity that she could assume if necessary, that at any rate they were both old enough to take rank as honorary grandparents.

"Donald and I did think—we did hope," she said. "But we stopped hoping and then we stopped thinking. And we were so *very* happy."

"Good girl, Margot," said Dr. Ford, kindly patting her knee. "Well, we all have our disappointments. But you're a fine girl, Margot. If we all knew the troubles our friends have had we'd be a gloomy lot. Bite on the bullet. That's the way. I did once think—" and he stopped.

"What did you think?" said Mrs. Macfadyen, not from idle curiosity, but Dr. Ford was an old and trusted friend who had given—as all good doctors do—far more of his long knowledge and his valuable time to the Phelpses than anyone would ever know, and not to the Phelpses only, but to all who needed him, whether rich or poor.

"Well, it was all a long time ago and what I thought doesn't matter now," said Dr. Ford. "A quarter of a century ago."

"That makes it sound very historical," said Mrs. Macfadyen. "Couldn't you say twenty-five years?"

"Certainly," said Dr. Ford. "Twenty-five years it is. But it was bad while it lasted. *You* don't talk, Margot, and no one cares now. It was George Knox's wife. I loved her when she was Anne Todd, making a martyr of herself to her selfish old mother, but George got in first. And I got over it."

"And you never wanted to marry anyone else?" said Mrs. Macfadyen.

"Once or twice I thought I did and then I decided I didn't," said Dr. Ford. "Time does help, you know. You don't like it at first, but you grow a new skin and life goes on."

Mrs. Macfadyen said Like a pearl in an oyster.

"More like a bit of grit in your eye," said Dr. Ford unsympathetically. "But I'm a tough bloke and I've got friends all over the place. That's one advantage of being a doctor. If you've done your best you find people give you the best. And I never think of those old troubles now—unless it's that they come up by chance. There are a lot of people going about, Margot, with broken hearts, but they put a stitch here and a bit of disinfectant there and a nice antiseptic dressing and gradually the heart forgets it is broken. Mine has—long ago. There's a friend of ours with a heart that got a knock-back somewhere, sometime. He never mentions it, but sometimes we've got talking if I was dining with him and he has dropped a word here and there. I never ask questions of course."

No woman could resist asking more about so romantic a person and Mrs. Macfadyen was still at heart very young and liked romance.

"Who is it, Dr. Ford?" she said.

"Who is who?" said Dr. Ford. "Oh, you mean the chap that got the knock-back. Old Tubby Fewling. We've often dined together and exchanged grouses. He has never told me any-thing, but he lets things drop sometimes and I'm pretty sure he was turned down by someone. Who it was I haven't an idea and I'm not going to ask. Some people think he's a professional celibate because he's so High, but that's nothing to do with it."

"What an extraordinary thing," said Mrs. Macfadyen. "I've known Tubby for years—ever since father retired from the Navy and we came here—but I never imagined him being in love with anyone. I wonder who it was."

"Probably one of those women who go all out for these High Church services," said Dr. Ford unchivalrously. "When he was at Northbridge, before he came here, he had all the old tabbies after him. Married, unmarried, widows too. Oh, sorry, Mar-got."

Mrs. Macfadyen could not think why he should be sorry. Then suddenly it dawned on her that she was a widow.

"Good gracious, Dr. Ford," she said. "*I* don't mind what you say about widows. I don't feel like one. I mean it isn't that I don't miss Donald—quite dreadfully sometimes—but I feel very much the same as I've always been."

"Good old Margot," said Dr. Ford. "Widows don't look like widows now. I can remember the black crape when I was a boy—we kept the old fashions up in the country. There was still a real hearse with two black horses with black plumes on their heads and the men had crape round their top hats—you don't often see a topper now. One of the most becoming hats to men that knew how to wear them. In the Barchester Race week Lord Stoke used to wear a grey topper and all the little boys cheered whenever he came out. Well, that's all over."

"It's like the *Heir of Redclyffe*," said Mrs. Macfadyen. "Did you ever read it? The hero who is very young *will* go to nurse his Wicked Cousin who has caught fever somewhere abroad and the heroine who is very young too and they are on their honeymoon, goes with him and the hero gets the Wicked Cousin's fever and dies and the Wicked Cousin lives and has terrific repentance. And the heroine's parents rush out to help her and she is all in white because they were up in the Alps or somewhere where you can't buy mourning and it is all very beautiful and the wicked cousin becomes good and leads a life of Remorse and when the heroine comes home and can get to the shops she goes into the black crape that she will never leave off till she dies."

Dr. Ford, in a very unfeeling way, said it sounded fine but it wasn't his style. And, he said, he had read a modern novel about what happened to the heroine afterwards and when she had mourned a decent length of time and the crape was getting under control, she met a very High Anglican clergyman who was a peer's son and married him.

"It sounds like Lord William Harcourt," said Mrs. Macfadyen, for the engagement of the Duke of Towers's younger brother with sir Robert and Lady Graham's youngest daughter Edith had given great satisfaction to the whole county, or at any rate to all who were interested in it.

"Well, look Tubby up sometimes," said Dr. Ford. "He's not

the kind of man to push where he isn't invited. I know he has
been over here quite often to see your people when you and
Donald were abroad. He'd like it. And where are you going to
live? Have you any plans?"

Mrs. Macfadyen said she wanted to find a small house for
herself with two or three bedrooms and a cook-housekeeper if
such a thing could still be found.

"If only I were a widower, or even a bachelor," she said, "I'd
have hundreds of applications at once, but no one seems to want
to work for women. And the annoying part is that I can do all
the work *much* better than they can. But it's no good being a
slave to one's house. What do you think of the parents or
present?"

So suddenly challenged, Dr. Ford had to decide quickly what
best to say and so quickly did he think that Mrs. Macfadyen was
barely sensible of the phase before he answered.

"They aren't getting any younger," he said.

"*Really*, Dr. Ford!" said Mrs. Macfadyen. "I could have told
you that myself. None of us are."

"Oh, all right," said Dr. Ford. "Your mother's heart is pretty
steady and she is very sensible about resting. Your father isn't so
good. But so long as he doesn't racket about to Old Pals'
Reunions or whatever the Navy have, he'll be all right. And the
more people visit him the better. He must have fought the Battle
of Jutland about a thousand times by now."

Mrs. Macfadyen felt and looked relieved.

"I suppose I ought to be with them more," she said.

"Now, Margot, just listen to me," said Dr. Ford. "You've been
enough with them, my girl. If Macfadyen hadn't turned up,
you'd still be the cook and the captain bold and the mate of the
Nancy brig. Macfadyen just saved you alive. Your parents
weren't a penny the worse for your going. They missed you a bit,
but they soon got used to it and there are plenty of friends ready
to help. The Carters come quite a lot. Miss Hampton and Miss
Bent drop in and they always bring a bottle of something. Crofts

comes up and when he and your father get going with the Battle
of Jutland on one side and the Massacre of Cawnpore or
whatever it was Crofts did in India on the other, it's what Wicks
calls a fair go and a ding-dong go. Wicks drops in too. In fact
they see far more life here than they would in Southsea, or
wherever the old sailors retire to. You come over when you can
and if there's any trouble I'll let you know at once."

"And you'll go on sending the bills to me, won't you?" said
Mrs. Macfadyen. "If you go on telling Father it's all on the
Health Service he'll believe you."

"You're a good girl, Margot. *I* shan't forget," said Dr. Ford.
"Let me know when you find a house and I'll come over whenever you need me, which I hope you won't."

Mrs. Macfadyen thanked him warmly. She had, she said,
been having Dr. Perry because he was nearer Greshamsbury, but
she was sure he would understand.

"And so will you?" she said.

Dr. Ford replied Not to be a fool and of course he would
always come if he was wanted and if Perry didn't like it he could
lump it.

"But you can't do better than Perry if you live over that way,"
he said, "and he has the advantage of one son in partnership.
Always have a doctor with a young partner. Are you on the
Health?"

Mrs. Macfadyen said Certainly not. She preferred to pay for
what she wanted so long as she could afford it, and it was very
improbable that she would outlive young Dr. Perry. Then Dr.
Ford, having happily wasted a good deal of his valuable time,
went away.

Mrs. Macfadyen went into the kitchen where so much of her
life had been spent and was glad to find everything neat and
clean. The village woman who helped in the morning was
evidently a conscientious worker, for the coal-scuttle and its
friend the coke-scuttle were filled, the hearthstone was white
and clean and several newly washed cloths and dusters were

drying in the yard outside. Mrs. Macfadyen almost automatically fell back into the past, fetched the cloths which luckily were not quite dry, rolled them, put two irons on the stove and the ironing-blanket on the kitchen table. While the irons were heating she went down to the hens and found everything in order. A man's form bending over a hen-coop straightened itself as she came near, revealing Mr. Wickham.

"Well, well, Margot," he said. "What are you doing here?"

Mrs. Macfadyen said she was paying a call on her parents and was delighted to find her father having a good sleep and had sent her mother upstairs for her usual rest.

"I'm still looking for a house, Wicks," she said. "Two living-rooms, two or three bedrooms, all mod. con., a really good light kitchen and a nice scullery with a copper and enough garden to have a lawn and grow some vegetables."

"'Four colley birds, Three French hens, Two turtle-doves And a Partridge in a Pear Tree' is what you want, my girl," said Mr. Wickham. "Well, we can't have everything but just as well to mention what you need. You've been over at Harefield, haven't you?"

Mrs. Macfadyen said Yes, she was staying with the Beltons and they had explored the attics at Harefield House and found six statues that used to be on the roof and were going to put them in those niches in the two colonnades.

"But the boys weren't back yet," she said. "I would like to have seen them. When I got married the only thing I missed was the boys that used to come here from the School. I really ought to have been Matron of a boys' school. I *do* like little boys."

"Never mind the little boys," said Mr. Wickham. "What you need first is a house—a home. If you can give me a figure and say where you want to be, I might hear of something. But mind, *not* in Southbridge. You'd be at Jutland Cottage all the time."

Mrs. Macfadyen said she would rather like Greshamsbury, because she would be near her parents and not too near and there were a number of nice people like the Leslies and the

Fairweathers and the Greshams and Umblebys and good old Tubby. Mr. Wickham approved this plan and said he often heard things when he was going about and would keep his ears open.

Then they went back to the house and found that the Admiral had woken up and Mrs. Phelps had come downstairs, so Mrs. Macfadyen took the irons off the stove and they sat in the kitchen till the kettle boiled and Mrs. Macfadyen said Why not all have tea in the kitchen.

"Sensible girl," said Mr. Wickham. "These English summers are the devil. You do nothing but wear out your winter clothes before the winter," so Mrs. Macfadyen laid the table and collected her parents and the party sat down to tea.

The smaller a society the most fascinating the gossip and Mrs. Macfadyen very much enjoyed hearing the latest news about the Carters and how Matron had been to Ostend for her holiday with her eldest nephew who was head wireless operator on one of the largest Atlantic liners and was on leave, and how Jessie the hideous head housemaid had a complete new set of teeth on the Health Service and only wore them on Sundays because they were so uncomfortable, and how Snow, the School carpenter, had been over to Pomfret Towers to exchange gossip with the estate carpenter and brought back a load of good parquet flooring from some of the rooms that were being modernized as offices by Mr. Adams the great ironmaster and his co-father-in-law Mr. Pilward of Pilward's Entire.

"I get over to the Towers off and on," said Mr. Wickham. "They all miss your husband, Margot. Amalgamated Vedge still have their offices there, but they say it isn't the same without Macfadyen. How's Amalgamated Vedge doing?" which was the most helpful question he could have asked, leading the talk from personalities (where Mr. Wickham felt that Mrs. Macfadyen might feel her loss again) to business, which remains business.

Mrs. Macfadyen said she was a director and had learnt a good deal from her Donald and meant to go on directing, and things were going satisfactorily.

"You see, I got to know Donald's business friends in Holland and Belgium pretty well," she said, "and I think they know they can trust me. And the directors here are very helpful and don't mind having a woman on the board."

Mr. Wickham said he was all for having women aboard and was frowned at by the Admiral who took it almost as an affront to the Royal Navy.

"Much better when they used to smuggle a woman or two aboard," said Mr. Wickham. "Or a dozen or two in port. Makes everything more shipshape and respectable," to which Mrs. Macfadyen answered, sotto voce, that it was a sad day when Black-Eyed Susan wasn't allowed to stay on board any more and Admiral Phelps said what were they talking about.

"About my looking for a nice small house for myself, father," said Mrs. Macfadyen, which was a false move, leading Mrs. Phelps (ably supported and/or contradicted by her husband) to recollections of Flinders, Trincomalee, Malta, Cape Town, Rio and other ports where her husband had been stationed and she (with Margot at different stages of growing-up-ness) had made homes and had always managed to have a Christmas-tree, or an Easter Egg Hunt, or a Token Harvest Celebration.

"*How* we got about then," said the Admiral. "And here we are now," which was perfectly true.

"Well, father, if you had a wooden leg and could stump up and down, or fire a small gun like Wemmick, would you really be happier?" said his daughter, to which the Admiral replied that he would leave that to Mr. Wickham, and Mr. Wickham said if he were Wemmick then Margot must be Miss Skiffins and they all talked at once and if Mr. Charles Dickens from some heavenly Gadshill was listening we are sure he was pleased. For the fires of writers do not live in their ashes, but in their words which—if they are great enough and human enough—

become part of the English heritage and its all-embracing, ever-changing language.

Presently Mr. Wickham went away. Mrs. Macfadyen, although she rather wanted to get back to Harefield, stayed on with her parents in case they were lonely. But as Colonel Crofts looked in and said his wife was coming down later if that was all right, and the Carters looked in en route to her mother Mrs. Keith, and Lady Cora Waring with her ex-sailor husband Sir Cecil Waring and two of their children paid a short visit on their way to the Southbridge Flower Show and Gymkhana, Mrs. Macfadyen thought how peaceful her married life had been, quietly at Framley and then with slow journeys abroad, meeting people with the measured speech of those who live on and by the soul. Last, but far from loneliest or loveliest, came Miss Hampton and Miss Bent, with offerings of curaçao and Vanderhum which the Admiral—who did not care for thimblefuls of liqueurs—ceremoniously put into a glass-fronted cupboard which he locked.

Both the ladies were delighted to meet Mrs. Macfadyen again and pressed her to come back to Adelina Cottage and sample some punch which they had made from an Indian recipe given to them by Colonel Crofts's ex-batman, who was confusingly called Bateman. But time was getting on and she said good-bye to the party and drove herself away.

As she was going by Greshamsbury she stopped to see if Rose Fairweather was at home and ask her to let her know if she ever heard of a suitable small house in or near the Old Town. Rose was at home and with her were her younger sister Geraldine who was married to Rose's brother-in-law, Major Geoffrey Fairweather, and Mrs. John Leslie. Mrs. Macfadyen said she was house-hunting and did anyone know of a nice house to let, small but not poky. Anything to do with houses, whether hunting them, letting them, or moving them, is of interest and all three ladies talked at once while Mrs. Macfadyen sat quietly and let the waves surge and break. Each of them of course hadn't heard of *anything* to let and with a rapid volte-face could recommend at least three delightful houses of complete unsuitability. And it was not much help when the Greshams came in and said there are no chance of a flat in Greshmasbury House at all, for as Mrs. Macfadyen didn't want a flat this news did not affect her. Then all the visitors went away with promises to keep their ears open for the perfect house.

Rose, who was far more practical and kind-hearted than most people in spite of her air of helpless beauty, asked Mrs. Macfadyen to tell her *exactly* what she wanted. Mrs. Macfadyen said—as she had said a good many times lately and felt she would go on saying to all eternity—that she would like to find a house with two good bedrooms and a third not so good for a possible resident maid; dining-room, preferably next to kitchen so that she could knock a hole through the wall for serving meals; some garden, all mains services, a really nice bathroom and a proper scullery, and of course a drawing-room or sitting-room and how nice if it had French windows opening onto a garden which must be neither so small as to be poky nor too big for her to manage. And of course some kind of central heating even if it isn't all over the house.

"Well, Margot," said Rose, "—you don't mind my saying Margot, do you—"

Mrs. Macfadyen said considering she had known Rose for nearly twenty years off and on she wouldn't mind at all.

"Of course we all called you Margot in Southbridge," said Rose. "But then you got married. Everyone calls me Rose except the ones that call me Mrs. John, but that's rather muddling because Mrs. Leslie is Mrs. John only people don't call her that," and Mrs. Macfadyen felt, as all Mrs. Fairweather's friends had felt for many years, that she would go mad if she lived with her. But as none of them were going to live with her it didn't matter and her sometimes exhausting ways were entirely forgotten in her beauty and her real kindness and her readiness to help.

"Well, Margot," Rose went on, "I can't think of a house at the moment. But I'll write down everything you want. I suppose you wouldn't think of the New Town?"

Mrs. Macfadyen said certainly not. Her only reason for house-hunting in Greshamsbury Old Town was that she had friends there.

"And if I did go to the New Town," she said, "I might begin to wear a raffia hat and a flowered smock and sandals. By the way, Mr. Belton knows Mrs. Welk—the father of that nice clergy-wife in the New Town. What *is* her name? Hopkinson?"

Rose said Parkinson and as nice as she could be.

"And so's her husband," she added. "Only she knows where she stands and he doesn't."

Mrs. Macfadyen asked her to explain. Rose said it was so difficult to explain, because when you said something you knew what you meant, but if other people couldn't understand it you began to get muddled too and wondered if you meant what you said. All of which fable strikes home to Us, for how often have we not heard our own voice uttering words which do not in the least represent what we want to say.

"I mean she and her husband aren't like us. I really don't know how to explain without sounding stuck-up and silly, but they *aren't*; only Mrs. Parkinson *is*," said Rose, "because her father Mr. Welk who is an undertaker knows all about wood and he can still use an axe and a saw and an adze, and he's friends with all the half-gypsy people up the woods. Sir Edmund Pridham says he is the old English thane in modern dress, like Cedric the Saxon in Ivanhoe."

"I'm so glad you don't say Seedric," said Mrs. Macfadyen. "Hardly anyone says anything right now, like the B.B.C. saying contróversy and exquízzite and Cavalléeria Rusticana and orrigo."

Rose, impressed and rather bewildered, asked what orrigo was.

"Well, to be truthful, I wouldn't have known that one myself," said Mrs. Macfadyen, "but Donald told me. He said it was orīgo and you couldn't mistake it because it came into a Latin poem and the Romans *had* to pronounce their words properly or they wouldn't fit into the hexameters or whatever they are."

"Well, I'll most certainly keep a look-out for a house," said Rose (who we think had abstracted her mind during Mrs. Macfadyen's brief excursion into antiquity) and we are certain that she not only meant it, but would carry out her word. "I'll ask Tubby's Mrs. Hicks. She knows everything," which Mrs. Macfadyen could not quite believe, but she felt cheered.

"Why don't you come here for a bit?" said Rose. "I'd love to have you and we could house-hunt. I adore poking into other people's houses. I'm sure there must be something up the road, near the Umblebys and Greshamsbury Park. I'll start looking for you."

Normally, we think, Mrs. Macfadyen would have thanked Rose very truly and said she would like to look for herself, but the offer was so kindly and generously made that she could only accept it.

"If I may really come to you when I leave Mrs. Belton next week I would love it," she said. "I do want to be settled and I know Donald would want it.'"

Rose who, as we ought to know by now, had a great deal of world-sense under her vague and easy-going manner, had a strong conviction that though Mr. Macfadyen would certainly want his widow to be in her own comfortable home if he were alive, it was not probable that he would go on wanting it when he was dead.

But this is not a subject to argue, as there are no premises. So she said the obvious thing, that she was sure he would, and a day was fixed for Mrs. Macfadyen's visit, with no mention of how long it would be.

"You are a *kind* girl, Rose," said Mrs. Macfadyen. "You always were, even when you were an awful flapper. Father always said you would turn out a swan—not that you were an *ugly* duckling," she added.

"Yes, I was. I was *ghastly*," said Rose, with apparent pride. "I can't think how Mummy and Daddy could bear me—or John either."

"You always had a heart, Rose," said Mrs. Macfadyen. "And it has got bigger and bigger. I think mine gets smaller and smaller."

"But that's only because it has nothing to eat," said Rose. "I don't mean beer or cakes—I mean things like being fond of people and taking care of them. If I hadn't John and the children to take care of I'd be *ghastly*."

"And I haven't Donald to take care of," said Mrs. Macfadyen, with no bitterness, just as a statement of fact. "You see, Rose, I've always looked after father and mother and then when I married I looked after Donald. Only he looked after me as well, so it was perfect."

"But now you haven't got him which is quite *ghastly*," said Rose, with a real sympathy that her catchword could not hide. "If John were dead I'd be *awful*."

"No you wouldn't. You'd have the children," said Mrs. Macfadyen.

"And that would be the *limit*," said Rose, at which comment from an excellent and devoted mother Mrs. Macfadyen had to laugh and then said she must go at once or she would be late for the evening meal and the Pomfrets were coming.

What with Summer Time, which is so welcome and in many ways such a nuisance, and Mr. Belton who was up in the park with the woodsmen and the gypsies, and Lady Pomfret having rung up to say she was delayed at a meeting of the West Barsetshire Hospital Association and had to fetch her husband from the Barsetshire County Club Committee meeting which always lasted too long, Mrs. Belton had put dinner off till eight, so Mrs. Macfadyen was in plenty of time. Already the evenings were noticeably drawing in. The central heating was comfortably on and Mrs. Belton was wearing a warm woollen dress. Mrs. Macfadyen said she was sorry she was rather late, but as everyone else was she need not have apologized. By the time she also had changed into a warm woollen dress and had come down again, a kind of delicious mildness was pervading the atmosphere, and in the drawing-room she found Mrs. Belton adding logs to a lovely crackling fire.

"I couldn't stand it any longer," said Mrs. Belton. "And after all we've got plenty of wood. Come and warm yourself. You are looking very nice, Margot," which she said not only with approval, but also with a very faint hint of surprise.

Mrs. Macfadyen laughed and said she must have caught a small germ from Rose Fairweather who was more good-looking than ever.

"And," she added, "Rose asked me to visit her when I leave you next week. I shall miss you and Mr. Belton. You have been so very kind to me."

Mrs. Belton said it had been a great pleasure to both of them and it was obvious that she meant it. Then she asked after her guest's parents whom she knew slightly and Mrs. Macfadyen told her what Dr. Ford had said and praised his kindness.

"The kindness of doctors!" said Mrs. Belton. "What they give over and above what is their duty and what they are paid has always made me feel very humble. I don't know Dr. Ford well, but I expect he is not unlike Dr. Perry—always putting the patient first."

"And he was *very* nice about Dr. Perry," said Mrs. Macfadyen. "He said a doctor who had a son practicing with him was worth his weight in gold," which was a gross exaggeration of Dr. Ford's words. But Mrs. Belton was quite capable of adding an adequate grain of salt, and thought none the less well of Dr. Ford.

Mr. Belton then came in rather dirty and dishevelled after an afternoon up on the hill with the men and the circular saw, and was sent away by his wife to tidy himself as the Pomfrets were coming and Mr. Oriel, but no one was dressing.

"All right, all right, my dear," said Mr. Belton, whose attitude to any piece of domestic advice was in the nature of "Connu!" or "Me you can tell nozzing." "You know it doesn't take me long to change so long as the buttons aren't off my clean shirts," and he took himself off.

"The buttons have only once been off his clean shirt within mortal memory," said Mrs. Belton calmly. "That sounds like the Pomfrets."

Wheeler opened the drawing-room door, said "It's Lord and Lady Pomfret," banged the front door shut and went back to her kitchen, leaving the guests to look after themselves.

What old Lord Pomfret would have said, what old Lady Pomfret would have looked, what both would have felt, is a thing imagination boggles at. But all that is only part of history now. The present Earl and Countess in ordinary day clothes came in and kissed their kinswoman. Mrs. Macfadyen was introduced and Lady Pomfret at once remembered meeting Mr. Macfadyen on various Barsetshire Committees and said how much his help was missed. And though she had taught herself to say the right things in the right way, those who knew her well could always catch the authentic ring when her heart was speaking as well as her mind, which we think in this case it was.

The last guest, Mr. Oriel, was celebrated for his absence of mind but just as Mrs. Belton was wondering exactly how much umbrage Wheeler would take if Her Dinner had to be kept back much longer, the front door bell was heard. After a short pause Wheeler opened the door, let Mr. Oriel in, shut the door again and went back to her kitchen, much to the relief of her mistress who had expected her either to leave the door open or to bang it; such being her primitive way of showing disapproval of people who were late and of employers who asked people who were late to dinner.

We have known Mr. Oriel for a long time now—ever since the year when the Hosiers' Girls' School was first evacuated to Harefield—and he must be of a considerable age, but in Barsetshire age comes dropping slow, with no nonsense about noon

being a purple glow or evening full of the linnet's wings—both
things that Mr. Oriel would have disliked very much. As he had
always looked older than he was and now in his later years was
still very active, no one bothered about his age. And if it comes
to that all our friends in Barsetshire, some of whom were not
even born when we began to explore that part of the world, are
older than they were. Some who were already old have died and
their places been filled. Some of those are almost forgotten.
Others—and we think the greater number of them—were
remembered faithfully year by year. Mrs. Charles Belton, once
Clarissa Graham, did not mourn for her beloved grandmother
Lady Emily Leslie, but every now and then something reminded her that such things were and her husband said sympathetically "Thinking of the old 'un" which made them both
laugh, and in their kind laughter there is also a tribute to Charles
Dickens who has given us the most just for almost every possible
occasion.

Mr. Oriel was once described by Mr. Carton as drying up
nicely, which words were not unkindly meant and describe him
very well. He must have been extremely handsome as a young
man. Now it was his fine bones that made his looks, which were
enhanced by his silver-grey hair whose tide was only now
beginning to ebb from his forehead. He had been married at
least a dozen times to various county ladies by his friends and
parishioners but we do not think he had ever really wanted to
marry. Partly because he had never fallen in love, partly because
his excellent cook-housekeeper Mrs. Powlett looked after his
comfort with ceaseless zeal, and partly because—being rather a
dreamer and behind the times—he vaguely thought that one
still had to give up one's college fellowship on marriage, a ruling
which had some good points, as many dons and undergraduates
at Lazarus could tell from their galling experience of the Monstrous Regiment of the Master's Wife including her odious
habit of sleeping on a camp-bed in the Master's garden in warm
weather, thus severely hampering the Alpine excursions of such

undergraduates as preferred to go to their rooms over the college roofs.

There were very few people in the county that the Pomfrets did not know and it was one of Lord Pomfret's self-imposed duties to try to remember names and faces. His wife luckily had extremely good social sense, and had known every farmer, cottager, hound and fox from childhood upwards. She it was who had backed young Mr. Foster—as the present Earl then was—about stopping the earths in Hamaker Spinney, a work of national importance that was being held up by a row between the Hunt Secretary and the old Earl's agent Mr. Hoare. Now there were very few useful hard-working committees of which she was not President or Vice-President and much as she loved Barsetshire she was sometimes glad to get to London when Parliament was sitting and see more of her husband—in spite of his regular attendance in the House of Lords—than she normally did at home.

The sherry-drinking was now interrupted by the return of Mr. Belton looking more than ever the Fine Old English Gentleman in a black velvet coat, trousers with a very wide braid stripe down the legs and a soft shirt with his tie pulled through an old signet ring. He greeted Lady Pomfret with an affectionate courtesy which rather touched her, though on reflection she realized that she had but been the gate to Paradise, namely for Mr. Belton to talk to Lord Pomfret through most of dinner about what the West Barsetshire County Council were doing over at Starveacres, which he proceeded to do across Mrs. Macfadyen. Mrs. Belton looked at Lord Pomfret and if one could so far presume as to say that Lord Pomfret winked at her, that was what he did.

"What I have been wanting to do for a long time, Lord Pomfret," said Mrs. Belton, "is to disentangle our connection. Mr. Carton once did it, I think, years ago and then when I tried I went mad," which statement Lord Pomfret appeared to find perfectly reasonable.

"I'm fairly good at family trees," he said, "but I'm not sure if I can. I'd like to have a connection with you."

"I *think*," said Mrs. Belton, "it's something to do with Thornes."

"In that case," said Lord Pomfret, "you would be some sort of millionth cousin once removed of some of the old Thornes over at Greshamsbury, all pretty well extinct now I think. My aunt, old Lady Pomfret, was a Thorne. I've tried to work it out myself but every time I try to get it all straight I have a letter from some complete stranger giving me some brand-new information— mostly, I must say, correct. I have a very good secretary now, a Miss Updike, who has been most helpful. She knows how to keep papers tidy and she has made a splendid list for me with cross-references and I can nearly always find what I want now. And she puts all the papers she is working on in the safe at night and won't let me have the key," which last statement he made with a kind of proud satisfaction.

Mrs. Belton said she knew the Updikes very well and liked them, but why wouldn't Miss Updike let Lord Pomfret have the key.

"Oh, because I would only use it if she did," said Lord Pomfret, to which Mrs. Belton replied, quite sensibly, that if it was his key she didn't see why he shouldn't use it. Lord Pomfret said it was because his wife didn't want him to look at papers out of office hours, but he said it with a tone of love, for ever since young Mr. Foster had proposed to Miss Sally Wicklow in the agent's room at Pomfret Towers, now so many years ago, he had known that in her was the rock, the fortress and the might that would never fail him.

"I only wish Sally wouldn't work *quite* so hard," he said. "I sometimes think that if I hadn't been Uncle Giles's heir, we might have been happier. I don't mean in each other," he added quickly, "but we would have had a little more time to ourselves. It's only when we get away to the villa at Cap Ferrat that we can live ordinary lives."

Half of Mrs. Belton wanted to take Lord Pomfret on her knees (figuratively speaking) and tell him to Hush him, hush him, and not fret him, Or the Nervous Breakdown would undoubtedly get him, while the other half thought she had certainly better not do so. But we all have to carry our cross in our own way and some people's crosses would appear to be of aluminum while others are stone sheathed in lead. So she did the next best thing which was to ask after his elder son Lord Mellings.

"Oh, Ludo is really doing very well now," said Lord Pomfret. "We were afraid that he mightn't be up to the standard of the Brigade, but he is enjoying it all like anything and putting on weight and seeing life. We can never be grateful enough to Aubrey Clover."

"What on *earth* do you mean, Gillie?" said Mrs. Belton.

"Oh it's quite an old story now," said Lord Pomfret. "It was the Coronation Entertainment at Northbridge. Aubrey Clover and Jessica did a little one-act play and by great luck he saw Ludo and asked him to take the third part which was a young man in love with an actress who is living with a roué."

"How *heavenly*," said Mrs. Belton. "Go on."

"Well unfortunately Sally and I were in London for the Coronation—I mean as an Earl and a Countess—so we didn't see Ludo. But apparently he brought the house down and the success made all the difference to him. In fact if I died tomorrow he would be able to take over. And I should be delighted if he did. But I don't want him to be pushed into a responsible position too young—as I was," Lord Pomfret went on, almost to himself. "Sorry, Cousin Lucy."

Mrs. Belton, more moved than she would have liked to admit, said she wished she had seen the little play. She had heard a record of that song, with Aubrey Clover singing it, and wished she could have heard Ludo. Lord Pomfret, pleased with her wish, said she must come over to the Towers next time Ludo was on leave, and then with exquisite timing they looked at each other questioningly and each set to the other partner, which threw Lord Pomfret into Mrs. Macfadyen's arms. Nor was she sorry, for much as she liked and respected Mr. Belton, she did feel that there were one or two other subjects for talk beyond the trees up in the park and the bodgers and the circular saw. But guests must be content. And as Mr. Belton was a great admirer of Lady Pomfret—not so much for her undoubted looks and kind ways as for her knowledge of West Barsetshire and her excellent seat on horseback—he was able to talk to her very comfortably, by which our reader will understand that he did the talking and she listened with a flattering air of attention that did not prevent her catching Mrs. Belton's eye from time to time in the conspiracy of women.

After a little talk of an exploring nature, kept up most con-scientiously on both sides, Lord Pomfret said there was some-thing he would very much like to ask Mrs. Macfadyen, but didn't know if he really could. To which she answered, very sensibly, that if he would tell her what it was he wanted to ask she would at once tell him if she could answer it. This appeared to throw him into acute embarrassment, but he had trained himself to pretend not to be shy about talking and asked Mrs. Macfadyen if she remembered the chapel at the Towers. The one his cousin, old Lady Pomfret, at least she was a somethingth cousin something removed, had done up with Italian workmen and a marble pavement. He then felt that he had muddled everything. But that nice Mrs. Macfadyen said she had once been over the Towers with her husband when he was alive and had one of his offices there, and had admired the Chapel so much.

"And so did Donald," she said. "The lovely windows and the floor with the pattern of lapis lazuli and white marble. And those beautiful seats with the carved ends."

"Well, that's exactly it," said Lord Pomfret. "I mean the choir stalls. I don't know when it happened, as we are most particular about not letting visitors in except with the guide, but some devil

did a bit of amateur carving on the high seat—the one the
bishop would use if there ever *were* a bishop one could safely
invite—and the estate carpenter can't match the wood. I don't
know much about wood, but your husband did say once that he
was interested in it. My carpenter could do the job quite well if
he could get the right wood."

"Now, wait a minute," said Mrs. Macfadyen, quite forgetting
that she was talking to an earl whom she hardly knew. "Donald
did know quite a lot about wood—you see trees are a kind of
vegetable after all and some trees will do in a vegetable garden
and some wouldn't fit at all. But there's someone almost on the
spot who can tell you everything. That's Mr. Welk, he's an
undertaker, that's why he knows wood."

Lord Pomfret was not often taken aback, but this sudden
irruption of graves and worms and epitaphs was too much for
him and he began to laugh. Lady Pomfret looked across the
table with a pleasure that she rarely had, for her husband seemed
to have less and less time, and even energy, to have the silly
hearty laugh occasionally which does one so much good.

"But he really does, Lord Pomfret," said Mrs. Macfadyen,
who was now laughing herself. "And he's up in the park here
most days just now with the gypsies from where the woods come
down by Gundric's Fossway. Mr. Belton is having some timber
thinned."

"And I thought I knew West Barsetshire," said Lord Pomfret.
"The half was not told me."

"Chronicles—and a dull book a lot of it is—Book Two,
Chapter Nine, I think. Can't be sure of the verse," said Mr.
Belton.

"There was a complete silence; mostly, we think, of a kind of
shame, for the number of people who can quote chapter and
verse is not so large. Among them we sadly number ourself, but
we are lucky enough to possess an 1875 edition of Cruden's
Concordance with the front cover missing, even from Abase to
Zuzims.

"I don't know if this is any use to you, Pomfret," said Mr. Belton, "but I happen to know that Welk is at the Nabob's Arms this evening. He's got a head like teak. I'll send up and get him to come here if you like."

As the gilded youth of England may feel when it has its first trousers, so may Lord Pomfret have felt when it was suggested that a real wood expert should be routed out from his port of call and summoned to Arcot House. But he also thought it unsuitable that a man who really knew wood should have his evening spoiled and very courageously asked if he couldn't go up to the Nabob, using the specious argument that Mr. Welk would probably be in a friendly condition by now. Mr. Belton looked at Lady Pomfret, who shrugged her shoulders and looked amused.

"By all means," he said. "I'll take you up and leave you to it," and without more ado he rose from his seat, bowed a kind of excuse to the ladies and to Mr. Oriel and went out followed by Lord Pomfret.

The three ladies laughed and Mrs. Belton asked Mr. Oriel if he would join them in the drawing-room or have another glass of port by himself. Or would he, she added, bring the glass of port in with him. There was something rather dashing about this which appealed to Mr. Oriel's bachelor mind so they all went into the drawing-room where Wheeler had kept up a good fire and talked very comfortably. Mr. Oriel asked Mrs. Macfadyen what her plans were and she told him that she was looking for a small house where she could have a guest if she wished and one living-in maid if she could find her.

Near Harefield, Mr. Oriel hoped.

In many ways she would have liked that, said Mrs. Macfadyen, but as her parents were getting on in years and not always in the best of health she was trying to find a house in Greshamsbury where she had a number of friends and would be within easy reach of her parents should any emergency arise, which filial attitude was much approved by the rest of the party.

"There's one thing about not having any children," said Mrs.

Macfadyen. "You don't have to worry. If Donald and I had had any I suppose we would have worried like anything. Now I have nothing to worry about."

Mr. Oriel, feeling that as a clergyman he ought to deal with this, tried to think of the right thing to say, but not finding it he very sensibly kept his peace.

"But I shall find something quite easily," said Mrs. Macfadyen in a hopeful voice. "Of course Father and Mother are always a bit of an anxiety, but I shall be near them at Greshamsbury. Tubby—I mean Canon Fewling—can do it in seven minutes, but his car is *terrific* and he's a frightfully good driver. Next best to Lady Cora Waring. Of course the police wouldn't ever meddle with her—they all adore her."

Mrs. Belton said she hoped the police liked Canon Fewling.

"Oh, of course they do," said Mrs. Macfadyen. "His nice housekeeper Mrs. Hicks has a cousin who is the policeman over at Southbridge, Haig Brown his name is, and he wouldn't *dream* of bothering Tubby."

"Tubby?" said Mr. Oriel.

"Well, really *you* ought to know, Mr. Oriel," said Mrs. Macfadyen. "Canon Fewling. He was in the Navy before he took Holy Orders and he was always called Tubby in the Navy and most of his old friends call him that—like Wicks."

Mr. Oriel, in a kind of scholarly bewilderment, asked what kind of a wick. He had heard, through his housekeeper Mrs. Powlett, of candlewick bedspreads which seemed to have tufts all over them as if they were moulting.

"Mr. Wickham. The Mertons' agent," said Mrs. Macfadyen. "He is so good about coming to see Father and always brings him some real navy rum."

Mr. Oriel asked how the Admiral was. Mrs. Macfadyen said up and down, but Dr. Ford said he must go slow. Luckily her mother kept quite well so long as she didn't do too much, but they had some help now and everyone was so kind about coming in.

Then Mrs. Belton and Lady Pomfret who had been talking Committees joined their talk and soon the travellers returned from the Nabob where Mr. Welk, who had only got to his sixth beer, had given Lord Pomfret a great deal of information, some of it really useful. So the Pomfrets said good night and went away, as did Mr. Oriel.

"Thank you for *such* a nice evening," said Mrs. Macfadyen.

"You must come again soon," said Mr. Belton, who hardly ever gave such an invitation. "I'll take you up to the woodmen's camp. You'd like to see the circular saw at work."

So they all went to bed.

CHAPTER 7

Mrs. Macfadyen had enjoyed her visit to Harefield very much. We cannot say that it had brought her complete peace and happiness, but every day had made the feeling of loss less bitter. Not that she had ever brooded—the heritage of the British Navy in her made her ready to rise and fight again—but every day the past was a day further away. And a line came back to her now and again—words from a poet who was also a seer and prophet—words that had been very well put to music though now no longer sung. But her mother had sung it to her in nursery years and now, for no reason at all, the words echoed in her mind. "The dead they cannot rise and you'd better dry your eyes. . . ." Her eyes were dried now, the sad fountains wept no more. But the poem had gone on, "And you'd best take me for your new love." And at this, even when only thinking of it without saying the words aloud, she suddenly had to laugh, all alone, at herself, for thinking of new loves. Not that Donald would mind, of that she felt sure. But such a thing would be too ridiculous at her age—and in any case it wasn't going to happen.

The Updikes gave a party for her on the eve of her departure and apart from Mrs. Updike cutting her finger and showering blood over a plate of cake, everything had gone extremely well.

We think that when Mrs. Macfadyen came to the Beltons Harefield had stood a little aloof, not in dislike or distrust, but just to observe. The result of the observations was in her favour with not a single dissentient voice and the party went on till nearly twelve o'clock; late hours for Harefield.

"Come again soon, Mrs. Macfadyen," said Mr. Belton as he squired her into her car next day. At least we think that was what he felt he was doing, but to give a lady your hand as she steps into her victoria, or open landau, is very different from seeing little of her as she gets into the car except the vision of Moses on Mount Sinai.

"I would like to—very much," said Mrs. Macfadyen as soon as she was settled at the wheel, and off she went. As she passed the drive gates at Harefield House the Winters were coming out and waved to her, so she drove on her way with a warm heart.

At Harefield most of the Beltons' friends were older than Mrs. Macfadyen and she had rather enjoyed having the status of a younger woman. Up at the School she had felt distinctly elderly in that atmosphere of looking to the future rather than remembering the past. And suddenly she saw before her the question was she to go on as the widowed Mrs. Macfadyen, a middle-aged woman, independent as far as money went, used to travelling, making her home here and there as the whim moved her. Or was she to be Mrs. Macfadyen whose husband had died and left her well off and dwell among her own people. To and fro her mind went over this choice as she drove and—which is so like one's mind—came to no decision at all. But luckily at this moment a herd of cows came out of a field and—as had happened so often in country lanes—her whole mind had to be directed to driving fast enough to make a little progress yet slowly enough for the small boy who was directing them to keep ahead of her. Luckily the farmyard was only a few yards away and she was able to pursue her journey. But the thread of her self-examination was broken and a good thing too, for we know very little of ourselves and often what we think we know is not in the least what our parents, children, friends, bank manager think they see. Sometimes it almost boils down to the nursery question—which seemed to us incredibly witty then—"Would you rather be a greater fool than you look, or look a greater fool than you are?"; and whichever one chose, the reply was "Impossible."

So she came to Greshamsbury, and there was her bedroom waiting with its own bathroom and a comfortable bed. And what was more, a bookcase with quite a number of books in it. Not what Charles Lamb calls biblia abiblia, not The Book of The Fortnight, nor The Teenager Looks at Life, nor By the Sweat of Thy Loins; but Mrs. Morland's new Madame Koska book, *Horror in the Hatshop*, and a new thriller by Lisa Bedale (whom most people now knew to be Lady Silverbridge), *Which Way Up*, and several pleasant travel books which were no trouble to read and could easily be forgotten and then read again. Also another novel by Mrs. Rivers about a beautiful South American señorita (if that is what they are called) who married a Canadian and pined away in Calgary till her husband found out what was biting her and got a job in Uruguay and on the way there in the plane (or one of the planes possibly) she met an English Diplomat who was Correct but with the Heart of a Boy and owing to being in a plane their love could never be consummated. But once a year he sent her a cable signed Forever and she sent him back a faded rose and her husband could not have cared less which made it Far Worse for her because to be Misunderstood would have given her just the pep she needed. But one can't have everything.

Rose was out, but by the time Mrs. Macfadyen had unpacked her suitcase and put everything in its place her hostess was at home again and delighted to see her.

"Now, do tell me all about Harefield," said Rose when they were settled for their tea. But Mrs. Macfadyen had not travelled all over the place with her husband for nothing and knew quite well that the people who ask you with yearning eyes to tell them what you have been doing are really waiting to Pounce at the first pause and tell you what they have been doing. There was a light and pleasant story by a writer now dead called *Listener's Lure* in which the nice quiet heroine gets the right husband simply by letting him talk, which makes him feel how truly intelligent (as well as desirable) she is. So she gave Rose a very brief sketch of her meeting with the Winters and how pleasant it had been with the Beltons and then asked her how things were in Greshamsbury.

The Leslies were all away, Rose said, and so were the Greshams, but everyone else was quite well.

"We were going to Majorca," she went on, "but John can't because he's got to entertain a Mixo-Lydian Admiral, so we sent all the children there with the Greshams and it's perfect heaven without them."

Mrs. Macfadyen asked if the Mixo-Lydian Admiral was coming to Greshamsbury.

"I'm afraid he is," said Rose. "Ackcherly we've had to invite him to supper tonight. John is in Barchester today, so he'll bring him out. But the Mixo-Lydian Ambassadress—you know, the one that was the Fieldings' cook in the war—says she will rescue us if he is a nuisance. She is staying in Barchester at the White Hart and she's coming too."

Mrs. Macfadyen said she didn't know Mixo-Lydia had a navy. If it had, her father would surely have known about it.

"John says it isn't really a navy at all," said Rose. "He says it's one very out-of-date English gunboat on a lake, and it has a cannon that can be fired only it usually bursts. Oh, and I went over to Southbridge while you were away and saw your people. They both looked pretty well and your mother said would I tell you that she was remembering to rest every afternoon and thought it really did her good."

Mrs. Macfadyen was truly moved by Rose's thoughtfulness and felt—as more than one person had felt and said—that beauty lived with kindness. Without exactly using these words she managed to convey something of her feelings to her hostess who, like Tennyson's Maud, took the compliment sedately, but we think she was pleased.

"I've asked those clergy-friends of Tubby's from the New Town," said Rose, "so I asked Tubby to come too because I am sure he can deal with Mixo-Lydians. Sailors can do anything. Mrs. Parkinson is getting on very well. She's got the Mothers' Union and the Townswomen's Guild right under her thumb. I wonder where she learnt it."

"I heard a lot about her father, Mr. Welk, at Harefield," said Mrs. Macfadyen. "Sir Edmund Pridham said he is a descendant of Cedric the Saxon."

"Well, Mrs. Parkinson is a descendant of William the Conqueror," said Rose. "Her children do what she tells them and so does her husband. But she's awfully kind to him," at which Mrs. Macfadyen couldn't help laughing.

"Tubby's been a bit off-colour," said Rose. "I know, because he plays the piano such a lot. I know *exactly* what he feels like. I was like that before I got engaged to John. I was perfectly *awful* to my people and played my ocarina all the time. But as soon as we were married John took it away from me and then I had the babies and I forgot all about it till Mrs. Carter found it in the front of the house among the shrubs. John threw it there because he didn't think it was the right thing for our honeymoon," and she looked so angelic as she said these words that the inelegant word Soppy came into Mrs. Macfadyen's mind.

"And don't bother about dressing," said Rose, which phrase, far from describing a nudist colony, now only means that you will change into the sort of dress you wouldn't wear at a real slap-up party such as the Deanery still gave.

"I think I have the right kind of dress," said Mrs. Macfadyen, quite calmly and kindly.

"Oh! I didn't mean—" Rose began, suddenly realizing that she was perhaps putting her foot in it.

"And I didn't think you did," said Mrs. Macfadyen. "After all, Rose, it was you that showed me how to dress. I mean before I was married and you and Lady Cora made me wear a proper belt—only corsets is what I called them—and have a proper hair-do and make my face up a bit. Donald loved clothes and he helped me to choose things that suited me."

"I hope you brought some. I'd simply adore to see them," said Rose. "Not if—I mean—" and her voice tailed away; a most unusual occurrence with Rose who probably knew what to say and how and when to say it as well as any wife in the British Navy.

"Yes, Donald did choose them and they remind me of him and that's why I like them," said Mrs. Macfadyen calmly. "We usually did some shopping in Paris and I got some very good things in Brussels. I didn't care for Florence so much, except one shop."

"Not Padella!" said Rose, mentioning a House that chose its own clients and had turned down several Royalties and South American millionaires and—to the ill-concealed joy of the whole county—Victoria, Lady Norton, who had walked in, demanded to be shown some nice evening gowns not too expensive and not vulgarly smart and been most politely and sweetly squeezed out into the Via Abbandonata so that she couldn't find the taxi which she had left in the Via Perduta.

"Yes, that was the one," said Mrs. Macfadyen. "They were *most* sympathetic and when Donald said he was an amateur of flowers and of very young vegetables for the market, they all fell in love with him and found some most suitable dresses for me."

"You don't mean *dowdy*, do you?" said Rose, anxiously.

"Oh no. Just dresses that were quite right for a woman of my age who isn't young and isn't slim," said Mrs. Macfadyen. "I will wear one tonight. Only demi-toilette, I suppose," and if this sounds a little unkind it was only with a view to showing Rose that though a widow and not very young she was quite capable of looking after herself. "I haven't worn it in England yet."

"Well, goodness knows what the Mixo-Lydian Ambassadress will be wearing," said Rose.

"That doesn't really matter," said Mrs. Macfadyen.

"But what does matter," said Rose, "is Mrs. Parkinson. I mean I would hate it if she felt a disadvantage because her dress wasn't up-to-date. I know they aren't very well off and she *is* so nice."

Mrs. Macfadyen said she would consider that too.

Rose, who recognized defeat, hauled down her flag and a truce was called. Not with any ill-feeling, for Rose, who had in the years when her husband was on various foreign stations learned to accommodate herself to every kind of company, recognized that Margot Phelps, the Admiral's stout, hard-working unmarried daughter, had become a Person in her own right with quite a good deal of worldly knowledge, not to speak of worldly goods.

The afternoon went peacefully by with a little gardening and after tea some records on Rose's long-playing gramophone and then they went upstairs to dress for dinner. Rose was down first and we need not describe her appearance for we have met her so often and admired her young beauty as much as we now admire the slightly riper charms of a wife, mother, and excellent hostess from Portsmouth to Hong Kong or wherever else. Their Lordships of the Admiralty sent her husband and allowed her to join him. We will merely state that though she was now nearly forty she was looking not much more than twenty-five in a deep pink which was her favourite colour. Then Mrs. Macfadyen came down in a dress of soft grey silk pleated from neck to hem with hanging pleated sleeves and a wide belt of soft silver leather.

"I *say*," said Rose. "That *must* be Padella! Gosh!"

"Yes, Donald chose it for me in Florence," said Mrs. Macfadyen with a touch of melancholy. "I haven't any taste, but I have all the clothes I need for the rest of my life."

"Now, *don't* talk like that, Margot," said Rose. "How old *are* you?"

Mrs. Macfadyen said getting on for fifty.

"But you don't look it a *bit*," said Rose.

Mrs. Macfadyen laughed and said Rose didn't look a bit like

nearer forty than thirty, which indeed she did not. Excellent health, a very kind firm husband, always quite enough money and good well-behaved children do not age a woman and we think Rose will always be beautiful because she was as kind as she was fair, and had the good bones which age can hardly touch. As for silliness it can be most attractive in small quantities and Captain Fairweather would not have had his Rose in any way altered for the world.

Then the roaring sound of his car was heard and the even more roaring sound of a second car. There was a noise of voices in the hall and in came Captain Fairweather with the Mixo-Lydian Ambassadress and a naval officer with a great deal of gold braid, a thick crop of short hair standing up all over his head, a very fine moustache and a spade beard: a phenomenon almost unknown to us now.

"Hah!" said the Ambassadress. "Bog! which pleasure, which joy! I am enchanted of meetink you, Prodska Fairweather. Or correctly I should say re-meetink for our preview meetink was in the past. Your Osbond which is oll kindness was offerink me to be lifted and ollso the Admiral, but we had his car so we came in both. I shall presentink him."

"No you won't, Gradka," said Captain Fairweather, who had known the Ambassadress for some time and enjoyed her conversation. "I say, sir, what *is* your name? Gradka did tell me and I'm frightfully sorry I didn't quite catch it. We English aren't good at languages."

The Admiral bowed, took a large card-case from a pocket, pulled out a card and presented it ceremoniously to Captain Fairweather.

"Sorry, sir, but I can't read it," said the Captain.

"Naturally not, because is in Mixo-Lydian," said the Admiral. "Is Prsvb."

This monosyllable Captain Fairweather repeated to the best of his ability and everyone said what a pleasure it was and the Admiral bowed to the ladies.

The parlourmaid, who had taken offence at the unceremoni-
ous arrival of her employer and his guests, now came in and
announced Mr. and Mrs. Parkinson and Canon Fewling. Rose
welcomed them with her usual warmth, explained to the Admiral that Canon Fewling used to be in the Royal Navy and
handed the Ambassadress over to Mrs. Parkinson who took her
on just as she would have taken on any other piece of parish work
that came her way. Canon Fewling said how glad he was to see
Mrs. Macfadyen again and hoped she had enjoyed herself at
Harefield. She also was glad to see him, but couldn't help feeling
that there was a difference in his manner.

"I say, Tubby, there isn't anything wrong, is there?" she said.
"I mean Mrs. Hicks hasn't given notice or anything?"

Canon Fewling said Oh dear, no. "But what I was wondering," he said, "was about that dress you are wearing. I don't know
much about clothes, but it is perfectly lovely—like something in
a picture—an old Italian picture."

"If I said it was a Padella dress I don't suppose you'd be much
wiser," said Mrs. Macfadyen. "It's a firm in Florence and they
won't sell any of their models unless they like the customer. Old
Lady Norton went there and the head vendeuse said they
couldn't do justice to the Contessa's figure and she had better go
to the Trois Quartiers in Paris. So she did."

"Then *that*," said Canon Fewling, "accounts for her appearance at the Mayor of Barchester's Soirée," which made them
both laugh.

Meanwhile the Ambassadress had seized Mr. Parkinson that
she might discuss with him the differences between the Church
of England and the Orthodox church to which Mixo-Lydia still
adhered in spite of efforts from Slavo-Lydia to impress a heresy
of their own upon her. But Mr. Parkinson, partly through some
serious talks with the Dean who was godfather to Master Josiah
Parkinson, and partly by his own reading and judgment, was
prepared for most adversaries and entirely refused to go into the
matter, though with a reservation in petto that people who

crossed themselves in what Mrs. Morland had once described as a very upside down and unreligious kind of way, could have little hope of salvation here or elsewhere. He had been rather afraid that he would find himself next to the Ambassadress at dinner, but much to his relief had Rose on one side and Mrs. Macfadyen on the other.

Mrs. Macfadyen was also pleased to have him for her neighbour and glad to find Canon Fewling on the other side.

Rose as a good hostess first took on the Mixo-Lydian Admiral, and did her best to make conversation. But for once her efforts were entirely wasted, for the Admiral had not come to talk.

"Am not good to spik," he said, wiping the soup from his heavy moustache. "Am good for eat—yes. You are good for look at. I look and I eat—yes. But spik—not!"

Rose said she absolutely agreed with him and in England they called the Navy the Silent Service.

"Is good," said the Admiral. "Shall tellink my navy to be silent. If not silent, be hang from farmyard—yes?"

"Of *course*," said Rose. "How marvellous. But we say Yardarm."

"Bog! which opdownside!" said the Admiral and went on with his soup. Rose, not sorry to be free of him, turned to Mr. Parkinson and asked him about the children, knowing that she would be rather bored but—which was far more important— that he would be at his ease.

We are glad to say that the news was all good and Master Parkinson had been already nominated by his godfather for a good grammar school of which he was a governor. And if Master Parkinson went on as he had begun he would probably in the end get a scholarship to a University as well, for the school was well endowed with special places for sons of the clergy.

"Of course that won't be just yet," said Mr. Parkinson, "but it's a weight off our mind," and Rose said Mrs. Macfadyen had been at Harefield lately and had met Mr. Parkinson's father-in-law,

Mr. Welk, who was with the woodmen up in Harefield Park having a busman's holiday.

"There's one thing, Mrs. Fairweather," said Mr. Parkinson in a lower voice. "The Ambassadress and the Admiral, what would they be?"

Rose found the question baffling. As far as she knew they were themselves and what else could Mr. Parkinson imagine they would be. Then a light broke on her.

"Oh, you mean what *church*," she said, also lowering her voice, though by now the noise of eight respectable people at dinner made this hardly necessary.

Mr. Parkinson said he had nothing against the Roman church, but it was obvious that he had mental reservations, so Rose hurried on to explain that she didn't quite know, but they crossed themselves the wrong way round.

"Ah!" said Mr. Parkinson. "That alters matters. Greek Orthodox probably."

"Not *Greek*, Mr. Parkinson," said Rose. "Mixo-Lydian. Quite a long way from Greece."

Mr. Parkinson gave it up and said how nice it was to see that nice Mrs. Macfadyen again.

"And what's even nicer," said Rose, "she is looking for a house here. She wants to settle down here. If you hear of anything I can tell you what she wants," and she outlined Mrs. Macfadyen's requirements (which we already know) and the rent she would be prepared to pay, or the price she could give if she bought a house.

"I wish I could suggest the New Town," said Mr. Parkinson. "There are some really good houses being built there now. But I don't think it would do. She is Old Town."

For once Rose was at a loss for an answer. What Mr. Parkinson said was perfectly true. Margot wasn't New Town and never could be, but how did Mr. Parkinson know it?

"But I'll tell Mavis," said Mr. Parkinson. "She often hears about things before I do, and of course Mr. Welk in his profession often hears of something coming into the market before it's made public. If Mavis can help she will, Mrs. Fairweather. We know what it's like not having your own home and we are ever so lucky to have a nice house now. Where we were at Pomfret Madrigal the kitchen range simply ate the coal and there wasn't any electric light only gas, and if I had to slap Joe once for turning the gas taps on I had to slap him ten times."

"Oh I *am* glad you smack them," said Rose, her lovely face animated by this conversation. "One smack is worthy twenty scoldings. There's something about it in the Bible."

"Proverbs Thirteen, verse—well I'm not sure but it's right at the end of the chapter—he that spareth the rod hateth his son," said Mr. Parkinson.

"How on *earth* do you know that?" said Rose, opening her lovely eyes wider than ever. But Mr. Parkinson did not answer— simply, we think, because he felt he was showing off and wanted to withdraw, and luckily at the same moment there was a setting to-and-from-partners and he had to turn to Mrs. Macfadyen who had been talking very comfortably with Canon Fewling.

This threw Canon Fewling into the arms of the Ambassadress. They were slightly acquainted, for in her refugee days during the war she had been cook to Sir Robert and Lady Fielding and acquired a fluent if peculiar knowledge of English and—partly thanks to their old governess, Miss Bunting—had passed with high credit the Society for the Propagation of English Examination by Correspondence Course, become a well-known authority on education in Mixo-Lydia, and so risen to Ambassadorial rank and been posted to the Court of St. James's. In this position she had been for some years, but spent a good deal of her time in Barsetshire, which she found more sympathetic than London, having many old war-time friends there from Greta Tory the postwoman at Hallbury, niece of Admiral Palliser's cook, to Ernie Freeman who drove the baker's van.

"I hope your Excellency is not to be posted abroad yet," said

Canon Fewling. "Barsetshire appreciates your visits here so much."

"Excuse, pliss," said Gradka (as we cannot help calling her, having known her for so long), "if I laugh, for posted is to me highly laughable. I am en poste here—in the post you say—and hope to remain."

"And pray excuse *me*, your Excellency," said Canon Fewling, "but if you were *in* the post you would be a letter," and he paused, rather doubtful as to how the Ambassadress would take his comment. Much to his relief she burst out laughing and then, rather to his alarm, smacked the back of his hand in a motherly way.

"Aha! you are the Joker," she said. "So will we joke together. I should perhaps say *on* the post."

"Not quite that either," said Canon Fewling. "It is a curious thing that English, perhaps the most flexible language in the world with a very large vocabulary, has to borrow from France to express certain feelings."

"Ah, les Français!" said Gradka. "T'as de cochons! They have riffuse to lend us a loan. We ask sixty million lydions—but a mere drop in the bucket—and they riffuse. On va leur en dire des nouvelles. On a des alliés—allez."

"Who *are* your allies, Excellency?" said Canon Fewling, who was immensely enjoying his companion's talk.

"Weech gives us most, that is our ally," said Gradka. "Que ce soit les Russes ou les Turcs, c'est égal. Bot we mosst have an identity—a large one."

"Possibly your Excellency means indemnity?" said Canon Fewling.

"L'un en vaut bien l'autre," said Gradka. "Bot we will not spik of such smallnesses. I will spik of you. You are celebrated—yes, no?"

For a fleeting moment Canon Fewling wondered if a report of his Easter sermon (over which he had taken a great deal of trouble and earned the Dean's approval) had somehow reached ambassadorial circles, but it did not seem probable.

"I don't think so," he said. "Or only in a very small way."

"Ha! Sly Boots," said the Ambassadress. "You do not have a wife, no? You have a little friend, yes?"

"Good gracious, no!" said Canon Fewling, suddenly realizing what his neighbour meant. "The clergy don't, you know. But I am not a professional bachelor myself. I just happen never to have got married. And, if I may presume, the word is celibate. Celebrated means very famous."

"Then am I ollso right," said Gradka. "You are celibate because you do not have a wife and you are celebrated because you spik well from your chair."

"From the pulpit I hope, your Excellency," said Canon Fewling. "Oh, I beg your pardon, I see what you meant."

"In Mixo-Lydia must the priest have one wife," said Gradka, "so that he may not wish to be seducting. And if his wife dies, he must marry again if he has children, a widow this time, bot without children and outside parturiating, for if he and the widow have children so is there strife of the two offsprings, like Kine and Abeel."

"I'm afraid I don't quite understand," said Canon Fewling.

"Hah! see mc this one weech does not know his Bible," said the Ambassadress in a voice which temporarily silenced the rest of the guests. "I shall be tellink you—" but her voice was drowned by the Mixo-Lydian Admiral saying "Czy, próvka, próvka, próvka." He then raised his glass, drank ceremoniously to her, wiped his beard and moustache, uttered a few more words in Mixo-Lydian and went on with his dinner. It speaks much for the self-control of Rose's guests that nobody laughed.

"He says Komm off it, ees enough," said Gradka mildly and then turned to Captain Fairweather who, having entertained foreigners all over the world from Powder-Monkey to Admiral (figuratively speaking), at once made himself extremely agreeable to her and they talked about the new film at the Barchester

Odean *Daughter of the Pyramids* in which Glamora Tudor was starring as Cleopatra with her latest co-star Hank Hawksfoot.

"Eet is of high grandness that film," said Gradka. "Cleopatra is beautiful eef you wish, yes, but to me is her style repugnating. Bot I am ollso sorry for her to have her face made oll black every night and to have to take it off again."

"There are two answers to that, Ambassadress," said Captain Fairweather. "The first is that she only had to be black while she was being filmed. The second that the people who made the film were as ignorant and conceited as those people mostly are. Cleopatra wasn't black, or even dusky. She was a Ptolemy, a Greek. But even Lord Tennyson made that mistake—your Excellency doubtless knows some of his poems. He describes her as A queen with swarthy cheeks and bold black eyes."

"In Mixo-Lydia would sotch a woman not obtain a osband," said Gradka. "In Slavo-Lydia perhaps, yes. Bot how are you knowink of soch things? In our Navy are all sailors unliteral, for if they could read they would waste their time, ollso they might try to spy upon the Captain and read the letters which oll his little friends write to him. You Enklish say A wife in every port. We do not have a sea in Mixo-Lydia, but oll round the great lake where is our navy is small little towns—omelettes you say—"

"Or hamlets, Excellency," said Captain Fairweather.

"Ah, now do we spik of literature," said Gradka. "Your Shikspere, weech is not of value now, has a tragedy of Omlet, which is much performed in Mixo-Lydia. We have Slavo-Lydian actors so that oll can be d'après nature and Omlet can veritably kill Polonius and his Onkel—and ollso has our best dramaturge Krcks made a better writing of the play that Ophelia is not drowned, so can Omlet kill her too. Is hig-leaf," by which, we think, she was using the French equivalent of High Life.

The Silent Navy can also, if it gives its mind to it, be the Deaf Navy and Captain Fairweather had abstracted his mind to the new bino-therapeutic-conglomerate compass about which he had made one or two suggestions that their Lordships of the Admiralty were seriously considering. Several people were now talking across the table, though not noisily. Rose looked at the Mixo-Lydian Ambassadress, who at once took the hint. The two ladies got up and followed by Mrs. Macfadyen and Mrs. Parkinson went into the drawing-room, where the fire was burning brightly and one could forget the cold leaden sky outside.

Rose, who had done some serious thinking while the Mixo-Lydian Admiral talked to her, asked Mrs. Parkinson to come and sit by Her Excellency who was deeply interested in English country life and would like to exchange views on Women's Institutes and the Townswomen's Guild. Mrs. Parkinson, always ready to help in a good cause, took possession of the Ambassadress who, to put it vulgarly, never got a look in. Mrs. Parkinson, with the kindest manner, tanked right over her Excellency, and gave her a great deal of practical and useful information about organized life in a small urban community and whenever Gradka showed signs of wishing to speak, paid no attention at all. And as Mrs. Parkinson had a pleasant voice and an air of effortless authority, we think that the Mixo-Lydian Ambassadress began to realize, for almost the first time, the immense power behind the throne in English country life as organized today—and also its value.

"I am thanking you, Prodska Parkinson," she said. "I shall visit you—yes?—and learn of your organizings, yes?"

Mrs. Parkinson with her eminently practical mind at once closed with this offer and before the Ambassadress knew where she was she had promised to come to the next Townswomen's Guild meeting and give a talk on the Arts Neo-Paysans in Mixo-Lydia. Then the men came in.

"And now must I go," she said, "for the Admiral is to drive me back," and beckoning the Admiral she spoke to him rapidly in Mixo-Lydian. As so often happens when one hears foreigners speaking their conversation sounded like what in English would be a first-class row, but all was well. Good-byes were said, Captain Fairweather took them to the front door and the roaring of their car died away on the Barchester road.

"Sorry," said Captain Fairweather. "I had to ask them," and he gave himself a stiffish whiskey and soda.

"I say, Tubby," said Rose. "Be an angel and play to us. We need a little soothing. It's still quite early, thank goodness."

Canon Fewling laughed and went over to the piano. It was a very good one, almost as good as his own, and he lovingly amused himself on it while the rest of the party talked quietly, or were glad not to talk for a few moments.

Inevitably their peace was disturbed by the telephone. Captain Fairweather went to its help.

"It's for you, Margot," he said. "Your father wants to speak to you."

"Father must be at a *very* loose end," said Mrs. Macfadyen as she came across the room. "He *loathes* telephoning. Hullo, father. How are you? WHAT? Just hang on one moment."

She put the receiver down, covered the mouthpiece with her hand and said "I must go over. Mother is dead."

"Oh, *Margot!*" said Rose.

"I will drive you over," said Canon Fewling quietly. "I'll bring the car round to the gate," and he went out of the room.

"Get some warm things on," said Rose. "I'll come up with you," and Mrs. Macfadyen, grateful for her company, quickly put on some day clothes, shoved a nightgown and a hot bottle and a few other things into a little suitcase in case of emergency and came downstairs.

"I'll ring you up as soon as I can," she said. "I might have to stay the night," and she went out to where the car was waiting. Canon Fewling was celebrated all through West Barsetshire for his driving, but never had he driven as he did on this chill autumn night. Luckily there was little or no traffic and they were very soon at Jutland Cottage.

"I shall wait here till you want me," said Canon Fewling. "I will take you back to Rose or, if you want to stay here, I can fetch anything you need. Take care of yourself and God bless you."

Mrs. Macfadyen thanked him, got out and hurried up the path with her suitcase. The door was ajar. She went in and was met by Matron from Southbridge School.

"Oh how *good* of you to be here, Matron," said Mrs. Macfadyen.

"I *am* glad you could come," said Matron. "The Admiral rang me up. There's not much I could do, and Mr. and Mrs. Carter are away, so I rang up Mr. Crofts to tell him, but he and Mrs. Crofts were away so I just put a few things in a bag and came round here. Your mother was dead, Mrs. Macfadyen. It was her heart of course. I got on to Dr. Ford and luckily he was in and he'll be here now any minute. And I know Mr. Crofts would have come at once if he had been at home."

"Thank you more than I can say, Matron. How *good* you are," said Mrs. Macfadyen. "I think I had better see Mother and then I'll go to my father."

From this point the bad dream which had begun in Greshamsbury seemed to Mrs. Macfadyen to go on unrolling itself for ever. The noise of a rattling old car outside heralded Dr. Ford who came in with a pleasant-looking middle-aged woman.

"I'm sorry this happened so suddenly, Margot," he said. "We all knew it might happen. Will you take us upstairs, Matron? Good of you to take charge. I rang up Sister Chiffinch and luckily she could come over. You remember her, Margot?"

Mrs. Macfadyen well remembered the kind and efficient Sister Chiffinch who was now more or less retired from her profession but would take on a case in an emergency, especially if she knew the patient. To see her in the little house already made things feel more normal. There was a brief greeting and Dr. Ford with Sister Chiffinch went upstairs.

"I expect the Admiral would like to see you, Mrs. Macfadyen," said Matron, and opened the study door.

The Admiral was sitting in his own special chair, near the fire, with a book on his lap. When he heard the sound of voices at the door he looked up.

"Is that you, Margot?" he said. "Good girl. I knew you would come. You know your Mother has gone, Margot. She has left me—for ever. I shall go to her some day, God willing, but she will never come back to me."

"*Poor* father," said Mrs. Macfadyen. "It wasn't like her to leave you—but she couldn't help it. She would have stayed if she could. Oh father, I am so dreadfully sorry. Had she been ill?" not that she wanted to hear about it very much, for nothing seemed to matter now; but she hoped that her father would feel less alone if he could talk about it all.

"No, not ill," said the Admiral. "She hadn't been very well for a long time now, but she wasn't ill. Ford told me she might go suddenly. That's how I'd like to go when my time comes. I always thought I should go first. But she has gone before me—before me. If we were at sea there would be a light that I could follow, but here, on land, there's nothing. Nothing."

The words fell as heavily as Lear's fivefold Never.

"But there will be something, father," said his daughter, searching for a word of comfort. "When Donald died it was like the end of everything, but really it wasn't. And you and mother were so good to me. I'll do my best, father, I truly will."

"Yes, you have had your sorrow, Margot," said the Admiral. "And you have always been so good to us and I know you will be good to me. But I must be good to you, too. Old people get selfish," which generous words nearly made his daughter cry, but most luckily Dr. Ford came down and with a sort of brusque kindness—far easier for the Admiral than any show of sympathy—said if they wanted to go upstairs everything was in order.

Whether one wants to look on the beloved dead or not, it is a kind of ritual which has its place and its meaning and must be duly performed. The Admiral got up very slowly and went to the door, deliberately ignoring the arm that Dr. Ford offered him.

But when he got to the bottom of the steep little flight of stairs he paused.

"I hope I wasn't being conceited," he said. "I thought I could go upstairs by myself but I can't." Without any fuss Sister Chiffinch gently put her hand under his arm and went up the stairs with him. Mrs. Macfadyen and Canon Fewling followed.

The tired body of the wife and mother through so many years was lying on the bed, very composedly, with nothing now to fear. Her husband and her daughter knelt beside the bed. What is there to say at this time? Mrs. Macfadyen heard herself saying aloud in a soft voice "Oh, please, *please*," but what she meant she did not know. The Admiral had risen and was standing to attention, waiting for his orders. Canon Fewling said a very short prayer. There was a silence and then they went down the steep stair again to the Admiral's room. Dr. Ford and Sister Chiffinch were talking together. Matron had quietly gone back to the School to collect her nightgown and a few necessary toilet articles, having arranged to keep Sister Chiffinch company for the night. The Admiral's daughter sat down, suddenly very tired and very unwilling to begin to think of the future.

Presently Canon Fewling came in.

"I don't want to bother you, Margot," he said, "but it's the question of your father. He can't be alone here and you can't manage him single-handed without a house of your own. My house has—I hope—a door open always for friends in need. I have suggested to Dr. Ford and Sister Chiffinch—what a nice woman—that we should take him back to Greshamsbury as soon as possible. My spare room is always ready. Mrs. Hicks will be delighted to look after so distinguished a patient and Ford says he will come over as often as he is needed. And when you have found your house, which I do hope for your sake will be soon, he can consider whether he would like to live with you or with me."

"But why should he live with *you*, Tubby?" said Mrs. Macfadyen. "You are an angel, but to land yourself with Father—oh, I am so confused."

"The worst of death," said Canon Fewling, his sailor's gaze fixed on some far horizon, "is that it always creates fresh muddles. But in this case I think we can make it simple. If you will allow me the privilege of giving what help and comfort I can to your father, I shall be grateful. Heaven has been kind to me in many ways—not in all, but probably I got what I deserved. As one old sailor to another I offer your father my house as his home so long as he likes it. If he doesn't we must try something else. When I say We," he added, "I am treating you as a partner in the Society of Friends of Admiral Phelps."

Before this calm reasoned pleading what could Mrs. Macfadyen do? After all Tubby was a very old friend, an ex-officer of Her Majesty's Navy, known to be comfortably off.

"Tubby, you are an angel," she said. "And too generous. It's my business to look after father really. But if he could come to you while I am looking for a house, I think he would be contented. It's no further for Dr. Ford to come. And if you are busy I could always take him somewhere for a bit—Portsmouth perhaps and he could tell everyone how he was in the cockpit with Nelson at Trafalgar. And I'm sure I'll find a house soon. Mrs. Parkinson is looking out for me," and then she told Canon Fewling how Mrs. Parkinson got special knowledge of houses that would probably be in the market through her father who was Mr. Welk the undertaker, at which Canon Fewling laughed in a most uncanonical way.

"Well, it's a bargain, Margot," he said. "I shall be glad to have your father to stay at the Rectory—if he consents that is—until you have found a house and are comfortably settled. Bring him over as soon as you can."

"You are an *angel*, Tubby," said Mrs. Macfadyen. "And father will jolly well *have* to say yes. Mother would have said yes for him at once—so I shall have to say it. I'll ring you up tomorrow. God bless you. Tubby, you are a friend."

"And you too—the blessing and the friend," said Canon Fewling, which sounds a little complicated but really isn't. "I'll be ready to drive you back as soon as Sister Chiffinch gives the word."

While she was talking with Canon Fewling another talk had been going on between Sister Chiffinch and the Admiral. That admirable woman had gone into the kitchen, at once found everything necessary for making tea, and had brought into his study or den a tray with a large kitchen teapot and some large kitchen cups, a kettle which she put near the fire to keep warm and some biscuits, and there they were talking away like old friends.

"When in doubt the answer's always tea," said Sister Chiffinch. "The Admiral's had two nice cups already and we're going to have another, aren't we?"

What with grief, fatigue and a kind of stunned feeling the Admiral would probably have preferred to go to bed, but there was something soothing about this nice woman and cups of hot sweet tea. And presently his wife would feel better and come downstairs. His daughter quickly realized this and was surprised to find how happily and comfortably they could all talk and thanked heaven for it.

Presently Mrs. Macfadyen managed to get Sister Chiffinch to herself to discuss the matter of beds for the night.

"Would you mind being here alone, Sister?" she said. "I thought I should have to stay with father, but I can't do anything. The little bedroom I used to have has a very comfortable bed and I see it is made up. If you are here I'm not really much use and neither of us wants to sleep on the floor. I'll be over again tomorrow. And if you need me, ring me up at Mrs. Fairweather's."

But Sister Chiffinch said she would be quite all right as Matron was coming over for the night and she had seen quite a lot of Mrs. Morland's books in Mrs. Phelps's room and might she take one to bed, which seemed a very small thing to ask.

So Mrs. Macfadyen and Canon Fewling drove back to Greshamsbury. There was very little to say, so they did not say it, for which she was grateful, for she was suddenly so tired that she felt she might begin to cry or make a fool of herself. Rose had not gone to bed, which Mrs. Macfadyen could not understand till she realized that (*a*) her hostess might have been sitting up in case she came back—which she had—and (*b*) that in spite of all that had happened since Admiral Phelps's telephone call, it was not so very late, though to her ten years of years had passed.

Rose listened kindly to Mrs. Macfadyen's account of what had happened and then said "Bed."

Only at this magic word did Mrs. Macfadyen realize how much she had gone through within the last—the last what? By the clock it could not have been much more than two hours. By one's own feelings it had been thousands of years. Her mother was dead. She had seen her, looking like and unlike the mother she had known. Her father would be very safe with kind Sister Chiffinch. And from now onwards her father must be her special care.

"Oh, I do *wish* Donald were here," she said aloud to herself. But no wishing can bring a loved husband from the ninefold Styx, and the dead they cannot rise and you'd better dry your eyes. Life. And Death. It was all too confusing and she was thankful for the refuge of bed.

CHAPTER 8

After a night's sleep Mrs. Macfadyen woke with an uncomfortable feeling that something had happened. All too soon she remembered what it was and wished she hadn't, but nothing could put the clock back, so she dressed and came downstairs as usual. In the dining-room she found Rose drinking her coffee with one hand and reading *The Times* with the other. Without wasting time on sympathy Rose poured out coffee and milk—which were warming their feet on a four-legged electric dish-warmer on the sideboard—and asked Margot if she had slept.

"Like anything," said Mrs. Macfadyen. "I suppose I was tired. I wonder what I have to do today. When Donald died his secretary did all the arranging—all I had to do was to be the widow. Poor mother. I'm glad she didn't have to be a widow. And I wish father didn't have to be a widower, but there it is."

"And what about *you* being a widow, Margot," said Rose almost severely. "You've been one for quite a bit, you know," which somehow struck Mrs. Macfadyen as rather funny and they both laughed.

"Who's your people's lawyer?" said Rose.

Mrs. Macfadyen said Mr. Keith in Barchester, Lady Merton's brother. "I suppose I'd better tell him," she added, "because Father won't know what to do," to which Rose replied that she had better ring up Jutland Cottage and speak to Sister

Chiffinch. That estimable woman said the Admiral had slept quite well as she had slipped a little sleepy stuff into his grog.

"I don't quite understand," said Mrs. Macfadyen. "Grog did you say?"

"Well, Mrs. Macfadyen, it was very hot rum and water with a slice of lemon and some sugar," said Sister Chiffinch. "Of course we all know rum isn't what it used to be, but when I suggested it the Admiral seemed quite pleased and wanted me to have some too. So just to humour him I had some in the tooth-glass and it really tasted quite nice. Not like whiskey which is really poison to me."

"I like rum too," said Mrs. Macfadyen, "and so did my husband, though he really preferred whiskey because he was Scotch."

Sister Chiffinch said one quite understood that and when she went on a coach tour to Edinburgh and the bonnie banks of Loch Lomond she had taken her dochandorus with the rest every day before supper and felt quite like a Scotch lassie or one of the Dagenham girl pipers, at which point Mrs. Macfadyen had to disguise her laugh as a cough and then felt rather ashamed, because kind Sister Chiffinch said she must take care of herself now.

"And what she meant by 'now' I cannot think," she said, when repeating this conversation to Rose.

Rose, applying her common sense to the question, said it was quite obvious that Sister Chiffinch, who was also an excellent maternity nurse, thought that widows always had a baby after their husbands' deaths and must have mixed it up with her mother's death, which reminded Mrs. Macfadyen of the *Heir of Redclyffe* and she laughed so much that she couldn't explain why she was laughing.

"And I told Sister Chiffinch that Mrs. Keith would be coming out to do any business that has to be done," said Mrs. Macfadyen. "I suppose I'd better ring Colonel Crofts up about the service," for Colonel the Reverend Edward Crofts was still mostly known by his military title. "Oh no, he and his wife are away, I'd forgotten. Perhaps they're back now though."

"Now, Margot, don't worry so much," said Rose. "Robert Keith will see about everything. Lawyers always do. It's no good having a dog and barking yourself," which very true remark made Mrs. Macfadyen laugh and did her a great deal of good.

"What you've got to do, Margot," said Rose firmly and kindly, "is to think of yourself for a moment. Get on with your house-hunting and decide if you will have your father to live with you—at least if you'll live together."

"But what else *can* I do?" said Mrs. Macfadyen. "Father is my responsibility now."

"But does he *want* to be?" said Rose. "Look here, Margot, don't go and be like Cordelia with that dreadful old King Lear—not that your father who is a darling is in the *least* like King Lear—and feel you've got to haul him about all over the place. Find a house as soon as you can and settle him there and butter his paws. He can't live alone, that's obvious, besides they always marry their housekeeper which would be such a bore."

"Well, Tubby lives alone," said Mrs. Macfadyen.

Rose said that was quite another thing, as indeed it was, for apart from their both being naval men there was a good deal of difference between a retired Admiral with little besides his pension and a priest who had once been a Commander in the Royal Navy and still had that peculiarly firm and unbending stoutness which so often goes with the quarterdeck, not to speak of a handsome private income.

"Anyway I'd better go on house-hunting," said Mrs. Macfadyen. "I must live somewhere," which was reasonable. "And I hope I shall be able to make father happy."

Rose, with her usual common sense, said the great thing with men was to make them *comfortable*. Then, she said, the happiness would come of itself.

"If father were just a rating with a wooden leg," said Mrs. Macfadyen, showing a sad want of filial respect, "it would be

much easier. Then he could spend all his pension at the Red
Lion and tell people how he remembered being held up by his
mother to see Nelson go by."

Rose said one couldn't hurry things and if one waited they
usually came of themselves and what about the burial and the
funeral service for her mother.

"Oh dear, I'd forgotten about that," said Mrs. Macfadyen.

Rose, a fearless if rather sketchy thinker, said it was all very
well about the dead burying their dead, but they couldn't; and
what about Mr. Welk, Mrs. Parkinson's father. But at that
moment there was a telephone call from the office of Robert
Keith, the Admiral's lawyer, and Mrs. Macfadyen found that,
subject to her approval, everything was being arranged and
Colonel Crofts who was now at home would feel honoured to
take the service, and had named a day and an hour subject to
Mrs. Macfadyen's approval, which of course she gave, thankful
to be spared any further decisions. Mr. Keith, said a clerk
speaking in his name, had gone over to Southbridge and everything was well in hand and perhaps Mrs. Macfadyen would like
to speak to Colonel Crofts herself, as well.

There were many things that Mrs. Macfadyen would have
liked better, but business is business whatever one's heart may be
feeling, so she rang up Colonel Crofts, who was most comfortable and reassuring and also said everything was well in hand
and any day that best suited Mrs. Macfadyen would suit everyone else. She answered in similar terms that any day he named
would have her approval and wondered how many other things
she would have to approve without really caring much one way
or the other. Donald had gone and a good deal of her life with
him. Now her mother had gone. She blamed herself for not
being more unhappy. But when you have seen someone you love
overburdened by life, it would be selfish to grudge the rest that
we must all some day have, young or old, rich or poor, quarter-
deck or ordinary seaman. And the wheels of life must go on

turning whatever loves or births or deaths they go over as they turn.

Death—except for people like Mrs. Hoare at Dowlah Cottage who throve on bequests of unidentifiable curios and pictures, or people who really enjoy funerals as such—is a bewildering experience. Not so much because of grief, which must have its course, but because nothing feels real. One is partly numb; another bit of one knows that it isn't true; another bit is intensely interested in what is happening; another bit is wondering where on earth it left the library book and another bit is trying to find words to express what it feels and like man Friday can only say Oh.

But the Law and the Church come to the rescue of the sometimes rather bewildered survivor and both do their best to see that things are decently appointed. There were only old friends and some of the village people at the ceremony. When it was over Admiral Phelps shook hands with everyone. Mrs. Crofts, by a private arrangement with Mrs. Macfadyen, invited the Admiral to come up to the Vicarage for a little rest. With his usual courtesy he accepted her invitation, though it was clear to his daughter that he would rather have gone home—if home it could be called now. But when he was at the Vicarage with old friends near him and a glass of Colonel Crofts's extremely good sherry at his elbow, he began to come alive and was genuinely pleased to see Mr. Wickham who had been unable to get to the service in time and had brought an offering of a bottle of rum.

"This is good of you, Wicks," said the Admiral. "The best medicine I know. You know my wife, God bless her, is dead."

"I was sorry to hear it, sir," said Mr. Wickham. "Very sorry. Lord! I'll never forget how she and Margot ran that Christmas party for the evacuee children in the war. That's a long time ago now."

"Yes, it is a long time," said the Admiral. " A long time since I have seen her. I haven't seen her for several days. But I expect she is waiting for me," to which Mr. Wickham replied with great truth that he was sure she was. "And bless my soul," he added, "if it isn't Sister Chiffinch. Here's to your bright eyes, Sister. Any good operations lately? Been sewing up the appendix patients with a plug of tobacco and a crooked sixpence inside them?" which rather schoolboy form of humour appeared to suit her nicely.

"But we mustn't get overtired," said Sister Chiffinch, looking towards the Admiral and speaking for his benefit, as it were. "You know that nice Canon Fewling has invited us over to Greshamsbury. Quite a little outing it will be for the Admiral and a change always does them good after a shock like this."

"Look here, Sister. As man to man," said Mr. Wickham, jerking his hand towards the Admiral, "what about it?"

"Well, Mr. Wickham, it's not for me to say," said Sister Chiffinch. "You'd better ask Dr. Ford. He's over there, talking to Mrs. Carter."

So Mr. Wickham, taking a glass of sherry with him, went across the room and was warmly received by Mrs. Carter and Dr. Ford, who were also holding each a glass of sherry.

"Rum thing about sherry, Mrs. Carter," said Mr. Wickham.

Mrs. Carter said Why not sherry thing about rum, which went down very well.

"But what I mean is," said Mr. Wickham, becoming serious, "rum's a much better drink than sherry, but it hasn't made the grade."

Mrs. Carter asked what he meant.

"Well, it's difficult to explain," said Mr. Wickham. "I mean you throw a sherry party—at least I don't, because it's only cat-lap—and everyone comes along and they think sherry isn't drinking. They're right in principle, but that's not what they mean. But call it a rum party and they may come or they mayn't. Still," said Mr. Wickham philosophically, "rum likes me and I like it. Well, here's mud in old Nasser's eye," a toast which was drunk with curses not only loud but deep upon half-castes who upset half the world.

"But the lame-footed goddess will get him by the short hairs some day," said Mr. Wickham, skilfully combining the classics with rather unrefined slang. "Here's mud in ALL his eyes."

Mrs. Macfadyen had been feeling more and more nervous as the party went on, because the moment would come when she would have to take her father away, and was wondering how she could best explain to him some time that Canon Fewling really wanted him as a guest. But she need not have feared, for he accepted what she said with a childlike faith which touched her and yet—so contrary we are—slightly annoyed her. We think it was a sudden realization of what she had undertaken to do and wondering—not unnaturally—how long and how much she would be tied to her filial duties. She blamed herself for this, but there it was and all one could do was to live for the hour, the day, the week—perhaps the years—and remember God's commandments on that subject, repeated through both Testaments from Exodus to Ephesians. Meanwhile the immediate present was all that mattered.

Sister Chiffinch had packed the Admiral's clothes and would come over to Greshamsbury, in her own car, and see the Admiral installed and stay for a time.

"Once I've settled him he'll be much better on his own, Mrs. Macfadyen," she said. "If you need help later on, give me a ring and if I'm not free, there are my pals Wardy and Heathy—the ones I share the cottage with over at Northbridge. They only take special cases now but one of them would always come to you if I'm engaged."

Mrs. Macfadyen thanked Sister Chiffinch warmly and went over to her father who was sitting in a comfortable chair comparing notes with Colonel Crofts on Trincomalee (which Colonel Crofts had never visited) and the North-West Frontier (where Admiral Phelps had never been) so that each gentleman was able to talk undisputed on his own subject. We may add that Colonel Crofts did the most of the talking with apparent interest and real kindness. But the Admiral looked tired and was becoming a little confused, so Sister Chiffinch came over to him and said in her kind yet immensely authoritative voice that Mrs. Macfadyen was rather tired and wanted to get home and would the Admiral come now. So like a good child he said good-bye to the Croftses and one or two other people. Sister Chiffinch helped him into his coat and walked to the gate with him, where her own car was standing.

"We are going back to Jutland Cottage to tell your mother all about the party, aren't we?" said Admiral Phelps. His daughter said Yes, for it was impossible to begin explaining and she had already realized that everything would have to be repeated several times and even then he might not understand.

"Can you get in, father?" she said, without any trace of impatience, ready to help if need were. But need wasn't; the Admiral got on board unaided, his daughter got into her own seat and drove off through the dusk, Sister Chiffinch following in her own car. The Admiral was very quiet on the journey, rather to his daughter's relief who was tired and did not much want to talk. When they got to Jutland Cottage Mrs. Macfadyen drove in by the orchard gate, ran the car into a kind of garage-cum-gardener's-toolshed, and walked up to the house with her arm through her father's, Sister Chiffinch following.

"A very pleasant party," said the Admiral. "I expect your mother will stay the night there. I shall go to bed. I am rather tired. You mother has gone to bed and I don't want to wake her."

For twopence Mrs. Macfadyen could have laughed—or cried—she did not know which. Sister Chiffinch said What a good idea and she could do with a bit of shut-eye herself. And as the Admiral had suddenly become a very tired old man she gently took him upstairs while Mrs. Macfadyen looked about in the kitchen, found eggs and bacon rashers and a loaf, pulled out the damper of the old-fashioned kitchen range and put a frying-pan on it to heat, and when Sister Chiffinch came down a delicious supper of eggs and bacon and fried bread was perfuming the air.

"He's gone straight off to sleep like a baby," said Sister Chiffinch. "Now, Mrs. Macfadyen, you've done quite enough. You go back to Greshamsbury. I'll ring you up first thing tomorrow morning and if the Admiral feels like it I'll bring him over."

"You are kind, Sister," said Mrs. Macfadyen. "Will you be all right?"

Sister Chiffinch said she had had a good look round the kitchen and there was plenty for breakfast and she had rinsed the empty milk bottles and put them outside the kitchen door where the milkman would see them and Mrs. Macfadyen wasn't to worry because there was always the phone.

Mrs. Macfadyen felt rather like a soldier deserting his post, but she was too tired to argue with Sister Chiffinch and after thanking her again she got into her car.

"Now, don't you commence to worry, Mrs. Macfadyen," were Sister Chiffinch's parting words. "The phone's there and there's plenty for breakfast and if I know these little towns, half the population will be round the back-door asking if they can help and hoping to see the Admiral. I'll ring Canon Fewling up tomorrow before we start. And I'll pack some things for the Admiral and the photos of Mrs. Phelps that he has by his bed."

When Mrs. Macfadyen got back to Greshamsbury her hostess took one look at her and said, "Bed." Never had Mrs. Macfadyen been so glad to have things arranged for her. With a great effort she kept awake just long enough to have a bath and almost fell into the soft embraces of Rose's super-comfortable bed and knew nothing more till it was broad daylight and Rose was drawing the curtains.

"Oh, hullo," said Rose. "I didn't wake you because you were asleep. Sister Chiffinch has rung up and your father slept like a baby she said and she has given him his breakfast. Oh, and Tubby rang up and said Mrs. Hicks was thrilled about it and is airing all the best sheets and wants to know if she is to put the central heating on and if the Admiral needs a spare pair of pyjamas to let her know."

"She is a good woman," said Mrs. Macfadyen.

"Well, so are you, Margot," said Rose. "It's funny how if you call a person a good woman it sounds like someone not quite our sort, but if you said a good lady it would sound like people who go about being charitable. What do you want to do today? Tubby rang up and he will be in all morning if you want to ring him up. Anyway have your breakfast in peace. I've brought a tray up. I say, I wish my hair had a wave like yours."

"It's your doing," said Mrs. Macfadyen. "You remember before I was married how awful I looked and you made me go to the Maison Tozier and get a proper set and ever since then I've gone there about every four weeks to have it trimmed and set. I couldn't afford it when I was at Jutland Cottage, but Donald liked me to go. He was so understanding and he did like me to be well turned out."

"So do we all," said Rose.

"I know you do," said Mrs. Macfadyen. "And I always feel grateful to you. Oh dear! I suppose I'd better get up."

"All right, but no need to hurry," said Rose. "Chiffy will bring your father over to the Rectory in her car and she won't leave him till she has seen every room and had a heart-to-heart with Mrs. Hicks. And a glass of sherry with Tubby if I am not mistaken. Oh, and Mrs. Parkinson rang up to ask about the funeral. Her father would have liked to do it, but Keith and Keith had arranged it already, so I said it was a shame and whenever I heard of anyone dying I'd let her know," which made Mrs. Macfadyen laugh. Then Rose went away and left her guest to get dressed.

In the middle of the morning Sister Chiffinch rang up to say that the Admiral had had a good night and eaten a good breakfast and was looking forward to his visit to Canon Fewling.

"He's so sweet," she said. "He said I was like Florence Nightingale and I said wasn't it dreadful the way she was really quite mental at the end and he said anyone could see I had all my wits about me. He's really an old pet. Well, I must hie me to my car and see if I need any more petrol."

"Do you think he would like me to be at the Rectory when he comes?" said Mrs. Macfadyen.

"Well, if I may just put in an oar, professionally," said Sister Chiffinch, "I think better not. He's a little excited and after the drive I think a little lunch and a rest. But if you could come over for an early tea perhaps? The Rector has most kindly asked me to stay on here for a bit and I think it would be just as well, in case the Admiral doesn't quite know where he is. One often doesn't when one's away, as I know from my own experience, for sometimes when I've been staying with a friend at Southend I've woken up the first morning and felt quite strange till I remembered where I was. Funny the way things go. Still, that's life," with which philosophical reflection she rang off.

Rose, who to the surprise of those who did not know her well always managed to combine a great deal of efficiency with her apparently careless way of life, was going down to the New Town to see Mrs. Parkinson about some eggs, for quite undeterred by a busy husband who came home to homecooked meals, three children with the average amount of the devil in them and the parochial duties which she took seriously, she was now setting up a duckery—if there is such a word—as well as hens; and having acquired a professional mother-duck wanted to keep her fully occupied. Rose had been able to get, via Mrs. Gresham who knew a duck at Hallbury, some eggs in search of a mother. So they drove up to Greshamsbury House, collected the eggs and took them down to the New Town.

Mrs. Macfadyen, who had a fair experience of fowls of all kinds, was of the opinion that the duck would at once spot them as interlopers, children basely introduced in a warming-pan, and throw them all out of the window. But though hens are feathered fools, ducks are, if possible, even sillier. The eggs were put in the nest—a most unpleasant object but ducks are like

that—and the mother coaxed to go near it. It was quite obvious
that her first words were, "Oh Lord! here are all those children
back again, what a bore," but this fine and most natural impulse
was overruled by the duck's hope—never yet realized—of
hatching out a two-headed (or otherwise deformed) duckling
whom she could exhibit to visitors at sixpence a time and then
hire another duck as Sitter while she went to the cinema, better
known to her unfeathered friends as that filthy green puddle
down by the allotments I can't think why the Council don't clear
it away. But we may be pretty sure that any subversive plans of
the foster-duck will be nipped in the bud by Mrs. Parkinson.

After lunch Rose had to go into Barchester and Mrs. Macfadyen was alone till it was time to go to the Rectory. She would
rather not have been alone, because she didn't much want to
think of the new life that was before her. Much as she had loved
her parents and dutifully and cheerfully as she had worked for
them, her married life had been a most happy escape and when
she thought of her husband the words often came into her head,
"Whose service is perfect freedom." Donald had given her so
much and never had she felt in any way fettered by his wishes,
while doing all she could to make him happy. Well, that was
over and she had known earthly happiness—she had lived and
loved. Now she must use her love to help her father as a means
to his happiness. If in so doing she could also find happiness for
herself, all the better, but in any case she would do it. She must
go more firmly into the matter of a house. One could not impose
on Tubby's kindness indefinitely. And she must remind herself
that from a worldly point of view she was well off—by her own
standards rich—and could do everything for her father that he
wanted or needed—though as for wants, his were very few.

If nettles are to be grasped, the sooner the better. At four
o'clock she went over to the Rectory where Mrs. Hicks opened
the door—which was quite unnecessary for all the Rector's
friends came in and out as they pleased in country fashion—
bursting with importance.

"The Admiral's doing nicely, madam," said Mrs. Hicks, which nearly made Mrs. Macfadyen have the giggles. "And Sister Chiffinch is ever so nice. I had a nice lunch ready when they came and they thoroughly enjoyed it. The Canon has gone out, but he'll be back soon and I'll tell Sister you are here. Come into the drawing-room."

So Mrs. Macfadyen followed Mrs. Hicks into the drawing-room where the Admiral was sitting in a large comfortable chair, not too low, with a padded back and wings. Beside him was a small table where lay his pipe, his tobacco pouch, matches and some books. And in another comfortable chair was Sister Chiffinch looking exactly like herself—as she always did whether in or out of uniform, at Gatherum or in a cottage—knitting a scarf.

"How nice to see you, father," said Mrs. Macfadyen, kissing him. "And Sister Chiffinch. I hope you had a good drive coming over."

Sister Chiffinch answered for both that it was a nice drive and Canon Fewling had met them at the front gate and the Admiral had an ever so nice room looking over the church-yard with all the afternoon sun and he could hear the church clock striking the hours—a phenomenon she seemed to find unusual in a Rectory.

Her father appeared glad to see Mrs. Macfadyen and asked where she and Donald had been. "Because you are always going abroad," he said. "I was out of England a great deal when I was at sea. But it's nice to be at home again. Your mother is resting—isn't she, Sister?"

Sister Chiffinch did not have to tell a lie or invent an answer when she said that Mrs. Phelps was resting very peacefully.

"And Fewling is a very good fellow," said the Admiral. "He has some books about Nelson that I shall enjoy. And I heard the church bells this morning. I suppose Crofts was having an early service. But that wasn't here. I was at home. Why am I here?"

Mrs. Macfadyen looked at Sister Chiffinch while her heart sank.

"And now you are here again, Margot. That is very nice," said her father. "Did anyone feed the hens while you were away?"

Mrs. Macfadyen could have sat down and cried. Her father was somewhere else and she could not reach him. There was the sound of a car outside and Dr. Ford came in.

"Well, Admiral, I said I would come over and here I am," he said. "And how did you sleep?"

The Admiral said very well. The ship had rolled a bit, but he was an old sailor and had turned over and gone to sleep again.

"You said you wanted to see me about your cough, Mrs. Macfadyen," said Dr. Ford, which was of course a whacking lie. "So I came over. Shall we go into the other room? I'll be back, Admiral."

Mrs. Macfadyen got up and followed Dr. Ford to Canon Fewling's study.

"You're a good girl, Margot," said Dr. Ford. "It's the shock of your Mother's death. He may get over it and be quite normal till he dies. Or he may not."

"But I can't let Canon Fewling go on having him for ever," said Mrs. Macfadyen. "I am trying to get a house and then I can have him with me. I must try some other agents. Poor father. I'm so glad mother can't see him. Will he ever get better?"

"That's a thing that even a doctor can't say," said Dr. Ford. "He might go on. He mightn't. You're a good girl and a sensible girl, and I can only tell you the truth. As far as I can tell your mother's death has affected his mind. Whether his health will be affected too I can't say yet. But you must be prepared for it."

"Does Tubby know?" said Mrs. Macfadyen.

"If he doesn't, he will," said Dr. Ford. "You don't deal with people for years as Fewling has, at sea and on shore, without knowing something of reaction. And he's had some pretty hard knocks himself and got through them under his own steam. Something happened four or five years ago—I don't know what it was—but he fought it all right. And the Admiral would go down standing on the bridge with his flag flying, if he were himself."

"But he isn't," said Mrs. Macfadyen, just stopping herself from laughing at the remembrance of a film about Kind Hearts and Coronets in which a bearded Admiral deliberately goes down with his ship (which is sinking through his own error of judgment) in slow motion on the bridge, to the intense joy of all viewers. "I didn't know that till just now. He sometimes thinks he is in a ship and she was rolling last night."

"Well, I'll see Chiffinch and give her something stronger to make him sleep," said Dr. Ford. "Then we'll see. And I think she had better stay here for the present. Fewling won't mind. He's a remarkably good fellow and a first-rate parson and a good Christian," which may seem a curious judgment for a doctor to pass on a clergyman, but there was very little that Dr. Ford did not know and understand.

"But, Dr. Ford," said Mrs. Macfadyen, "we can't impose on Tubby like that. You know I am really very well off and I am looking for a house anyway, and I could make father comfortable—as for happy, I don't think he'll be happy ever again without mother. You know, he thinks she is still alive and will turn up at any moment."

"Just as well," said Dr. Ford. "Now, Margot, listen to me. The Admiral has been failing for some time. Then he had the shock of your mother's death. And now, mercifully for him, something has given way and he doesn't realize what has happened. It's no good saying what *will* happen because one doesn't know, but—as far as a great many years of general practice can guide me—apart from a miracle, which no one can expect, he will go on sinking. I can't tell you how long it will be. Sorry, Margot."

"That's all I wanted to know, Dr. Ford. Thank you," said Mrs. Macfadyen. "I've told the house-agents to give their minds to finding me a house. I can always get help round here and I hate to think of Tubby being imposed on."

"I don't think you, or anyone else, could impose on him," said Dr. Ford. "He sees where he is going and follows the road. Like Christian; but you young people don't read your *Pilgrim's Progress.*"

"Indeed we do!" said Mrs. Macfadyen indignantly. "And what's more father has the same old edition that Stevenson wrote something about somewhere, and the good people have speckled tunics and the wicked people plain tunics, or cutaway coats and top hats. And what is more, father has *always* followed the road, which is more than Christian did," at which tirade or outburst Dr. Ford laughed like anything and then said she was a good girl and she must send for him whenever she wanted him.

"I'm not taking new patients now," he said, "except a few whose parents used to come to me. But I'll come over to your father whenever you want me. Now, don't worry about Fewling. He's like Mrs. Gamp."

Surprised and interested, Mrs. Macfadyen asked how.

"Dear me, it's my habit of quoting Dickens," said Dr. Ford. "It's Mrs. Harris who—according to Mrs. Gamp—said If ever a woman lived as would see her feller creeturs into fits to serve her friends, well do I know that woman's name is Sairey Gamp. Fewling is just the same, if you see what I mean," and Mrs. Macfadyen couldn't help laughing and said she quite saw it.

"Mind," said Dr. Ford, "Fewling would be kind, but he wouldn't be weak. It will give him real pleasure to have your father here and if there were difficulties he would tell you. But I don't think there will be."

"You mean that father might die," said Mrs. Macfadyen. "I mean soon."

"I can't tell you that, nor can anyone else," said Dr. Ford. "But he is a sailor and you are a sailor's daughter, Margot. You would rather know. That's all I know and all I can tell you. I won't tell you anything but the truth—as soon as I know it."

Mrs. Macfadyen thanked him. He had a short talk with Sister Chiffinch and went away. The Admiral had been dozing, so

Mrs. Macfadyen said she would go, when who should come in but Mrs. Parkinson, bringing some fresh eggs from her hens and full of kind enquiries.

Then the Admiral un-dozed—for we cannot think of a better description of his slow emergence from wherever he had been—and his daughter told him that this was the daughter of Mr. Welk who knew all the gypsies up in the woods, and the Admiral came alive and asked Mrs. Parkinson if she would like to see over the ship. It does the greatest credit to Mrs. Parkinson that she at once grasped the situation and said she would love to another day, but she had to go home and give her children their tea. The Admiral was showing signs of trying to get up to say good-bye to her, but she was by his side before he could move, took his hand, thanked him for seeing her and said she would like to come again.

"I've been on to the agents about your house, Mrs. Macfadyen," she said when they were out of earshot, "but they've still not got anything on their books that you would really like."

Mrs. Macfadyen thanked her and said she must go on looking till she found something.

"And Teddy says if the Admiral ever would like to see him, he'd come over any time," said Mrs. Parkinson, "but with Canon Fewling there he wouldn't wish to intrude," and Mrs. Macfadyen, very sensible of the kindness and delicacy of Mr. Parkinson's offer, said she would most certainly let him know if he could help.

There had been for some time in the Close a growing feeling that Canon Fewling should leave Greshamsbury, where he had faithfully and zealously laboured, to become a resident in the Close. Who began it we do not know, but it was strongly supported by Canon Joram, the Chancellor Sir Robert Fielding and the Dean. One of the houses in the Close had lately come into the market and there was a rumour about that Victoria, Lady Norton, was making an offer for it. As her ladyship had (to the great annoyance of her son and daughter-in-law) an ample jointure and could afford what she wanted, there seemed to be a horrid possibility—nay, probability—that she might become a resident.

Canon Joram, who was a great hand at crossword puzzles, had tried to make an anagram (preferably of an opprobrious nature) on her name with no success at all and a Minor Canon with a turn for light verse had gone so far as the first lines of a limerick, running,

> There was an old Dowager Norton
> Whom no one would ever have thought on—

but here his Muse failed him, largely, we think, because her eight sisters said, with one octuple voice, that it was a Cockney rhyme.

"No, it won't do," said the Dean, when it had been explained to him with a good deal of what he considered rather senseless laughter among some of his grown-up grandchildren. "But there must be some other rhyme."

A grandson who was still at his public school said Bourton (on the Water), Porton (a junction not far from Barchester), Wart On if you had a wart on your hand—at which point his grandfather said That was enough, but the grandson had to say Moreton-in-the-Marsh and Morton's Fork, at which point an elder brother and a female cousin of about his own age seized him and squashed a cushion over his face. Then even their grandmother said That was enough, and their grandfather gave them a short, pungent address on Cockney rhymes by which they were entirely unimpressed. But the youngest grandson committed it all to memory so that he could show off in the literature lesson at school—which he did with such a horrid affectation of angelic innocence that his long-suffering form-master could not find an outwardly valid excuse for keeping him in. But he evened the score by putting in the term's report that

Crawley, S. A. (Septimus Arabin) would do better if he did not try to be funny.

It was, we think, the Reverend Lord William Harcourt, a younger brother of the present Duke of Omnium, who first brought the matter to the attention of the Cathedral Chapter and warned them about Victoria, Lady Norton. Not that he knew her ladyship more than the merest civility demands, while his mother the Dowager Duchess and both his elder sisters were even more united in their dislike of her. His wife's family, the Grahams, had always refused to know her ladyship except on the most ordinary terms of social civility. Canon Joram, the ex-Bishop of Mngangaland, and his wife who had been Mrs. Brandon were also of one voice about her. And what was even more comforting, the whole body of servants in the Close (where by a kind of miracle that vanishing race still existed) were united in dislike of her ladyship's airs and her stinginess. And the final word against her went forth when Simnet, butler to Canon Joram and a pillar of the Close, gave it as his opinion at the Club that no head servant, no nor no footman, no nor housemaid neether, could demean themselves by working in a house where the tea was weighed out and Someone bought marge and wrapped it up in butter wrappers for the kitchen.

"I think, my dear," said the Dean to his wife, "we might ask Fewling to lunch. If he comes to the Close, as I hope he will, he might want to see where he can live before he decides."

"*Really*, Josiah!" said his wife. "Oh well, I daresay you are right. But men never look at the servants' quarters."

"Well, my dear, if he is really coming here you can look at them with him," said the Dean. "I'd like to have him here. It's a pity he isn't married. A middle-aged celibate canon has such an attraction for elderly spinsters," on hearing which words his spouse blamed him for his selfishness.

"You are really most unfair, Josiah," she said. "At least the canons are. The least they could do would be to marry some of the older girls and settle down. Look at those Harcourt girls for instance. The Duchess never bothered about them and when anyone did propose to them she squashed it and they haven't a chance now. Your Canon Fewling must be pretty well off. I mean he doesn't live on his stipend."

"One often wonders," said Dr. Crawley in an off-hand way, "what one's friends *do* live on."

"Snob!" said his wife. "But he did tell me once that his father was in business of some sort at Plymouth and that was why he wanted to go to sea. I forget about his mother. Oh no, I don't. She was a clergyman's daughter and I think she died when he was quite small. Canon Fewling wasn't well off till quite lately when he inherited something from an old uncle and aunt. He used to be in the navy. It was after the war that he felt a call to the ministry—"

The Dean said sailors often did.

"—and if only you wouldn't interrupt me, Josiah," said his wife, "I would have gone on to say that it is a great pity he doesn't marry. He is too nice to be a bachelor."

"I rather agree, my dear," said the Dean. "But on the other hand think how useful a bachelor Canon would be in the Close where one is always wanting an odd man for dinner parties."

"Yes, but if he were in the Close he would get married at once," said Mrs. Crawley, "Look at Doctor Joram."

"Well, I married you, my dear, I am glad to say," said the Dean. "And Joram seems extremely happy. You must look for someone for Fewling. What about one of the Harcourt girls?" for the Dowager Duchess of Towers had two unmarried daughters.

"That is an idea," said his wife. "Lady Elaine was engaged to a man, but he broke his neck hunting, and Lady Gwendolen has a passion for the celibate clergy."

"But surely Fewling is a celibate," said the Dean.

"Don't quibble, Dean," said his wife. "Canon Fewling isn't a professional celibate—he has just never happened to meet someone he wanted to marry."

"Or else he did meet someone and she became the Bride of Another," said the Dean, quoting from that beautiful lost lyric, "We met, 'twas in a crowd."

"Well, the great thing is to get him here as soon as possible," said Mrs. Crawley firmly. "And then we can think about your Mr. Parkinson."

But the Dean said Festina Lente was a good motto and Mr. Parkinson and his wife were doing such excellent work in Greshamsbury New Town that it would be a great pity to disturb them yet and would his wife kindly remember that the patronage of the living in the Old Town was not in his hands. But they agreed that to have Canon Fewling in the Close would be both agreeable and useful and if he had Acacia House (so called because there had been for many years an acacia tree in front of the house, which tree had not been judiciously pruned and had grown very high with a lot of dead wood in it and made the house in summer like living under the water with the green light) and were married to someone suitable, not too young, he would be a tower of strength against the Palace.

"And I gather that he isn't badly off," said the Dean, "from what you said. Just as well in the Close," and if our reader thinks he was snobbish and not taking a properly religious view of Poverty, we must remind her of the Reverend (and Dreadful) Amos Barton, who was most suitably poor and had not only a wretched stipend but was also a very selfish unpleasant character and practically killed his wife and kept his eldest daughter as his slave till the end of his life; and we always hope that the rest of his family deserted him and ran away to sea, or married a tallow-chandler and went to live in a different part of the country. But it was all very well for Miss Mary Anne Evans to invent a perfect woman and praise her, when she herself lived in dull intellectual sin with a gentleman from whose eyes, ears, nose, cheeks and chin more hair sprouted—if we are to believe contemporary portraits—than is humanly possible, and herself looked like a large, sad and not very intelligent horse, with drooping ringlets; that is in face—but otherwise with a total wacancy of hoofs.

"Well, Josiah, it is no business of mine," said Mrs. Crawley, "but it would be just as well to have Canon Fewling's appointment settled before the Palace gets in. It might be someone like that dreadful Mr. Slope that you said your grandmother used to talk about."

The Dean laughed and said at least Mr. Slope, or so his grandmother had told him, had said a very few well-chosen words to the Bishop before he left the Close and shortly afterwards the city.

We are not well enough acquainted with the internal politics of the Close to know exactly what was done, but whatever it was, the Dean saw to it that it was well done and Canon Fewling was asked to lunch at the Deanery. There were not any other guests and after lunch Mrs. Crawley went away and the two clerical gentlemen got down to brass tacks.

Canon Fewling listened with interest to the Dean. He had for some time been aware that life was changing and he wondered if he was being rather a comfortable old stick-in-the-mud, doing his not very onerous duties in Greshamsbury. And now that the New Town had its new vicar, with energy and goodwill and the backing of the Deanery and—possibly more important than anything else—a wife of good unblemished Barsetshire background whose ancestors had probably worshipped Woden and Thor and before that heaven knows what strange British deities, things would be well ordered.

As the angler dangles the fly, or tickles the trout, or does whatever else anglers do, so did the Dean dangle Acacia House before his guest, who showed distinct signs of rising to the bait.

"Well, Fewling, I don't want to hurry you," said Dr. Crawley. "Think it over. If you do come to the Close there is quite a good house vacant that you might like to look at. Not one of the big houses like the Fieldings', but very well arranged. If you aren't in a hurry we might go and look at it. I've got a set of keys."

Canon Fewling said Certainly there would be no harm in going over the house though it seemed rather like counting one's chickens before they were hatched, but he did like looking at houses. So the Dean put the keys in his pocket and they walked down the Close. The elms were blazing in bronze and gold and the acacia which gave its name to the house was beginning to look pretty bald. Behind it the house was waiting to be looked at. Good red brick, a front door in the middle, a high window on each side, two storeys above it and a stone parapet along the top.

The Dean unlocked the door and they went in. From this point Canon Fewling, who was an enthusiastic collector of Barsetshire tradition, felt that he was rather in the position of Dean Arabin when Dr. Grantly told him exactly what he must do in his new vicarage, even down to the kind of dining-table and the throwing out of a wing. But Dr. Crawley was of milder mood and reserved his suggestions entirely for the kitchen regions.

These were pleasant, for though the front part was semi-basement the ground behind sloped away towards the river, so that the back rooms were on ground level but, we are glad to say, with a little walled courtyard outside them so that the gentry need not be offended by the sight of what are known as The Clorths hanging out to dry— nor the more intimate garments of the staff—if any.

"Would your housekeeper come with you, Fewling?" said the Dean.

Canon Fewling said he would cross that bridge when he came to it and then they went to the ground floor with a good hall, a dining-room which looked onto the Close and had a service lift from the basement, and behind it a smaller room which Canon Fewling at once saw as his study. Then up the staircase—not so noble as Canon Joram's but a good civilized flight of stairs—to an L-shaped drawing-room that ran right through the house so that it got the afternoon sun and a view over the garden to the river and away beyond it to where, we regret to say, a new suburb was rising. But the willows and poplars at the far side of the meadows made a summer screen, and as the land was cathedral property there would be no nonsense about lopping and dismembering; only judicious pruning.

On the floor above was a master-bedroom (as house-agents will call it) with a dressing-room opening off it, another smaller bedroom and a good bathroom. Above this again were two good bedrooms, another bathroom and two less-good bedrooms where servants could sleep and a small room which would do very well for luggage and anything that wasn't needed downstairs.

"And a fire-escape," said the Dean proudly. "If the house is on fire and of course the staircase too, you run upstairs, open the window and turn this handle—" and he proceeded to explain the mechanism to Canon Fewling who did not quite grasp it and was determined not to try. The Dean looked rather disappointed.

"It is only a matter of trusting the machinery," he said.

"It's not the machinery, it's me," said the Canon firmly, allowing his grammar to collapse. "I *cannot* see myself trusting that affair. Besides, Crawley, I shouldn't be sleeping up here. I would be on the floor below. It will be my guests and the servants—if any—who will have to escape. If my bedroom were on fire I should probably be able to get downstairs. You know, in the new buildings at Southbridge School the stairs to the dormitories are of very thick seasoned wood. The Barchester Fire Brigade told the Headmaster it was safer than an iron stair in case of fire, because the wood only smoulders very slowly and if the alarm is given the stair can be used, but iron stairs get red hot almost at once."

The Dean said there was an iron staircase outside the Palace at the back and appeared to be lost in a delightful dream of the Bishop with his wife and gaiters being grilled like St. Lawrence while trying to escape from a doom which in any case was waiting for them in the next world.

Then they walked back to the Deanery. The future was not discussed again, but evidently the Dean was hoping and also doing some wishful thinking which might help to the required result.

"You remember Admiral Phelps at Southbridge," said Canon Fewling. "His wife died—rather suddenly—and I suggested that he and the very nice nurse, Sister Chiffinch, should stay with me for a time till his daughter—she is the widow of Macfadyen, the big market gardener and an unusually delightful woman and extremely competent—has found a house for herself where she can have her father under her eye. He is quite broken by his wife's death, but extremely good and patient and we talk about the Navy when he feels up to talking."

The Dean said he was sorry about the Admiral and expressed a hope that Mrs. Macfadyen might find something in Barchester where the Admiral could more easily have a few old friends from the County Club to look him up.

"I don't know," said Canon Fewling. "He mostly thinks he is in his own flagship and sometimes I feel rather like Captain Cuttle myself only I haven't got a hook instead of a hand. Well, thank you, Crawley. I'll ask my lawyers to go into the question of Acacia House—that is if things go as we hope."

"Oh, things will go all right," said the Dean, with the fine confidence we all have in other people's luck—whereas we know that we were overlooked at our christening by a Wicked Fairy. "By the way, Fewling," he added, "I am working on St. Paul's Epistle to the Mixo-Lydians. It is very little known and probably spurious and I shall be glad of any further light on it. I don't suppose that is your subject?"

Canon Fewling said it wasn't, but he knew the Mixo-Lydian Ambassadress who was much interested in English studies and had founded a college for women in Mixo-Lydia called Bunting College after the Fieldings' old governess who had helped her with her English studies when she was a refugee during the war.

Dr. Crawley asked for her address and wrote it, in his neat scholarly handwriting, in a small pocket-book.

"By the way, the Mixo-Lydians are not of the Roman faith, are they?" said the Dean suspiciously.

Canon Fewling said as far as they were anything they tended towards the Greek Orthodox Church and crossed themselves the wrong way round.

The Dean said "Ha!" but Canon Fewling had known him too long to be impressed, and they parted.

When Canon Fewling got home he met Mr. Parkinson just outside the house.

"Mrs. Macfadyen asked me to look up her father," said Mr. Parkinson. "I don't mean professionally—just as a friend while that nice Sister Chiffinch went out for a bit. What a dear old man he is. He told me quite a lot about the Navy, I couldn't follow much of it but he liked talking," and Canon Fewling at once gave Mr. Parkinson an Alpha Plus for his intelligent and sympathetic attitude towards the Admiral. "And then he asked me to read to him out of the Bible, only he said not out of Revelation because he couldn't believe there would be no more sea. So I took the liberty—I do hope you won't mind—of taking out one of your Kipling volumes with the verses about all the seamen who didn't like the idea of heaven without any sea and how the Lord called the good sea up to Him, and 'stablished its borders unto all eternity. 'The Last Chantey,' it's called. I think he liked it."

"A fine poem if ever there was one," said Canon Fewling, "and I was a sailor myself. How good of you to take so much trouble."

"But I liked it," said Mr. Parkinson. "Admiral Phelps is so good and patient that I felt quite small."

"Well, Parkinson, inasmuch as you have done it—I needn't go on."

"Matthew twenty-five," said Mr. Parkinson. "But that's too much, sir, I mean, what else could I do?"

"Well, when you have done what is best and kindest there really isn't anything else you can do," said Canon Fewling. "The Dean was asking after his godson. Come again if you feel like it. You will always be welcome here," and then Mr. Parkinson got onto his bicycle and went back to the New Town.

The Dean, with the whole-hearted support of the Close, then took up the question of Acacia House and—in the words of old Canon Thorne who was now immune to all mundane matters except his meals and the intromissions of the Bishop—girded his heavenly armour on and wore it ever night and day. And when pressed by his friends he admitted that the third line of that verse was eminently applicable to the Bishop; adding as a rider that if whom the Lord loveth He chasteneth was true, the Close was singularly favoured by heaven. Everything moved slowly, but there was no hurry. We do not, in Mrs. Gamp's fine phrase, seek to participate, but we can assure our reader, if she is curious, that all will go well and Greshamsbury will also have a pastor suitable to its status and inhabitants. But that is still far away.

Mrs. Macfadyen had, up till now, had no luck in finding a suitable house, and so distressed was she by the thought of Canon Fewling being landed, as it were, with a nurse and an invalid who was gently preparing for his last voyage, that she seriously considered moving into Barchester where was an excellent nursing home which would take permanent cases and she could ask one or two old friends to visit him—if their visits could give him any pleasure; and that was something that no one knew. But she was a very sensible woman and did not talk about it, nor try to hurry it; only made her plans and went to look at the nursing home on the pretext of visiting the rather dotty widow of a deceased Canon and thought well of it.

She also consulted Dr. Ford, who said that no one—not even if they had, in Mr. Samuel Weller's words, a pair of patent double million magnifying gas microscopes of hextra power—

could say what the Admiral felt, what he thought of, if he knew where he was, or would mind or notice much any change of place. As he had settled down apparently contented in Canon Fewling's house, there was no reason why he should not settle anywhere else where he could have kind attention and his daughter to see him often. Mrs. Macfadyen was—as any daughter would be—torn between the duty which she felt must tie her to her father and the fact that he hardly noticed her now and would be better cared for by kind professional hands; for Sister Chiffinch could not stay with him for ever.

Of late Canon Fewling and Mrs. Macfadyen had necessarily been together a good deal and had enjoyed talking about the earlier days when Father Fewling—as he then called himself, not yet a Canon—had only lately come to Greshamsbury from Northbridge, and Margot Phelps, as the Admiral's daughter was then, was working most valiantly in farm and farmyard in most unbecoming trousers. Each liked the other's company and felt comfortably free to talk or be silent. Rose Fairweather, who liked having Mrs. Macfadyen as her guest, looked on and said nothing, with the strange worldly wisdom that went with her apparent easy carelessness.

Dr. Ford, when asked by Mrs. Macfadyen for his opinion, said that there would be no unkindness in a nursing home and more security; provided always that his daughter could often visit him, which she would most certainly do.

One late afternoon, shortly after Canon Fewling's visit to Barchester, Mrs. Macfadyen came over as usual to sit with her father who was vaguely pleased to see her, though whether he thought she was his wife, or herself, or just a kind friend who had looked in, we do not know. He dozed for much of the day now and was glad to stay in bed in the mornings, but still insisted on coming downstairs for tea, which Sister Chiffinch said was very good for him. It was one of those afternoons of autumn when the days are drawing in faster than one realizes.

There was a good fire and the curtains not yet drawn. The Admiral was in his usual chair with his daughter beside him while Canon Fewling played his piano softly to himself and sometimes sang to himself in his pleasant baritone voice, but softly, lest the Admiral should think it was 'God Save the Queen" (which he was apt to do) and try to stand up. Then the Admiral dozed off and Canon Fewling described to Mrs. Macfadyen the charms of Acacia House and how with luck he would be moving into the Close and asked if she would like to go over it; an invitation no woman can resist.

"I would like," he said, "to ask you to bring your father and spend a week or two there when I am settled. If we get him as far as the Close, he might visit the nursing home and get to know the Matron—in case it were better for him to go there."

There was a chill about the thought, but Mrs. Macfadyen knew it was not intentional and realized the kindness that lay behind it.

It was the hour for evening service. Sister Chiffinch came back from a visit to Rose Fairweather and took charge of the Admiral, who was gently pleased to see her, though very vague as to who she was. Canon Fewling and Mrs. Macfadyen walked across the garden and up the path to the church where there was a sufficiency of worshippers and—partly owing to the new heating apparatus—a feeling of comfort and peace. When the service was over Mrs. Macfadyen remained in the pew, trying to concentrate on prayer for her father and to beg God to do whatever was best for him. She then felt that it was not her business to interfere and asked to be pardoned if she was too importunate. But there was precedent for importunity in a Book.

The sexton had turned nearly all the lights out. Canon Fewling came out of the vestry and joined Mrs. Macfadyen in the church porch.

"I do like this church," she said.

"So do I," said Canon Fewling, "and I shall miss it. I have

never come here without having some burden lifted from me. There was a burden—some years ago—that I thought I could not bear. But I brought it here and I was helped."

Mrs. Macfadyen, with a sense of guilt or responsibility for which she could not account, asked what it was.

"You told me that you had promised to marry Donald Macfadyen," said Canon Fewling.

"And you congratulated me so kindly," she said.

Canon Fewling did not answer.

"Oh no! It couldn't be *that*," said Mrs. Macfadyen. "I didn't guess. How could I? And you were—"

"Yes, I was," said Canon Fewling. "And you married the better man."

"I never knew. I never knew," she said, on the verge of tears.

"But I did find comfort here," said Canon Fewling. "And I had a reward. I knew that you were happy. Shall we go back to your father? Perhaps, some day, you will let me speak of it again. Acacia House will need a mistress."

"Oh, let me come!" she said.

Meanwhile Sister Chiffinch had gently roused the Admiral from one of his many dozes that she might take him upstairs, so Canon Fewling and Mrs. Macfadyen found the drawing-room empty. There was no need for more words at the moment. Canon Fewling went to his beloved piano. While he was softly playing Sister Chiffinch came in and sat by Mrs. Macfadyen.

"The Admiral has died, Mrs. Macfadyen," she said quietly. "He was very tired and then he said the Captain wanted him on the bridge, so I helped him upstairs and then his heart gave out. Dr. Ford knew it would."

"Oh, poor father. I am so glad for him," said Mrs. Macfadyen, but softly, so that the music would cover her voice.

Sister Chiffinch went away to do whatever had to be done and to let Dr. Ford know. Mrs. Macfadyen sat quietly letting the music flow over her. Then it stopped and Canon Fewling came across to where she sat.

"Father is dead," she said.

"God bless him," said Canon Fewling. "You looked after him with courage and faith and kindness."

"I don't know. I did try," said Mrs. Macfadyen. "And I shall do my best to look after you with true love. Here, or in the Close, or wherever you are. Only *please* don't die before I do. I couldn't bear it twice," and when Sister Chiffinch came back she found them laughing. But, as she truly remarked to her pals Wardy and Heathy that she shared the cottage with, you never know the way things will take people.

COLOPHON

This book is being reissued as part of Moyer
Bell's Angela Thirkell Series. If you are interested
in Angela Thirkell, contact the Angela Thirkell
Society, P.O. Box 7798, San Diego, CA 92167 or
email JOINATS@aol.com.

The text of this book was set in Caslon, a typeface
designed by William Caslon I (1692-1766). This
face designed in 1725 has gone through many
incarnations. It was the mainstay of British print-
ers for over one hundred years and remains very
popular today. The version used here is Adobe
Caslon. The display faces are Adobe Caslon
Outline, Calligraphic 421, and Adobe Caslon.

Close Quarters was typeset by Alabama Book
Composition, Deatsville, Alabama and printed by
Edwards Brothers, Inc., Lillington, North
Carolina, on acid-free paper.

Moyer Bell
54 Phillips Street
Wickford, RI 02852
info@moyerbell.com